DEALING WITH DEMONS

ALSO BY
MELISSA HAAG

THE JUDGEMENT OF THE SIX

JUDGEMENT OF THE SIX COMPANIONS

OF FATES AND FURIES

DEALING
WITH
DEMONS

MELISSA HAAG

Shattered Glass
— PUBLISHING —

He wasn't the creature of mist and shadows that I remembered. Normal, pitch-black hair fell in soft short waves around his head. However, his hair wasn't long enough to conceal the last inch of his pointed, very non-human ears.

His eyes captivated me. Swirling prisms of color, his irises contrasted the muddied backdrop of the whites of his eyes. The difference between the two was as scary as it was beautiful.

His warm fingers closed around my own, and he gently tugged me to my feet. He didn't release my hand. Instead, he pulled it up toward his chest while gently turning it so my palm would make first contact. Before I even touched him, I felt the heat radiating from his skin.

Without removing my hand, I looked up into his strange eyes.

"Have I met my part of the deal?"

MELISSA HAAG

DEALING
WITH
DEMONS

DEALING
WITH
DEMONS

Chapter One

LIGHT SPILLED ONTO THE BED WHERE I LAY CURLED ON MY SIDE. For a moment, Brian stood unsteadily in the doorway. Then, sweeping a hand through his hair, he sighed, turned off the hall light, and made a noisy attempt at creeping into the room. We both knew I wasn't asleep, but neither of us spoke.

In the next bedroom, our daughter slept, oblivious to her father's infidelity and, later, his alcohol-induced death.

STANDING in the senior hallway of Middlelyn High School, I dipped my shoulder, shrugging off Brian's warm hand and the remnants of the vision.

"Tessa?" he asked. He stood close to me, waiting for my answer.

Revulsion filled me as the bitter tang of stale alcohol lingered in my nose. I managed a smile and answered his question with a lie.

"A movie and dinner would be great, but I'm not allowed to date. Sorry, Brian."

He shifted his stance and tucked his hand into the front pocket of his fashionably worn jeans.

"I could come over and maybe help with homework or something."

Animated conversations from the kids flowing around us muted his suggestion. It didn't help that the school secretary's voice also blared over the intercom system with the end of the day announcements and joined the cacophony of noise. None of it really registered, though, as I studied Brian's expectant face.

With his messy, light brown hair, chiseled classic features, bold blue eyes, and buff body, he could have his pick of dates.

"Brian, I have to be honest. I don't trust you or your sudden interest. What's up? Really."

When I first moved to Middlelyn months ago, the boys asked me out based on genuine interest. Because of my blonde hair, deep brown eyes, trim figure, and oval face, I passed as attractive. Add to that the fact I didn't grow up with any of them and witness their awkward stages of puberty, nor they mine, and I stood out even more. Fresh meat. However, after I'd declined to go out with every boy who'd asked, the requests had tapered off, and I'd been labeled a prude. Just one of many labels I now carried.

The sudden interest of one of the most sought-after seniors didn't fit.

Brian flashed his cocky I'm-hot-and-you're-not grin before answering.

"Fifty bucks for the first one to get you on a date. Say *yes*, and I'll split it with you."

Hurt, but not willing to show it, I turned away and stacked the textbooks into my locker. He didn't leave, most likely because he thought the money would tempt me to change my mind.

In a school this size, everyone knew where I lived and that my family didn't have much. Brian probably didn't even realize how cruel his words sounded. It annoyed me how callous boys could be. Dating was all a game to them. Then again, I'd witnessed girls acting as bad. In fact, I knew I could be one of those girls on occasion. I didn't like it, but sometimes I didn't have a choice.

"Wow. So tempting," I said, still facing the locker. "But if I take half, it won't leave much for the booze you're thinking about buying."

Glancing his way, I caught his startled look before he schooled his features. I immediately regretted my temper. Annoyed or not, I should have kept my thoughts to myself.

"You're a freak," he said as if just now believing the rumors circulating about me.

I hated the rumors but couldn't claim them untrue. My mouth often got me into trouble. Might as well finish with flare.

"Yep, and the freak thanks you for asking her on a date, Brian."

Grabbing my jacket and bag, I closed the locker door with a metallic clang and walked away. A few of my schoolmates hurried out of my path. I ignored them and their careful avoidance of me.

As much as I tried to keep what I saw to myself, sometimes I failed. And, that's how the rumors about me seeing someone's death started to circulate around school. People didn't like hearing how they were going to die. It didn't matter that I was trying to helpfully warn them. They only saw me as a freak when I knew things I shouldn't. Yet, how could I keep quiet when I saw so much death that I might be able to stop if I just said something? I still wasn't sure if I had that kind of influence over their fates, but it didn't stop me from trying.

The glimpse of my life with Brian replayed in my head. Although it wasn't pretty, it remained consistent with most of my visions. Not horrible, but not great either. At least, not for Brian. If I dated him, he'd drink himself to death. But what if I didn't date him? Given his reaction to my suggestion that splitting the winnings would cut into his drinking money, I'd guessed accurately about his current drinking habits. Would my sarcastic comment change anything? Despite his attitude, I hoped it would.

I let myself out of the main doors and immediately smelled bus exhaust tainting the clean, cool, fall air. Other students jostled around me as I headed toward the end of the line and boarded my bus. The warmth was welcome.

The driver used her mirror to watch the trouble underway in the back of the bus and ignored me as I sat near the front with the younger kids. They were less irritating, and that made the forty-minute bus ride tolerable.

The flow of kids leaving the school slowed, and the first bus in line finally pulled away. The rest of the line slowly followed.

Taking the bus sucked at my age, especially when I already had my license. Even with both Mom and Aunt Grace pooling their incomes, there just wasn't any extra money for even the crappiest of a second car for my family. I hated the limitations that came from living so far out of town.

The young boy next to me tapped my arm and asked me to tie his shoe. I smiled at him then showed him how to make bunny ears out of the laces. Little boys were cute until they learned to care what their peers thought of them.

At one of the first few stops, I moved to let him out. After that, I stared out the window and watched the trees pass in a blur of brown.

When the bus emptied of a few of the more obnoxious older kids, I pulled out my homework. I always finished my assignments on the bus, which worked out well. Despite the long ride, I usually beat my mom and aunt home. With my homework done, I could help out Gran a little more.

Two minutes after finishing my last math problem, the bus slowed for my stop. Gravel crunched under my feet as I stepped down from the bus, and a crisp breeze swept past.

I went to the mailbox to do my one true chore in winter, and quickly placed the mail under one arm before returning my hand to my pocket. The air that had felt cool and refreshing after school now just felt chilly.

Eyeing the distance to the house, I again wondered how we

would manage to shovel our long driveway. Naked trees and long, dormant grass crowded the narrow drive. Small hills and valleys in the gravel made for a bumpy ride or a slow walk. It would be a challenge to navigate with a shovel. But, the house made up for the driveway.

From a distance, the faded green paint that coated the wood siding of the two-story farmhouse didn't look bad. Up close, you could see the crackled pattern in the paint that stubbornly clung to the old boards. Other than being drafty and needing paint, the house remained in good shape, and low rent made it worthwhile.

I spotted my great-grandma waiting for me on the porch and hurried my steps. Her stark white hair stood out against the green paint behind her as she rocked slowly in an old wicker chair. She had no jacket on, just a blanket wrapped around her shoulders.

In her early seventies, though she looked the grandmotherly part, she didn't always act like it. Her life had been hard early on, especially after the death of my grandmother. It had taken its toll. She'd told me repeatedly that my birth had breathed life back into the family. Life that she embraced with every breath.

"Gran, it's getting too cold to sit and watch for me."

She laughed away my concern.

"The cold won't be what kills me. How does spaghetti sound for dinner?"

"Great." I helped her from the chair, and we both went into the house.

It wasn't much warmer indoors, but I still peeled off my jacket before I followed her to the kitchen. I knew the small, cheery room would warm up as soon as we started cooking.

I moved to the butcher's block, and she went to the pantry.

"Anything interesting happen at school today?" she asked, returning with an onion for me to peel and chop.

"Brian asked me out. Touched me. With me, he'd be a drunk and a cheat until the day he dies."

"Any kids?" Gran asked absently, moving the empty pot from the stovetop to the sink.

The image of a sweet, cherub face invaded my mind, and I suffered a pang of loss. The visions, along with their emotional attachments, always stayed with me for a few days.

Gran set the pot full of water on the stove and pulled out another pan, jarring me from the fake memory.

"One." I grabbed some garlic to mince while she prepped the sauté pan with oil.

"Hold out for at least two."

I didn't bother answering. That's what my mother, the aunts, and grandma always said. Not, "Hold out for a guy who will live to see his hair turn white," or, "Wait for the right one. Someone who makes your toes curl." No. Instead, their suggestions all revolved around holding out to make the best of a horrible fate. After all, that's what they'd all done.

Understanding their stance didn't stop their answers from frustrating me. I didn't want to make the best of things. I wanted life to go easy on us all for a little while.

I could feel Gran's eyes on me while I chopped in silence.

"Tessa, honey, you know we want you to be happy. We've all tried to find what happiness we could. When you lose your man, you'll at least have your daughters. That's why we say to wait."

The onions and the garlic made my eyes water so when I answered, I sniffled a little. "I know, Gran. I just don't understand why this happens to us."

"All we have is what is in Belinda's book," she said sadly before turning to pour the noodles into the boiling water.

Belinda, the first of our line, had created an unpretentious, small book that detailed the basics of her life and gave us a few slivers of knowledge.

All the women of our line had a gift. With a single touch, we could see a glimpse of our future with the man we were touching. The touch only worked on men, and it manifested exactly on our twelfth birthday. Belinda's book warned that we had until our seventeenth birthday to choose our future partners, and that gift would disappear when we made our choice.

It sounded simple. A wonderful gift that would enable the women in my family to avoid the cheaters and the unmotivated and search for the one who could make us truly happy. Who wouldn't want that? However, there was a catch. None of us would ever be happy because the gift came at a price. The one we chose would always die young. If we were lucky, we'd have a daughter or two before that time. Only daughters, never sons.

Belinda's book left so much for us to guess. What would

happen if we didn't choose? Neither she nor any of her descendants ever noted an answer. Only that we *must* choose.

In the back of the book, Belinda had started a family tree of sorts. Mothers noted the birth of their daughters by entering their names. Many branches just stopped. Like Great-Aunt Danielle's, Gran's twin. She never had a daughter. No one ever talked about who she'd chosen or what had happened. My mom had warned me at an early age not to bring it up. Mostly, Aunt Danielle sat quietly on the chair in the corner of the living room, her haunted eyes staring off into space. I suspected she lost a daughter long ago along with her husband.

Aunt Grace, my mother's sister, had chosen a man who wouldn't give her children. Unlike Aunt Danielle, Aunt Grace spoke about her decision once when just the two of us were home. She hadn't wanted to condemn her child to our shared fate of the visions and forced choice. But after helping to raise me, she regretted her choice because now, only one branch remained active in the book. My mother's. Everything rested on me. I'd have no cousins to share my burden when I had children of my own.

Gran and I worked in silence. The smell of fresh basil, plucked from the herb pot in the window, filled the room. Water bubbled on the stove and slowly heated the kitchen. Gran added the chopped ingredients into the frying pan, and I moved to sit at the table. I buttered bread, cut each slice in half, and set them to the side. I enjoyed working in the kitchen because of the warmth and light.

"Looks like it will be dark early tonight," she said with a glance at the cloud-laden sky through the window by the sink. "Homework done?"

"Yeah."

I already missed summer and its long hours of daylight.

Only in winter did I truly resent the rules in Belinda's book. Actually, not all the rules. Mainly just the one that stated those with the gift had to be home before dark. The book gave no explanation why. Just simple instructions to secure the house before the sun sank below the horizon. A brief note stated that shutters worked best to block out the night.

Between school and the bus ride, I never had much spare time in winter. In late fall through early spring, the monotonous events of my short days made me want to scream. Get up and race to school. Do homework while riding the bus home. Make dinner with grandma, eat, and get ready for bed. No time remained for anything else.

Mom and Aunt Grace arrived home just as Gran and I put supper on the table. As usual, Aunt Danielle didn't join us. However, Mom and Aunt Grace didn't seem overly worried about her. As Gran's identical twin, I supposed they would worry if she started to look thinner than Gran.

After supper, we all got ready for bed. I had priority on the shower since I wouldn't wake before seven. Another lovely rule. To protect any daughters from the night, the daughters slept until the sun's first ray crested the horizon. In winter, that rule made it a tight race to get to school on time.

Mom knocked on the door.

"Fifteen minutes until dusk. We're starting now."

"Okay," I called back, turning off the water.

I hurried to pull on my pajamas. The material stuck on my damp skin a few times, and as a result, I rushed out the bathroom door with clothes that felt slightly twisted.

The tightly closed shutters blocked out the fading light and cast most of the house into darkness. Using my hand as an anchor on the hallway wall, I moved to the living room where everyone waited.

They sat on their heels in a small circle in the middle of the living room floor. Their quiet murmurs filled the house as each spoke the words of protection from Belinda's book. This was the one time of day Aunt Danielle always joined us.

Outside, I could feel the sun setting and a cold, scary presence growing. I stepped between Mom and Gran to stand in the middle of their circle. As one, they rose and reached their right hands toward me. Their fingertips brushed my bare arms, and lethargy set in, cocooning me in safety.

"Sleep tight, Tessa," my mom whispered as she wrapped an arm around my shoulders.

She led me to my room. I struggled to keep my eyelids open so I didn't run into my bed. Waking up with a bruised shin made me grumpy.

Yep, I hated winter, weirdly induced sleep, and boys who died after committing their lives to me.

I WOKE ABRUPTLY and glanced at my mute alarm clock. Seven a.m. Mom stood by my bed with a plate of toast.

The cycle began anew.

With a sigh, I sat up and shoved a huge bite of toast into my mouth. Though cheap and filling, I disliked toast. Probably because I had it every weekday during the school year. I'd tried cereal, but I made an awful mess in my rush to get ready and usually wore milk dribbles to school. Now, cereal remained reserved for the weekends.

While I chewed, I tossed on clothes then grabbed my bag.

Within five minutes, I sat in the back seat of mom's rusted out car. It had long ago lost its emblem identifying the make and model. The cracked leather seats quickly warmed on the fifteen-minute drive to town. As usual, I dwelled on the unfairness that it took fifteen minutes to get to school and forty to get home.

She and Aunt Grace dropped me off near the front steps of Middlelyn High. Only a few other late arrivals still rushed through the main doors. It meant fighting my way to my locker through crowded hallways.

As I trudged forward, I felt more than the usual stares boring into my back. Glancing around, I saw Brian and a group of boys talking quietly. They all watched my progress. Great. By rejecting Brian, I'd made matters worse and made myself more of a challenge to them.

With a mental sigh, I hurried to my locker, placed the books I'd taken home inside, and pulled out the books for my first two classes. Less locker time would be a good thing today.

Predictably, one of the boys broke away from the group and approached me. I cut him off when he opened his mouth to say something.

"Don't waste your energy."

I closed my locker and walked away.

The day crawled by as Brian's group of friends took every opportunity to speak to me. My patience wore thin when one of them approached at lunch. I sat alone at the table and tried to ignore Clavin as he invaded my solitude and graced me with his magnificent presence. The mockery in his voice as he suggested we "get it on in the supply closet" pushed me too far.

My words carried to the next table when I told him to sit on a broom handle instead. Everyone at that table snickered. Clavin's face infused with red, and his eyes narrowed before he stormed off. His look promised retribution.

By the end of the day, I'd managed to offend each member of Brian's circle. Not intentionally though. But after the cafeteria incident, it didn't matter what I said. They all got angry, and I hated their stupid bet and callous attitudes even more.

The last bell rang, and I left the chemistry lab to merge with the other students who poured into the halls. My mind was on what Gran and I would make for dinner, and I didn't notice Clavin until he bumped into me. The nudge was hard enough that I lost my balance and stumbled into a side hall we were passing.

Tripping over my own feet, I struggled to regain my balance. My bag almost fell off my shoulder in the process, and I narrowly avoided a face plant to the floor. A pair of shoes, attached to familiar legs, registered as I caught myself. Heart thumping, I looked up and saw Brian standing next to a door.

Before I could do anything, he opened the supply closet and Clavin pushed me in. The door slammed shut behind me.

The sudden absence of light startled me as much as the abruptly cut-off laughter worried me.

A thin band of light at the bottom of the door did little to illuminate the small space that smelled of cleaning supplies and old mop water. I dropped my bag and grabbed the door handle. It didn't move.

"Real mature." I pounded a fist on the door. "Let me out." No response.

If they thought this would turn me into a crying mess, they needed to think again.

Pausing, I listened for an indication the boys waited outside the door. In the distance, I heard other students as they left the school. No sounds came from nearby. The school had almost emptied already. My stomach did a crazy flip, and fear slid into my belly. I needed to get out soon or I'd miss the bus. Home before dark...

The handle still didn't budge.

I pounded and kicked the door, hoping someone from the main hall would hear me. Somebody had to have seen what happened. Before that hope took hold, I realized no one would care.

I changed strategies, knowing it was time to be smart, not panic.

Feeling along the door, I searched for a switch. I felt nothing to either side but shelves. Raising my hands above my head, I waved them around, feeling for a string. Something brushed my fingertips. I slowed down the waving and tried again with success.

With the string between my fingers, I gave a gentle tug. Light flooded the space, and I blinked away the pain as my eyes watered. Between blinks, I studied the tiny area.

Mounted to the wall, a small utility sink occupied the back of the room. In front of it sat the janitor's mop and bucket filled with cold, dirty water. I wrinkled my nose. The shelves held cleaning supplies, and bags of liquid absorbent lay stacked on the floor. There was nothing I could use to open the door.

Turning, I studied the doorknob. The lock was on the inside. I frowned at the lock and stepped forward to try the handle once more. It gave a little before stopping. They hadn't locked me in. Someone held the knob from the outside.

Angry, I gripped the knob tightly. Whoever stood outside held it steady.

I closed my eyes. I'd only ever gotten visions when touching skin to skin, but I concentrated anyway, hoping I could figure out who held the door closed. I breathed slowly, cleared my mind, and willed a vision to appear.

Nothing happened.

Outside the door, the sounds of leaving students faded to

an eerie quiet. The thought of the buses leaving made me desperate. So I guessed.

"Brian, I know it's you holding the handle," I spoke with a false calm as I placed my ear against the wood to listen. "I know it's you just like I know you're going to grow up to be a raging alcoholic who dies in his sleep."

The doorknob twisted sharply, and because of my tight grip, my knuckles scraped on the frame. As I gasped at the pain, the door jerked outward a few inches. Just enough for me to lose my balance and catch sight of Brian's startled face peering back at me.

Before I recovered my balance, he slammed the door shut again. The side of my face smacked against the wood with a crack. The cheap door gave under the pressure, splitting before my cheekbone did.

I cried out and pressed a hand to my face. Heat radiated into my palm, and my eyes watered from the pain.

Fury cut through the urge to cry, and I grabbed for the knob again. This time, I met no resistance when I pushed the door open. The sound of my tormentor's rapidly retreating feet assured me I need not worry that they lingered.

Further down the hall, a janitor turned the corner. He pushed a mop and bucket identical to the one already in the supply closet. Before he spotted me, I grabbed my bag and darted out, my hand still pressed to my face.

The deserted halls echoed with my racing footsteps. Each footfall sent a jolt through my throbbing cheek. The pain, which started near my earlobe, seared through the bone to carve a slow, brutal path to the base of my eye. Too angry to cry, I didn't pause to look for Brian and Clavin and focused on getting out of the building.

Afternoon sunlight poured into the main lobby, an atrium with display cases for the school's sports trophies. It usually felt warm and welcoming. Not today. The doors flew wide open as I raced through them.

The empty drive in front of the school confirmed my guess that I'd missed the buses. Since we only had the one car, calling Gran wouldn't do me any good, and I didn't want to call Mom at work. She'd insist I wait at the school. I couldn't tell her why I didn't want to do that. We had enough to deal with.

I glanced at the overcast sky, shouldered my bag, and set off at a brisk pace. I estimated we lived about seven miles from school. It was probably almost three o'clock. That'd give me two hours to get home.

Plenty of time, I tried to assure myself. *And, when the bus passes the house without stopping, Gran will call Mom, and she and Aunt Grace will watch for me on their way home.*

An icy breeze played with my hair. Lifting the strands, it swept over the back of my neck and made me cringe. Forty minutes until Gran called Mom. I could handle the cold that long.

I'd made it across the staff parking lot when I noticed a mustard yellow car idling in the student lot. Like my mom's car, what it lacked in newness it had in character. Too far away to see the people inside, I only spared it a passing glance as I cut across the lot to the school's main access road.

It wasn't a big school or a big town, so the sidewalk disappeared just before I hit the southern outskirts. I walked the graveled shoulder at a steady pace and kept a careful eye on the ditch that dropped a few feet before it sloped away into fallow fields. My face hurt enough without me falling and landing on the clumps of dirt that poked up in frozen disarray.

A shiver stole through me, and I curled deeper into my light jacket while using my freezing digits to soothe the hot ache in my face. My cheek helped keep my fingers warm, but I worried what the extreme heat meant and began to regret what I'd said to Brian. I should have kept my mouth shut.

At the last school I'd attended, just an hour away, I'd finished the year as a complete outcast. I hadn't liked it, but at least the bullying there hadn't escalated past nasty words exchanged in the halls.

Lightly touching my cheek, I hoped it wouldn't bruise. My mom would flip if she found out just how bad things had gotten and would want to move. Again. In my life, we'd moved eleven times. Seven of those occurred since I'd turned thirteen. We usually moved at the end of the school year, stayed somewhere for the summer, and moved again before the next school year started. Every year, a different school.

According to Belinda's book, moving often protected us. From what? I was sure that Gran and Aunt Danielle knew. They always instigated the talk of moving. Their primary argument centered on the fact that moving meant new boys to meet. After all, finding "the right one" remained our priority.

Once I made my selection, we'd all be free until my fatherless daughter turned twelve.

I wished I could be like other kids at school. The normal drama of who dated whom and what so-and-so said to what's-her-name appealed to me. *Heck, just having someone willing to sit with me at lunch would be nice*, I thought. *But, did I want that bad enough to move again so soon?*

Even if we did move, the chances of finding a friend willing to deal with my weirdness was low. No, it was better to stay with the devils I knew. If I beat Mom home, I could try to use makeup to hide whatever mark might be on my cheek.

Hopefully, the problem with Brian and Clavin would die down on its own.

Lost in thought, it took me a moment to hear the sound of a car approaching from behind. Already on the shoulder, I took another step away from the road as I turned to look back. The large, faded yellow car from the student lot approached fast. I squinted, trying to see the driver, which hurt my cheek. Absently, I touched my cool fingers to it.

The fire in my cheek dulled in comparison to my anger when I recognized Brian driving. His glare and white-knuckled grip on the wheel had me spinning away. I jumped the ditch and landed in the field. Trying to run and keep my balance while avoiding the frozen, tilled clumps of dirt proved almost impossible, and I stopped after I'd only made it about five feet.

A large, overturned stone lay loosely on top of the hard ground near my feet. I grabbed it and faced the road.

The car flew past with Clavin's arm hanging out the passenger window. He flipped me off.

Heart hammering from the scare, I stayed in the frozen field and watched them disappear over the next slight rise.

The fields eventually gave way to woods in the direction they'd headed. The same direction I needed to go. My eyes lingered on the distant, dense trees on either side of the long, remote road home. Tops barren, their thick trunks still afforded protection if I needed it. If I could reach them before the boys returned, the trees would give me a chance to run.

Without any other option, I moved back to the road. I still clutched the rock. Heavy and about the size of a hardball, the rock was better than nothing. I could try to throw it at the windshield if they came back before I reached the trees. Deciding not to take a chance on my aim, I started to jog.

My cold hands warmed, and sweat started to dampen the small of my back and underarms. My face hurt, and without my cool hands to help it, I could feel my cheek start to swell.

When I topped the next rise, I spotted the car parked on the west side of the road, a fair distance beyond the start of the trees. Dread filled me.

Apparently, Brian and Clavin weren't ready to forgive and forget.

I couldn't tell if the pair waited in the car or if they already hid in the woods. I stopped my approach and glanced right then left. Neither side of the road presented a better option. Both were still three fields deep before the nearest tree line. Brian and Clavin would spot me before I made it very far and could easily cut off any attempt to avoid them. They probably watched me standing on the rise now. If I turned around, they'd likely just follow.

My stomach churned. I hated my life, but not enough to walk willingly into a fight I'd lose. They'd already injured my face. What would they do to me next? I couldn't imagine it would be an apology.

I eyed the clouds. Dusk stole closer. I didn't have time to stand still and debate my next move. They were determined to confront me again, and I didn't see that I had any other option.

Taking a deep breath and gripping my rock, I started the long walk forward. The wind blew across the fields, playing with my hair and tickling my ears. The sweat I'd worked up cooled too quickly. At least the chill felt good on my face.

When I was close enough to hear the rattle of the barren branches, I saw the outline of the car's two occupants. I stayed focused on them and kept walking.

Both car doors creaked as Brian and Clavin opened them and got out.

I didn't stop.

At about twenty feet away I called, "How much do you like your car?"

"How much do you like your teeth?" Clavin asked.

Well, that made their intent very clear. I pulled back my arm and threw the rock at the car's back window.

My plan? Throw the rock as a distraction, run past Brian who'd presumably freak about his car, and bolt into the trees in the general direction of home.

Instead, I watched in horror as the rock flew straight at Clavin. Despite what they'd done to me, I didn't want to hurt either of them in return. Clavin saw the rock sailing toward him and tried to dodge. The stone clipped his hip with a deep, muffled sound. He folded over.

Brian stood frozen in shock for a moment. Then he ran around the car to check on Clavin.

What had I just done? I shook myself so I could shed the brief paralysis.

I'd created the distraction I needed. The realization motivated me.

I sprinted across the road and cleared the tree line opposite the car. If they caught me—I cringed at the thought and ran faster, dodging around trees to move deeper into cover. Despite my fear, I focused to maintain a sense of direction instead of running blindly. The cloud-filled sky made it difficult, though.

Too soon, I had to stop because of a stitch in my side and the ache in my face. Bent over and gasping for air near a clump of bramble, I tried to listen for pursuit. Voices echoed distantly from the direction I'd run. I couldn't see the boys though.

Shaking with adrenaline and fear, I wanted to cry. Instead, I changed direction and forced myself to walk softly over the leaf-strewn ground. I snuck from tree to tree, making my way back toward the road where the trees thinned. After a few moments of quiet movement, I noticed their yelling had stopped. Hopefully, they would believe I was still running straight toward my house and would keep heading in that direction.

By the time I neared the road, I could breathe semi-normally. The wind swept harder over me through the thinning trees. I stopped walking and leaned against the trunk of one. The dry, rough bark bit into my palms as I risked a look around it. In the distance to the right, Brian's car still sat on the shoulder. At least I'd passed it.

I listened for another moment. Hearing nothing, I sprinted across the road and leapt back into the cover of the trees on the other side. A broken branch, half-covered by fallen leaves, tripped me. Going down hard, I skinned the palm of my right hand.

Immediately scrambling to a crouch, I held my breath and listened again. Nothing. The silence wasn't necessarily a good sign, however. They could be anywhere. Quietly, I made my way farther into the trees and started to follow the general direction of the road. I had no idea how much time had passed, but the fading light spurred me on.

Tired and sore, I jogged when I could and walked when I couldn't, making slow progress. Several times in the distance, I heard a car on the road and quickly dropped to the ground. I wasn't sure how far into the trees they'd be able to see when they drove past, but I didn't want to take a chance.

After a while, the long shadows in the trees forced me to the road, which proved fortunate. I recognized the familiar bend where I emerged. I was so close to home.

I wanted to laugh, but a vibrant orange streaked the sky,

announcing the sun's final rays. Fear, instilled by every lecture from my mother, great-grandmother, and aunts, had me sprinting over the blacktop and down the treacherous gravel driveway.

My house waited ahead, shutters already drawn. The front door stood open, light filling it from the inside. I wheezed for air but didn't slow my pace.

Behind me, the cadence of running feet harshly hitting the crushed gravel grew in volume. Another spike of adrenaline filled me. Even this close to home, within sight of my family, I didn't trust Brian or Clavin to leave me alone. I just hoped it wasn't Brian behind me. Clavin, heavier and less fit than Brian, meant I'd have a chance to reach safety.

My mother stood in the doorway, shouting for me to hurry. She had her arms outstretched to catch me. Worry etched her face.

While my legs continued to eat the distance between me and the house, I looked back. My eyes widened, and I cried out for the second time that afternoon.

Behind me, a dark creature with glowing green eyes and horns galloped on two hooved feet. It seemed more shadow than reality, and I couldn't process what chased me.

My mom's voice called my attention. I quickly focused on her instead of the thing behind me. I sprinted up the steps then through the open door and fell to my knees just inside. The door thumped closed, muffling the sound of the creature reaching the steps.

I never got off my knees before I felt the first, light touch on my skin.

"No," I tried to whisper.

I needed to know what waited outside our door before they forced me to sleep.

Too bad I never seemed to get what I wanted.

Chapter Two

WHEN I WOKE, I SAW WEAK MORNING LIGHT FILTERING THROUGH my curtains and turned my head to check the clock.

My cheek brushed the pillow, and I clenched my teeth against the pain, only to immediately regret my reaction. Even my teeth hurt this morning.

The time on the clock face swam in and out of focus as I struggled to concentrate on anything beyond the throbbing pulse in my cheek. I'd woken at seven, as usual, but there was no toast bearer present. I glanced at my bedroom door. Did that mean no school, either?

Considering the way my face hurt, it wouldn't bother me a bit to stay home. I didn't particularly want to encounter either Brian or Clavin so soon. If they'd hated me because of what I'd said at school, they'd really have it in for me after I hit Clavin with that rock.

Warm under the blankets piled on my bed, I considered closing my eyes and going back to sleep. But I didn't. Not after sleeping for almost fourteen hours.

Ready to face the inevitable, I pulled back the covers and

sat up. My head thumped painfully, and I gently touched my cheek. The skin felt hot, tight, and very puffy. Maybe I had broken something more than the door.

I swung my legs over the side of the bed and stood. Even that simple move induced a wince. My thighs and calves ached like the devil from all the running the day before.

Moving gingerly, I made my way to the bathroom and turned on the light only to quickly switch it off again. Squinting hurt too much.

In the semi-gloom, I scowled at the mirror. A big purple-black bruise covered my right cheekbone and partially surrounded my eye. No wonder my face hurt. Spitefully, I hoped I'd bruised Clavin's hip just as bad. The jerk.

The bruise wasn't the only thing on my face. Dirt streaked my forehead, and I still wore the same mud-caked clothes, right down to the socks. I didn't blame my mom for not changing me but wished she would have. Now, I'd need to clean myself up. Only a good scrub could resolve the mess staring back at me, but the muscles in my legs protested at the thought. A quick rinse would have to do.

I hurried through my shower and cringed whenever the water hit my face, palm, or scraped knuckles. Once I turned off the water, I noticed the house still remained unusually quiet. Typically, we all rushed to get me out the door on time.

After painfully getting dressed, I made my way to the kitchen. The echo of my growling stomach followed me down the hallway.

Everyone, except Aunt Danielle, sat around the table and

quietly watched my approach. My steps slowed at the strange sight. Gran looked sad and slightly worried while my mom and Aunt Grace looked upset.

I opened my mouth to ask what was going on, but my mom cut me off.

"We've read Belinda's book to you since you were born. You know the rules. Home before dark. Perform the ritual. Sleep. What you did last night is unforgivable."

My mouth fell open in shock. It remained like that for a heartbeat before I snapped it shut angrily. The move only hurt me more and fueled my temper.

"I can't believe you think I did that on purpose. Do you see my face?" I waved at my vividly colored cheek. "I was locked in a supply closet, missed the bus, and then had to run home through the woods to avoid the same assholes who did this."

I was so mad I actually swore in front of my mother for the first time. She didn't seem to notice.

"Why, after four and a half years of following the rules, would you think I'd suddenly decide to rebel against the way I've been taught—since I was born—how my life would be?" The yelling hurt my face, but I didn't care. I'd suffered enough abuse in the last twenty-four hours. I didn't need it from my mother or anyone else.

"Thanks for the trust and sympathy, Mom."

Her angry expression cracked to show a small bit of concern. It wasn't good enough though. With angry tears in my eyes, I grabbed my coat and headed out the door. Going to school didn't seem like a bad idea anymore.

Outside, I paused to consider the family car parked on the side of the house, then the long road to school. Even though I should have felt safe in daylight, I wasn't ready to walk that road again. I also didn't want to go back in and ask for a ride after yelling like that.

Life sucked.

The door opened behind me, and I turned to glare at whoever dared approach.

Gran walked out, wearing a warm jacket. Her purse hung from her shoulder and keys jingled in one hand. In the other, she held my bag. Her calm expression melted a tiny bit of my anger as did the way she handed over my bag and the keys.

"You drive to school, and I'll drive back home. One of us will pick you up this afternoon."

I nodded. Gran didn't like to drive, but she would if she had to. She followed me to the car and settled into the passenger seat while I slid in behind the wheel.

About halfway to school, my anger faded, and I started to feel guilty.

"I'm sorry for yelling," I said grudgingly, still feeling like the innocent person in the whole mess. "I was just so mad that Mom didn't even ask me what happened."

"She's sorry, too, honey. When we put you to bed, no one noticed your face. It hadn't yet bruised. You shocked us all this morning and reminded us we need to trust each other. Especially now." She looked straight ahead, watching the road.

Her words brought forward the image of whatever had chased me. I shivered.

"What was that thing?"

"What thing?" She gave me a worried look.

"The black thing with horns that chased me. It couldn't have been so dark that you couldn't see it."

"We didn't see anything, honey, but it sounds like you saw the reason you need to be inside and sleeping at night." She sighed, and a slight quaver of fear escaped with the sound.

"If you didn't see anything, why did you say 'especially now'?" I asked, confused.

"Before you woke, Danielle predicted we'd need to move again. It's why everyone stayed home." Gran paused, and I could feel her studying me. "Given the bullying you received, you won't mind moving, will you?"

Bullying seemed an understatement, given the state of my face. What I'd suffered was abuse, plain and simple, and it reminded me far too much of the time I'd touched a boy and saw my fate as an abused wife. That vision had scared me so bad I'd stayed home for two days then avoided him for the rest of the school year.

In answer to Gran's question, I shook my head.

Even with the many rumors that started no matter where we went, we'd never moved once school started. I'd always managed to hang in there for the long-term even though Gran had suggested leaving early a few times.

There would be no managing. Not this time. After what Clavin and Brian had done to me, I wanted to leave.

Maybe I would have a chance for a friend at the new school, I thought to myself, refusing to revisit my thoughts of the day before. *It has to be better at a new school, not worse.*

"If we're moving, do I really need to go to school today?" I still didn't want to face Clavin and Brian. Hurting Clavin as I had would only make him meaner. Also, my face looked horrible.

"No, I was going to the office to get your records. You can wait in the car if you want."

I thought about her offer. The idea of avoiding everyone had appeal. But why should I be the one to run and hide? Hadn't I done enough of that in my life? Especially last night? Besides, there were books I should return and a final paper I wanted to turn in. I spent a lot of time on it and knew it would earn an A.

Sighing, I declined the easy out.

I turned into the staff lot and parked in a visitor space since she wouldn't be staying long. Then, Gran and I walked to the office together so I could get a late slip.

The state of my face shocked the office secretaries. More so when Gran told them that kids at school did it to me and I wanted to transfer because of it. I flushed as Gran spoke. I hadn't planned to discuss what had happened to my face but understood why Gran said something. It was a convenient and realistic reason for a sudden upheaval. Moving because of a book written by a centuries-old ancestor, or because a monster with glowing green eyes had found me, didn't seem as plausible.

After talking to the principal, Mr. Jameson, for twenty

minutes, I finally made my way to class. I gave the teacher my late slip and ignored everyone's stares as I took a seat.

Barely a heartbeat later, Brian and Clavin's names were called over the loudspeakers. Behind me, someone whispered, "snitch."

Did all the students know what happened? Could my day get worse? Probably.

Although the students seemed to side with Clavin and Brian's actions, the faculty did not.

At the end of first and second hours, I turned in the required textbook and explained that I wouldn't be back. My second-hour teacher glanced at my face sympathetically before nodding. I figured word had already spread through the faculty regarding the reason behind my impending departure.

My stomach began to rumble during third hour. I had lost the chance to eat dinner the night before, and in my rush to leave the house, I'd forgotten breakfast, too. When the lunch bell finally rang, I hurried toward the cafeteria and ignored the students' stares. The presence of additional teachers in the hallway didn't escape my notice though. Bodyguards. Nice.

In line, I piled on as much food as the lunch ladies would allow me. Being poor meant I didn't need to worry about paying, but I was still limited regarding what I could take. Today, though, I had their sympathy, and my bruised face earned me a double scoop of mashed potatoes.

Mouth watering, I made my way through the sea of filling tables. Conversations quieted as I neared some tables and escalated again after I passed.

Close to the table where I usually sat, I saw Brian and Clavin unobtrusively speaking to a group of girls. The pair's gazes darted my direction, but they didn't make a move toward me.

Before I could decide what to do, Mr. Jameson approached me.

"Mind if I sit with you?" he asked. He had a tray of food in his hands as well.

Sit with the principal or risk more Brian and Clavin quality time? I really didn't have much of a choice.

"Not at all," I answered quickly.

Together we walked the rest of the way to the table of isolation; no one approached us the entire lunch hour. Mr. Jameson kept a light, one-sided conversation going. He didn't mention "the incident" or ask to which school I would be transferring. He rambled on about his love of winter and snow. I appreciated his effort and nodded or made non-committal noises when necessary.

As I forked the last bite of food into my mouth, his demeanor changed. He stopped talking and just watched me, his expression hard to read.

I glanced around us, looking for what may have caused the difference. Everything seemed normal to me. Most of the other students had finished eating and had already left the cafeteria, including Brian and Clavin.

Curious, I glanced back at the principal.

"Is there a problem, Mr. Jameson?"

He didn't immediately answer me. Instead, he reached

across the table and lightly touched my bruise. The gesture shocked me.

"Who did this?" he asked before I could react.

I froze. I'd spoken to him, in detail, about what had happened. But his sudden memory lapse didn't concern me. His voice did. It softly echoed, sounding as if two people said the words at the same time. One was Mr. Jameson's voice. The other was deeper, quieter. And it didn't belong. A cold dread spread through me.

His finger stroked my bruised flesh once more, without inflicting pain, before he withdrew his hand. I stared at him, not knowing what to do. First, some kind of phantom monster had chased me home, and now, my principal spoke as if he was possessed. Unrelated? Definitely not.

I opened my mouth to ask who I was speaking to, but the rapid click of heels on the tiled floor interrupted me. My English teacher approached the table, her hard gaze on Mr. Jameson.

She frowned at him several long moments before addressing me.

"I'll walk you to class, Tessa."

I kept my attention on Mr. Jameson as I stood, so I didn't miss the change. He seemed to deflate ever so slightly, his shoulders tilting forward in a subtle hunch. Then he blinked twice and looked down at his food as if lost in thought.

I didn't hesitate; I fled with my English teacher.

FOR THE REST of the day, I watched everyone around me. I knew my peers perceived my actions as weirder than normal, but I couldn't help it.

Some*thing* had taken over Mr. Jameson for a minute. If not for the voice change, I never would have known the difference. Its ability to possess people scared me. It could be anywhere, in anyone. But what did it want...other than to know who bruised my face? And why did it care about that? Why had it chased me last night?

Its appearance at dusk, given the book's rules and warnings, made far more sense than its appearance at school. Why did we need to hide from it at night if it could find us during the day?

Uncertain about the answers to my questions, all I could do was watch and listen for the remainder of the day.

For my seventh hour, I had a study hall. With nothing to do since the homework didn't apply to me, I asked to go to the library to research this new phenomenon in my life. I doubted the school library would have anything related to demon possession, but it didn't hurt to look.

Wandering the racks of books, I didn't at first notice Clavin on the other side of the bookshelf. When he spoke, I nearly screamed.

"Don't do this to us, Tessa," he whispered.

After what had happened at lunch, I'd almost forgotten about my problems with Brian and Clavin.

Annoyed, I pulled a book out so I could see him better. He did the same.

"Do what?" I asked.

"They are talking about you pressing charges. They said we're old enough to be treated as adults. It was a stupid accident, Tessa. We let you out."

His ridiculous statement had me rolling my eyes.

"And what about following me in your car? Chasing me through the woods? Were those accidents, too?"

He looked close to tears as he rubbed his face in frustration.

I felt no pity and didn't stop.

"We both know the only reason you're even slightly remorseful is because you were caught. Look at my face. What you did was not a funny prank. You were angry, and you were cruel. I have to live with the consequence of your actions. You should, too."

I pushed the book back into place and walked away to find the librarian. I'd thrown a rock at Clavin and hurt him. Then, I threw his plea for forgiveness back at him. If he'd been mad before, he'd be furious now.

After my last class, the teacher walked me to my locker. I didn't mind. Students made way for us in the hallway, and Brian and Clavin remained scarce. As I bent to clean out my locker, I wondered if they were even still in school.

Mrs. Wrightly watched me impassively as I put my notebooks and folders in my backpack. Up until today, she had been my least favorite teacher. Older and starchier, she'd lost her tolerance of youths long ago. But I found it hard to dislike her when she diligently watched my back.

I stood and smiled at her.

"Thanks, Mrs. Wrightly. I'm all set."

"I'll walk you to the bus." She didn't wait for my reply but set out in the direction of the main entry. Her sensible pumps announced our approach and cleared a path.

Appreciating the escort, I didn't tell her that my mom's car would be out there somewhere.

In the atrium, Mrs. Wrightly stopped so abruptly I almost collided with her. Wary that whatever happened to Mr. Jameson had gotten to her, too, I stepped around so I could see her face. But, she appeared fine as she stared with tightly compressed lips at the outer doors. Her gaze narrowed behind her overly large glasses.

Turning to see what she was looking at, I saw Brian and Clavin outside. Brian looked worried while Clavin looked angry. Brian reached out, grabbed Clavin's jacket sleeve, and pulled Clavin close to speak in his ear. Whatever they said to each other, they were trying to be quiet about it.

As I watched, Clavin shook off Brian's hand and pushed through the atrium doors. He walked in our direction.

"Should we go to the office?" I asked Mrs. Wrightly.

She no longer looked at Clavin but, instead, studied me. She didn't look as upset as she had a moment ago.

"He looks mad," I said, just in case she'd missed that detail.

She opened her mouth to say something, but Clavin interrupted.

"Mrs. Wrightly, I'm not going to cause any trouble. I just want to talk to Tessa."

I turned away from Mrs. Wrightly, who hadn't even blinked in Clavin's direction, to gape at Clavin.

"What more do you need to say that you didn't say in the library?" I asked.

"Tessa, please. Talk to Mr. Jameson for us."

"Us? Brian's not with you."

Behind Clavin, I caught Brian's gaze through the glass. Brian raised his hands in an apologetic gesture then ran his fingers through his hair. He looked at Clavin, then toward the buses. After one more glance, he walked away. The majority of the students who still lingered inside seemed to sense a confrontation brewing and hurried out the doors to the idling buses too.

Unaware of Brian's desertion and the rapidly emptying atrium, Clavin again glanced at Mrs. Wrightly.

So did I.

Her unwavering gaze met mine. The realization that she'd not once looked away sent a shiver through me.

I took a cautious step back, moving away from both Clavin and Mrs. Wrightly. Clavin grew more agitated with my retreat and kept talking, unaware he no longer spoke to a teacher.

"It was an accident, Mrs. Wrightly. We opened the door to let her out of the closet but then heard someone coming down the hall. That's why we closed the door again."

For the first time, the older woman looked away from me. Her gaze fell on Clavin.

"You?" Her voice echoed oddly.

My heart picked up speed at the proof that Mrs. Wrightly

was no longer herself, and I glanced at Clavin. He didn't seem any more disturbed than he had before, so I doubted he'd heard the echo in her voice.

I prudently took another step back.

Clavin, thinking I meant to leave, reached out to stop me. At the same time, Mrs. Wrightly pivoted and moved between us. Clavin's hand met with Mrs. Wrightly's chest instead of my arm. I continued to back away while watching them.

Clavin stared at his hand in absolute horror and started to stammer an apology. While Clavin looked ready to pass out, Mrs. Wrightly's focus didn't shift. She appeared completely unconcerned with the fact Clavin had yet to remove his hand.

"Did you bruise her?" she asked in a deceptively calm manner.

The thing possessing Mrs. Wrightly had asked just about the same question at lunch.

"It was an accident," Clavin said.

Like before, I saw the change as it jumped bodies. Mrs. Wrightly relaxed slightly as Clavin tensed. They were like two balloons deflating and inflating simultaneously. Clavin immediately focused on me.

Confused by the reason for the switch, I stopped backing up.

"Clavin? What are you doing here?" Mrs. Wrightly demanded as she looked for me.

She frowned when she spotted me ten steps behind her. I barely paid her any attention because Clavin had yet to look away.

When he answered, his words rang with double voices.

"Making amends. Atoning for misdeeds."

I didn't like the sound of that. I waited for the thing to come for me but it surprised me by turning and walking outside. Through the glass doors, I saw the first bus pull away. The rest followed in slow procession.

Clavin kept a steady pace as he crossed the large, cement quad that separated the school's entrance from the parking lane. The final bus departed, and student cars started to drive past. He didn't turn to walk on the sidewalk but walked straight toward the line of traffic.

Alarm pooled and solidified in my stomach.

"No!" I yelled, running forward.

Behind me, Mrs. Wrightly gasped as she, too, realized what Clavin meant to do.

As I pushed through the door, Clavin stepped off the curb in front of a car. The driver, busy with the radio, didn't react in time. The thud of Clavin's body hitting the hood and the squeal of tires covered my second cry. The impact knocked Clavin back a few feet. He collapsed to the ground.

I fell to my knees by his side but didn't touch him, unsure if the thing had released Clavin yet. The cold asphalt bit into my knees as I studied him.

He calmly looked up at me without speaking. Blood streamed from his head where it had connected with the ground. The people surrounding us began to yell for help. Teachers poured from the school as they shouted for the students to move away.

The engine of the car that had hit him quieted. Someone else knelt beside him and started to ask him questions. Neither of us paid any attention.

The thing hadn't yet left Clavin.

"Who are you?" I whispered.

He smiled and reached up to touch my face. I flinched away, and he dropped his hand.

"Now that I found you, I will take care..." Clavin's voice was only a rasp, but the echo behind it came through strong and clear.

"Take care of what?" I asked.

His eyes rolled back in a faint. The teachers swarmed around Clavin, trying to revive him.

I stood, heart racing, and scanned those in the group surrounding us. The thing's ability to jump from person to person terrified me. I spun a slow circle, searching for it. Everyone looked away as soon as I made eye contact. Where did it go?

"Tessa!"

I turned at the sound of my name.

Gran stood outside the crowd, trying to get to me. I ran to her, and the frightened crowd shuffled to give me a wide berth. When I reached her, I didn't slow, but grabbed her arm and pulled her away from the accident. No one moved to stop us.

"We need to get out of here, now." I kept my voice low and quiet. "I'll drive." I held my hand out. My fingers trembled badly, but she willingly surrendered the keys.

Gran hurried to her side of the car as I slid behind the wheel.

Sweat beaded on my upper lip. Something out there watched me, wanted to hurt people who hurt me, and was able to hop from body to body. And, apparently, only I could perceive it.

Shaking, I fumbled with the ignition and, after several attempts, managed to insert the keys.

I buckled as I navigated the visitor lot. In the distance, sirens blared, but I didn't worry about them. I needed to get Gran as far away from that thing as possible. What would it do if it possessed her?

Despite the fear that still shook me, I controlled my use of the gas pedal when I really wanted to floor it. I took an indirect way home, winding through back roads until I felt certain no one followed.

Gran said nothing the entire time.

When I glanced over, I saw her gripping her purse straps tightly and eased off the gas. At some point, I'd begun using it liberally. At least, I now knew she wasn't possessed.

Gradually, the shakes eased and the sweat dried. With only an hour of daylight to spare, I stopped driving aimlessly and headed home.

As soon as I skidded to a dusty stop in front of the house, the front door flew open. My mom hurried down the steps with a scowl.

"Inside," I said without preamble, waving her toward the

house while I moved around the car to help Gran. She was out before I reached her.

"Excuse me?" Mom looked seriously pissed.

I didn't stop to argue with her. Didn't need to. Gran piped up with a sharp, "Get in the house, Clare," and beat me to the door.

Inside, boxes partially covered the table and lined the wall. Many of the cupboards stood open in various states of emptiness. Small things like throw pillows, pictures, and knickknacks no longer decorated the living room. Aunt Danielle sat in her chair with her eyes closed.

"What on earth is going on, Tessa? You were driving like a maniac. That's the only car we have."

"Sorry, Mom."

I let my bag slide to the floor as I dropped into a kitchen chair. I'd thought the shaking was finished, but now, safe at home, it reclaimed me. I leaned forward, braced my elbows on my quaking knees, and rested my head in my hands.

My hand trembled so badly I hurt my own cheek, and the pain finally penetrated my shock.

The silence in the room cocooned me, but it gave me a moment to think. Inside before dark. Sleep until seven. Move often. Pick a boy before my seventeenth birthday. Have a baby, or babies, young. Watch my husband die prematurely.

What happens if I'm out after dark? Something finds me and starts to talk to me through other people. What did it want? Could it find me here? Why was it out during the day? I thought I was safe when it was light outside; otherwise, what was the point of knocking me out each night?

"Baby?"

I raised my head at the gentle touch on my shoulder. My mom stood beside me, watching me with concern.

"Please. What happened?" she asked, all anger absent from her expression.

I looked at Gran, who sat nearby, and Aunt Grace, who had just walked into the room. They all waited. Unsure of what Gran had already told them, I started with what I knew.

"When I was running for the door yesterday, it wasn't just because of sunset. I heard something behind me. Gran says none of you saw it, but when I turned to look back, I did. It had horns on each side of its head, dark shifting skin like black smoke, and glowing green eyes."

No one said anything, but I saw alarm creep into each of their faces. I swallowed hard around my own fear.

"Today at school, something took over Mr. Jameson's body." My hand drifted to my cheek as I remembered its touch. "It wanted to know who bruised me. Before I could say anything, another teacher came over to walk me to class, and it released Mr. Jameson. I watched for it, after that but didn't see it again until the end of the day when it took over Mrs. Wrightly.

"Then, Clavin showed up." My voice broke as I relived the terror.

"It asked if he was the one who bruised me. Clavin tried saying it was an accident. But I don't think it cared. It jumped from Mrs. Wrightly to Clavin. Then, it walked Clavin right in front of a moving car. It said Clavin needed to atone for misdeeds." I took a deep breath and finished on a whisper. "I think it hurt Clavin because Clavin hurt me."

My mom sat heavily in a chair near mine.

"What is it?" I asked, looking at Gran.

"It's what we hide from, obviously," Aunt Danielle said. Her peacefully closed eyes belied her awareness.

We all watched her as we waited for more, but she said nothing.

"Well, we have a lot of packing to do." Mom stood, nervously wiped her hands on her faded jeans, and viewed the enormity of our task before moving toward the dishes. She took a piece of newspaper from the pile on the table and went to the mismatched glasses on the counter.

When she reached for a glass, her fingers brushed its neighbor and nudged it off the edge. I watched it drop to the floor. The tinkling shatter sounded anticlimactic to me. Given my day, it should have been more of an explosion.

Staring at the sparkling splinters that dusted the floor, I thought of birthday candles and wondered if I'd make it another five months.

SINCE MOM ALREADY HAD A HOUSE LINED UP IN THE NEXT county, she and Aunt Grace took the breakables to the new place at first light. A shallow trunk and a short back seat didn't leave room for much else for the initial load. But that was okay. We'd learned over the years that the breakables had a better chance of survival on their own in the car.

To save gas and time, we wouldn't use the car to move everything, though. One of Aunt Grace's co-workers, who owned a pickup and trailer, would stop by the old place after lunch for the bigger pieces.

Because of the short distance, we should be able to move everything in one day. We had talked about possibly moving farther away, but the cost of gas and Mom and Aunt Grace's current jobs just didn't make it feasible. And, finding another employer wanting to hire two people at a comparable pay was out of the question.

While they were gone, Gran and I kept working. We packed up my bedroom. Then I focused on taking apart the beds. Mattresses lined the living room by lunchtime.

Lacking anywhere to sit comfortably for a break, I took my sandwich out to the porch. My breath fogged the air as I sat in Gran's chair and took in the dormant landscape. I'd been looking forward to seeing what this house would be like blanketed in white at Christmas, which was only a few weeks away. If only the snow hadn't stubbornly refused to fall yet.

I watched the frozen branches sway and ate my sandwich. Chewing still sent little twinges of pain into my cheek, but it wasn't enough to stop me from eating. The subtle ache was enough of a reminder, though, for me to almost choke on my bite of sandwich when Clavin's shiny, cherry red car turned onto our drive.

Fear slithered down my spine. Who was really driving? Clavin or what possessed him yesterday?

Through the windshield, Clavin watched me before glancing at the house. The change in his attention was a good sign. No burning fixation that I'd noticed during a possession.

While I was terrified of the thing that had hurt Clavin, I also wisely acknowledged Clavin was a danger to me, too. My face still vibrantly displayed a reminder of how far he could go.

I set my sandwich aside and stood. The sooner I dealt with Clavin, the sooner he could leave before that thing returned.

As he parked, I studied him for any sign of aggression. The last time I'd made him mad, he'd been flushed with anger. He didn't appear flushed now, just pale. Despite his apparent calm, I still hoped Gran wouldn't notice his arrival. I didn't want her hurt.

He opened the car door and used the frame to attempt to leverage himself from the seat. It took several tries before he managed to pull himself upright. He paused for a moment and rubbed his forehead tiredly, which called attention to his tousled hair. It stood out in different directions with the strands in front sticking up from the bandage at his hairline.

With an awkward hobble, he got out of the way to close the door then kept a hand on the hood to make his way toward me. As he rounded the front of the car, the reason for his struggling progress became clear. A cast covered his leg from toe to mid-thigh.

The memory of the car hitting him changed my self-concern to pity.

"Are you supposed to be walking around on that leg?" I asked.

He stopped his approach, his fingertips on the hood for balance, to glance down at his leg.

"No, but I had to come."

When he met my gaze again, I saw panic in his eyes.

"I think I'm going crazy, Tessa. When I woke up this morning, there was a note by my bed. It looked like I wrote it, but I don't remember doing it."

A chill ran through me, and it had nothing to do with the cold.

"What did the note say?"

"It was about you, but I don't understand it." His voice quavered. Balancing against the hood, he reached into his pocket, pulled out a crumpled piece of paper, and offered it to me.

Hoping I wasn't making a huge mistake, I left the porch and grabbed the note.

"You need to sit down." I helped him over to the bottom step. By the time he was sitting, he looked like he was about to throw up.

Giving him a moment, I skimmed the page.

Go to her. Apologize. Without her forgiveness, your other leg is next.

I sat heavily next to Clavin and met his watery gaze.

He cleared his throat and swallowed hard.

"When I came to at the hospital, they told me I walked right in front of the car. The doctor said I was lucky the car wasn't going faster. Brian was there. He said he called my name as soon as I walked out the doors, but I didn't even look at him. I don't remember any of it."

Clavin looked down at his hands, and I saw a tear fall onto his sleeve.

"At school, the rumor is that you can see the future."

I flinched a little.

"Do you know what's going on?" he asked, his words laced with desperation.

My stomach flipped with relief. For a moment, I'd thought he would accuse me of controlling the thing, or maybe even him, and causing his accident.

"I wish I did know," I said, looking toward the trees to give him a minute to wipe his face.

I grew up knowing that I was different. My weird family history made it marginally easier to deal with the possibility that something was out there possessing people. However, poor Clavin had to be going crazy with fear.

"I forgive you, Clavin. Whether what happened was an accident or a malicious plan, I forgive you." I hoped that speaking the words would spare him any further involvement.

Clavin's tears started falling in earnest. He nodded then awkwardly pulled himself to his feet. Without saying anything further, he limped back to his car.

As I watched him struggle, I didn't ask if he was okay to drive or if he wanted to stay. Forgiving him didn't mean I liked him. I sat on the step until he pulled onto the road then went back to Gran's chair and my sandwich, thankful she hadn't come outside. The turkey and cheese didn't appeal to me anymore, but I still munched on it while staring at the note I'd kept.

When the thing had used Mr. Jameson, it had wanted to know who hurt me; and when it found out, it had hurt the person back. Was that protective or possessive? I needed to figure out what the thing was and what it wanted.

Popping the last bite into my mouth, I stood and tucked the folded paper into my pocket.

Mom and Aunt Grace returned just a few minutes later, and their friend arrived not long afterward. We loaded as much as we could on the trailer and more into our car since they would follow him to the new place.

I waved as they left then went back into the house. Looking

at the piles of belongings that remained, I estimated we would need another two trips with the truck, which meant they would make it back from the last trip just before dark. The house would be empty of everything but cleaning supplies, sleeping bags, a few blankets, and Aunt Danielle's chair. The chair always went last.

The prospect of a night in an empty house unsettled me because now I knew what waited out there in the dark. Somehow, the furniture and our things made the house feel safer.

BY THE TIME we finished stacking the final load onto the trailer, every muscle ached, especially in my legs. I'd overused them in the last few days, and they were letting me know, loud and clear, that they wouldn't put up with anything tomorrow. That meant finishing the bathroom today.

Kneeling on the floor to scrub around the toilet would probably send my legs into a state of mutiny. I could picture my legs detaching themselves in a cartoonish way and walking off without me.

Smiling at the possibility, I went back to work.

"Tessa, honey, you look exhausted," Mom said a long while later. "I think you should get ready for bed now."

Glancing up from the dustpan I held, I nodded and wondered when they'd returned. Too tired to ask, I finished sweeping the corners of the last vacant room and joined Aunt

Grace in the living room. Without furnishings, the house echoed loudly, and chilly drafts drifted along the floor where she'd made everyone blanket beds. Though I wouldn't notice any of the discomfort once they knocked me out, I wondered what the rest of my family would do.

I collapsed onto my blanket and listened to them move around as they closed up the house for the night.

Finally, the lights clicked off, leaving only the glow of the candle that burned near Aunt Danielle. I blinked my eyes slowly as the flickering light played tricks with me. For a second, I thought I saw the outline of the chair handle through her hand.

Everyone gathered around me, and the familiar words filled the space. Comforting. My eyes drifted shut before their first touch.

THE NEXT DAY, my legs stayed attached even though they hurt. By nine, we all piled in the car. I sat in front with Mom while Aunt Grace, Aunt Danielle, and Gran rode in the back. Everything we'd kept with us, including Aunt Danielle's chair, fit into the twine-tied trunk.

Unable to help myself, I looked back as we pulled away. Something told me that moving wouldn't be enough this time.

It took about forty-five minutes to reach our new home. The updated ranch, with a paved driveway and a garage, was located in a quiet neighborhood of a small town. The light grey siding and professional landscaping looked established. The dark grey shutters on the windows appeared new though. The house was a definite upgrade for us, and I sent my mom a puzzled look.

"My boss," she said by way of explanation. "When I told him why I needed a few days off and what happened at school, he offered this place. I couldn't say no. The rent is reasonable, and it's still close to work. Plus, being in town will be an advantage. You can walk places easily and won't have to spend so much time on the bus."

"And the shutters?"

"A special request that he didn't mind. I said it was a religious thing."

Aunt Grace took me on a tour of the house while Mom and Gran helped Aunt Danielle inside.

No old planks covered the floors in this house. We'd been upgraded to tiles in the kitchen and carpet in the living room. It continued down the hall to the left of the kitchen and in all three bedrooms.

The master suite, which Mom and Grace would claim, had its own bathroom. Gran, Aunt Danielle, and I would share the one in the hall. While the rest were sharing bedrooms, I'd get my own. They always made sure I had a room to myself.

In every room, light, welcoming colors coated the walls.

Even in an obvious state of disarray with boxes everywhere, the place felt homey.

Wasting no time, we began unpacking. The pile of empty boxes on the curb began to grow by lunch.

Over lunch, Mom and I debated whether I should go to school that afternoon.

"I have enough going against me. Do I need to add a bad first impression to the list?"

She eyed my purple cheek and grudgingly agreed.

We used the weekend to finish settling in, and by the third day in the new house, everything was back to business as usual, except for school. Though I appreciated the decreased swelling around my eye, the coloring remained so vivid in one small area that concealer did nothing to hide it.

With nothing better to do, I lay on the couch with one of my legs hooked over the arm and studied Belinda's book. It worried me that the creature seemed to have taken an interest in me, and I hoped I might find a clue somewhere in the worn pages.

However, the familiar words didn't tell me anything new, so I started studying the book as a whole. On the first page, scrawled in shaky penmanship, Belinda wrote the date August 17, 1798. The penmanship varied in several areas of the book, but none of it was dated as the original pages had been. Obviously, Belinda's descendants had added to it at some point.

Despite its age and all the evidence of its use, the book had held together remarkably well with only a few signs of repair.

The list of descendants in the back of the book didn't note any dates of births or deaths. That missing information, along with no last names, made doing research very difficult. All the moving around everyone had done didn't help either.

The book never said, "Don't write a last name," or, "Don't enter any dates," so why didn't we put them in there? My thoughts went to the possibility of someone reading it. Given the odd rules and ambiguous reasons for them, who would take any of it seriously? Even if they did take it seriously, who would be able to gain any information from it to track down any of us?

Studying the family tree, I noticed a pattern. I knew we only bore daughters and that not all daughters branched out.

Now, I noticed that only one daughter out of each generation went on to have children. If Aunt Danielle had a baby, that child's name had never been entered. And, I knew from talking to Aunt Grace that she'd purposely chosen a match where there wouldn't be children. Was that what had been happening for over two hundred years? I counted generations. I was the fifteenth. I cringed at how young some of the women had to have been when they gave birth.

"If you keep frowning at that book, it'll burst into flames," Gran said as she walked into the living room.

"I can't believe there's so little information to go by. If it weren't for the chant and me sleeping until sunup every day, I'd think this whole thing a fake."

Gran made an agreeing noise.

"You should go for a walk. It's not bad outside, and the fresh air will clear your head."

"Our ideas of cold are very different," I said, already going to bundle up.

Armed with a button-up grey woolen coat, thick cream-colored mittens, and a cute knit earflap hat with a tassel, I stepped outside. The bright sun fought to warm my face, despite the chill. Gran, as usual, was right. It wasn't bad out.

I mentally let go of Belinda's puzzle and just enjoyed my freedom as I walked toward the downtown area.

A little coffee shop set in the lower half of a narrow, two-story brick building caught my eye. The door and two picture windows took up the front of the shop. The right window sported a white, painted outline of an old-fashioned coffee cup complete with wisps of steam. Above the cup, the words "Coffee Shop" clearly identified the type of establishment within.

A handwritten sign was taped to the inside of the window. In black marker, it stated, "Weekend Help Needed." Normally, I wouldn't pay attention to a job posting, but the hours held my attention. Seven-thirty in the morning until one.

The bell above the door jingled as I let myself in, and coffee-scented heat enveloped me. Pulling off my hat and mittens, I closed my eyes in bliss. The taste of coffee didn't do much for me without a lot of cream and sugar, but I loved the smell of it. I exhaled slowly and looked around.

Seven small, glass-topped tables crowded the dining area. The top half of the interior walls matched the brick outside while taupe paneling capped with a chair rail covered the bottom half. Someone had managed to hang a few pictures and decorations in the mortar. The space felt cozy and welcomed people to sit and read a paper while they drank.

The L-shaped service counter quartered off the back of the

room. On the longer stretch of the L sat a register along with a variety of coffee-making equipment.

At the sound of the bell, a middle-aged woman leaned against the counter. She wore a printed t-shirt tucked into jeans and had a fluff of orange hair that haloed her head.

"You can order up here and sit anywhere you like," she said with a friendly smile.

Thankful for the change in my pocket, I ordered then asked about the sign while I watched her make my drink. She explained she just needed help during the weekends because that was when she served sandwiches. While the food was delicious, making it slowed her down. So she needed someone to take orders at the counter and deliver them to the tables.

"I have to be honest. The pay will suck. It'd be server wages because of the tables and tips. I've had a few kids try it, but they usually leave for something that pays minimum wage." She handed me the application. "Bring it back if you're interested."

I smiled my thanks and took the sheet and my coffee.

"I'm Mona, by the way," she said, introducing herself.

I offered my hand.

"Tessa."

"I have to ask. What happened to your eye?"

"I'm probably one of the few people that can honestly say I ran into a door."

"Clumsy?" she asked, her gaze flicking to the application.

I laughed.

"Not usually." Hiring a clumsy person in a coffee shop

wouldn't do much for the already slow business. "If I can borrow a pen, I'll fill this out now."

Thankfully, the simple form didn't ask for any prior employment references. When I handed it back to her along with my empty cup, she looked over the application.

"First job?" she asked.

"Yeah. I don't own a car, and you're within walking distance from my house."

She nodded while reading.

"This looks good. If you're up for it, let's give it a try this Saturday. Be here by seven-thirty. Wear comfortable shoes, jeans, and a t-shirt. Nothing freaky. We'll see how that goes."

I agreed, said goodbye, and left with a smile. Mom would flip and probably not in a good way. Outside, a bus drove past, and I realized I'd stayed longer than I thought. I set out at a brisk pace and made it home in seven minutes.

Gran was quietly talking to Aunt Danielle when I opened the front door. The book lay in Gran's hands. When they saw me, Gran smiled widely and stood.

"You look much better. Happy. What happened?" She took my hat and mittens and put them in the hanging basket under my coat hook.

"I got a job," I said with a small smile as I hung my jacket.

I moved to the fridge and started to pull out dinner ingredients. The growing silence wasn't unexpected.

Spontaneity wasn't our thing. We were careful people. We talked, planned, and then decided together if the plan would work.

Setting everything on the counter, I grinned at Gran.

"Seriously. It was as if it was meant to be. It's only on the weekends from seven-thirty until one. The owner, Mona, admitted the pay sucks, but it seems like it'd be a good first job. And it sounds like a few kids left the job already, so if it doesn't work out, I doubt she'll be surprised if I quit."

Gran nodded and helped me put a salad together for dinner. When Mom came home, she wasn't as surprised about the job as I'd thought. She smiled and said she knew moving was the right thing.

MY BRUISE HAD FADED enough by the next morning that I could hide its remnants with the heavy concealer. Having done my fair share of first days, I wasn't nervous. Since Mom had already stopped by the school to get me registered, I walked through the doors with my schedule in hand, ready to try again.

The main entrance opened to a modest lobby that smelled like wet sneakers. Two primary hallways branched from the lobby. I spotted the office to the right and went to check in.

Another student dressed in a red, black, and grey plaid, pleated skirt and solid grey sweater layered over a white collared button-up already stood in the office. She leaned comfortably against the counter as she talked to the secretary. I wondered if this school encouraged uniforms.

The secretary looked up at me, and I gave my name. She

smiled in welcome, asked the girl to give me a brief tour, and handed us both late slips. Popping a tutti-frutti scented bubble between her teeth, the girl nodded her mostly blonde head and motioned for me to follow. The pink and purple dyed strips of her hair contrasted her otherwise school-girl look.

With a welcoming smile, she introduced herself as Beatriz. After showing me my locker, we went down my list of scheduled classes, finding each room in relation to my locker.

Beatriz's relaxed manner and easy monologue about the school had me wishing for a friend. Oh, I knew how to make friends. I just knew that I couldn't keep them. Friends eventually wanted to come over or go out at night. They also eventually asked hard questions I couldn't answer. At least, not without sounding crazy.

So, when she concluded the tour, I smiled and thanked her but didn't start up any additional conversation. Instead, I turned and began to put my things into my locker. The tactic usually drove people away from me. Not Beatriz.

"You know, I'm going to like you," she said from just behind me.

I glanced over my shoulder at her, trying to figure out why she was still there.

"Simple things. Nothing pretentious." She nodded at the stuff in my locker.

I studied my school supplies. Cheap and bought in bulk, the supplies hadn't ever warranted much thought. I did my homework with them and moved on to other things. There and gone again.

"You can tell a lot about a person by their locker," she said. "I'm taking a guess here, but you keep to yourself and don't really care what people think about you." She didn't give me a chance to answer. "Come on. We have first hour together. We can catch the last few minutes."

It turned out that we had several classes together. Beatriz talked to me in the hall when she had a chance and introduced me to a few other students. Overall, it easily ranked as the best first day ever. I didn't have to touch a boy once.

That night when my mom got home, she asked if I met anyone interesting. I mentioned Beatriz even though I knew she meant boys. She gave me a level look and told me I needed to put more effort into choosing a boy. I didn't need the reminder. I knew my seventeenth birthday loomed on the horizon, making my time left to decide short.

I nodded in agreement while I wondered again what would happen to me if I just didn't choose.

Chapter Four

THE SECOND DAY OF SCHOOL DIDN'T GO AS WELL.

After lunch, Jess, a boy in my geometry class, stopped me outside of the cafeteria. While the majority of students still milled around us in the hallway, he awkwardly asked if I had plans on Saturday.

I wanted to lie and say I did, but I knew I was running out of time to make my choice. In a friendly and hopefully non-suggestive manner, I touched his arm, briefly letting the vision wash over me before giving my regrets.

His face fell slightly, and a flush started to creep up his neck. I thought my rejection had hurt his feelings, but then he stood straighter, and his previously downcast gaze met mine directly.

"Tell me. What did you see?"

The echo in Jess's voice stole my breath and lights danced before my eyes as nausea rose. The thing was back.

"You don't look well. Come. Sit." The thing that wore Jess motioned me into the quieter lunchroom, where the lunch-ladies were already starting to wash tables, and waited expectantly for me to move.

I hesitated to do anything he suggested but knew I didn't really have much of a choice. After all, he could jump bodies, follow me, and possibly hurt the person he controlled. A thought struck me. If I didn't listen, could he control me?

I woodenly moved into the large space then faced him. "Who—what are you? What do you want?" My voice came out strong, surprising me since my insides felt like jelly.

"Don't you know?" he asked. For the first time, an expression leaked through the face of the person he controlled. He appeared puzzled. "Did you lose the book?"

My mouth popped open. How could he know about the book? He watched me patiently, his observant gaze never wavering.

When I didn't speak, he answered my last question.

"I am here to collect on the bargain Belinda's father made."

"What bargain? What are you collecting?" My voice rose in fear.

"Excuse me, you two," one of the lunch ladies boldly interrupted. I swung my shocked gaze in her direction. "You'll have to take your drama somewhere else. The bell rang, and we need to clean up."

I barely managed a nod. When I turned back to Jess, he frowned at me in confusion.

"How did we get here?" he asked without an echo to his voice.

It had left. Relief flooded me along with a healthy dose of

frustration. Whatever that thing was, it had answers my family needed. Answers I needed. I had to speak to it again. The thought made my stomach dip dangerously.

Jess blinked at me, waiting for an answer, and not wanting to ruin a potentially good school, I lied like a pro. "Are you okay, Jess? You asked me if I had plans on Saturday and kinda blanked on me for a minute. Want me to walk you to the nurse's office?"

It took effort to sound concerned and caring when bigger problems floated around in my head, but I managed. Jess shook his head, and I watched him slowly walk off before I hurried to my next class. I'd been right about the move. Nothing had changed except for maybe keeping me safe from bullies.

For the rest of the day, I debated whether I should keep what had happened in the cafeteria to myself as I had with Clavin's visit and the note. I knew it hurt to keep secrets, but I knew what my family would want to do when they found out. And I didn't think another move was the answer. If the thing had followed us from the other house, what would keep it from doing so again? But I worried that staying might mean that it could find a way to hurt my family like it had Clavin. I had to trust that the precautions we used—locking up the house at night and the chant—would be enough to keep us safe.

When the final bell rang, I put my books in my locker with relief. There had been no sign of any possessions since lunch. Then again, I didn't have much of an idea of what I was looking for. I thought about checking out the school's library. There wasn't much hope that this library would have more than the last school, but I figured I'd try. Besides, asking for books about demon possession would cause less suspicion at this school. My reputation hadn't yet had time to grow. Plus, I could easily walk home now. Easily, but maybe not comfortably, I thought as I recalled the brisk walk home from the Coffee Shop.

Walking home from school would be just as chilly. If I saved what I made working, I would need to talk Mom into taking me to the thrift store. The image of a thick, fluffy jacket popped into my head, but I hesitated to get excited over it. My current jacket had been a gift from everyone at home. Would purchasing a new one hurt their feelings?

"Doesn't that hurt?"

I spun around, recognizing both the voices that spoke.

Beatriz stood beside me, studying me. Her animated expressions from the day before were absent as her calm hazel eyes studied me.

"What?" My response came out as more of a croak, and I quickly looked around to see who stood close enough to hear our conversation.

"Biting your lip. Doesn't that hurt?" It tilted Beatriz's head and pointedly looked at my mouth.

"Uh, I'm careful?" I hadn't even known I was biting my lip.

The thing nodded Beatriz's head as if it understood, but it didn't relax its searching gaze or alert stance.

"What did Belinda write in her book?"

That question surprised me. When it mentioned the book before, I thought it knew something more than I did. If not, then how did it even know about Belinda's book? I wondered what I should reveal. Should I pretend I didn't understand the question? Was there something in the book that could hurt us if I shared the information? I didn't think so. The fact that the information was unhelpful in my own search for answers prodded me to answer honestly, yet vaguely.

"Rules and everyone's first name. Like a family tree. That's all."

"What rules?"

After a lifetime of secrecy, talking about our weird rules in public unnerved me. In my mind, I imagined everyone around us hearing everything even though I spoke softly.

"Home before dark. Close up the house. Sleep." I didn't elaborate on that part. "And choose a boy before we turn seventeen."

It was quiet for a long moment and actually broke eye contact to look away with an unfocused gaze. "Haven't you ever wondered why you're choosing a boy?" The last word was said with contempt.

I wondered about its distaste for the word but could only nod. Yes, I did wonder why. I wanted to know badly but wasn't sure if I should trust anything the not-Beatriz before me said.

Her eyes focused on me, and whatever controlled her answered as if it had seen my nod. "I'll sit with you tomorrow at lunch. We'll talk more then."

Again, I was left feeling torn and dealing with a confused person.

Tomorrow would be a good day to pretend to be sick.

NO MATTER how much I didn't want to go to school, I couldn't come up with a good reason for my mom to let me stay home. Or, at least, one that didn't involve the truth. Though I didn't want to keep what happened from my family, I knew how they would react. I could imagine my mom telling her boss we needed to move already, less than a week after we'd arrived. The thought made me cringe for her. How awkward would her work relationship be after that? Especially when he'd been so nice about setting up this place for us. No, I firmly decided to keep my problem to myself.

When the bell rang for lunch, I approached the cafeteria with caution. Beatriz caught up with me in line, and we chatted about our English assignment as I covertly watched everyone around us.

After the lunch ladies filled my tray, Beatriz and I found a table. She sat next to me, still talking. Jess seemed to consider joining us but changed his mind at the last minute, which was for the best. With him, I would have four kids in three years. One set of twins. He would die in a car accident, leaving me heart-broken because I would have loved him. That, along with the idea of four kids, scared me. None of the existing branches showed four. Three topped it. The life expectancy of our men, along with the gestation period, made having more children nearly impossible.

As soon as Beatriz finished her lunch, her entire demeanor changed, and I knew she was no longer Beatriz.

"You look well today," the thing controlling her said with an indecipherable expression.

Maybe because I'd been expecting its appearance, or maybe because I'd already spoken to it several times, I didn't feel the usual spike of numbing fear. Oh, the idea that something was following me and possessing people still scared me, just not enough to paralyze me.

"Thank you," I said hesitantly. "Not to be rude, but what are you?"

"A creature created long ago when nature was corrupt with other influences."

That told me nothing. I toyed with my fork as I tried to gain the courage I needed to be more direct. Given how quickly it tended to disappear, I didn't want to let this chance to get a meaningful answer slip by.

So, I took a calming breath and forced myself to just start talking.

"What bargain were you referring to yesterday?"

I startled a little when it reached over and removed the fork from my hands. A small smile played on its lips. Setting the fork on its own tray, it leaned toward me and spoke softly.

"Belinda grew up without a mother. Her father, who loved her very much, worked hard to provide for them but could never earn enough to improve their circumstances. He worried about what would become of Belinda if something should happen to him. He tried to arrange a match for her, but she didn't like her options. To be honest, I don't think her father did either, but with so little money back then, there wasn't much choice. So he called on me. He asked for—"

"Wait, he called on you?" The story sounded a lot like a fairy tale I once read. "What does that mean? Did he know you?" It shook Beatriz's head. "Then how did he call on you?"

"Let's save that for another time. We don't have much left today."

I looked around, noted the emptying cafeteria, and nodded.

It gazed thoughtfully at me then continued its story.

"He asked for money. Just enough to secure a future for Belinda." At my puzzled look, it explained before I could interrupt again. "I can make deals. Pacts. I have the power to grant requests, but there's always a price. The price was Belinda."

My mouth popped open. No wonder she'd been hiding. But why leave a book telling us we needed to hide, too, if she was the price?

"I wanted a companion. Someone to talk to. In my mind, I could provide her with security no human could. At that point in my existence, I'd had little exposure to humans and didn't fully understand...well, I didn't understand much. However, I did want a companion who would come to me by choice.

"We struck a deal. I could spend time with Belinda to present myself to her as a choice. Because I'm not very patient,

I set a limit to the amount of time she had to decide. She had until her seventeenth birthday. In the event that she didn't choose me, I added a clause allowing me to present myself to any descended from her line under the same conditions until someone did choose me."

The bell rang, startling me. I looked around. The cleaning crew began to make their way along the tables. Voices from the steady stream of students in the hallway drifted in. When I looked back, Beatriz stood and grabbed her tray.

"Tomorrow."

After that word, it left. And I still didn't know what it was. Could I trust what it said? The information all seemed to fit and explained why Belinda wrote the book; she'd made her choice and left the rest of us to suffer the consequences.

AFTER SCHOOL, I headed to the library to do some research like I'd wanted to do the day before. As I'd suspected, there wasn't much to be found, and what little there was mostly pointed to demonic possession. There were only a few references to mental illness. I ruled out mental illness right away. There was no way so many people in my family could fall victim to spontaneous, temporary mental illness. It would be too much of a coincidence.

Then, a thought occurred to me. What if they weren't the ill ones?

The common factor in all of the occurrences was me. I

remained the only one to see the thing. And for all of the people it had possessed, only I seemed to hear it. My ability to glimpse my future, coupled with the sleep thing, wasn't normal. Growing up, I'd been told repeatedly to keep that part of who I was to myself. What if my family just wanted to protect me from myself and this was all in my head?

Deep in thought, I left the library and started the seven-block walk home. The overcast sky matched my troubled mood. Just in case my psyche wasn't the issue, I needed to categorize the questions I had and decide which one was the most important. Then, I would know what to ask first the next time I had a chance.

I really wanted a better explanation of what it was. But did that matter more than finding out what it wanted? After our talk today, I had a general idea. Yet, I needed to know what, exactly, presenting itself to me as a choice meant. He'd said he wanted a companion. But why? That brought me back to who it was. Was it a he? A she? Did it even have a gender? What was its name? The questions started to pile up.

Taking a deep breath, I cleared my mind and started again. What is your name, and what does it mean to choose you? Good.

As I neared the house, I slowed down and circled back to my original thought. Could I trust anything it said? The only person who could verify the thing's story died almost two hundred years ago. All I had to go on was its word, which might even be a figment of my deranged mind.

Red-nosed and weary, I pushed open the front door and

called out a less than chipper greeting. Gran responded from the back of the house.

"I was wondering where you were. Did you run into trouble?" She moved toward the kitchen with a concerned expression and looked me over for any new marks of trauma. She wouldn't see them. They were well hidden in my mind.

"I was doing some research at the library. Mom's right. Living in town is kind of nice." I made an effort to sound happy as I peeled off my jacket, hat, and mittens.

Gran stepped aside so I could put them away.

"As long as you're safe, that's all that really matters." She grinned at me impishly and then added, "Your mom was right about town. I do like having neighbors again."

Moving to the stove, she stirred the browning ground meat. While we put together the fixings for tacos, she told me about the widower two houses down who'd stopped by to offer his help when it snowed.

"I assured him that with all of us girls working, we'd be fine on our own, but he insisted. He has one of those machines to clear away the snow. Said he'd be happy to do it in exchange for some cocoa."

I looked up at Gran, astonished as something clicked into place. The book said we needed to choose before seventeen. After we chose, we lost our gift and no longer needed to hide until our daughters turned twelve. Oh, and our husbands were short-lived. Why, then, hadn't anyone ever remarried? Based on her comments, Gran was still interested.

Before I could ask her, the door opened, and Mom and

Aunt Grace walked in. It wasn't a topic I wanted to bring up in front of everyone. So I kept quiet.

As I waited in the lunch line, the question repeated in my mind. What is your name, and what does it mean for me to choose you? Even though I still wasn't sure if I would believe the answers it might give, I wanted to be ready.

"I like how you dress."

I turned and saw Beatriz standing just behind me. Since I'd been watching for the thing, I had no idea how not-Beatriz had managed to sneak up on me.

The boy who was behind me eyed her oddly, and I realized how the compliment must have sounded. Having a rumor that I was a lesbian floating around school would be a new one for me.

Since not-Beatriz stood awkwardly to the side, I handed her a tray and motioned for her to step in line. The boy behind us didn't object but watched us closely.

Moving with the line, I watched her out of the corner of my eye. Whatever controlled her did everything I did, asked for what I asked for, and studied how I interacted with people. If the thing wanted to learn social skills, I'd have to let it know I'd be a bad choice for a role model.

"I dress like everyone else," I said as we waited for the register.

"No. You don't."

I glanced at it questioningly.

"You dress for yourself. They dress for everyone else."

For the first time, I really noticed what I wore and compared my clothes to everyone around me. Sure, I wore the same worn and holey style of jeans, but that was easy to do when you were poor. My style similarity stopped there, though. I didn't own the cute little flats or the high heels that some wore. I owned sneakers. One pair. That's what I wore. My mom and I wore the same size tops, so we swapped around our clothes to keep a bigger selection. She didn't work anywhere with a dress code, so cumulatively, we owned t-shirts, long and short-sleeved, and a few sweaters.

Mostly, I layered the t-shirts and wore a hoodie when it got too cold. I didn't wear makeup. I didn't have enough time in the morning, thanks to the curse. And jewelry, even the cheap stuff, felt like a waste of money.

After taking inventory, I felt decidedly inferior. Yet, not-Beatriz liked that. Why? Did it think my poverty made me more desperate?

Leading the way to the table, I put down my tray and sat stiffly. "They have money. I don't."

It quietly watched me take a bite. "You're upset. Why?"

"You just told me I dress like a..." I was at a loss for the word then thought of one Gran used. "A schlub."

Beatriz's brown eyes remained focused on my face as if it gleaned information from me that way, and it canted her head at me. "Is that a word?"

"It is in my house," I mumbled, looking down. I forked in

another bite of food and took a moment to taste what I was eating. Alfredo. Glancing at my tray, I grabbed a breadstick and dipped it in the sauce.

"I think you misunderstood me. I like how you dress. I wasn't hinting at anything with my words."

I glanced up but couldn't read anything in Beatriz's expression. "Fine. Let's just forget it." Was I really getting moody with the unknown creature sitting inside Beatriz's body? My questions. I needed to focus.

"What is your name, and what does it mean to choose you?"

A choking noise to my right distracted me. The boy who'd been behind us in line sat a few seats away. Although he sat partially turned away from us, he'd obviously been listening. I narrowed my gaze, thought about what we'd said so far, then rolled my eyes. Yep, by tomorrow, I'd be a confirmed lesbian. That'd put a damper on meeting new boys.

"Morik," not-Beatriz said, answering my question. "And choosing me means time with me. As I said, I've been alone a long—"

I held up my hand when the boy made another sniggering noise, and I pointedly darted my gaze toward our eavesdropper. Beatriz's flat gaze shifted to the boy. In an instant, the thing left Beatriz then entered the boy. I felt horrible and didn't know what to do. Would it hurt him? What could I say to prevent that from happening? Call it back, maybe?

The boy picked up his tray and stood.

"Tessa, I don't feel good," Beatriz said quietly.

Forcing my gaze away from the boy, I noted Beatriz's pale complexion. I'd completely forgotten about her. She looked more scared than sick, though.

"I don't remember how I got here." Her voice warbled with barely suppressed tears.

"Oh, honey, we walked together." My pitying look wasn't fake. I hated lying, but the truth was worse.

Before I could say more, it returned. Beatriz's expression of fear faded into the calm mask of someone possessed by that thing. Morik.

I looked around and spotted the boy. He sat further away and was looking around, puzzled.

"You need to stop doing that," I said, focusing on Beatriz again.

Her eyes shifted from me to the boy it'd placed across the cafeteria. The boy looked back at us in confusion, and I averted my gaze.

"All the people you keep popping into are going to think they're crazy," I said.

"I am willing to spend time with you in my true form, but I do not think you are ready."

The image of its glowing green eyes crossed my mind. Morik was right. I wasn't ready and didn't think I ever would be.

Obviously, now that Morik had found me, he wanted to be around me until I made my choice. And, for now, he would be in other people's bodies. I shivered, thinking of later. Is that why Belinda chose a boy? To get rid of him? No wonder she said to hide. That thought made me pause. How had he found me in the first place? Was it really because I'd been out at dusk? I opened my mouth to ask, but he interrupted me.

"We will talk more later." Then, Morik was gone.

Frustrated, I sighed before realizing Beatriz was back and in need of comfort.

"You're not going crazy—I can see that's what you're thinking, so stop. You probably had a lot on your mind when we walked here. It's not like we were talking. I've walked myself to the kitchen hundreds of times and then wondered how I got there."

She studied me for a moment, probably looking for sincerity, then started to eat her untouched lunch. I dug into my own.

These quick conversations with Morik weren't answering my questions, but they did hint at one thing: He didn't want to harm me. I needed more time with him to get the information I wanted in full detail. Maybe that was his plan. Tease me with information so I'd willingly spend time with him.

Barely suppressing a sigh, I also realized that if I wanted to spend the time with him to get my answer, I needed a host for him. Beatriz was out. So was talking during school. After school then. But with who? I looked around. The boy who'd been watching us still sat where Morik had left him. He wouldn't work, either. Too many weird things that could relate back to me would fuel the gossip fire, and that boy already had enough fuel. I needed someone outside of school.

For the rest of the day, I concentrated on my problem but found no solution. Everyone I knew, I liked so far, and I didn't want that thing messing with their heads. Which left me only one option. I needed to face him, the real him, if I wanted more of an explanation without jeopardizing someone else's mental stability.

My nightly curse-induced sleep made it hard to wake with a "destiny be damned" attitude. Yet, that Saturday, the first day of my first job, I managed to make an exception.

I opened my eyes right on time and immediately hopped out of bed to get ready. Anticipation filled me with enthusiasm. Mostly because I was tired of all the restrictions in my life and very much looking forward to the small measure of financial freedom I'd gain by having a job.

Dressing in a nicer pair of jeans and an old video game t-shirt, I pulled my hair back into a ponytail. A few of the shorter strands of hair around my face refused to comply, so I left them to hang in a light wave. Mom watched me from the doorway of the bathroom and promised the wisps looked cute even though I thought they made me look slightly deranged.

Just before I left the house, Mom snapped a picture of me and made me promise to let her take an "after" picture when I got home. She had a small scrapbook of pictures from my big moments and wanted to add both photos to it. While I didn't understand why she needed an after picture, I was willing to humor her.

I called out a quick goodbye and rushed out the door.

Since it was still snow-free, I'd worn my sneakers. I knew they'd be far more comfortable than borrowing a pair of boots. However, by the time I reached the coffee shop, the tips of my fingers and toes stung with cold. Any hope I had of warming up with a cup of coffee died when I glanced through the shop's windows and saw that more than half of the tables were already occupied.

Busy was good, though. It meant more tips. My toes and fingers would warm as I worked.

I pushed open the door and inhaled the welcoming scent of roasted coffee.

From behind the counter, Mona greeted me with a smile and nodded toward the closed door behind her, labeled with an "employees only" sign. I started to pull off my mittens as I weaved my way around the tables.

"There's a place to hang up your things back there," she said when I neared. "I'll join you in a minute." She didn't pause in her task of making a coffee for the man who waited.

Following her instructions, I stepped around the end of the counter and opened the door that led to a spacious hallway. Just inside the employee entrance, Mona had several coat hooks and a rubber mat just below it. Boots rested on it, which meant I'd be able to wear boots to work and have somewhere to keep them after I changed to sneakers.

I hung my things on an available hook then looked around.

The first door to the left was a small bathroom for employees. Further down the hall, also on the left, a supply room door stood open. Peeking inside, I saw storage racks and a counter and prep sink on the adjoining wall. The doors to the right led to a utility room and an office.

Mona stepped into the hall a minute later.

"There's a steady stream of customers who come in throughout the day. For now, I could use your help prepping for the sandwiches I offer." She pointed to the supply room with the sink. "This is where I do the prep work. The actual assembly I do out front." She quickly went over what needed to be sliced or diced and how to store it. Then, she told me to get her when I finished.

After she left, I doubtfully looked at what she'd set out. There were five tomatoes and a head of lettuce to dice thinly, an avocado to cut into wedges, and sprouts to wash. I hoped she had more work than that. Fifteen minutes of pay wouldn't go very far. I washed everything, set it aside to drain, then fetched the clear containers she used for her under-the-counter refrigerators out front. Her knives were much better than ours at home and cut through everything with ease. I carefully avoided my fingers.

When I had one large container and two small ones filled with produce and covered with plastic wrap, I washed my hands and ventured out to the counter.

Mona seemed surprised to see me so soon but directed me where to place everything and then told me to watch her for a while. She certainly had a rhythm for what she did. No move was wasted.

Most of the customers ordered some variety of coffee. I tried to memorize the different ingredients and, within an hour, felt I understood the basics. Every now and again, someone ordered a sandwich from Mona's limited menu. Each sandwich sounded great. The turkey avocado one made my stomach growl, and she grinned at me.

By lunch, I no longer just watched but helpfully passed her cups and kept pace with her. She took a quick break to eat at a table with a friend while I manned the machines. The register took some getting used to, but it appeared simple enough with a cheat sheet next to it, indicating which buttons to push.

Mona flipped the sign from "open" to "closed" at ten after one as the last customer climbed into his grey car parked on the street outside the picture window.

"You did great," she said with a huge smile. She moved behind the counter and started putting together a sandwich. Turkey Avocado.

Although she'd given me an opportunity for a break, I'd only used it to go to the bathroom. I hadn't brought money to eat because I figured I'd eat when I got home.

"So what do you think?" she asked while she worked. "Want to give the Sunday crowd a try?"

I didn't think I'd been overly useful but agreed since she invited me back. I moved behind the counter and grabbed a washcloth and the cleaning spray to wipe down the tables like I'd done periodically throughout the day when I could.

"You are a gem, Tessa," she said, walking around the counter with the plated sandwich in one hand and the tip jar in the other. "Most of the time, you're doing stuff before I even tell you to do it. You read minds?"

I contained my startled laugh. Barely.

"No. I guess you can thank my great-grandmother. We make dinner together every night. So I'm used to the prep, serve, and cleanup process."

"Leave the rest of those tables for me, and come sit." She set the sandwich on the table I had just finished wiping down. "This is for you. Let me know what you think."

She sat in the chair across from me, dumped the contents of the tip jar on the table, and started counting. I joined her, too hungry to decline, and took a bite of the sandwich. She smiled at my expression as I savored the delicious flavors.

While I ate, I watched her count.

"I have to admit this is more than usual. Don't get your hopes up that it'll be this much tomorrow. Someone tossed in a five." She handed me nineteen dollars and some change. Half of the tip jar for doing less than half of the work.

I wanted to protest, but I needed the money. I knew my future. I'd be alone, raising kids in just a few short years. Well, not alone. I'd have my mom just like my mom had Gran. So, I nodded my thanks to Mona and pocketed the money. Then, I finished my sandwich.

When I stepped outside, the wind buffeted me. Despite the cold, I looked up at the overcast sky, hoping for snow. A Christmas without snow just didn't feel like Christmas. The money in my pocket called to me wistfully. It'd be nice to earn enough to buy everyone real presents, but we had a standing rule in our house. No purchased gifts. Everything had to be homemade.

Lost in thought, I didn't hear someone calling my name at first. The second time it rang out, it registered, and I turned around. I spotted Clavin's car parked a few feet behind me.

Clavin opened the driver's side door and struggled to get out. He looked pale and unhappy as he limped toward me and wordlessly handed me a note. As soon as his hands were empty, he shoved them into his pockets and ducked his head in an attempt to keep his ears warm.

Curious, I scanned the words.

Go to her. She's at the Coffee Shop. She will help you get the rest you need.

Say what? I read it again then looked up at Clavin and studied his face. The sunken, dark flesh around his eyes, the hollowness of his cheeks. He didn't look well.

"Are you having problems sleeping?"

When he next spoke, I had to strain to hear his words.

"Every time I close my eyes, I see its eyes...its horns..." His voice quavered.

So he dreamt of Morik. But why would Morik send him to me? I thought Morik didn't like Clavin. Wasn't the idea to prevent me from picking a boy? Although I'd forgiven Clavin, there was still no way I would ever choose him. Maybe Morik knew that. But it didn't explain why he had sent Clavin to me. Did Morik really care that the guy wasn't getting any sleep? My eyes flicked to Clavin's cast. Maybe he felt guilty for walking Clavin in front of a car.

While I debated, Clavin started to shiver.

"Fine," I said with a sigh. "Give me the keys, and I'll drive us to my house." He handed them over willingly. I hadn't thought he would. "You really look like crap."

Taking pity on him, I helped him to the passenger door.

"I'll let you sleep at my house for a while, but I'm kicking you out in an hour. Got it?"

He nodded, his relief plain on his face.

I parked in front of the house a few minutes later and listened to Clavin's hobble as he followed me to the door. I dreaded what Gran would say. Yet, when I opened the door, silence greeted me, and Danielle's chair sat empty.

I called out a hello as we removed our jackets, but no one answered. At first, I thought they'd gone to visit the widower Gran had mentioned. However, a note from Mom and Aunt Grace waited on the table. It said they'd gone shopping and would be home before dark. I shook my head at the last part. Of course, they would. Mom had also asked me to take a picture of myself. The camera lay on the table. I ignored it.

After hanging Clavin's coat over mine, I led him to my room and waved him toward my bed. I stayed far away while he wearily lay back. A boy in my bed. I couldn't quite process the thought. A boy I didn't really care for. I still questioned why he was even here.

I watched him pull a quilt over himself, and trying to stay in a charitable mindset, I didn't think about how I would need to wash my bedding quickly before dark. Well, I didn't think about it much.

Clavin had barely closed his eyes when his breathing deepened. Tired from work, I turned to leave the room and relax on the couch.

Morik's voice stopped me.

"I trust you don't mind if I use Clavin?"

I spun around and stared as Clavin sat up. It was one thing for me to talk to Morik at school. Talking to him here, in my room, made my heart jump in fear. I'd brought this unknown creature into my house. I backed toward the door and was suddenly very glad no one else was home.

"How did you know where I was? Where I would be?" My voice remained steadier than my pulse.

"Since I found you, I've never lost track of you." He stood and walked toward me.

I backed through the doorway, pivoted, and quickly went to the living room. Although I wanted to run, I didn't. He'd had plenty of opportunities to hurt me before if that had been his intent. It just felt so violating that he knew where I lived now... that he'd never lost track of me.

In the living room, I paused for a moment. I could hear him stop walking behind me, too. What did he expect me to do now? I took a deep breath to calm down and decided to try treating him as a guest, without getting too close. Guests needed beverages.

"How did you find me the first time?" I asked as I nervously got us each a glass of water.

When I turned, he already sat at the table and waited for me expectantly. Hesitantly, I joined him and passed him his drink. Just like at school. A conversation across the table.

"I felt you the moment he bruised you. Your pain was my beacon." He took a drink of water. "I feel every birth and death in Belinda's line, but those are weak signals compared to when one of you is hurt. It's because of those faint signals that I lost track of Belinda's descendants at times."

I tried to piece together what purpose there might be to him feeling our pain, birth, or death, but couldn't think of any.

"Why do you feel us?"

"How else would I keep track of all of you throughout the years? Especially when you move around so much? It also helps me know how many of you are approaching your seventeenth birthday."

I thought of the family tree in the back of Belinda's book. Perhaps the dead branches weren't dead after all but branches that had moved away for safety. They could have made a copy of the book to pass down through the daughters of their branch.

"Are there others then? Other descendants of Belinda?"

He shook his head sadly.

"The four of you in this house are the last of her line. You are the only one of age."

"Five, you mean."

He canted his head to the side.

"No. Four. I am not mistaken."

The certainty of his tone had me frowning. Playing with

my half-empty glass, I stared at the clear water, deep in thought. Without a doubt, there were five of us in this house or my mind wasn't the only one in question. Maybe, somehow, we'd managed to hide one of us from him.

The obvious answer was Gran and Aunt Danielle. Twins. He'd probably only sensed a single birth since they'd been born so close together.

I glanced back up at him. He watched me closely, and I tried to keep my expression blank. They were both gone, but for how long? I wanted to get answers, but his presence could jeopardize their secret. However, given their age, did their secret even matter?

The biggest question still remained. Did Morik pose a threat to us? That clearly wasn't a question I could just ask him. After all, he'd walked Clavin into traffic.

While Morik had made it clear the act had been because Clavin had hurt me, his reason didn't make Morik less dangerous. What would Morik do to Brian if he knew about Brian's involvement? I hoped he would do nothing.

Since hurting Clavin, Morik hadn't done anything more than possess people to talk to me. And even then, when I'd pointed out he was upsetting the people he possessed, he'd found a way around that by using Clavin in a way that Clavin wouldn't question. After all, it was easy to lose track of time when napping. I sighed. Why couldn't I detect lies instead of seeing the future?

"Why do I see my future when I touch a boy? Where does that come into all this?"

When he replied, he seemed a bit sad.

"Once Belinda's father made the deal, she chose a suitor. That had been a disappointment, but she bore a daughter. It gave me hope that maybe her daughter wouldn't be so opposed to the idea since she would be raised knowing I waited to meet her.

"But Belinda sought to make a different deal with another of my kind. She wanted her deal with me removed. Ahgred's price was too high—her life to spare her daughter from the choices she faced. Since my deal with Belinda was complete, I couldn't interfere. However, I was near and listened to the bargain she made. I will never understand why she agreed.

"As a wedding gift, Belinda's father had given the couple the money he had obtained through his deal with me. A lazy man, her new husband lavishly spent the money and did nothing to earn more. She quickly grew to despise him. Because of her mistake in choosing him, she asked Ahgred that her daughter be granted a glimpse of what her life would be like if she were to choose the man she touched. Ahgred was a fair broker, but such a gift, used repeatedly, required a high price."

I leaned forward in my chair, caught up in his retelling. I could easily imagine a young woman dressed in a fine dress, angry at the world.

Morik took a sip of water, his gaze never leaving my face.

"The man chosen by the use of that gift would have a short life. Belinda agreed then asked for more. She knew I sensed her best at night. So she asked for a way to hide her daughter from me during that time. Ahgred taught her a simple chant that would force sleep through a touch. The price for Belinda was easily paid. She surrendered what money remained of the gift given to her by her father and relished telling her husband of the loss."

I pictured Belinda gloating while she held her baby as everything of value disappeared from her house. I wondered how long it took Belinda to realize her situation. I'd been poor my whole life, and it wasn't a fun thing.

"Her father heard what she had done and grieved over his misjudgment. His bargain with me, made in an effort to ease her life, had only caused her hardship. He called me once more and asked that I take his life and break our deal. Since he did not value his life, I could not either; I cannot make a deal without a payment. He died a few days later in his sleep, brokenhearted. Belinda's husband, hopeful of a small inheritance, hung himself when the news reached him that her father had nothing left. Belinda, penniless and without a husband, suffered a hard life of her own making."

Stunned, I leaned back and took a small sip of now tepid water. How had Belinda not recognized her mistakes? She had condemned her daughter to an even worse fate by making the second deal.

"I just don't understand," I said. "Why was she so afraid of you?"

Morik laughed. The sound of it startled me.

"That you asked means you do not view my existence as she did. She feared the concept of me. In her mind, a creature so unlike herself could only be the work of evil. Her view never angered me. I tried to speak to her, but she saw the practice of using someone else's body, as I am doing now, as proof of evil."

"Well, it's not nice," I agreed.

"As you've mentioned before." He gave me a level look, and I decided it would be wise to refrain from repeating my opinions. "I don't like occupying others, but it's my best chance to speak with you."

I studied him and wondered why a companion was so important to him. But I didn't ask. He had been annoyed when I mentioned the possession. A show of annoyance meant he could be angered as well. Though he seemed fine answering questions about my history, I didn't want to push too far and find out the full extent of his capabilities. Besides, I needed time to think about what I'd already learned.

Noting the dark circles that underscored Clavin's eyes, I said, "Clavin really doesn't look good. Would you mind letting him sleep now? There's not much time left before I have to boot him out."

Morik agreed and walked back to my bedroom. Within seconds, Clavin slept peacefully while I wondered where Morik went when he left a body.

THE NEXT DAY, MORIK'S STORY TWISTED AND TURNED IN MY mind as I walked around with the coffee pots to offer refills.

I pitied Belinda's father, and though Belinda had been a self-centered woman, I understood her hesitation about choosing Morik. I wasn't sure I could have, either. But to make that second deal? She'd condemned countless boys to a premature death instead of sacrificing herself, and she'd robbed all of her descendants of any chance of true happiness.

My mom had always said my dad had been a good man. She'd told me stories about his kindness and his willingness to help others. I'd never known him because he'd died before my second birthday, but from her, I knew he'd loved me very much. I'd once asked my mom why she'd picked him if she'd known he was such a good man. She'd smiled sadly and said she'd loved him, and he'd loved her. It wasn't much of an answer.

Mona didn't seem to notice my distraction. Like the day before, we worked in tandem, taking and making orders. I did most of the serving while she stayed behind the counter assembling the sandwich orders. After a particularly grueling rush, I went back behind the counter and found half a ham and Swiss sandwich plated with a cappuccino next to it.

I looked up at Mona questioningly, and she answered with a grin.

"If we're lucky, we'll get about a ten-minute lull. Enjoy it while you can." She pulled out a bar stool from the dark recesses under the counter, sat down, and propped her feet on a down-turned, empty five-gallon bucket.

The smell of the rye bread teased me, and my stomach rumbled. The bowl of cereal I'd eaten for breakfast was just a memory. I leaned against the counter, glanced at the handful of people still sipping their coffee, then took a quick bite. The tang of the brown mustard blended perfectly with the other flavors. I sighed happily then quickly devoured my lunch.

Within minutes, the bell above the door started to jingle once more. I greeted the new customers with a smile and started the second round of taking and making orders.

As soon as the flow slowed around one, I wrapped up a few of the less common sandwich ingredients and started to wash the tables. Since Mona had everything under control at the counter, I went in back and wiped everything down in the supply room. Turning off the lights, I went to the coat rack to grab my jacket. When I came back out, the sign said closed, and Mona sat at a table, counting the tips.

"Everything in back is wiped down. And we're out of tomatoes." I put on my jacket and pulled the mittens out of the pocket.

"Not so fast," she said, looking up. From under the table, she used her foot to nudge out a chair. "Have a seat."

I sat, and she finished counting. At least, today I felt like I'd done more work.

"Looks like you're a keeper, Tessa." She handed me twenty-five dollars with a wide smile. "We're serving people faster than they're used to, and they like it. It doesn't hurt that you're nice and smile," she added with a laugh. "I was toying with the idea of staying open for the afterschool crowd. Would you be willing to help out if I do?"

Inside, I frowned. Working after school wouldn't be a problem in fall or spring. It was just the wrong time of year for that.

"I'm sorry, Mona. I have to be home before dark every night. My great-grandma and great-aunt live with us, and I have to help out at home." I hated using the religious excuse that my mom used. It made us sound weird. In reality, we were weird enough without adding to it.

"That's what makes you such a good worker. You know your responsibilities. If things change, let me know. Otherwise, we'll keep it just like this weekend."

I nodded in agreement and stood. She walked me to the door and locked up behind me.

A strong northern wind swept down the street and robbed me of breath. The brave souls who walked the sidewalks downtown did so at a brisk pace. It wasn't the weather for leisurely strolls.

I spotted Clavin's car a short distance away and headed

straight for it. Not bothering to knock on the window, I tugged open the door and slid in. Sure, he helped bash my face into a door, but he'd also cried in front of me and had come to me for help.

Closing the door with a heavy thud, I turned toward Clavin, who watched me tiredly. Heat surrounded me.

"Need sleep?" I asked as I removed my mittens.

He nodded.

"My mom's home this time," I said, "but she'll be okay with it."

I didn't add why she'd be okay with it. Yesterday, I'd barely gotten him out of the house before everyone came home. No one said where they'd been, and I didn't ask. I'd been too distracted by worrying that they would see something out of place or that they'd smell his cologne in my room.

Inwardly, I cringed at the hopeful excitement his presence would bring everyone else.

"I brought homework just in case we needed a reason," he added helpfully as he pulled onto the road. With that comment, he broke down a little bit more of my deep aversion to him.

We parked in front of the house, and Clavin grabbed his bag. I reached out to stop him from taking his homework inside, and my bare hand skimmed his wrist. Our future together bulleted into my brain. I gasped softly.

As Clavin turned toward me, Morik took over.

"What did you see?" he asked.

"You've got to stop doing that!"

He watched me patiently, waiting for me to answer his question.

"I'll tell you what I saw if you tell me how you always know just when to pop into someone."

"I stay close. I watch." He spoke as if the answer should have been obvious to me.

"All the time?" I asked.

He nodded.

The thought of him constantly watching me unsettled me, so I changed the subject.

"It wasn't what I saw as much as what changed. It's never done that before."

I looked out the window toward the house and noticed a curtain move. My mom had seen me. I wondered if she recognized the car. My family knew of Clavin's involvement in the bruising of my face. Would they try to discourage me from choosing him?

"What changed?" Morik asked quietly as if sensing my distraction.

I tugged on my mittens as I turned back toward him.

"Before, Clavin would have been a jerk, not mean but selfish. Now, it looked like he'd be nice and very considerate of me."

For a brief moment, Morik frowned before schooling Clavin's features. He made no comment, but I knew he didn't like the shift in Clavin's personality.

"I guess getting hit by a car changes a person," I said.

Morik studied me a moment before answering.

"Perhaps you're right. I'll refrain from making undesirables more desirable in the future."

I grinned at him, glad he'd caught on. It wasn't that I might actually consider Clavin. I just didn't want to see anyone hit by a car ever again.

"There's no way I can bring you into the house with everyone home. It's time for you to go."

Without a word, Morik left, and Clavin blinked at me with confused eyes. He no longer held his bag.

"Come on, you. You're way too tired."

I opened my door, wondering what he noticed. That he didn't have his bag, that my mittens were now on, or maybe the cooler temperature in a car he thought he'd just turned off? He didn't say anything. Instead, he just followed me as he'd done the day before.

My mom had the front door open before we reached it. She eyed Clavin's cast for a moment then flicked a questioning gaze at me. I ignored the look and motioned for Clavin to come inside.

She shut the door behind us as I started to take off my jacket. I felt the curious gazes of the whole family on us. Gran stood in the kitchen, checking on an apple pie in the oven. Aunt Grace sat on the couch, knitting.

They waited for me to say something. I turned to Clavin, who again looked close to tears. He wasn't oblivious to the tension.

"Everyone, this is Clavin. I invited him over for a few hours. We'll be in my bedroom."

Clavin grunted in surprise, and I hid my grin. It was probably the first house he'd been to where the girl announced she was taking a boy back to her bedroom unsupervised.

"Mom, can you take Clavin's coat while I get us a snack?" I didn't want to touch him again so soon.

Mom hesitated then smiled tentatively at Clavin as she took his things. He looked at me helplessly as I walked away. They'd figure it out. Being nice shouldn't be so hard for people.

I opened cupboards with no luck before whispering to Gran to see if she had an idea. She offered to bring in pie when it finished baking. I shook my head. No interruptions. Her eyes widened for a moment, but she nodded. I'd just given Gran the impression we'd be getting busy back there. I wanted to groan and hide my face. Instead, cherry red, I led Clavin back to my room without a snack.

As soon as I closed the door, I motioned for him to take my bed.

"Are you sure this is okay?" he whispered. "They know who I am. Your mom didn't look too happy."

"It's fine. Don't worry. I'll protect you from them while you sleep."

I changed my socks to the heavy wool ones I saved for at home and threw on a sweater. Mom kept the house set to fifty-five in winter to reduce the heating bill. It made working at the Coffee Shop and going to school that much more enjoyable.

Clavin kicked off his shoes, crawled into my bed, and

pulled the black and white, paisley-patterned quilt over himself. His breathing slowed to a steady cadence in seconds. I moved to my desk and pulled out my homework, looking for something to do.

I tried playing solitaire with the dog-eared deck of cards I had buried in a desk drawer. Then, Clavin started to snore.

I looked at my bedroom door wistfully even though I knew it wasn't an option. If I walked out, they would pounce on me with questions I couldn't answer. They would want to know why I'd chosen him. And when I told them I hadn't, they'd want to know why I brought him here. Telling the truth, that I'd taken pity on him because he was having bad dreams, wouldn't go over well. Everyone would want to know why he thought I could do something about them. Sure, I could go into the whole guilty mind and needing forgiveness thing, but I hated lying.

The more I lied, the worse it would be when I came clean. And, I knew I eventually would tell them everything. I just didn't want to yet. I needed to figure more out. I needed to decide if I could trust Morik.

After a while, I fought to keep my eyes open despite my good night's sleep. All the running around at work, or maybe just listening to Clavin's relaxed soft snores, made me tired. Clavin had rolled toward the wall. It left enough room for me to lie next to him, but I hesitated. I slept too much the way it was. If I fell asleep now, that would set me up for a headache tomorrow morning. I rubbed my hands over my face and went back to my cards. The suits gradually started to swim before my eyes, and I tossed them down.

Giving in, I lay on top of the covers next to Clavin, my back toward him. The chilly room would ensure I didn't sleep too deeply or for too long.

HEAT ENVELOPED ME. I snuggled in with a sigh before my eyes popped open from the wrongness of it. Blankets covered me, and I lay on my side, facing Clavin, his face inches from mine. The way he studied me gave away that it wasn't Clavin.

"How long have you been here?" I asked, staring into his eyes. Morik wasn't touching me, just watching me intently.

"Since you fell asleep." I frowned at him, and he quickly added, "Clavin will not know the difference. He will feel rested. And those living here do not know."

I didn't ask why he'd waited to appear. I didn't want the question to be interpreted as an invitation for him to pop in whenever he wanted. Perhaps the delay was because he had a little bit of pity for Clavin. I doubted that idea as soon as I had the thought. Morik's reaction in the car made it obvious he didn't like me seeing Clavin in a positive light. So I asked about something else that still wasn't clear.

"What will you do once you have your companion?"

He sighed and closed his eyes. "I won't need to hide who I am. I will talk to her and spend time with her freely." He opened his eyes, looking right at me.

"Why limit yourself to one family? There are millions of girls out there, and you could probably be with one already."

"Even in the beginning, nature had rules and limits. Made by nature, I too have rules and limits. Your race, created so long after mine, is off-limits to my kind unless invited. When Belinda's father called on me, it was the invitation I needed though it was only to make a deal. As I've said, there were rules to that deal."

"So, you're stuck with me. Have you ever seen another girl who you liked? Maybe I could help you make a deal with her." Something in his expression changed. I couldn't tell if he was upset or laughing at me. "I'm not trying to get rid of you or get out of Belinda's deal or anything. I just don't think it's fair that you don't have a choice when I do."

He closed his eyes again.

"I will make do. Dusk is coming soon. Be ready for Clavin."

"Wait," I squeaked, scrambling to get out of the bed. No way did I want Clavin to wake up with me snuggled under the covers with him. I saw Morik quickly smother a grin and frowned at him. "Not nice," I mumbled.

A moment later, he left. Clavin stretched with a yawn, and I hurriedly ran my hands over my hair.

"You have to get up, Clavin. I need you out of here in two minutes." I darted my eyes toward the window. Light still shone through it, but dimmer. Morik was right. Dusk approached. I had about forty minutes before dark.

Clavin sat up and struggled out from under the blankets.

"Thanks again, Tessa," he said groggily. "I feel like I actually slept this time."

"No problem. I hope you sleep better this week so you don't have to drive all the way out here." I walked to the bedroom door, trying to hurry him along.

He looked up at me with a slightly hurt expression. "You'd rather not see me?"

"It's not that, Clavin. I just don't think this is good for you. Coming here, I mean. I think you're having bad dreams because you're feeling guilty, and I'm wondering if seeing me might just make it worse. I already forgave you. All you need to do is forgive yourself, and I'm sure the dreams will stop." I hoped Morik would hear and get the message.

Clavin nodded and stood, leaving my bed a rumpled mess. I wondered if I'd have time to change the sheets before dark. Did it really matter though when I'd been in it with him already?

I pulled open the door and led him out. The house didn't smell like cooking food as it usually did. Not even the baked apple pie smell lingered. Everyone sat in the living room, watching our tiny old television. From the sound of it, they focused on the evening news. We didn't watch the news in our house. I understood what they were doing. They were making the house as unappealing as possible for lingering visitors. But why would they do that if they thought I'd made my choice?

I didn't say anything, just walked to the coat hooks and handed Clavin his things.

"Good luck," I said quietly before he walked out the door.

He nodded but didn't look back at me. I had a feeling I was seeing the last of Clavin.

I stayed by the door, peeking through the curtain high at the top of the door, until his car pulled away. Turning, I faced three sets of eyes. Aunt Danielle lounged back in her chair, eyes closed, ignoring us all.

"He's feeling guilty and not sleeping. I couldn't say no."

Gran shook her head while Mom scowled at me.

"Yes, you could have said no," Mom said. "You just chose not to. You're wasting your time with him instead of trying to meet a boy—"

"Now is not the time," Gran interjected. Mom closed her mouth with an angry snap.

All this pressure to make a choice that I didn't want to make weighed on me. Gran looked at me with a tender expression, and I loved her more for her intervention.

"Tessa, there's some food warming in the oven for you. Eat. You don't have much time."

I nodded and took a page from Danielle's book; I ignored everyone for the remainder of the night.

The next morning, Gran gave me an apologetic look when I saw her standing next to my bed, holding breakfast. She didn't need to say why she was there instead of Mom. Mom was still mad at me and had left before I woke up.

While I understood her stance, her anger didn't help matters. What did she expect me to do? Of my ten waking hours, I spent the majority in school. It would have been a lot easier to choose a boy if I could have actually spent time with them outside of school. Sure, I should have used the summer, but I'd thought I'd have plenty of time and pushed it off.

So, I accepted my toast, hurried to get ready, and walked to school while freezing my butt off.

Beatriz lounged against a neighboring locker when I finally got to school. She looked mildly amused.

"You'll never guess what rumor is floating around school," she said as I started to peel off a few layers of clothing. "Apparently, I'm gay and have a girlfriend. One I totally admire, especially her sense of fashion."

I pulled out what I needed for first hour and closed the locker, giving her my full attention.

"It's you!" she laughed as we started walking through the crowded halls.

Given my weekend, I'd forgotten about the boy at lunch. Though I liked that Beatriz took the rumor with a sense of humor, the timing of it couldn't have been worse, considering my mom's anger over my lack of effort to choose.

"It doesn't really bother you, does it?" Beatriz asked, and for a moment, I was confused. "A rumor today is forgotten tomorrow. It's no big deal."

Understanding, I smiled and assured her it didn't bother me.

"Great. We should hang out after school sometime. I think you'd like my brother. He graduated last year." She studied my face for a moment. "We could spread the word about your interest in him and put an end to the rumors."

I upped the wattage on my lackluster smile and shook my

head at her offer, assuring her the rumor didn't bother me. But I did wonder if I could talk Mom out of the chanting thing so I could go out at night. It wasn't as if they were really protecting me from anything. Morik visited me at will. They didn't know that, though. I thought of all the things I missed about the night. To see the stars again...I hadn't seen them in years.

"Okay. You could still just come over to hang out," Beatriz offered again, a persistent glint in her eye.

I gave my standard lame answer.

"It sounds fun, but my great-grandma and great-aunt live with us, and I have to go home right away to help out."

Already grumpy because of the pressure from Mom and the forced walk to school, the reminder of all the things I couldn't do until I made my choice put me over the edge enough to allow an epiphany.

Morik, the dealmaker, was the key. I could make a deal with him to remove the effect of the chant, win my freedom, and prove what he said was true. Or, at least, the part where he could make deals. I wanted to believe everything he shared just so I had an explanation for my life. Except, he'd been wrong regarding how many of us were alive. So, I hesitated to believe the whole thing, even with the possibility that Gran and Aunt Danielle being twins confused him.

Yet, if I did make a deal, I needed to be careful. I didn't want to do something that would hurt anyone else like Belinda had. Maybe only temporarily remove the chant so the price wasn't so high. But how would I pay? I needed to find out what

Morik valued, other than a companion. He said that he could only make deals of equal value.

My plan sounded good. However, the more I thought about it, the more I worried. I was considering making a deal with a creature that had walked Clavin in front of a moving car to break his leg. Then, that same creature had threatened Clavin's other leg. Did I really want to mess with that? I liked my legs just the way they were.

"What about after that?"

I looked up at Beatriz, confused again.

"After you help out at home," she said. "We're usually up until ten or eleven."

For a moment, I'd thought she'd wanted to know what I'd do after my legs were broken. I really needed to pay more attention.

"Not tonight, but I'll talk to my mom and see if I can maybe work something out."

I just wanted a small taste of what it would be like to be a typical teen before I went and got myself knocked up. The irony of my thought wasn't lost on me as I walked past a senior well into her third trimester.

When Morik joined me for lunch, thanks again to Beatriz, I initiated the conversation I'd been plotting over the last few hours.

"You said you weren't upset with Belinda when she didn't choose you. What about her descendants? Did you ever get upset with them? Or maybe do something to their husbands to help along their passing?" I needed to know what type of person...er, creature, he was.

He gave me a dark, disapproving look as if I just said something rude.

"No. The rules are clear. They have a free choice."

"Why did you hurt Clavin, then?"

He gave an exasperated sigh.

"I regret that completely." When I said nothing, he explained further. "I saw your face, felt your pain, and was angry. Until you choose someone else, I consider you mine to protect."

Wasn't expecting that. If he considered me his, how would he not get mad when he lost me to someone else? I didn't want to push that point further, though, so I redirected my thoughts.

While he'd admitted his regret, he hadn't explained why. Was his regret because he knew I didn't like what he'd done or because of his own feelings on the matter?

"Do you like hurting people?"

"I protect what is mine. What I like comes second to your safety."

So he didn't like to hurt people but did what he had to do. And his attitude made some sense. He only had access to Belinda's line. If any of us died and failed to have a baby, it limited his chances. Now that he was down to just me, well, I guessed I would be pretty important to him.

"Okay. I'm important to you as a potential companion. I get that. What else is important to you?" This was the part of the conversation I really cared about.

"Nothing."

I fought not to wrinkle my nose at his answer.

"There has to be something you think about. What about the things you would do once you have a companion?"

"We're out of time. Tomorrow." He left as quickly as he'd appeared.

I looked around the cafeteria. There were still students lingering over half-eaten lunches. We'd had plenty of time. I scowled at my food. He'd run, the chicken. Whatever was important to him, he didn't want to admit. That made it harder to make a deal with him, but not impossible. I'd just have to lay the cards on the table and see what price he demanded. If the price was too steep, I'd walk away.

Decided, I finished my lunch and chatted with Beatriz, who didn't seem to notice the gap in time.

MORIK STAYED AWAY for two days. I hadn't realized how interesting he'd made my life until he stopped appearing.

During his absence, my highlight in excitement occurred when a boy stopped me in the hallway to ask if I really preferred girls. Beatriz, right by my side, had laughed so hard she'd cried.

By lunch on Thursday, I couldn't decide which emotion ran stronger. Annoyance or boredom. When he finally took over Beatriz after she finished eating, I'd just about given up hope that I'd see him.

"It's about time! You're a liar, you know that?"

Beatriz's eyes rounded in surprise, and I wished I knew how he'd look if he were in front of me and not in her.

"You said tomorrow. That was two days ago." He opened her mouth to speak, but I didn't give him a chance. "I'd been trying to have a serious conversation with you. You can't just take off in the middle of it."

Taking a slow calming breath, I closed my eyes and rolled my shoulders. Definitely annoyed. Bored went out the window as soon as he showed. Crabbing at him wasn't a good opening for a deal, though.

I opened my eyes and started again.

"I'm sorry for jumping down your throat."

"You're right. I apologize for leaving as I did."

"It's okay. We all have things we don't want to talk about. If I hit a nerve, just say so. I'll back off. Since we have limited time to talk, I'd prefer if you didn't just leave." His apologetic expression faded to a carefully blank mask, so I quickly changed subjects.

"But I do have something I want to talk about." He nodded, encouraging me to continue. "I was asking what was important to you because I was hoping we could make a deal."

He frowned.

"Nothing big like my ancestors," I said. "They made enough of a mess. I just..." I looked down at my hands, busily turning my unused spoon in the silverware trench of the tray.

Forcing myself to stop, I again met his gaze.

"I want ten days where I can pretend I'm normal. I want to

go to a friend's house and not worry about when it's getting dark. I want to see the stars again. I just wanted to know if there was something I could help you with, something you would value as much as I would ten days of freedom."

He bowed Beatriz's head for a moment, deep in thought. When he looked at me, his intense gaze drew me forward. Whatever he had in mind meant a lot to him.

"Ten days. I can release you from the chant, but not from our bargain or the touch."

I nodded. I could live with that. The idea of no curfew really appealed to me.

"Your price?"

"I want you to look upon me as I really am and touch me without fear."

Through our interactions, I'd gained bits of knowledge about him, and the memory of the shadowy green-eyed creature frightened me less after our time together. However, I still struggled to think of him as a person.

"Just one touch?" I needed to be sure I understood the scope of the bargain since that was the basic thing that Belinda had failed to do.

"Yes, but for each day, you must spend an hour with me as I am."

"Okay, but how are we going to do that without people freaking out?"

He grinned slightly.

"I will blend."

I thought about it, trying to see it from every angle.

"Help me out here. Are you tricking me in some way? Is there something that I should be asking or thinking of? If your price is really to touch you once and spend an hour a day with you for ten days while I'm allowed to stay up as late as I want, with no backlash, I'd agree. But is someone going to die because of this? Am I going to fall into a coma for ten days after or something weird like that? Or will this affect my children someday if I don't choose you?"

He watched me carefully as I spoke. I thought the last comment would bother him, but he took it without reaction.

"No. The terms are as simple as they sound."

Taking a deep breath, I agreed to the deal and waited expectantly for a swirling of pixie dust around my head or something, but nothing happened. Instead, Morik flashed a triumphant smile.

"I will see you tonight. After the chant, you will feel sleepy, but will stay awake until you see me. Do not fear me. Tonight will be the first night of ten." He faded as the last group of students rose from their table.

"Come on, Beatriz," I said when she blinked at the suddenly empty cafeteria. I didn't let her dwell on it. "Do you have plans for Saturday? I was thinking of trying to talk my mom into a little free time."

She perked up, and we started to make some potential plans. All I had to do was get through tonight without screaming and running away when Morik showed up. I hoped there were no hidden terms to the deal—like my imminent death.

Chapter Seven

IT TOOK EFFORT TO HIDE MY TENSION FROM GRAN WHILE WE prepared dinner. Anticipation warred with trepidation. Would I be able to touch Morik without fear? I wasn't sure I would even manage to look at him without wanting to run and hide.

Gran looked at me questioningly a few times when my thoughts slowed me, but I smiled and diverted her attention with different topics. The most distracting one being that of our elderly neighbor, who had invited her to a card party. I grinned and asked if she would go. The happiness on her face dimmed just a little when she said the party didn't start until dark. After that, we both quietly withdrew to our own thoughts.

I wanted happiness for all of my family, but until I chose, they had no freedom. Once they put me to bed, the house and everyone in it remained under lockdown until sunup.

Those limitations just made my deal with Morik that much more important. If I could pull off meeting him in the flesh, his new deal with me would be the proof I needed to believe his story enough to tell my family everything. Then, I might not be the only one making plans for the weekend.

Sitting through dinner tested my patience. I couldn't ever remember looking forward to the evening chant. Yet, I was careful not to give anything away.

I forced myself to eat slowly and listened to my mom talk about her boss's invitation to a seminar that she had turned down. Something in her tone caught my attention briefly, and I wondered if she might actually be interested in her boss.

When I finished my meal, I excused myself from the clean-up process to shower and get ready for bed. As I changed, Morik's words repeated in my mind, and I started to panic. Was he going to knock on the door after they put me to bed? They didn't answer the door for anyone. I could miss my chance to complete my end of the deal.

I looked around my room, trying to think of a solution. He said I would feel sleepy but stay awake. Maybe that was so I could sneak to the door and slip out. If I had to sneak out, I'd need more than pajamas, but Mom would be suspicious if I dressed in anything else.

I set clothes out on the chair near my bed. If I didn't pass out, I'd change then listen for my chance to get to the front door. Warmth was good, but I'd need light to go outside. Using a drink of water as an excuse, I went to the kitchen and took a book light out of the drawer we used to store emergency supplies. No one noticed me sneak it back to my room.

"You're very quiet tonight," Mom said when she came to get me.

"A lot on my mind with school," I said, too nervous to come up with anything better.

She stopped in the hallway and turned toward me, forcing me to stop as well.

"Are you being bullied again?" Concern laced her voice.

All the resentment over the yelling we'd done at each other vanished when I saw the fear in her eyes. I gave her a reassuring hug.

"No, Mom. It's just regular school stuff."

She nodded, and I felt guilty for the secrets I was keeping as I followed her to the living room. There were still too many reasons not to tell her everything, though. One more night, I promised myself. If the deal went as simply as Morik said it would, I'd have more trust in the legitimacy of the story he'd told me and be able to share it.

My family's chanting surrounded me, and I closed my eyes. I bit my lip to keep from smiling as anticipation finally won over trepidation. Whatever happened tonight would be the result of a deal of my own making, not someone else's. I felt each light touch on my bare arms. Mom's, strong and sure; Aunt Grace's light and shy; Aunt Danielle's quick and cool; Gran's soft and gentle. Then it was over.

With a steady arm wrapped around my shoulders, Mom led me to my room, pulled back the quilts, and helped me into bed. I didn't feel any different. The strange compulsion to sleep gripped me as usual. I struggled to keep my eyes open as she turned off the light and closed the door.

Frustrated, I rubbed my eyes. But that meant closing them.

And once they closed, they refused to reopen. I hovered on the verge of sleep.

Time slipped away from me until I heard a slight noise from the direction of the chair.

"Tessa," a deep, rumbling voice quietly drifted to me, "It's Morik. Open your eyes."

My heart gave a little flutter at the sudden sound. I took a calming breath, pushed aside any fear I had, and tried to open my eyes as he said. To my surprise, it worked.

I waited for them to adjust to the darkened room. However, the light coming from under the bedroom door just wasn't enough to see a thing. So I listened. I couldn't hear any noises inside my room but did hear the TV in the living room. That surprised me. I'd always thought everyone else went to bed after I did.

"Can you turn on the book light on my desk?" I whispered, not wanting to turn on the bedroom light.

A quiet click later, the dim yellow glow from the light blinded me.

I sat up and mentally braced myself. No fear. I could do this. I swung my legs over the edge of the mattress and turned toward the light.

I held still and focused on slow, even breathing while I studied Morik.

He wasn't the creature of mist and shadows that I remembered. At first glance, he was solid and very human-looking. But that was due to the small light that he still held loosely in his hand. It cast shadows over the features that made him not human.

In the dim light, the color of his skin hinted at Native American but with a subtle greyish undertone. Normal, pitch-black hair fell in soft short waves around his head. However, his hair wasn't long enough to conceal the last inch of his pointed, very non-human ears.

I swallowed hard and pulled my gaze from them to the two worry lines that marred his smooth, wide brow. The sight of his concern gave me the courage to continue, and I met his gaze.

His eyes captivated me. Swirling prisms of color, his irises contrasted the muddied backdrop of the whites of his eyes. The difference between the two was as scary as it was beautiful.

He held himself still as I continued to study him though his wide, full lips turned down in a slight frown. I noticed his lower lip protruded slightly as if he had an underbite. Before I had time to study his mouth further, I discerned a slight dent in his chin. Not quite a butt chin but still a strong one. My gaze drifted further down.

He wasn't wearing a shirt. Why wasn't he wearing a shirt?

I did a quick peek lower, and I breathed in relief at the sight of khaki cargo pants. Calmer, I went back to his chest. No hair sprinkled his skin there, everything lean muscle. He was right. He did blend well. Better than my first glimpse of him. I forced my eyes back up to his face, not wanting to be rude.

Seeing the real him without fear? Check.

"So, where exactly am I supposed to touch you?" I kept my voice low so no one would hear.

At the sound of my voice, the worry lines disappeared, and he smiled. When he did, I saw the reason behind the prominence of his lower lip. His lower two canines, longer than the rest, extended just enough to overlap his top teeth. The slight curve of them pushed against his lip, giving the illusion of an underbite. Definitely not human teeth.

He stepped forward and extended a hand to help me stand.

Fine, dark hair dusted the back of his hand. Normal enough. Sharp, black nails neatly tipped each digit. Not normal. I stared at them for a moment and struggled to push back at my rising fear. He patiently waited with his hand outstretched.

Please don't shred me with those nails, I thought as I hesitantly lifted my hand.

His warm fingers closed around my own, and he gently tugged me to my feet. Since he was taller than me by a foot, I found myself staring at his chest. He didn't release my hand. Instead, he pulled it up toward his chest while gently turning it so my palm would make first contact. Before I even touched him, I felt the heat radiating from his skin.

Once he placed my hand over his heart, he let go again and stood still for my inspection. The texture of his skin distracted me from my embarrassment.

I moved my fingers slightly to test what I felt. Soft, smooth skin covered hard muscle and the steady beat of his heart.

Most women would kill for skin like that. The thought made me internally cringe. The women in our family had killed enough without envy of skin texture.

I became aware that I just stood there, lightly running my fingertips over his chest, and quickly stilled my movement. The last thing I needed was a mix-up in signals.

Without removing my hand, I looked up into his strange eyes.

"Have I met my part of the deal?"

"Almost," he said quietly, flashing me another triumphant smile as he quickly stepped away from me. "Now, I get an hour of your time." He reached behind him and lifted a shirt off the chair. I hadn't even noticed he had clothes there.

The shirt mussed his hair when he tugged it over his head, and I noticed his ears weren't the only thing hidden in those waves.

He had horns. A dull, black horn adorned each side of his head. The base of each, barely hidden within his hair, started at the edge of his temple. From there, the horn arched up and then back down before tilting up once more just at the end. Channels ringed the horns and almost gave them a carved look.

Given the color of his hair and the way it fell, the horns had been easy to overlook the first time. Now that I'd spotted them, though, I couldn't unsee their impressive lengths or how the point of each ear only reached the middle of the horn.

The worry lines returned in his forehead, and I met his gaze as I scrambled for something to say.

"What are we going to do now?"

He stepped close and tilted his head to study me, his face now carefully blank.

"Are you frightened?"

"No," I answered quickly. And I wasn't. Not really. I liked this version of Morik. At least, I liked it a lot more than the shadowy one and the body-snatching one. But the sight of his horns had me wondering if there were other versions of Morik I hadn't yet seen.

He continued to study me closely.

"You touched me without fear, but this," he reached up with his right hand and ran his fingers over a horn, "bothers you?"

As he spoke, his long teeth played peekaboo with me. He was so different. There was so much to look at that it was hard not to stare at any one thing.

"You're just different from what I imagined." I dropped my eyes to his shirt. Fabric was safe. It was some vintage band t-shirt, and I wondered if he got it when the band was new. He was old enough.

"I'm sorry for staring," I added, hoping the apology would help.

"I like when you look at me, Tessa. But I don't want you to fear me."

Cautiously, I met his eyes. We watched each other for a few minutes as the silence grew uncomfortable. My skin started to prickle in the cool room.

Though his gaze never left my face, I still felt weird

standing in front of him in only my pajamas when he was now fully dressed. Not that I wanted him to take his shirt off again. That had been worse. My attention drifted to the sweatshirt on the chair behind him as I struggled for something safe to say.

"What do you do when you're not busy with Belinda's line?" I asked.

"I broker deals when called," he said softly, regaining my attention.

"People still call you? Do you always have to answer? Like a genie or something?" I glanced at the sweatshirt again, wishing I were brave enough to reach around him and grab it.

"People will always know how to call me, and no, I don't have to answer; but I usually do. It's the only way I can interact with your kind."

He watched me expectantly, a slight smile on his lips. It began to make me nervous. Wrapping my arms around myself, I sat on the edge of my bed and contemplated pulling a blanket over my shoulders.

He turned and grabbed my sweatshirt. He looked at it for a moment before stepping forward to hand it to me. "Why didn't you just ask for it?"

"Uh..."

"I saw you look at it. You're cold. Why didn't you ask me to hand it to you? Or, why not reach for it yourself?"

I plucked the sweatshirt from his hands and quickly tugged it over my head. My words were briefly muffled.

"Because I don't know the rules. If I ask you for something, am I making a deal with you? I don't want to do what Belinda did and compound an already difficult situation with bad choices." I couldn't bring myself to answer his last question and hoped he wouldn't notice. The truth was that the combination of his eyes, horns, off-colored skin, and ears unnerved me.

"Difficult situation?" he asked.

"I'm sure you've noticed that not every girl has to sleep when it's dark out or touch a boy to figure out what kind of life she'll have with him. My life is a difficult situation. I don't want to make it worse."

He nodded, sat down on the bed next to me, shoulder to shoulder, and set the light to the side. Shadow covered the side of his head facing me and hid his horn.

"You can ask me for anything, and I will try to do as you request. A deal isn't necessary unless you want one. The only thing I cannot do is cancel a deal already made before a new deal replaces it."

Averting my eyes, I changed the subject.

"So what do people usually ask you for?"

"Money."

Involuntarily, I glanced back at him. "Where do you get the money from?"

I was curious how a being who couldn't interact with the human world unless through a deal could get his hands on any currency. My guess was that his deals weren't just limited to the US.

"That's not an issue. I have existed for so long and made

deals for so many different things that I can always trade what I have for what I need to meet a deal's demands."

"What was the first deal you ever made?"

"A boy wanted to marry a girl several steps above him. He asked for a way to become wealthy enough to marry her. I showed him how to carve combs from shells scavenged from the sea near his home. Once he mastered that, I taught him to adorn them with decorative carvings. We worked together at night for weeks. Many of his attempts broke. But, when he had three sets of hair combs, he was considered wealthier than anyone in the village." Morik smiled at me and shrugged. "Instead of offering for the girl, he went to a bigger town to sell what he'd made."

"How long ago was that?"

His eyes lost focus for a moment.

"More than four thousand years ago."

"Holy crap!" I clapped a hand over my mouth and looked at the door, holding my breath. I felt him turn and look at me.

"No one heard," he assured me. The light under the door remained unchanged as did the volume of the TV.

"What would you ask for?" he asked hesitantly.

When I focused on him again, he watched me with cautious eyes, and it took me a moment to realize why.

"Don't worry, I wouldn't ask for money. That kind of deal has done nothing but cause me problems."

A relieved smile flashed at me, an abrupt showing of white in the darkness. Then, we both grew quiet.

I'd only asked what he usually did when not chasing us

down to see what he might have planned for his hour. Brokering deals was obviously out. Since I'd pretty much used up my conversation, I had no idea what else to do. I glanced at the clock. Only fifteen minutes had passed.

"Do you want to do something?" I asked, hoping he had an idea.

"What do you have in mind?"

Deflated, I shrugged. With the TV still on, leaving the room wasn't an option. Whoever sat out there would freak out if they saw me still awake. I looked around the dark room, searching for anything. What would a four-thousand-year-old creature want to do?

On my shelf, I had games but games required light. Then I saw a box label glowing lightly. Perfect. Old people loved puzzles.

"Want to put together a glow-in-the-dark puzzle?"

"We can do whatever you like," he said quietly.

I moved to the shelf, pulled down the puzzle, then cleared space on my desk. Every noise made me cringe. I probably had the only mom in the world who'd be okay with finding a boy in my room after dark. Yet, when it came to finding a...whatever he was...demon, possibly? Well, she'd act like any other mom and start screaming. Maybe worse.

Once the pieces were spread across the desktop, I turned to look at Morik. Only he wasn't sitting on my rumpled blankets anymore. He stood just behind me, so when I turned I bumped into him.

"Sorry," I mumbled.

He reached around me and started to sift through the pieces, his arm brushing mine. I stepped to the side to give him more space. Not that there was much to give. With a long and narrow room, the bed took up most of the width between the door and the desk. The desk occupied the wall under the window. What little room remained, the chair and shelves claimed, leaving only a comfortable walkway throughout.

Looking at Morik, the chair, and the puzzle on the desk, I saw my mistake. One of us would be standing for the next half hour.

"I didn't really think this through," I whispered to him. A low rumbling laugh sounded from his direction, but I ignored it. "Maybe we should plan better for tomorrow. What time did you want to hang out?"

"After school."

I hesitated to agree.

"I need some time to talk to my mom. How about you come over for dinner?" I paused. "Do you eat?"

He chuckled again but stayed focused on the puzzle.

"Yes. I eat. Are you sure your family is ready to meet me?"

"Now? No. But they will be by tomorrow night. If not, we can go somewhere else and grab something to eat." Whether dinner here or dinner somewhere else, it was an easy hour. Much better than doing a puzzle with him in a dark bedroom.

The book light, still on the bed, created a sphere of light that didn't quite reach where he stood. I wondered how much of the puzzle Morik really saw. He continued moving puzzle pieces around on the desk. Even standing beside him, I couldn't see much of what he did. Was he just trying to look like he had something to do? Wasting time?

I remembered what he said when I was cold and decided to see how honest he'd been. "Would it be okay if we cut tonight short and make up the time tomorrow?"

That got his full attention. He turned to look at me, frowning slightly.

"You're nervous."

"No, I'm uncomfortable. There's a difference." He didn't move or say anything.

"Look, we're standing in my dark bedroom, whispering because I don't want to get caught before I have a chance to break...well, you...to my mom. It's like sneaking, and I don't like it. It makes me uncomfortable." And it did. Just not as much as those swirling multi-colored eyes or his horns or the lower canines that made surprise appearances. I needed time to adjust.

After a moment of silence, he nodded, and I relaxed slightly. However, with everything that happened, I doubted I would ever fall asleep tonight. Again, I tested his word to help me however he could without needing a deal.

"Hey, Morik? Would you chant me to sleep before you go? I don't want Mom to know about our deal until I get a chance to talk to her."

He walked toward me and gently nudged me toward the bed. As soon as the backs of my legs bumped the mattress, he stopped moving and started the chant. The rhythm matched what my family had spoken over me for years. Before he even touched me, I felt the tug of sleep. He helped me lay back and pulled the blankets over me.

When he bent down and leaned close to my face, my heart stuttered in fear. For a moment, I thought he would kiss me. Instead, he whispered in my ear.

"Tomorrow, I'll give you a ride to school."

Wait, what? I fell completely under the spell before I could say a word.

Chapter
Eight

THE MOMENT I WOKE, I TOSSED OFF THE COVERS AND SPRANG TO my feet. My mom's eyes rounded, and the toast almost fell off the plate she held as she stumbled back, but I didn't slow down. I had no idea what time Morik would arrive to take me to school, and I wanted to be out the door before he had a chance to knock on it.

I hurried to the clothes that were on the chair, thanks to my prep the night before.

"Mom, can you come home an hour early tonight? It's important."

As I tugged on my jeans, I glanced at my desk. More than half the puzzle lay pieced together. I paused with one leg in and one leg out, staring.

"Do you need me to stay home?" Mom asked, her voice laced with concern.

I tore my eyes from the puzzle and glanced at her while hopping around to get my other leg in. "No, I'm fine. I just want to talk to all of you, and there's not much time before dark lately."

"Okay. Today wouldn't be a bad idea for it anyway. The weather's going to turn. I think it's supposed to snow by lunch."

I grabbed the plate from her hand and kissed her cheek as I rushed by.

"Good. I'll see you later, then." As I headed toward the bathroom, I devoured the toast in four bites.

By the time I finished, Mom and Aunt Grace had already left. Coming home early meant they needed to get to the office early. Gran sat at the table, going through a cookbook, when I stepped into the kitchen.

"What's for dinner tonight?" I asked.

"I'm thinking something bigger since everyone will be home earlier. How about roasted chicken?" She thumbed through a few more pages while she spoke.

"Sounds good to me. Do we have a chicken?" I walked toward the door and grabbed my jacket.

"Nope. I'll walk to the store." She closed the book with a decisive snap and stood.

I handed her coat and scarf to her. We both bundled up. Gran moved to the door but laughed when I followed.

"I think you're forgetting something. Give me a kiss, then go get your books."

I quickly kissed Gran's warm cheek and said good-bye before running back to my room. My eyes once again fell on the puzzle. Although it'd been a glow-in-the-dark puzzle, the pieces hadn't glowed enough for me to see them. And the book light hadn't been bright enough to charge them. Not only were Morik's eyes abnormally—yet beautifully—colored, but he could also see in the dark. The differences between us amazed and troubled me. He wasn't human, and he'd never answered my question about what he was.

Shouldering my bag, I headed back toward the door and called good-bye to Aunt Danielle. She made a sound of acknowledgment from her chair but said nothing.

When I opened the door, I smiled wide. Gone was the dead brown grass of fall. A crisp, clean blanket of snow covered everything and muted the usual sounds of morning traffic. The world looked fresh and new. Peaceful. And the overcast sky promised more snow than the sample it'd already provided.

Clavin's car idled at the curb. After last night, I'd thought Morik would show up as himself. I'd made my opinion clear enough in regard to his body-snatching, but maybe he didn't have his own car. It made sense if he hardly interacted with humans. At least it was Clavin and not some random person.

I waved, gave him the universal just-a-minute sign, and moved toward the garage. With a ride, there was enough time for some snow removal. Three trails of footprints led away from the front door. Two veered toward the garage and the other toward the sidewalk.

I grabbed our cheap shovel and quickly cleaned the inch of snow from the path leading from the sidewalk to the front door. Gran would appreciate the effort when she returned laden with a chicken for dinner. Leaving the rest for later, I went to put away the shovel and paused at the garage door to stomp the snow from my feet.

Behind me, I heard the crunch of snow as someone approached. I hurried to the back of the garage, replaced the shovel, and turned with a smile on my face.

"Morning," I called.

Clavin paused mid-step but quickly recovered and continued through the door.

He didn't look well. Even darker circles haloed his bloodshot eyes, and his limp appeared more pronounced. But, more concerning was how he'd dressed himself today. His pale blue t-shirt peeked out through his unzipped jacket, and the fly of his jeans gaped open. The extremely slicked look of his neatly combed hair in contrast to the rest of him definitely gave off an "I'm crazy" vibe.

Before I could comment on Morik's poor choice of a host, Clavin spoke.

"I tried staying away." A hint of a whine came through with his words, but there was no echo.

It wasn't Morik; it was Clavin.

"The last five days have been hell. I can't sleep. I tried. I even took pills. Every time I close my eyes, I see him. His horns, his eyes. They won't leave me alone!"

He shuffled closer to me, and I backed a step farther into the dark recess of the garage.

"The only time they leave me alone is when I'm with you. I

did what you said. I forgave myself. It doesn't matter. They won't forgive me. Come with me." He held out his hand. "Please. I just want it to stop."

I didn't want to touch him, fearing what I'd see. Instead, I stalled, hoping Morik would appear.

"Where would we go, Clavin?"

He must have taken my words as my consent because his face lit with anticipation, and he moved closer. "It doesn't matter as long as we're together."

I stood my ground. The light from the bay door didn't reach any farther back into the garage. No one would see us.

"Clavin, you're scaring me. You need help." He stopped moving forward. "Have you talked to your parents or Brian about this?"

Hurt and something else replaced the anticipation on his face.

"Talk? What good is talking going to do? I wake up and find notes I've written while asleep, saying things I wouldn't write. Do you know what would happen if I told someone I was being haunted by horned demons?"

"Yes, you'd get the help you need," I answered calmly.

"You *are* the help I need."

He lunged for me. My pity for Clavin no longer outweighed my fear of him. I shrank back from his wild grab a moment before Morik appeared between us, a barrier dressed in denim and a leather jacket. My nose hovered an inch from his back.

I put my hands out, bracing myself on the soft leather, dizzy from his abrupt arrival. On contact, I felt Morik's muscles tense and quickly glanced around him. His odd eyes remained focused on Clavin, who stood before him with a gaping mouth. Morik felt me move and gently nudged me back behind him. Given Clavin's scary instability, I willingly hid.

"You're real," Clavin whispered. "Tessa, you see him, right?"

"Yeah, I see him," I said from behind Morik's back. "He's holding me prisoner, Clavin." I felt Morik's muscles twitch under my fingertips and quickly smoothed my hand over the spot, trying to tell him to wait. When he stayed where he was, I continued.

"You have to go to the police and tell them. But be careful, Clavin. He's not like us. You see his horns and eyes, right? Look at his nails and his teeth. Make sure you tell the police everything so they know how dangerous he is."

"Are you going to be okay?" Clavin asked with a quaver in his voice. I truly felt bad for him. Sure, he'd been an ass, but he didn't deserve what he was going through now.

I peeked around Morik again. Morik reached out protectively, so I didn't get too far.

"I'll be fine, Clavin. He treats me well."

Clavin nodded, pivoted, and rushed to his car, his hop-step-gimp comical if not for the seriousness of the situation. Morik stayed positioned in front of me until Clavin peeled away from the curb.

As the sound of Clavin's car faded, Morik slowly turned. I dropped my hands and stared up into his carefully blank expression.

"No, I don't think you're holding me prisoner," I said. "Clavin needs help, though. That far-fetched story will give the police a reason to look at Clavin closely. Maybe he'll get the help he needs." I sighed heavily and dropped my gaze to the zipper of Morik's jacket before admitting the downside. "Or he might come back and be worse than before."

Morik remained quiet, and I looked up again to gauge his reaction. He looked slightly amused.

"Are you ready for school?"

I couldn't help the small, hysterical laugh that escaped me. School? My hands still shook. "Not really, but I don't have much of a choice. If we don't hurry, I'll be late."

I leaned to look around him but didn't see another car parked on the street. The garage did limit my view a little, though.

Morik pulled a baseball cap from his front jacket pocket. It was worn and soft and easily fit over his horns and the tips of his ears. If I looked closely, I could see the outline of both, but to the casual observer, the cap would mask them. The bill also helped hide his eyes a bit.

He motioned for me to follow, and we walked from the garage side by side. Any of the neighbors who watched would wonder how he'd gotten in there. It occurred to me that I didn't know how he got into my room last night, either.

"So you can just pop into places? Just like you pop into

people?" Snow crunched under our feet as we walked down the driveway. I still didn't see a car.

"Yes," he said.

He didn't expand on his answer and seemed unusually reserved this morning.

"So, why didn't you pop in sooner?" Previously cool air felt frigid, now. I tucked my mittened hands into my pockets and dipped my chin into my jacket in an attempt to stay warm.

He turned to walk on the sidewalk, away from the direction of school. I stayed by his side.

"Because I wasn't sure if you wanted me to interfere. When you said he scared you, I considered it then. But when he moved toward you..." He didn't say more for a moment.

"Who's Brian?" he asked.

I missed a step and stumbled. Morik reached out a hand to steady me. As soon as I gained my footing, he let go and tucked his hands into his pockets. Our breaths puffed out in little clouds as we walked. I knew he waited for my answer, but I hesitated to give one.

He stopped walking and turned toward me, tipping the brim of his cap up so I could clearly see his eyes. I didn't say anything. We stood at the end of the block in a silent standoff.

Finally, I gave in.

"I don't want anyone else hurt. Look at what happened to Clavin." A snowflake drifted in the air between us. "Promise you won't hurt him for something that's in the past and forgiven."

Morik didn't answer immediately. More snowflakes drifted down, settling in my hair, on our shoulders, and on his hat.

He reached up and gently ran a finger over my cheek then down along my jaw, just as he'd done when he'd controlled Mr. Jameson. The heat from his fingers created a trail of warmth.

Finally, he dropped his hand.

"Were there more involved than Clavin and Brian?"

I shook my head slightly.

"If Brian continues to absence himself from your presence, I will do the same from his. I can't promise more than that."

Morik turned and walked toward a motorcycle parked around the corner. Snow was rapidly covering its seat. When he lifted a helmet toward me, my mouth popped open.

"Morik, you can't be serious. I'll freeze. Is it even legal to drive those things in winter?"

He flashed a smile. "You'll be fine. The school is just a few blocks away. I promise you won't be cold."

How could he possibly promise that when I was already freezing?

"This isn't a winter jacket. It won't protect me from the wind or the snow." Though the snow drifted lazily now, I knew it would bite into any exposed skin once we moved.

Undeterred by my argument, he stepped close and fitted the helmet on my head. His fingers were quick and his touch brief as he clasped it and closed the visor. Then, he removed a scarf from his pocket and double looped it around my neck before he tucked it into my jacket. I took over the tucking part. When I'd finished, he tested my bag to make sure it sat securely across my body.

I waited on the curb while he dusted off the seat and got on. He held out a hand. I only hesitated a moment before I wrapped my fingers around his and swung my leg over the bike. I bit my lip as cold air gusted up my pant leg. I was sure I would be a popsicle before we ever started moving. The cold leather seat had already started to sting my skin through my pants. This would never work.

He adjusted his hat, turning it backward, and slid on yellow sunglasses. A demon—I still didn't know what to call him—perfectly hidden in plain sight. Taking me by surprise, Morik reached back, captured both my hands, and pulled them forward to tuck into his jacket pockets. The position pressed my front closer to his back, and his heat warmed me. Everything, that is, except my legs and butt. I hoped it would be a short ride.

He pulled away from the curb with ease as if an inch of snow didn't still coat the road. I clutched at him nervously for the first minute, but he drove slowly enough that some of my tension lessened. That made it possible to notice other things, like the helmet smelled new, and the scarf matched my jacket. Had he purchased them just for me? Unsure how to feel about that, I focused on the sound of the snow as it hit the helmet with little pings and pops. I could only imagine how it would sting if it hit my skin and appreciated the visor even more. Morik's exposed face had to hurt.

In a few short minutes, he pulled in front of the school and held out an arm so I could get off. I managed that fine, but the first attempt to remove the helmet gave me a moment of claustrophobia. Morik reached out to help and quickly and painlessly extracted me from its confines.

Smoothing a hand over my hair, I thanked him.

"Do you still want to come to dinner? We're having roasted chicken. Do you like chicken?" I felt awkward and knew I rambled.

He smiled slightly as he answered.

"Yes, I like chicken. I'll see you at five."

That was too close to dark just in case something changed, like my mom's willingness to listen, and I still owed him extra time from last night.

"Can you make it four-thirty?" I asked.

He nodded, and I set the helmet on the back of the bike as it had been before I'd gotten on.

"Thanks for the ride. It was interesting."

I took a step back. He eyed me a moment more, seemingly puzzled, then pulled away.

I didn't spend any time staring after him. Our unusual arrival on a motorcycle during a flurry of snow had attracted too much attention. Thankfully, Beatriz was one of the many nearby witnesses and tugged me, arm in arm, into the school.

"You have to tell me. Are you two a thing? If not, can I have him?"

A thing? With Morik? My mind still struggled to adjust to the reality of his existence. I couldn't process any more than that. But her comment did give me something to think about. Other girls might be interested in Morik. Today's world was vastly different from Belinda's world. Maybe someone out there would be a better companion than I would. If Morik couldn't interact with them, nothing prevented me from talking to them. I could be his liaison. All he needed to do was tell me who interested him.

"We're friends," I said vaguely.

"He looks older. Obviously not in high school. Is he over twenty-one?"

I grinned. She had no idea just how far over twenty-one he was.

"I'm going to talk to my mom tonight about maybe going over to your house this weekend," I said instead of answering.

"Great. My brother's home, and my parents are out of town. It'll be fun."

WHEN I GOT HOME after school, the kitchen already smelled like roasted chicken. My mouth watered.

"Need any help?" I asked Gran as I quickly discarded my jacket.

"Nope. I did most of the work already, so I can sit when your mom and Aunt Grace get home. I don't want to miss whatever this talk is about." She slid another covered dish into the oven and reduced the temperature.

"Was that pie I just saw?" I sniffed the air theatrically.

"I'll make you a deal. I'll tell you what I made if you tell me what this conversation's about."

"No way. No deals. No thank you."

She gave me an odd look but didn't question my adamant response. Since everything was done already, we sat at the table to wait. Gran asked about my day, but I couldn't recall much since I had a hard time concentrating on anything but tonight's dinner while in school. I'd run the conversation I planned to have with my family through my head countless times during the day, and none of the imagined scenarios ever went well. I hoped the real one would go better.

Mom and Aunt Grace walked through the door just before four.

"What's going on?" Mom said, pulling off her gloves. They both hung their jackets while watching me expectantly.

Butterflies tickled my stomach as I met my mom's gaze.

"You might want to sit down. This is going to take a while. Just, please, wait until you hear everything before you freak out."

Mom's eyes narrowed, but she nodded. Aunt Danielle sat up in her chair, her eyes open and watching, but she didn't join us.

I got up, retrieved Belinda's book from Gran's bedroom, set it in the middle of the table, and sat down.

"Belinda was a young woman who lived around two hundred years ago." I flipped open to the back of the book and pointed to the line of descendants. "We already know this just by looking at the births in the tree. But I've learned more.

"Two hundred years ago, Belinda's father worried about her future. Since he was poor, he couldn't attract suitable prospects for her—you might say her *choices* were limited."

I paged back to the beginning of the book and eyed Belinda's first instruction.

"Belinda's father made a deal with a creature who had very limited contact with humans. This lonely creature saw an opportunity. Knowing we feared him, he asked for an unusual payment in exchange for the money Belinda's father requested. The creature wanted to present himself to Belinda as a possible companion. He hoped Belinda would consider him as an alternative to getting married. He offered to care for her in return for her company.

"He wasn't unfair or cruel in his fee. He didn't demand that Belinda choose him, only that she give him consideration. If she decided to choose another, he asked that he be allowed the same chance with any descendants of her line."

Gran and Aunt Grace looked interested, maybe even captivated by the details of our past, but Mom had a glint in her eye.

"Belinda's father agreed to the terms without consulting with her. As you can guess, Belinda rejected the creature's offer. She married and had a daughter. But, she was so angry that her daughter would have to face the same creature someday that she made a deal with another creature.

"In exchange for the return of the money her father had

given her—well, every penny he'd originally bargained for that she still had—she wanted the ability to hide her children from the creature. And hating her husband, she wanted her daughter to have foresight when choosing.

"This new creature agreed to the gift of foresight but demanded a high price in return. Each husband would die prematurely. Their lives for a glimpse of our futures. Belinda also learned a chant to protect her children at night when we are most easily found."

Now that I'd retold the story, I had more questions for Morik. If there were more creatures like him, why didn't he seek their company?

I closed the book and smoothed my hand over its worn cover before looking up at my mom. Her gaze pinned me to my chair. She knew the worst was coming.

"The first creature's name is Morik. And he followed us despite the move."

My mom gave a pained groan.

"He scared the bejesus out of me at first," I said quickly. "But, other than breaking Clavin's leg for hurting me, he hasn't done anything bad."

Aunt Danielle chuckled a little from her chair, but I ignored it. I knew breaking someone's leg was plenty bad.

"When he told me the story, everything fit. When I asked questions, he was right about everything, except for how many descendants are left." Everyone looked at me blankly.

"He said four," I clarified. "He can sense when something big happens to us...like when we're born, die or, in my case, when Clavin and Brian bashed my face, and I was in pain. I think because Gran and Aunt Danielle are twins, he counted the two of you as one."

"Why are you telling us this?" Mom asked quietly.

"Because I made a deal with him." At her horrified expression, I held up my hand. "A small one. Ten days of no forced sleep in exchange for an hour spent with him every day. I did it as a test to see if he was telling the truth about the touch, the chant...everything."

On a roll, I jumped in with what Mom would consider the worst part.

"I invited him to dinner." I said it quickly, like pulling off a Band-Aid.

"Tessa Bree Sole, you can't possibly be considering him as an option." Mom's vehement tone made me cringe.

Before I had a chance to respond, Aunt Danielle piped up.

"Why not? Would it be better that she make no choice at all? You know as well as I do that the choice isn't just in your head but in your heart as well."

My mom's expression paled, and I turned to look at Aunt Danielle as she stood and glided toward us.

"Pull out a chair for me, dear."

I did, and she carefully sat, lightly resting her arms on the top of the table.

"Your Gran made her choice already at sixteen. She knew what she wanted. But I was more like you. I didn't want to be forced into a choice, a choice no one ever explained."

I nodded my head, for the first time seeing someone who truly understood my position.

Aunt Danielle sighed.

"So I didn't choose, and on my seventeenth birthday, I died."

She said it quietly, watching me with her soft grey eyes, and I didn't believe her for a minute. Not until she moved her hand to cover mine. A chill penetrated my skin at the same time her hand passed through my own then through the table. I wanted to panic. Hyperventilate, maybe. But all I managed was a single tear. I thought back and recalled her touch as always cool, cold even. Since we were in a cold house, I'd never thought it odd.

She watched me sadly as I struggled with the truth. Death. If I choose a boy, he died. If I didn't choose, I died. Did Morik know the consequence of the time limit he set?

"If choosing Morik keeps you safe and happy, and no one else interests you, then you go ahead and choose him." She leaned close and kissed my cheek. Her cool lips didn't pass through me this time.

Choose Morik? No. There was a fourth option. Find someone else that Morik might be interested in who returns his interest. With a different companion, how could the original deal still stay intact?

Wiping the tear from my cheek, I glanced at Mom. It hurt to look at her tear-stained face. She and Gran clasped hands tightly, silently supporting each other. Aunt Grace smiled at me weakly, on the verge of tears herself.

"Thank you for telling me," I said to Aunt Danielle. To my mom, I added, "The pressure you've been putting on me to pick makes more sense now. But I'm not choosing anyone. At least, not yet. I have a few more months and will take it more seriously now."

I scrubbed my hands over my face before I glanced at the clock. We only had ten more minutes before Morik showed up. My stomach flipped when I thought of how he'd popped in last time.

"So, about Morik coming to dinner. He's different. Really different. Maybe even a little scary..." The more I thought about him suddenly appearing in the kitchen, the more I worried. "Just keep in mind that he hasn't interacted with people much. In fact, he might not know to knock on the door before popping in."

Gran gave Mom's hand a brief squeeze before letting it go.

"Don't worry. We're experts with the unusual and will deal with this just fine. We always do." Gran stood and briskly went about setting the table. Aunt Grace moved to help.

"Mom," I said cautiously. "Since I have ten days, I was wondering if maybe I could leave the house at night. There's this girl at school who invited me over tomorrow."

"As if I could say no. This might be your only chance at freedom." She got up and stretched across the table to kiss my forehead. "Just let me know who you'll be with, where, and when. I'll worry if you don't." She briefly touched my cheek as a reminder. Good thing she didn't know about Clavin's latest mental break. I wondered if he'd gone to the police as I suggested.

At exactly four-thirty, a brisk knock sounded at the front door. The table was already set, and the chicken rested on the stove, so Gran motioned for me to get the door. With my hand on the knob, I looked back at my family to make sure they were ready. They stood close to each other, near the table, watching me.

Taking a breath, I tugged the door open. Morik waited on the stoop. He was dressed as he'd been that morning, and I took a moment to study him, his real self still new to me. His cap hid his horns and ears while the yellow sunglasses slightly masked his eyes. Snow dusted his shoulders.

Behind him, more snow continued to fall, coating everything in white, including his motorcycle in the driveway

"There's room in the garage if you want to park in there," I offered as I stood back to let him in.

"It'll be fine," he said quietly. He looked at my face closely. "Crying?"

Uncomfortable with our audience, I gave a slight nod and softly said, "Not a bad thing."

He didn't look like he believed me and shifted his attention to my family. Would he consider hurting my family if he thought one of them upset me? I worried I might not like the answer.

"Can I take your jacket?" I asked to distract him.

The question won back his attention, and I breathed a little easier as he handed me his things. After hanging his coat,

I nervously started introductions. My family was understandably quiet to his polite greeting, and I hoped I hadn't made a mistake by inviting him to dinner.

From her chair in the living room, Aunt Danielle asked what no one else would.

"Why are you still wearing your hat and glasses, young man?"

He grinned, a flash of sharp canines, before he answered.

"I didn't want to frighten anyone with my looks."

"What's that hat hiding?"

"Horns and pointy ears."

"Show me."

Morik removed his hat and glasses and withstood her amused scrutiny. Being dead, she didn't have to worry about a monstrous creature attacking her. However, that fear seemed to be on everyone else's minds, based on their reactions. Mom's already pale face took on an ashen hue. Aunt Grace fearfully panted for air while Gran tightly gripped her hands together in front of her.

Morik's attention shifted to them.

"I truly thank you for inviting me into your home. I've never eaten dinner with anyone before and have been looking forward to it since Tessa made the offer. Is that chicken I smell?"

Gran found her voice.

"Chicken, garlic mashed potatoes, baby carrots, and pie for dessert."

"I've never before smelled food so tempting."

Gran gave a small smile and stepped aside to motion to the table.

"Please have a seat."

I sat next to Morik through a stilted dinner. As usual, the food was delicious even if the portions were a little small since I hadn't warned Gran we'd have company. Morik didn't seem to mind, though. He ate with perfect table manners. I wasn't sure what I had expected, but it wasn't what I saw.

By the time Gran served the pie, Mom had regained some of her color. I didn't blame her for her worry. I'd had the benefit of talking to Morik through familiar faces the first few times I met him. If our initial introduction had been face to face, it would have been a severe shock. I probably would have run, screaming. My family had all handled it much better than I would have.

After his last bite of pie, Morik thanked Gran for dinner then looked at Mom. She flinched when his gaze met hers, but she didn't look away.

"With your permission, I'd like to take Tessa out for a little while."

Mom tried speaking but had to clear her throat. "Where?"

"Just out in the front yard. In sight of this house."

Mom nodded reluctantly. I wasn't sure who to feel sorry for. Morik because people only looked at him when they wanted something, or my mom because she struggled to do what I'd asked even when everything in her wanted to take me and hide me away.

Before leaving, I helped clear the table for a change. Morik stayed out of the way, watching us move. When we'd cleared everything, everyone, except Aunt Danielle, quietly stood by the table as he and I put on our jackets. I glanced at the clock. Dusk. Too many years of rules drilled into my head made me hesitate at the door.

Morik reached around me and turned the knob. The move brought his mouth close to my ear.

"I'll keep you safe," he said quietly.

I stepped into the dusk with Morik close behind me. My feet wouldn't carry me any farther than the front step as my eyes drifted to the darkening horizon.

The sound of the door closing startled me. The last time I'd been out at this time of evening, I'd been running for home while a green-eyed shadow thing chased me. Tension skittered along my spine. While I knew Morik now, sort of, that didn't mean I wanted to see him like that again. I forced myself to look over my shoulder. Relief flooded me. No green-eyed shadow stood behind me, just the Morik I'd come to know. He'd replaced the cap but had tucked the glasses in his pocket so I could see his eyes clearly as he studied me.

"Look up," he said quietly.

I did and saw the first stars twinkling in the twilight. As I watched the sky fill with the sparkling lights, I made a heartfelt wish. Morik seemed nice, minus the whole Clavin thing. Nice people...er, beings, deserved friends. Although I didn't want to be that friend forever, my wish was to be enough of a friend to help him find what he sought.

"Are they as you remember?" He stepped next to me, tilting his head back to look at the sky with me.

"Yes. Thank you." I sighed in contentment before looking at him. My gaze met his.

"Would you like a ride to work tomorrow?" Though the question was delivered casually, I had a feeling he really wanted me to say yes.

I glanced at his bike and inwardly cringed before nodding. At least now, I knew what to expect and could dress in layers.

"Thank you for this evening." He looked toward the front window where the curtain moved. "It wasn't easy for them."

"No, it wasn't. But, I'm glad you came. And thanks for knocking."

When he grinned, there was a mischievous glint in his crystal eyes. "I've popped in unannounced before and learned that knocking is a necessary custom."

The sight of his sharp lower teeth caused my heart to skip a beat. His grin faded, and he pulled his glasses out of his pocket and put them on.

"Good night, Tessa." He opened the front door for me, holding it until I stepped inside.

"Night," I rushed to say as he started to close it.

He nodded once before the door clicked shut.

My stomach sank as I realized my reaction to his teeth had hurt his feelings. Outside, I heard the bike start and peeked out the window just in time to see him pull away. I wondered where he went. It couldn't be far since he said he was always near.

"I don't care what deal you made. I'd feel a lot safer if we shutter the windows now," Mom said from behind me.

I nodded and went to take a shower since I wanted to think. If I was going to be his friend, I needed to get over our differences and really start to get to know him. Once I knew Morik better, I'd know what type of person he would connect with and could start my search. With my birthday not far away, I didn't have much time.

Chapter Nine

"Up, lazy girl!" Aunt Danielle called from nearby.

Disoriented and groggy from a horrible night's sleep, I groaned as I rolled over in bed. Sunlight blinded me the moment I opened my eyes. Blinking, I tried to focus on Aunt Danielle, who watched me from my doorway.

"Morik is in the kitchen, waiting for you."

Her words acted like a shot of caffeine. My eyes opened wide, and I bolted out of bed in a panic. She grinned at my reaction.

"He's here?"

"Yes. In the kitchen."

I glanced at the clock and saw I had to be at work in seven minutes.

"I can't believe I overslept." I tugged on clothes at random, grabbing whatever was close.

"I heard you tossing and turning late, and I told your mom to let you sleep when she came to wake you." She moved aside as I rushed from my room to the bathroom.

I brushed my teeth, tossed my hair up into a messy bun, and flew out of the bathroom sixty seconds later.

Morik sat at the table. I smiled briefly as I ran past him to get my coat.

"I'm really sorry to rush you, but I have to be at work in four minutes."

He gracefully rose, donned his own jacket, and calmly tucked my scarf around me as he had the day before.

"Are you sure you want to be there in four minutes?" He grinned in response to my nod. "Come on, then."

I called a farewell to the house and strode determinedly out the door toward his motorcycle.

"Not that I'm ungrateful," I said over my shoulder, "but wouldn't a car be better in winter?"

"For humans, maybe."

"I *am* human." When I spun toward him, barely any space separated us, and I had an up-close view of the pointy teeth his teasing grin displayed. Seeing them didn't bother me as much today, and I rolled my eyes in response to his joking.

The playful smile remained in place as he reached around me and painlessly tugged the hair-tie from my hair. I held still, wondering what he was up to when he held the band out to me.

"Won't work with the helmet."

"Ah."

I twisted the hair-tie around my finger and waited for him to fit the helmet on my head. While he did that, I noticed the snow piled on the ground everywhere except the sidewalk and driveway.

"What's that face for?" he asked just before tapping the visor into place.

"I'm feeling guilty for oversleeping. I should have been up to help shovel."

He straddled the bike, started it, and held out his hand. "I didn't mind."

"You did this?" I clasped his arm and got on behind him. He nodded as he pulled my arms around his waist. I couldn't say more because he revved the motorcycle and swiftly pulled away.

Although the plow had been through, a thin layer of snow still coated the road. Fearing what an icy patch could do to us, I tightened my grip around his waist and closed my eyes. The stomach-churning ride lasted a few short minutes before he parked in front of the Coffee Shop. He'd maneuvered the roads expertly, but my legs still felt weak when I climbed off the back. He didn't wait for me to try to extract myself from the helmet but helped right away. It gave me a chance to calm down.

He'd parked right in front of the picture window, and I caught Mona doing a double-take once the helmet came off. I waved and hurriedly pulled my hair back, securing it once again with the hair tie.

"Thanks for the ride."

"Not a problem. I'll be back later." He started the bike again, but I didn't wait to see him leave. I hurried inside. The fresh brewed aroma of roasted coffee welcomed me as did the few patrons already seated, sipping their morning delight.

"Sorry I'm late, Mona. I overslept." I moved behind the counter and checked the coffee pots, starting another regular.

"You're right on time." She laughed at me as I opened the side door to rid myself of outdoor accessories.

I glanced at the clock in disbelief. He'd really done it. I didn't have a chance to overthink how fast we'd gone because a wave of customers poured in moments later.

Between rushes, Mona quizzed me on the "hottie with a crazy streak," proving that I wasn't the only one who thought a motorcycle in winter was weird. She said it made him dangerous and more compelling. I wondered if Morik had an age limit for companions. Mona sure seemed interested. Besides, it wasn't as if she was older than he was. While I waited on customers, I tried to think of a tactful way to ask him.

Morik walked in a little before noon. When he said he would see me later, I hadn't thought it would be a public appearance. However, covered with a cap and dark sunglasses, his differences didn't send the patrons screaming as he approached the counter. I couldn't hold back my smile as I thought of the chaos his appearance without the hat and glasses would cause.

Mona recognized him from earlier and stepped aside so I could wait on him. She took the coffee pots around the room for those with the bottomless cup.

"What can I get for you?" I asked.

"The coffee any good?"

"Like the coffee; love the sandwiches."

His lips twitched, and he ordered the bottomless cup with one of Mona's specialty sandwiches. He didn't linger at the counter after he ordered. Instead, he found a table and sat to sip his coffee while Mona made his sandwich.

I delivered his food but couldn't stay. We were in the middle of our lunch rush. Within thirty minutes, most of the tables would empty. Until they did, Mona and I took turns at the counter and running refills.

Mona caught me behind the counter during a breather. "Black nail polish? I would have never pictured you with a bad boy."

My eyes shot to Morik, but with those sunglasses on, I couldn't tell if we held his attention or not.

"We're friends," I said quietly.

She smiled knowingly but wisely said nothing more. There wasn't time. We faced the last rush together. Morik never moved. When the clock struck one, Mona didn't comment on his presence, just flipped the sign to "closed" and took the tip jar to the back. Taking the washcloth and sanitizer, I started the process of closing down.

"You like working here." His voice carried in the now quiet shop. It wasn't a question but a statement of fact. I nodded anyway. "Why?"

I moved to wipe down his table, and he surrendered his empty cup.

"What's not to like? I love the smells, the people are nice, and Mona's a great boss. Plus, I get paid."

Mona walked into the room saying, "Of course I'm a great boss! I can't afford to lose another employee to crappy wages."

She handed me a few folded bills, the outer one a single. I tucked it into my pocket and finished wiping the table.

"Get her out of here now. She's worked enough for today." She smiled at Morik, not commenting on his hat or glasses.

He smiled in return and stood. "Yes, ma'am."

I left Mona to chat with Morik while I grabbed my things. If only she knew what those glasses hid. Would she still talk to him?

Outside, the sun had melted the snow from the roads. Relieved, I willingly ducked into the helmet and climbed onto the back of the motorcycle. I still didn't like how cold I got, but at least our chances of crashing were lower.

On our way to my house, I thought of my plans for the rest of the day. I wasn't yet sure what we'd do for our time together, but no matter what we settled on, I'd ask Morik to help me sleep tonight. Another night tossing and turning didn't appeal to me.

Morik slowed as we approached the house, and I noted the garage's bay door stood open, its dim cavern empty. Puzzled, I wondered who had left. Usually, we spent Saturdays together. Last Saturday had been a welcomed oddity, but two Saturdays in a row? It didn't make sense.

I managed to tug the helmet off without hurting myself as

Morik kicked the stand into place. "Do you want to come in? I'm not sure who is home."

"Just your Aunt Danielle." He placed the helmet on the seat then joined me on the sidewalk.

"I was wondering...if Aunt Danielle died at seventeen, why does she look Gran's age?" We slowly walked to the front door.

"The same reason she's still here. They're linked. One soul in two bodies. When your Gran passes, so will Danielle."

It made me sad just thinking about it. I couldn't imagine my life without all of them. Mom had once told me that she and Dad had lived on their own for a bit with me. It was only after he'd passed away that she'd brought me back to Gran's house. Aunt Grace had already moved in with her by then, her own husband already gone. That was just what my family did when a husband died. They banded together to protect their children as best they could.

Lost in thought, I opened the door. Morik followed me in.

"'Bout time someone came home. It's boring without company," Aunt Danielle called from her chair, more animated now that she'd exposed her secret.

"Where is everyone?" My fingers warmed marginally when I tugged my mittens off.

"Your mom went to the office. Grace and your Gran walked to the store a little while ago."

"I'm going to change real quick," I said to Morik.

He nodded and looked at my . "If you'd like, I can join you."

She nodded with a grin. Removing his cap and glasses, he went to sit by her.

I walked to my room and put the twenty-six dollars from my pocket with the rest of the tip money I saved. I'd been honest with Morik. I couldn't have asked for a better job. If things didn't go as I hoped, at least I'd have a job after my nameless husband died.

Annoyed with my turn of thoughts, I focused on the present. Thanks to Morik, I was temporarily no longer bound to the "home by dusk" rule, and I planned to take advantage of that.

After changing, I used the phone in my mom's room to call Beatriz.

"Sorry I didn't call sooner. I have free time tonight if you still want to do something." I spoke quietly, not yet sure where Morik fit into my plans.

"Sure. With my parents gone, my brother's making some calls to his friends. There will be a lot of people here. You'll have a blast." She rattled off directions to her house and suggested I show up after dark.

I hung up the phone and glanced at the directions I'd written down. It didn't take a genius to point out what I'd be in for if I went. With a college-aged brother and no parents at home, the party would be large and a lot of people would be drinking.

While I'd liked the idea of spending one-on-one time with Beatriz, a party could work better for me and for Morik; no one would find a guy with a cap and sunglasses out of place.

They probably wouldn't even notice his horns or eyes without the cover if they had enough to drink. We could mingle with other people, and I could watch him. Not only would I be able to get to know him better, but I'd also be close if he showed interest in someone. My mom couldn't object because it presented me an opportunity to search out my choice.

Decided, I looked at the clock. Now, what would we do for the next few hours?

As soon as I walked back into the living room, the quiet conversation between Morik and Danielle stopped. They both turned to look at me even though I hadn't made a sound, and I felt as though I'd interrupted something.

Morik stood and joined me, watching me expectantly. I wondered if he'd somehow heard my end of the phone conversation.

"I was invited to a party tonight. Would you like to come with me? We could watch a movie here until it's time to go."

"I'll stay for the movie and give you a ride to the party, but I don't think I'll join you."

"All right," I said, hiding my disappointment. How would I match him up with a companion if he didn't mingle with people?

Aunt Danielle suggested a movie that we had. Morik obligingly started it for us while I settled on the couch. I had a whole movie to come up with a plan.

Two hours later, I scowled at the rolling credits. The stupid movie had distracted me from my plotting. Gran and Aunt

Grace, who'd arrived home mid-movie, had quietly put away groceries then joined us in the living room.

I looked over at Morik, who reclined on the other end of the couch. "Are you sure you don't want to come with me? There's going to be a lot of people there. You'll blend in fine."

"What are you up to?" Gran asked from a nearby chair.

Aunt Grace turned off the movie, and I had the room's attention.

"Beatriz from school invited me to her house. Her brother's home from college and is inviting a bunch of his friends over." Gran said nothing, but I could tell by her expression that she didn't think my going was a good idea. "Where's Mom? Isn't it a little late to be working?"

"She should be home soon. We'll start dinner. You two go find something to do." Gran shooed Morik and me away with her hands.

Smiling, I motioned for Morik to follow me to my room. Though he moved to join me, his expression was neutral.

At times, I could easily read his thoughts or feelings. Why did he sometimes mask them? Or maybe it wasn't masking. Maybe when he showed emotion, he made an effort to do so. After all, he did say he didn't interact with humans much.

In my room, I went straight for the desk and the incomplete puzzle. "You must see pretty well in the dark, huh?"

Focused on the puzzle, I half-listened to him follow me in. The snick of the closing door caught my attention, and I looked back at him. He ignored my look and joined me at the puzzle. Without hesitating, he started to place pieces.

"Have you done this one before?" I asked.

"Yes, I can see in the dark. No, I haven't done this one before," he said, answering my questions in order.

"How are you finding the right pieces so fast?" I leaned close to watch him and study his eyes as he searched for then placed the pieces together.

Tiny bits of bright green flared in his irises each time he found the piece he wanted. When he placed the piece, the green faded into silver, the primary color of his iris. Other colors danced in the silver pools, but the green caught my attention because it happened consistently. I wondered what it meant.

A sudden swirl of violet took me by surprise. I couldn't help but watch it flow around in the liquid silver background. Before it could fade, green and brown strands joined it. It took a moment for me to realize Morik had stopped looking at the puzzle and, instead, faced me with an amused expression. I couldn't look away.

"Your eyes are amazing to watch," I said without thinking. A blush immediately infused my cheeks, and I hoped he wouldn't read anything into what I'd said. "What do the different colors mean?"

"I don't know. You'll have to tell me when they change." He went back to finding puzzle pieces, still looking amused by my attention.

After a while, my mom called out a hello from the kitchen.

Not wanting Gran to tell Mom about my plans before I could, I hurried from the room and left Morik to follow me if he wanted.

Mom stood near the door in the process of removing her jacket when I found her. She didn't look like she'd been working all day. Her hair was still neat. Usually after work, her hair had little twisty spirals in it. She curled it around her fingers when lost in thought.

"Hey, Mom. Where were you?" I asked idly.

"Don't be nosy, Tessa." Her tone was a bit more abrupt than I thought the question warranted.

"Sorry. Beatriz invited me to her house tonight. I planned to head over there after dinner and to be back by ten. Her brother's home, so there should be a lot of people there." More people meant more guys, which meant more options—something my mom would like.

However, my mom didn't answer me. Instead, she looked past me to Morik.

"Morik, I don't want to subject you to a conversation that might lead to an argument."

He nodded respectfully to my mom then looked at me.

"I will be outside if you decide to go." He grabbed his jacket and was out the door before I could say anything.

I stared at my mom, appalled by her rudeness.

"He's standing outside in the snow. How could you do that? You didn't even ask him if he'd be cold!"

Gran and Aunt Grace drifted from the room. No doubt, they sensed a battle brewing.

"Will he be?" Mom asked as she took plates from the cabinet to set the table.

I thought back to when I'd touched him. He'd felt nicely warm to me despite the temperature of the house. No, he probably wouldn't be cold.

"That's beside the point! You were rude."

"I didn't want to argue in front of him." She didn't look at me but focused on counting out the forks we needed from the drawer.

"Argue about what? All I did was ask where you were."

"And you tried to tell me you're going to a party tonight."

"Tried?"

"You're not going." She said it casually as she took glasses from the drying rack next to the sink.

She'd been fine with the idea of my going out at night the day before. Since this was the first time I'd even spoken with her today, I didn't think her current snit related to me even though I felt the brunt of it.

"You've set one too many settings," I said quietly.

She looked up, surprised. Probably because I wasn't yelling but mostly because I'd contradicted her.

"You don't want me to choose Morik, but when I'm invited to a party where there'll be enough drinking that no one will notice the weird girl discreetly touching an arm here or a hand there, you want me to stay home. So what you're telling me is that you don't want me to choose at all."

I looked over at Aunt Danielle for a moment. She sat

quietly in her chair, her eyes closed, but I knew she listened. Turning back to my mom, I said what needed saying.

"How'd that work out for Aunt Danielle again?"

Mom paled, and her eyes grew watery. "I don't want you to get hurt."

"Then you shouldn't have had me," I said sadly, the words harsher than my tone. "Our choices are limited, but they're still there. Don't limit mine further. This is hard enough."

She set the stack of plates on the table and walked out of the room. I stared after her for a moment, feeling like crying myself.

"Don't cry, girl," Aunt Danielle said from beside me, making me jump a little. "The truth can be as hard to say as it is to hear, but it's always important."

I nodded and grabbed my jacket. Before opening the door, I looked back at Aunt Danielle. "Remind her I love her, okay?"

"I will, honey."

Shutting the door quickly to prevent a cold draft, I paused outside on the step and looked up at the indigo sky.

I hated when I argued with Mom. Knowingly saying something that would hurt her sucked. But she was being unreasonable. Nothing in this whole deal was easy or simple. So far, I'd voluntarily touched boys that I'd thought I might feel even the slightest interest in.

Granted, in cases like Brian and Clavin, it wasn't always voluntary. Regardless, I had been selective up until this point. Knowing that I'd die if I didn't choose soon helped lower my standards a bit to...oh, just about anyone being a possibility. I didn't want to go to a drinking party. But I'd spoken the truth. The possible benefits outweighed the risks.

With a sigh, I stepped off the stoop and headed toward Morik, who waited with my helmet tucked under his arm.

Seeing him distracted me from my musings.

"Why do you bother with a motorcycle if you can pop in and out of places?"

"Popping draws too much attention and scares people." He handed me the helmet.

"So does riding a motorcycle in the snow," I said under my breath, making him laugh as I settled the helmet on my head. "Are you sure you won't come to the party with me?"

"I'm sure." He got on the motorcycle and started it.

I climbed on and wrapped my arms around him without his prompting. Shouting her address to him over the noise, I wondered how long I'd last before my legs went numb.

Five minutes.

Piercing needles of pain danced over my thighs. Carefully, I removed one arm from his waist and laid it over my right leg for additional protection. It didn't help.

Morik took his hand from the throttle and reached back. I thought he was going to pull my arm around him again. Instead, he laid his hand on the coldest part of my leg. Heat seeped through the denim immediately. When he slowed too much, he switched hands to the other leg. I couldn't believe he rode without gloves and didn't have cold hands.

Warmed, I rode the final few minutes in relative comfort.

Beatriz stood at the door when we pulled up to the

sprawling two-story home. Several cars already lined the long driveway, and music pumped from the house. Since she lived outside of town, there weren't any nearby neighbors to complain.

Unstrapping the helmet, I handed it back to Morik. His expression was hard to read, and the glasses hid the color of his eyes.

"If you change your mind, just come in. Looks like the door will be open."

He nodded, hesitated a moment, then pulled away. Somehow, I felt as if I'd just disappointed him.

Chapter Ten

"Nooo!" Beatriz called playfully from the door. "Tell hottie to come back. He's way cuter than anything we'll see inside."

Turning, I smiled at Beatriz. She'd changed the color of her peekaboos and now sported a fluorescent orange.

"You're only saying that because you're related to one of them."

"Maybe." She grinned back at me.

The heat escaping the house warmed my cheeks before I even stepped inside. When I reached back to close the door and keep the warmth in, she stopped me.

"Don't bother. People will be coming and going all night." The sound of another car on the drive proved the truth of her statement.

"Come on. I'll show you around."

I quickly kicked off my shoes to add to the pile of discarded shoes already on the floor of the entryway and followed her. Bursts of laughter erupted from somewhere deeper within the house and grew louder when we entered the kitchen. She pointed out the well-laden snack counter then took me down to the finished basement, the source of the noise.

In the space to the right of the stairs, a guy made drinks from behind a fully stocked bar. The resemblance between him and Beatriz was unmistakable.

When he saw his sister, he motioned to her through the crowd. Between the conversation and the music, I couldn't hear all they said, but I did hear Beatriz shout my name and the name "Brad" by way of introduction. He motioned to a basket loaded with sets of keys behind the bar.

Beatriz shook her head at Brad then leaned in close so I could hear her.

"He wanted to know if you drove. If you had and wanted to drink, you would have had to hand over your keys to Brad."

"That's very responsible of him."

"Yeah, there's just less potential trouble that way. Do you want something to drink?"

"A soda would be good."

While she went to get one from her brother, I moved away from the bar to explore the rest of the basement. With the bar, pool table, and air hockey table to the right of the stairs, most of the crowd congregated there. To the left of the stairs, I found a quieter sitting area with a huge screen. A comedy played without sound. Turning to go back, I spotted a bathroom tucked under the stairs.

Beatriz, carrying my soda, found me looking around.

"You have the perfect setup down here," I said.

"Yeah, but don't use this bathroom. By the end of the night, it will be too gross. Best bet is the one all the way upstairs. Come on, I'll show you my room while this party winds up."

Her second-floor room had its own immaculately clean bathroom, which she said I could use. We sat on her bed and talked for close to an hour. Every now and again, we'd hear another car pull up, followed by a shout or two from the entryway. Each noise was a reminder that I needed to rejoin the party and use my gift. Yet, I lingered because I enjoyed Beatriz's company and felt as if I'd found a friend. That was very much a novelty in my life since any free time I had always went to finding the "right" guy. Briefly, I wondered what would happen to our friendship when my deal with Morik expired.

"Ready to head down?" she asked. "It will be way more crowded, but they're all nice. Especially to us because we're younger, and Brad will kick them out if they're not."

I didn't want to return to the party. The volume had increased, and it now sounded a little on the wild side. However, since Morik wasn't there and I couldn't focus my attention on finding him someone, I had to focus on finding someone for myself. And that meant I had to go where all the men were. Even though I would have preferred not to touch a bunch of drunken people, I nodded. I owed it to my family to make an effort.

In the packed basement, I enjoyed a certain freedom as I used my gift without anyone even noticing, thanks to Brad's generosity at the bar. Several visions later, I grew restless.

Since Beatriz had pulled one of her brother's friends to the air hockey table, I approached the bar on my own for a new drink. Brad spotted me, smiled, and handed me a cup with pink liquid. When I asked what it was, all I got from his explanation was the word punch. The rest of what he said blended with the noise of the room.

The fruity punch set my head spinning by the time I drank half of it. I should have known better. Warm and needing a drink of plain water, I wove through the crowd and made my way upstairs to the kitchen. People lingered by the snack table as they munched and talked.

I went to the sink and dumped the rest of my drink. As I ran the tap and waited for the water to turn cold, I looked out the kitchen window. Stars lined the sky. I'd never get tired of looking at them.

Away from the house, I caught a brief flicker of a green glow. Leaning toward the window, I scanned the dark. Had those been Morik's eyes? Was he out there waiting for me?

"Didn't like it?"

The voice startled me into yelping and jumping a little. With a hand over my wildly beating heart, I turned toward an amused Brad.

"The drink," he said, nodding toward the pink remains in the sink. "Didn't like it?"

"It was fine. I just have to work tomorrow morning."

"So do half the people here." He chuckled and leaned against the counter like he was settling in for a conversation.

"Who's behind the bar if you're up here?"

"Beatriz. She serves very good watered-down drinks. Keeps the party from getting out of hand." He reached back, grabbed a few chips to munch, and held out his hand to share. "I noticed you wandering around the room down there. You had a sort of lost look in your eyes. Not having fun?"

Crap. He'd been watching me? I'd bombarded myself with as many visions as I could in a short time just in case Beatriz called for my attention again. While envisioning the future, I probably did look a little lost. It was hard to process one future after another like that.

A few guys had been decent enough, but when I came to and actually looked at whom I touched, I felt nothing. I wanted a spark or my heart to skip a beat. Some kind of indication of an actual attraction on my part. Mean, I know, since they would die because of me, but I couldn't imagine making babies without some kind of affection. Instead, each time, there'd been nothing.

"No, not fun in the sense that they're having fun." I waved at a drunk pair who laughed uproariously over spilled beer. "But fun in my own way. Educational for sure." For example, I now had a "top ten reasons not to drink" list. But, I kept that to myself.

"Beatriz said you just moved here. You don't talk to anyone except her, you don't date, and you don't even hang out after school. But you do have a job. What do you do?"

His keen observation of me while I'd been swimming in visions downstairs and his secondhand knowledge of my life unnerved me.

"I just help out at the Coffee Shop on the weekends."

From the basement, angry shouting erupted. Brad moved

fast, dashing down the stairs. A clipped blast of an air horn sounded, then an eerie quiet descended. I stayed where I was, safe by the sink, and wondered what had happened.

"Tessa! Get the doors there," Brad yelled from below.

Looking around, I spotted the dining room's French doors as the noise picked up again. Warm from the drink, I didn't mind yanking them open. Behind me, I heard thumping on the steps and muffled curses.

Five guys carried another up the steps then maneuvered him outside. It wasn't an easy feat since he fought their hold and swore against the sock stuffed in his mouth the entire time.

Brad pulled out the gag as the rest of the group set him down. The guy came up swinging. Two guys caught his arms, and Brad started fast-talking.

Brad told him that he could calm down outside and drink some water or Brad would call him a ride. Angry but defeated, the guy slumped onto a snow-covered chair. I cringed, but he didn't seem to notice the cold.

Everyone except Brad and the guy in the chair came back in. I closed the doors behind them.

Beatriz sprinted up the stairs just then.

"Liquor is locked up," she showed me a little golden key, "and water is being served." She looked out the window at her brother. "Can you go to the closet by the front door and grab Brad a jacket while I get Tommy some water?"

Figuring Tommy was the drunk in the chair, I nodded. The front door no longer stood open, which explained why it felt warmer inside. I stepped over the randomly placed shoes and nudged the closet door open enough to pull out a worn canvas jacket.

Beatriz took both the jacket and the water outside. I watched through the window as Brad smiled his thanks. He took the water from her and offered it to Tommy. Tommy didn't appreciate the effort and started swearing again. With a dark look at Tommy, Brad sent Beatriz back in.

"He's going to be in for it in the morning," she said as she closed the doors.

"Which one?" I asked as I looked over the snacks. They'd been thoroughly picked through. Broken chip remains littered the bottoms of several bowls.

"Tommy. Brad's using his phone to record him." She snickered to herself and then caught my confused look. "He was swearing at me. Brad is *way* overprotective. But, he'll wait until Tommy's feeling better to talk to him about it. I'm betting I get breakfast out of this."

I checked the clock above the sink.

"I think I'm going to head out." Beatriz started to protest, but I cut her off with a hug good-bye. "I have to work in the morning. Thank you for inviting me. It's been fun."

"But we didn't get to challenge the drunks to air hockey…"

I laughed and shook my head.

"Next time."

"Promise?"

"Sure." I doubted there'd be a next time soon, though. She

walked me to the door and helped me find my shoes. Grudgingly, she retrieved my jacket, too.

"Do you need to call the hottie?" she asked as I bundled up.

It was a good question. I'd assumed he'd give me a ride home, but we never talked about it.

Something in my face gave away my thoughts because Beatriz gave a slow shake of her head. "You need a ride home, don't you?"

"I forgot to ask him. Can I use your phone to call my mom?" I didn't relish the idea but knew she'd come get me.

"Are you serious? This is an under-age party. She'll freak out. I don't want to get Brad in trouble." Beatriz started to look panicked.

"Don't worry. My mom's not like that at all. She already knows where I am and what I'm doing."

Beatriz didn't look convinced.

"You don't have that guy's number?"

"Morik," I said, supplying her with a name. "And no, I don't have his number. He always seems to show up just when I need him." At that moment, we caught the distant rumble of a motorcycle.

"You're not kidding." She smiled at me triumphantly and pulled open the door.

We both watched the single light turn into her driveway.

"Thanks again. It was fun." I left her at the door as Morik parked.

He handed me the helmet and didn't offer to help but watched me closely to make sure I put it on correctly.

As soon as I settled on the seat behind him, he started down the drive. I hid behind him as we sped down the salt-melted roads, but the pins and needles in my legs were inevitable.

He pulled in front of my house, killed the engine, and helped me from the back. Frozen and wanting to hurry inside, I handed him the helmet. But I hesitated when I noticed his eyes through his yellow sunglasses. Streaks of vibrant orange swirled in their mercury depths.

"Did you find what you were looking for?" he asked quietly.

"Looking for?" As I said it, what I'd done became clear, and I wanted to kick myself.

He'd spent a long time tracking me down. When he'd found me, he had waited to show me his true form because he'd been afraid that he would scare me, which he had, a little. Then, after I'd proven I could touch him and see him without fear, which had probably given him hope that I saw him as a choice, I had gone to a party where I could continue to search for an alternate choice.

"I don't know what I'm looking for," I admitted honestly. "None of this feels right to me. I know you're a choice. I'm not discounting you. I'm not discounting anyone." I stuffed my hands in my pockets in frustration. "I can't do what the women before me have done. They tell me to just pick someone. I don't want a stranger. I'm sorry my going to the party hurt you.

175

I didn't mean it that way. I just don't want to die and am looking for a way to make everyone happy."

He studied me for a moment. The orange in his eyes dimmed, but didn't recede completely.

"Need help getting to sleep?" he finally asked.

"Please," I said gratefully, not just for his offer but also for his understanding.

We walked together to the door. I let myself in. However, when I looked back, he was gone. The house was quiet, but my mom waited in the living room with Aunt Danielle.

"Everything go all right?" Mom asked quietly as she stood and unwrapped the knit blanket from her shoulders.

"From Beatriz's point of view, it did. Nothing much happened for me, though, but not from lack of trying,"

"I'm sorry you haven't connected with anyone yet, Tessa. I do worry about that constantly, but I want you to be happy, too."

I nodded and hugged her good night before I headed to my room. Behind me, Aunt Danielle's soft voice broke the silence though I couldn't hear what she said.

When I flicked on my light, I wasn't surprised to see Morik at the desk or that the puzzle was complete. I nudged the door closed with my heel and sat on the bed to peel off my socks. Everything was cold. My toes didn't want to move.

Picking up my pajamas, I went to the bathroom to change and brush my teeth. I let the water run hot just so I could warm my hands when I rinsed. The warmth didn't last long.

Wet fingers in a cold house didn't have a chance. The good news was that I wouldn't be awake much longer to notice it.

I hurried back to my bedroom, ready to get under the covers. Morik waited beside my bed. As soon as I entered, he started the chant. I barely made it to the bed before I felt the first pull of sleep. He helped me sit then lifted my legs in. The bed and blankets were already warm as if they'd just come out of the dryer. I smiled sleepily.

"Thank you, Morik. I love being warm." Then, I was out.

Chapter Eleven

LIKE THE DAY BEFORE, I WOKE UP LATE AND HAD TO SCRAMBLE TO get ready for work. However, everyone seemed more relaxed when I strode into the kitchen. Morik and Mom sat together at the table, and the lingering aroma of fried eggs hung in the air. My stomach growled, and I briefly wished I'd woken earlier.

Morik stood as I entered.

"I can't be late," I said instead of a polite good morning.

"Do you want to eat first?" Even as he asked, he moved with me.

"Can't." I called good-bye to my mom and rushed out the door.

Moments later, we raced through the streets. When he pulled in front of the Coffee Shop, I ripped off the helmet and dismounted. My hurried moves nearly tipped us over, but Morik quickly braced his feet on the ground and kept us upright.

"Sorry," I said, tossing him the helmet. "Lunch is on me if you want to stop in again." Not waiting for his answer, I raced inside.

"Tessa, I wish I had your luck," Mona said from behind the counter.

I hurried to the back hall and put my things away. "What do you mean?"

"To have a guy watch me like that..." The wistful note in her voice caught my attention as I pulled my hair back.

"Like what?" I glanced at the window across the shop, but Morik was already gone.

"Like he just saw something he had to have and was plotting a way to get it. It's the same look my ex had in his eye when he saw the pickup truck he now owns," she said with a grin.

I didn't want Morik to look at me like that. It made me feel guilty for going to the party last night. Thankfully, I didn't have time to dwell on it as customers filled the shop.

Toward noon, the rush died off until most of the tables were empty. The lull before the lunch crowd, if you could call it a crowd, gave Mona and me time to regroup. While Mona went to restock some of the sandwich ingredients in the back, I started wiping down the counter.

The bell above the door rang. I looked up with a ready smile on my lips. The smile grew when I saw it was Brad. His warm brown gaze found me, and he smiled in return as he made his way to the counter.

"So, you made it to work."

"Yeah, but barely. Thankfully, I have a friend who's willing to give me a ride."

"Well, you did better than half the people who came last

night. The last one woke up and left about an hour ago. Beatriz, Tommy, and I just finished cleaning up."

"How's Tommy doing this morning?" I asked, remembering how drunk he'd been.

"He's good. Groveling for Beatriz's forgiveness."

I could imagine Beatriz's reaction to the groveling and gave a small chuckle.

"What did he say that got him in so much trouble?"

Warming to the conversation, Brad leaned against the counter. "Ah, the lipping off wasn't as bad as throwing up in her bathroom."

I laughed. Just then, the bell rang again. I looked over in time to see Morik paused in the doorway, completely focused on Brad. It took effort not to let my worry show in my expression as Brad followed my gaze and nodded a brief greeting, not noticing Morik's intense regard.

Inwardly cringing over how this probably looked to Morik, I turned to Brad again. He appeared completely unaware of the tension he'd just caused.

"Are you looking for coffee to take back for everyone, then?" I didn't look up at the sound of the door closing.

"Sure, I'll have a cup to go. You choose the flavor. I'm not much of a connoisseur." As I started making his order, he added, "I actually just stopped in to make sure you got home okay last night. Beatriz told me how your friend picked you up on a motorcycle. Pretty dangerous, given the snow and how cold it was. No frostbite or spills?"

I kept my eyes on my task instead of checking on Morik's progress through the nearly empty room.

"I trust him completely or I wouldn't have gotten on the bike." I didn't say anything about the frostbite, though.

Brad nodded, seemingly satisfied, and I handed him his coffee in exchange for a five. When I moved to the register, he told me to put the change in the tip jar.

"I'm glad you and Beatriz are friends. See you around."

After Brad walked out the door, Morik stepped up to the counter. It was hard to guess his thoughts with his eyes covered. When he didn't immediately say something, I stretched forward, reaching over the counter to nudge his sunglasses down the bridge of his nose. He didn't try to stop me.

His usually multi-colored silver irises had disappeared in a sea of red with orange, stormy centers. No liquid silver remained. I didn't know what it meant, but I knew that whatever emotion those colors were tied to was a strong one. And, probably not a good one.

Thinking of Clavin's broken leg, I reached out with both hands and cupped Morik's face.

"Brad was just being nice to his kid sister's friend."

Morik closed his eyes but didn't move away. I waited, holding his face. He reached up, placed his hand over mine briefly, then pulled away entirely and pushed his sunglasses back into place. He ordered a coffee and sandwich as if nothing had happened then offered to wait to give me a ride home.

Mona didn't seem to mind his lingering presence while we cleaned up. Again, she disappeared into the back to count out the tips. When she handed them to me, she told me the Coffee Shop would be closed next weekend so we could enjoy Christmas.

UNLIKE THE DAY BEFORE, Morik left after he dropped me off at home. I watched the retreating motorcycle for a moment and re-evaluated my plan. Though he'd assured me that he would respect any choice I made, I worried about choosing someone else. He definitely didn't like other men around me. Despite my limited time, I'd have to hold off on my own search until I found someone for him.

"Where's Morik?" Aunt Danielle asked when I walked into the house.

"Not sure. He didn't say what his plans were." I hung up my things and moved to the couch to put my feet up. "Where's Mom?"

"Out with her boss, Stephen, again."

I sprang up from my relaxed position and swiveled toward her.

"What do you mean?"

"Lunch date, I think." Aunt Danielle became bored with the conversation and leaned back into her chair, closing her eyes.

My mom was on a date. I sat there frozen, trying to get past the shock. A date. Why didn't she say anything to me? I felt hurt. All her talk about being honest with each other obviously only applied to me.

"Don't be upset, dear. There are only a few short years they'll be free of obligation to you. Once your husband dies, they will band together again to help you. Don't begrudge them their happiness."

Them? Then, I remembered Gran talking about the elderly neighbor. It explained where she went without a car. Did that mean Aunt Grace had found someone, too? Were they all waiting for me to choose so they could have a normal life for a little while?

Quietly, I closed myself in my bedroom. There, I lay on my bed, curled on my side as I hugged my pillow and faced the wall. It was too much pressure. How did they deal with this when they were my age? Mom had made it sound like choosing my dad had been unintentional. I wished that would happen to me.

Part of my problem was the guilt I felt over knowingly condemning some poor man to an early grave. Now, I could add another scoop of guilt that I was holding the rest of the family back from having normal lives. What would happen if I weren't here? Would it be so bad not to choose? What was I saying?

Morik wanted a companion. I needed to stop running from it and do what Belinda couldn't.

I wondered if Morik really did listen all the time.

"Morik, what do I have to do to choose?"

A moment later, the mattress dipped as he sat next to me.

"Why are you asking?"

I didn't turn. Holding my pillow close, I continued to stare at the wall.

"According to Mom and Gran, it's not as simple as walking up to someone and saying 'I choose you.' But, most of the time, they make it sound like going on a date would be enough."

"You have to choose in your mind and your heart."

"How can that be? I've heard Gran talking about her husband. She didn't really like him."

"She saw her daughter, though. It was enough for her heart to choose."

Not a single, potential future I experienced had ever been enough for me. All those cute little cherub faces, even the ones that stayed with me for days afterward, hadn't been enough to outweigh the guilt I felt over causing someone's premature death. If it had, I would have chosen.

The phone rang, stopping my train of thought. Since I was the only one home, I forced myself to get up.

Morik stayed in my room while I went to answer it. Sitting on Mom's bed, I said a quiet hello.

Beatriz chirped a greeting.

"I'm bored, you're done with work, and it's light out. I think you should have hottie drive you over here. He can join the guys in their air hockey tournament while we spectate."

"I heard Tommy christened your bathroom," I said, ignoring her invitation. Going to her house again wouldn't be fair to Morik. I'd promised him an hour a day.

"Yeah, Brad mentioned he talked to you about that. I think he was worried you wouldn't come by again because last night got a little crazy. He thinks I need more friends." She snorted in disbelief. "Most everyone in our school is a backstabber or a gossip. No thanks. So, can you come over?"

I glanced at the open bedroom door and thought of Morik in my room; I knew I couldn't go. Given his attitude last night and his reaction to Brad's appearance at the Coffee Shop, it was safe to guess he wouldn't be happy about a repeat visit.

"I'm sorry, Beatriz, but I don't think Morik is in the company kind of mood today."

"Aw! That sucks. If you still want to come over, I can get Tommy or Brad to pick you up and take you back home."

I twisted my finger in the antiquated phone cord.

"Thanks Beatriz, but I ditched Morik last night. I can't do that to him two days in a row."

Morik's hand covered mine, stopping the agitated twisting. I looked up in surprise, not realizing he'd joined me.

"We'll be there in twenty minutes," he said.

Beatriz squealed loudly through the phone. I jerked it away from my ear with a wince. Obviously, I didn't need to relay what he'd said.

I mouthed "why?"

"You could use the fun," he said.

"He's right, you know," Beatriz said. "You're way too serious. Let him know that there will only be a few people here, nothing crazy like last night."

I agreed to tell him and quickly hung up the phone. Morik

and I stared at each other. I hadn't forgotten the conversation Beatriz's call had interrupted but wasn't sure if I wanted to revisit it. I felt like a failure just thinking about my inability to choose. How could the other women in my family so easily pick someone? Well, not everyone. Aunt Danielle understood.

Maybe Morik was right. Maybe I needed to relax a little and give nature a chance to work itself out.

"Still using the motorcycle?" He nodded. "Then I'm going to layer up so my legs don't freeze. Will you wait for me in the kitchen?"

I found a pair of leggings, a long-sleeved, V-neck shirt and, after I raided my mom's closet, an oversized sweater. Over the leggings, I added jeans. Nothing really matched, but it would keep me warm for a little while. I thought of adding another layer. However, other than my pajamas, nothing would fit over the jeans.

"You need to go shopping," Aunt Danielle commented when I stepped out into the living room.

I snorted and shook my head.

"It's not that bad. I just don't want to freeze again on the way over to Beatriz's. Can you let Mom know where I went? I'll be back before nine." Aunt Danielle promised she would give the message, and I put on my jacket.

Outside, when the wind bit into my skin, I appreciated that the helmet would, at least, keep my face warm. Even with the extra layers of clothing and the scarf tucked around my neck, I estimated I'd lose feeling in my feet and legs by the time we reached Beatriz's house.

"Remind me why this is the transportation of choice," I said as I slipped the helmet on.

"It's small enough that I can appear suddenly on the side of the road or in an alley with no one noticing. Cars are harder."

The visor on the helmet was still up when I paused to stare at him in surprise. I'd thought he'd picked it because it was faster or maybe just because he liked motorcycles.

"I didn't realize you get cold so easily. I'll look for some better clothes for you," he promised with a concerned glance at my jacket. His yellow glasses hid any color differences in his irises, but I wondered what colors I would see if he weren't wearing them.

"No, that's okay. We just won't plan any long rides until it warms up."

He didn't say anything. Instead, he carefully closed the visor and helped me onto the bike.

I took turns with one arm around his waist and the other on my legs to prevent them from getting cold. And it worked, for the most part. My legs were fine, but my hands froze quickly despite my knit mittens. I tried to warm them in his jacket pocket, but they remained frozen. Telling myself we were only a few minutes from Beatriz's house, I curled them into fists.

My pinky on both hands started to sting. I wiggled my hand out of the mitten, careful to keep my hand in his pocket. Without the mitten, some of his heat seeped through the lining but not enough to warm it. The sting intensified, and Brad's comment about frostbite rang in my ears.

Worried, I took a moment to deliberate another option to warm my hands. Morik hadn't seemed to mind when I touched him three nights ago. But, I hadn't been freezing cold then. Hoping he wouldn't be upset, or worse, drive us off the road, I quickly withdrew my hand from his pocket and slipped it under the jacket. The shirts he wore were both untucked and easy to get around.

I laid my hand on his bare skin. His stomach muscles twitched, but he didn't give any other indication that he'd noticed. And I was grateful because his heat immediately started to warm my fingers. I quickly shed my other mitten so that hand could join the first. I leaned closer to keep his jacket down and the cold air out. My hands slowly warmed, and pressed against him, my legs stayed warm, too.

I turned my hands over and couldn't help but notice again how smooth his skin felt.

He twitched again, and I supposed it didn't feel too good to keep moving my cold hands around like that. I didn't stop, though. He could scowl at me all he wanted when we got to Beatriz's.

Basking in his heat, I didn't immediately notice that the trees that had whipped past at a dizzying speed had slowed. No, we had slowed. The last flip to warm my hands had probably shocked him. At least, he hadn't run us into the trees.

"You okay?" I asked.

He nodded and sped up again.

With regret, I withdrew my hands and stuck them back in his jacket pockets. I stayed reasonably warm the last few minutes of the ride but was happy when I saw Beatriz's house ahead. Morik parked in the drive and kept the bike steady for me to dismount.

Unwilling to remove my mittens again, I waited for Morik to help me with the helmet. His eyes behind the yellow sunglasses appeared much darker than usual, tempting me to reach up and move the sunglasses out of the way. Not giving in, I held still for him. As soon as the helmet was off, I gave him a sheepish smile.

"I hope I didn't cross a line. My hands were cold."

He quirked a lopsided grin. "I know. I felt it. And no, you didn't cross any lines." He stepped close and gently smoothed my hair. "For you, I'll never draw any."

Something inside me squirmed a little. Not trusting myself to say the right thing, I only nodded.

Behind me, the front door opened, and Beatriz called out a greeting. I broke eye contact first to turn and wave to her.

"Twenty minutes on the dot," she said when we stepped inside. "You're good."

Her gaze wandered all over Morik. I hoped she wouldn't notice his eyes, horns, or ears. Or his nails. Hopefully, she'd think it was nail polish like Mona had. This wasn't a good idea. Hesitantly, I officially introduced the two.

I should have known that the girl who saw so much on my first day wouldn't miss a thing though.

"So, what's up with your eyes?" She watched him with

open curiosity while I fought not to cringe and fumbled for something to say.

"It's an eye condition," Morik said smoothly. "Several actually. The whites are discolored and the irises abnormal. I use the yellow driving glasses so people can still see my eyes but not all the detail. Less mass hysteria." He tucked his hands in his pockets in a relaxed pose and waited.

"Don't blame you. People freak out when you're different. That's why I like different colors in my hair. Distract them with the obvious so they don't notice the stuff I don't want them to." Beatriz held up her hand and splayed her fingers. Her pointer finger was a little shorter than it should be.

"I never noticed before, Beatriz."

"That's just one of many reasons why I call you friend." She grinned at me. "Let's go downstairs. They're already warming up. Are you any good at air hockey, Morik?"

"I've never played, but I'm a fast learner," he said, following us down the steps.

Beatriz gave him the same guided tour of the basement she'd given me then introduced him to Brad, Tommy, and Jay. Jay's face wasn't familiar so I guessed he must have missed last night's party. That or he showed up after I left.

Brad moved behind the bar and pulled cans of soda from the refrigerator.

"Tommy and I will play the first set. Best of three. Morik and Jay, you'll be next. Then, the winners of the two sets play. Anyone want anything to drink before we start?"

Beatriz and I stayed by the bar, drinking the soda and

munching on the bar mix set out in a bowl. Morik leaned against the pool table and watched the contenders closely until the first one scored. After that, he joined us.

Beatriz started up a conversation with him, completely at ease with his watchful gaze. She asked when he graduated in a very subtle attempt to determine his age.

He dodged the question, saying he hadn't made the best decisions about school and asked what she was interested in going to college for. She liked the idea of Interior design, which fit when I thought about her room and her bathroom.

"You look Native American, Morik. Where are you from?"

"I am native. This is my homeland. In fact, I grew up not too far from here."

Something about the way he said it had me thinking that was probably a very watered-down version of the truth.

Jay joined us and started asking Morik about his motorcycle. I took the opportunity to escape to the bathroom and peel off the extra layer of clothing I'd put on. Crazy how a girl who never seemed to get enough heat suddenly had a sweaty upper lip. Getting rid of the jeans and sweater left me in the V-neck shirt and the leggings. The clothes were comfortable, but I wasn't sure I was comfortable in them. Like the leggings, the v-neck hugged my curves.

I quickly switched the leggings for the jeans. More confident, I left my extra clothes in the basement living room area then rejoined the others. Morik eyed my change in clothes before turning back to Jay, who still dominated the conversation.

Beatriz, bored now that she no longer quizzed Morik, hopped down from her stool and dragged me toward the pool table.

"I suck at playing pool, but it's better than listening to mechanics."

I smiled, saying nothing because Morik needed this opportunity for regular conversation. He'd hinted that every interaction had been because of a deal. Even his interactions with me were due to one deal or another. Happy to give him his moment, I focused on the pool table.

"I've never played before. So, I doubt it will be much fun for you."

"It's easy," she assured me with a quick grin.

She racked the balls and grabbed us each cue sticks. At my blank look, she proceeded to show me how to play. I watched closely as she broke the triangle formation of the balls she'd racked. They scattered nicely and left me plenty of options. One of the striped balls came to a stop very near a pocket. I moved around the table and tried to mimic her bent-over stance and felt a little self-conscious when she giggled. She laughed when I tried doing the bridge she'd shown me.

"Play nice." I faked a scowl and pointed the cue at her.

Beatriz kept a smile on her face, and she attempted to show me, again, how to stand and use my hand to create a bridge. As I listened, I noticed that the conversation and good-natured taunting around us had come to a stop.

Beatriz noticed the same thing because she turned and glared at her brother.

"What? I'm showing her something wrong, aren't I?" She said the last as an angry statement, not a question.

Brad laughingly held up his hands. "Not going to interfere. Just watching."

"Back to your own game." She stood with her arms crossed and waited for them to comply. When they did, she leaned close to me and quietly demonstrated what to do.

"I'm probably showing you wrong. Just try to hit the white ball without tearing the cloth, and it'll be a good try."

She moved away, and I tried again. This time, I looked up for confirmation that I was doing it right. She smiled widely, clearly amused by my efforts, but nodded anyway.

I jabbed the cue forward in a parody of what she'd shown me. The tip missed the cue ball completely. Beatriz encouraged me to keep trying until I finally made contact. The ball I finally hit didn't go far, which was good since I'd moved it further from the pocket.

Beatriz expertly studied the table then moved into position and sunk her targeted ball into a side pocket. After counting the number of balls on the table and estimating how long each turn took me, I decided our pool game would take forever.

At the air hockey table, Tommy swore and Brad laughed, interrupting my concentration.

"Morik. Jay. Your turn," Brad said. Tommy moved behind the bar to get himself a soda while Brad took a seat to watch both games.

I paused in my turn to watch Morik and Jay begin. Jay watched Morik closely. Morik watched the puck. He unerringly caught it and sent it sailing back to Jay's goal without hesitating. Jay deflected, but to me, it looked like luck more than skill. Morik caught the rebounding puck and immediately shot it back to Jay's goal.

Suddenly, playing pool with Beatriz didn't seem so bad or as competitive. I went back to studying the pool table, spotted another ball close to a pocket, and bent down to take aim.

"Nope, not that one," Beatriz said, standing near the table and leaning on her cue to watch me. "The first kind of ball you sink is the one you aim for the rest of the game. I have solids. You have stripes."

I glanced at the balls again, focusing on the striped ones. Nothing else on the table looked remotely possible.

"Here, let me help," Brad offered.

He moved over to the table, directly across from me, ignoring his sister's cry of "no fair" to point out how to aim at the cue ball to make it veer in different directions. I paid close attention to his instruction.

He moved back from the table as I prepared to shoot. Since the previous ball I'd hit had barely moved, I put some extra force behind my thrust this time.

The cue ball flew but didn't go in the direction I wanted.

"Please, Bea," Brad begged his sister, "just let me help her for a few minutes so it's more fair."

"You make me sound like a shark. Fine. Help her." She sat down next to Tommy, sipped her soda, and watched.

Brad walked up to me, turned me slightly away from the table, and stood right behind me. From there, he showed me how to hold the cue, make the bridge, line up the cue stick with the cue ball, and use a smooth stroke to better control the outcome. It amazed me when I pocketed a ball with his help.

Behind us, Jay let out a yelp. "Dammit! That hit my knuckle!"

I turned in time to see him rub his hand for a moment before he grabbed the mallet again. Morik wasn't paying attention to Jay. He watched me. Or rather Brad, who stood inches from me, having just assisted me with my last shot. Morik's eyes swirled with vivid orange color, but no one seemed to notice over Jay's loud complaints.

Okay. No more help from Brad.

"I think I got it now, Brad. Thanks for the help."

He winked at me, assured me it wasn't a problem, and turned to sit back down.

Jay cried out again. "I think I'm bleeding. Man, you hit hard."

Tommy started to laugh. "How many times do we need to tell you to keep your fingers out of the way? You want Brad to show you how to hold the mallet?"

Jay told Tommy to piss off, which earned him a dark look from Brad, then gripped the mallet again.

This time, I watched Morik's play instead of Beatriz. He bent aggressively over the table, and I grew a little worried for Jay. When I noticed the red glint in Morik's eyes, I knew I needed to do something to prevent Jay from losing a finger.

"Is anyone else hungry?" I asked in an overly loud voice.

Jay straightened, obviously willing to take a break. Tommy perked up and nodded.

Brad looked at Beatriz.

"What do you think, pipsqueak? Delivery or create our own masterpiece?"

"Delivery," she said emphatically. Then she squealed, "Chinese!" She laughed when the other three groaned. "Fine. Pizza. What do you guys like on your pizza?" She looked at me then Morik.

I hoped she wouldn't notice his eyes. I had no idea how Jay hadn't noticed. Maybe he'd been too busy watching the puck.

I answered for both of us.

"Anything is fine. We're not picky."

Beatriz led the charge upstairs to make sure Brad ordered what she wanted. Tommy gave Jay a hard time about his injured fingers as they trailed behind.

I stayed downstairs with Morik, who still gripped the mallet.

Once everyone else was gone, I set my cue on the pool table and went over to him. Sliding down his glasses, I saw the same swirling red with a vivid orange center.

"I think I know what red and orange mean," I said softly to him, feeling the weight of his angry gaze. He closed his eyes and breathed deeply for a moment. I laid my hand over his and gently took the mallet out from underneath it. Fine fractures lined the high top.

"Do you want to go home?" He shook his head. "Brad won't help me anymore," I promised him quietly. I heard feet on the

196

stairs, patted his hand, and pushed his glasses back into place. I stepped back before Beatriz rounded the corner.

"Three extra larges on the way," Beatriz said, holding a bag of cheese-coated chips. "This will have to hold you over for now."

We stayed through the rest of the games, and Morik eventually beat Brad. Since Brad left me alone for the rest of the evening, Morik made an effort to be nice. When Brad laughed and called Morik "Yoda" before asking if he'd come back Friday night for his next party, Morik studied him for a heartbeat. Then, he shrugged and agreed that he'd let Brad know later.

Beatriz tried to talk me into staying for a movie. I knew she wanted an opportunity to get closer to Morik, but a movie would put me past the time I had promised to be home. Reluctantly, she let me change back into my layered outfit. However, we were delayed when I couldn't find my mittens. Everyone helped me look, but I noticed that Morik didn't seem very motivated.

After a few minutes, Beatriz gave up the search.

"Do you want to borrow a pair of mine? I'll keep looking for yours and bring them to school when I find them."

Morik answered before I could.

"I have something she can use on the bike. We'll be fine."

I looked at him, puzzled. All that he had was a helmet. Since the sun had set, the temperature had dropped. I worried that I'd be cold again, but his steady liquid silver gaze had me agreeing. He was up to something, but I didn't know what.

We stepped outside, and I took a moment to enjoy the stars while keeping my hands in my thin coat pockets. He patiently stood beside me, waiting. Missing the stars was the reason for our deal, after all. I didn't pause too long, though.

He helped me with the helmet so I could keep my hands in my pockets. He didn't offer me anything else. When I settled behind him, I had no choice but to tuck my hands in his pockets where I knew they'd be warmer.

The motorcycle snarled to life, and we left Beatriz's house behind. I'd enjoyed our time there and hoped that Morik would consider going back on Friday.

Within minutes, the cold penetrated my hands and numbed my fingers. Morik hadn't seemed to mind when I warmed them on the way to Beatriz's, so I didn't hesitate to use the same method. This time, I went for his sides just below the pockets.

When I touched his skin, my stomach did a crazy flip, unsettling me. I resisted the urge to move my fingers and, instead, rested them against his skin.

In just a few short days, I'd done what no other in my family could do before me. I'd spoken with Morik, faced him without fear, and willingly touched him. None of it bothered me, either. In fact, I liked spending time with him.

Silently warming my hands on his sides, I again acknowledged what I'd known since he'd told me Belinda's story. I didn't need to plot to find someone else for Morik. I just needed to do what Belinda hadn't. For my sake and the sake of my family.

Chapter Twelve

Monday morning, I opened my eyes to find no one standing beside my bed. I frowned at the lack of breakfast, especially when I could hear the low murmur of voices coming from the kitchen, but I rushed to get ready regardless.

When I emerged, I found Gran and Morik in the kitchen but no Mom or Aunt Grace.

"Where is everyone?"

"They already left since you have a ride," Gran said.

I hadn't had a chance to talk to them last night about their dates but guessed that it didn't really matter. Not if I could make it work with Morik. My gaze slid to his.

"Thanks. I really appreciate this. We better hurry, though."

When I started to move past him, he caught me by the hand and stopped me.

"I have something for you." He nodded to the pile of leather draped over the chair next to him. I'd thought it was only his coat. When I looked closer, I saw there were two.

He lifted the one on top and handed it to me. The weight

surprised me, and it almost hit the floor. He smiled, took the coat, and helped me into it. I felt the difference as soon as it settled on my shoulders.

"Are there plates in there?" I tapped an elbow and it made a thunk sound. It felt like there was one on my back as well.

"You worry about falling. I thought this type of jacket might make you feel safer while keeping you warmer, too." He unzipped the side pockets and pulled out new, black leather gloves. "And, these will protect your hands." He paused, met my eyes briefly, and gave a small smile. "Not that I minded cold hands on my skin."

I felt the blood rush to my face as I tugged the gloves on. They matched the black riding jacket.

He picked up his jacket and shrugged into it. I noticed that a red fleece scarf still hung over the back of the chair. The knit cloth matched the zipper material that ran down the front of my new jacket and the pockets on the front and the arms.

He smiled slightly when he noted me looking at it, and I tried not to flush further when he picked it up and looped it around my neck. Rather than focusing on the way he carefully tucked it in, I tried to focus on what these gifts meant. My upper body wouldn't get cold, but I didn't think my legs would be any better off.

He stepped back to eye his work.

"For the longer rides, I have insulated jeans, too, but didn't think you needed them to get to school."

"Thank you." His consideration meant more to me than the jacket did.

Gran whistled low. "That's a sharp sight."

I grinned and gave her a quick hug good-bye while Morik waited by the door.

"Don't you ever get cold?" I asked as we walked outside. The jacket and gloves were amazingly warm, but the cold air chilled my face.

"Rarely. If I do, something's usually wrong with me."

"What do you mean? You get sick?"

"Or hurt. It's happened a time or two."

The thought of him hurt or sick made him seem more human. And it worried me.

"You should be wearing a helmet, too, then," I said, settling behind him. He laughed and took off. My hands tightly circled his waist.

My arrival at school, decked out in form-fitting leather, drew more attention than I anticipated. When I handed the helmet to Morik, his eyes swirled with orange. No red.

"Will I see you after school?" I asked.

He nodded before he took off again, weaving through the morning school traffic.

"You are smokin' hot in that," Beatriz said, coming up behind me.

I smiled self-consciously.

"Friends share, right?" she prodded.

"Any time." Hopefully, Morik wouldn't mind if I loaned out the jacket when I didn't need it.

"Good." She sighed and stared off in the direction he'd disappeared. "I'll take him tomorrow."

I laughed. "You're on your own there. I don't control him." We started walking toward the school.

"Shows what you know. I saw the way he watched you yesterday. And how he got annoyed when Brad helped you. Brad noticed, too. He thinks Morik might be a little too old for you, though."

She had no idea.

"We're not together. Just friends."

"Right," she agreed sarcastically. "You and I both know that Morik would like to be more than just friends."

Yes, I knew what he wanted, and it still scared me. I didn't even know what it would mean to be with him. Rather than think about all of that, I changed the subject when we reached my locker.

"Any big plans over winter break?"

"Nope."

I knew a lot of families usually took the week that we had no school to go on vacation or spend it visiting every relative under the sun. Since neither of those was an option for my family, we typically didn't do anything, not even a big gift exchange, although we still had a family dinner. I never thought Beatriz's family might be like mine.

"Really? Nothing?"

"Not this year. At least, not for Brad and me. My parents had a chance to visit with my Dad's side of the family who live in England. They left last Thursday and won't be back until next Monday."

"That's a long time."

"Yep. That's why Brad's home to keep an eye on things. My parents didn't want me alone, especially over winter break, which starts this Friday." She paused for a moment. "Just in case you didn't know."

I smirked at her heavy hinting.

"Are you going to make me beg? Seriously, what time are you coming over? Say noon so you can help set up for the final party before my mom and dad come home."

"It'll depend on when Morik's available," I hedged. "So your parents won't be home for Christmas?"

"No, but Brad and I are okay with it. We could have gone with them, but I would have missed too much school. Oh, before I forget, what are you doing after school? I thought I'd go to the mall and do some shopping. Want to come with?"

"Morik is picking me up." Shopping would be fun now that I actually had money, but I wasn't about to go back on plans I'd already made with Morik.

"Perfect. We can ask him about the party on Friday and shopping tonight at the same time."

I shook my head in disbelief, and she just flashed me a triumphant grin. I'd thought I'd successfully put off her question about Friday. I should have known better. Beatriz was the little engine that could.

We barely made it to class before the second bell rang.

MORIK LEANED against his motorcycle while he waited for me, and he didn't seem too surprised to see Beatriz at my side when I approached him.

"Hello, Beatriz. What can I do for you?"

"We're having another get together at our house on Friday, and I'd really like for you and Tessa to be there. It'll be a lot of fun."

His gaze shifted to me before he answered.

"Tessa and I haven't yet made plans for Friday."

She grinned. "Perfect. And since Christmas is this weekend, I asked Tessa to keep me company tonight while I hit the mall to catch some of the last-minute deals. I thought she might have some shopping of her own to do."

"That sounds like a good idea," he agreed. "But the mall's too far for a ride on this."

"I have a ride for both of us. What time do you need to be home, Tessa?"

That reminded me of my promise to let my mom know who I was with and when I'd be home. Morik guessed my thoughts.

"I'll let Aunt Danielle know where you are."

Beatriz and I agreed that she'd have me home by seven. She walked away to find our ride and to give me a minute with Morik.

"Are you sure you're okay with this?"

"Yes. I'll see you at seven." He smiled easily, and his eyes gave nothing away until a car pulled up next to us with Beatriz in the passenger seat. Morik glanced at the driver and nodded. When he looked back at me, I saw tiny slivers of barely discernible orange behind his yellow driving glasses. While he casually reached into his pocket and changed to his sunglasses, I glanced at the car and saw Brad in the driver's seat.

"Not too late to change your mind," I said quietly to Morik.

"No. Go. I'll drop this off for you." Hidden behind the dark lenses, his eyes gave nothing away when he took my school bag.

Not knowing what else to do, I climbed into the back of the car and waved to Morik as Brad pulled away.

"Glad she could talk you into going. It saves me from having to wait outside of dressing rooms to give opinions," Brad said.

Beatriz chatted about school, the upcoming party, vacation, and the holiday during the thirty-minute drive and the ten minutes it took to find a place to park.

People bundled against the chill rushed in and out of the mall. The happy melody of a Christmas song drifted from inside when Brad held the door open for us. Garland and lights decorated the main entrance, which opened to the food court. The smells enticed me, and my stomach growled quietly.

"Time to split up. Stick together and meet me back here in two hours."

Beatriz rolled her eyes at Brad.

"We're not toddlers."

"Just stick together, Bea."

She didn't need any further prompting. She turned and led me to the first of many department stores.

Shopping with Beatriz was exactly what Brad had said it would be. I stood outside of the dressing room most of the time while she tried on various things. She did have a knack for finding amazing deals. Despite my family's no purchased gift rule, I bought a new top for my Aunt Grace. And further bending the gift rule, I shopped at a craft store for what I would need to make several pairs of earrings for everyone.

The checkout line moved slowly like every other store we'd visited. While we waited, I watched the flow of people that passed the store's window. Safe from the cold, they moved slower in the mall. The number of bags some of them carried astounded me.

The checkout line moved forward again, and I turned away from the view.

From the corner of my eye, I thought I caught a glimpse of Brian, but when I looked back, I didn't see anyone who looked remotely like him. My imagination was playing tricks on me. Probably because I was subconsciously wondering about Clavin. Shouldn't I have heard something by now, either from Clavin himself or the police? While trying to contact Clavin directly to check in on him was far too risky, calling Brian might work. I decided to give it a few more days.

After checking out, I tiredly followed Beatriz to the food court. Brad waved to us from a table he'd already claimed. A mound of bags took up the chair next to him. Beatriz piled our bags with his then pulled me into the lines for the restaurants lining the food court. First, we hit all the samples. Then, we selected one of the Chinese places. With a pile of food for seven dollars, we headed back to the table and watched the bags so Brad could order.

Brad teased Beatriz while we ate, saying he'd gotten her an amazing gift and wanted to know which of her bags contained his gift. Since I'd been with her, I knew she hadn't gotten him anything. She ate quickly and then declared she still had twenty minutes to shop before we needed to leave. Since Brad still didn't want to be stuck standing on the wrong side of a dressing room door, he insisted I go with Beatriz.

With a full stomach and laden with bags, I followed her as she made a beeline for a high-end store. She led me unerringly to the beauty department where she spoke to a sales associate and sniffed cologne samples. I mistakenly looked at a display case, and another sales associate swooped in and started asking me questions about the man I needed to buy for. I thought of Morik, but said I wasn't interested in anything. My modest budget couldn't handle this kind of store. Plus, he smelled good just the way he was. But, it did get me thinking about what I should get him.

After Beatriz selected and purchased a bottle of cologne, we met up with Brad again and made our way to the car. The sun had set, and I was exhausted. My energy would never match Beatriz's when it came to shopping.

While Brad stowed all their purchases in the trunk, I

paused by the car to look up at the stars. The light pollution muted their glow, though. Disappointed, I didn't linger in the cold.

As we pulled from the parking lot, I caught a flash of glowing green but lost it before I could catch a glimpse of Morik. I checked the clock on the dash and frowned. We weren't running late. I hoped Morik wasn't watching because I was with Brad.

Brad and Beatriz dropped me off just a few minutes before seven. Morik opened the door for me before I reached it, and I smiled at him even as I wondered how his jumping from place to place worked.

"How was shopping?" Mom asked from her place on the couch. She and the rest of my family all looked marginally relaxed in the living room. It made me wonder if Morik had been waiting with them or by the door. I knew better than to ask, though, given how Mom had previously treated him.

"Shopping was good. I'll be right back."

Morik stayed with them as I hid my bags in my room. After I returned, we all watched a movie together. When it was over, Morik discussed the movie's plot and inaccuracies with Mom. I could see her effort to make and maintain eye contact and knew he still made her nervous. Yet, that they were conversing at all was a marked improvement. I couldn't believe it'd only been a few days since he showed himself to me.

TUESDAY AFTER SCHOOL, Morik and I arrived home to find Aunt Danielle the sole occupant of the house. She informed us that Gran went to visit the neighbor again. I embraced the novel opportunity of having the house to myself and grabbed the craft bag from my room.

After swearing Aunt Danielle to secrecy, I used the kitchen table to spread out the materials I planned to use to make the earrings. Morik helped me separate everything until the crystals rested in groups on the wood surface and glittered in the afternoon light. I eyed them critically and tried to decide how I wanted the finished product to look. Not too long or wide. Not too much crystal.

I created two smaller piles and began to arrange them in a pattern, using metal beads to break up the crystal. Morik leaned in and caught my hand with his left one. Then, he reached under our joined hands and rearranged the existing piles.

After his story about the shell combs, I wasn't surprised when his arrangement looked amazing. Although his attention remained on the crystals, I became more aware of his hand still wrapped around mine.

I turned to thank him and withdraw my hand, but the words died in my throat.

Scant inches separated us. The shifting silver pools of his gaze swirled with green and brown, a mesmerizing display. Yet, it was the sight of his lips, as he gave a self-satisfied smile, that captivated me to the point I couldn't look away.

While I'd wondered about kissing before, I'd never seriously considered it. I'd always thought it was associated with choosing. However, if what Morik said was true, kissing wasn't choosing. My heart and mind had to agree on the choice.

There were no glimpses of my future with Morik to sway my heart, but maybe a kiss would help. All I needed to do was lean in.

Just lean in, Tessa.

Noting my long stare, he pulled his gaze from the beads to look at me.

A blush ignited my cheeks, and I quickly focused on the table while mentally scolding myself for not having the guts to steal a kiss. Maybe it would have been great. My stomach might have even done that crazy flip thing it did, like when we were on the motorcycle and I'd touched his skin. At the thought, my stomach did the funny little flip again, and my cheeks heated further.

I needed to stop thinking about kissing and touching. However, it was hard to do when he still held my hand. I tried to draw my hand away, but he didn't release it. Instead, he slowly pulled it closer.

Knowing my face glowed bright red, I hesitantly met his gaze. In just those few moments, his eyes had undergone a drastic change. The silver was completely absent, engulfed by a black void. The now black irises set against the brown-yellow of his sclera sent a shiver trailing down my spine. He looked intimidating like that.

"Never fear me," he whispered, noting the shiver. He leaned in, touched his forehead to mine, and closed his eyes. "Tell me. Please. What were you thinking just now when you were looking at me?"

I closed my eyes as well, trying to hide from my embarrassment and his question. Despite the quiet of the room, I was certain we had Aunt Danielle's undivided attention.

"Can we talk about this later?" I begged in a whisper as I opened my eyes to glance quickly at Aunt Danielle. As I'd suspected, she sat in her chair and watched us with unabashed amusement.

Morik caught my look and pulled back from me. Still holding my hand, he addressed Aunt Danielle.

"We'll be back in a moment. She is safe."

One moment, we sat in my kitchen at the table; the next, we stood in an unfamiliar living room. The abrupt change left me slightly dizzy. Morik wrapped an arm around me to steady me.

"Now tell me," he said in a coaxing voice.

"What just happened? Where are we?" I looked around the room. Large and open, it connected to a kitchen on one side and an open stairway on the other. Everything looked neat and new.

"My home. I apologize for bringing you here without asking. I thought you didn't want to speak in front of your aunt."

His voice, usually deep and smooth, now had a roughness

to it. Almost a growl. I focused on his eyes. They remained black, but the ochre from his sclera seemed to be blending with it.

I wasn't sure how to interpret the new color combination. Past interactions left me with the impression that brown meant he was happy, or at least content, while orange and red were angry or upset colors. Was ochre then the middle ground between the two color groups? What the heck did that mean? He was neutral?

"Are you mad at me?" I asked hesitantly. I wasn't afraid of him even when his eyes unnerved me a little, but I didn't like the idea of him being mad at me either.

"No, Tessa. You are frustrating me." He let go only to gently cup my head in his large hands. "Stop stalling, and tell me what was going through this precious head of yours."

"I wasn't stalling," I said before I could stop myself. More ochre pooled into his black irises. "Okay, okay."

My face, which had cooled slightly during my confusion, flared scarlet again. Four days wasn't enough time to really know someone I realized as panic started to rise inside me. Why had I even thought about kissing? Because I'd made up my mind to think of him as my choice. As my choice, wouldn't it be natural to wonder? I took a deep breath and closed my eyes, not wanting to see how my next words would affect the color swirling in his irises.

"I was wondering what kissing would be like. With you."

For a moment, nothing happened. His warm hands

remained cupped along my jaw, touching just below my ear and curving around the back of my neck. It made me feel small. While I waited, his fingers twitched slightly before stilling again.

When I opened my eyes, I was surprised to see him locked in place. Pure black once again claimed his irises. He looked slightly shocked, and I had a horrible sinking feeling I'd misunderstood the whole situation.

"Morik, it's no big deal. I'm not asking you to kiss me. I was just—"

He slowly moved his thumb over my bottom lip, silencing me. His gaze followed his thumb's back and forth movements.

"There are rules." His voice had dropped an octave, rumbling in his chest. "Because my abilities put humans at a disadvantage, nature created a few basic laws I can't break unless through an agreement."

"Like a deal?"

"Yes. A part of a deal. One of the rules is that I can't interact with humans unless they call on me. The deal with Belinda's father gave me a loophole to get around that rule in some circumstances. Another rule is that I can't touch humans. The original deal allows me to speak with you, to protect you, but not to touch you." He removed his hands. "But, our deal and your touch now allow me to." He ran his fingers through his hair then continued. "The rules are meant to protect you from my kind. To negate the natural advantages I might have."

I wasn't sure I followed his line of thinking and was afraid to ask the real question on my mind, which was whether he wanted to kiss me or not.

"So, if I want a kiss, I need to make a deal with you?" It'd be like forcing him to kiss me. I didn't want that.

"No. You only need to kiss me first."

"Oh." All the color that had flooded my face moments earlier drained. I'd have to initiate the kiss. My first kiss. What if I messed up?

He stood there, watching me expectantly.

Instead of doing the crazy little flip that got me into this mess, my stomach hatched an army of ninja-kicking butterflies. I didn't know what to do.

"I think I need to sit down."

Morik scooped me into his arms and moved to a large leather chair. Instead of setting me down, he sat with me on his lap. The butterflies didn't stop kicking.

"It's okay," he whispered and rubbed my back soothingly. "Kissing isn't part of the agreement, Tessa. I never thought it would be."

That killed every butterfly in my stomach. Did that mean he didn't expect me to kiss him but would like it if I did, or that he didn't want to kiss me and just told me how to kiss him because I had been curious? Having depleted my store of courage for the day, I didn't ask for clarification. I was too worried the answer would be the latter.

We sat quietly for a few moments. Slowly, my heart rate returned to normal.

"Would you like to see my home?" he asked.

Relief flooded me. If he was willing to drop the subject, so was I.

He led me through his house, which from the view out the window appeared to be in a suburb. Each room, spaciously built and tastefully decorated in light colors with vivid accents, drew my attention. With a total of three bedrooms and three baths, the house felt empty with only him living there. It lacked pictures or any other personal items to show he had a past. Everything was pretty, but nothing felt lived in.

The open kitchen with its large breakfast bar was made for entertaining. He had a television in the living room, and he mentioned several gaming consoles that he stored elsewhere.

"How did you get all of this? Deals?"

"No. The internet allows me to obtain what I want without actually interacting with humans. Another loophole in nature's rule."

At the end of the tour, Morik took me home just in time to clean up the jewelry in progress before everyone returned. He stayed for dinner and another movie. While I sat beside him, my mind continued to dwell on my newest problem.

When I'd had my brilliant thought to help prod my heart along, I'd never dreamed I'd need to be the one to make the first move. What if he wasn't interested in me like that? Not only would I be mortified if I tried kissing him and he freaked out, but I also doubted I'd be able to choose with my heart after that.

Before he left, I asked for his help to put me to sleep; I wouldn't be able to turn off my thoughts on my own.

One thought stayed with me as I drifted off with the low murmur of his voice teasing my ears.

If I didn't want to end up like Aunt Danielle, I needed to figure out a way to choose Morik.

Chapter Thirteen

WHEN I OPENED MY EYES THE NEXT MORNING, I STAYED IN BED. I knew I'd be late for school but didn't care. Thinking about Morik, and how he felt about kissing me, took priority.

Taking risks wasn't easy for me. All the rules I'd grown up with stressed the need to exercise caution. Just being with him broke that mold. I could kid myself and say this uncharted course didn't scare me, but it did. I wasn't afraid of a fanged, horned being with constantly changing eyes, but I was afraid of what he represented. An unknown future.

With a sigh, I got out of bed. I didn't rush. Instead, I let my mind wander as I pulled on faded jeans, a cami, and a University of Hawaii thrift store hoodie.

As I brushed my teeth, I realized what I was doing. Stalling. I'd always known where I stood with a boy, thanks to my touch. This time, I was in the dark, and it sucked.

I rinsed then stared at myself in the mirror and wondered how Morik saw me. Was I interesting to him? Did he hope that I wouldn't choose him? I cringed at myself in the mirror, grabbed my mom's makeup bag, and rifled through the contents. I usually didn't take the time to wear make-up, but since I'd need a late note anyway, I smudged on some eyeliner and brushed on mascara. Then, I stood there, hesitating.

A knock on the bathroom door almost made me scream. I opened it quickly and surprised Gran.

"Are you okay?" she asked. When she studied my eyes, she smiled lovingly. "You look very pretty."

I hugged her and whispered that I was fine.

"Morik's been waiting for you. I think he's getting worried that it's taking so long. I took pity on him and said I'd check on you."

I nodded and turned off the light before I followed her to the kitchen. Morik stood near the table, my jacket in his hands. I couldn't meet his eyes. Instead, I looked at the scarf, gloves, and school bag that lay in a pile on the table.

"Sorry I took so long." I took the jacket from him and quickly put it on before grabbing the scarf.

"It's no problem." He handed me the gloves. "Everything all right?"

I took the gloves and shouldered my bag.

"Yep. All set. You ready?" I forced myself to meet his curious gaze. He studied me for a moment and then nodded.

He led the way out the door and held it for me as I called good-bye to Gran. The motorcycle waited as usual. My uncertainty ate at me as I sat behind him with my arms wrapped around his waist.

He pulled in front of an unusually quiet school. Obviously, the second bell had already rung. I got off the back of the bike and handed him the helmet with a quick thanks. He caught my hand as I turned away.

"Are you going to tell me what's bothering you?"

"No." The answer popped out before I could stop it. "I'm late. I have to go."

He released me, and I made my escape into the school. Some of the guys I passed gave me weird looks. After the lesbian rumor, I'd gotten some strange looks, but this was different. It wasn't until a boy from my English class made a second attempt to start a conversation that I remembered I'd worn makeup.

Despite the confusing attention, my runaway thoughts continued at school. Even if Morik were interested in kissing me, it didn't stop my worry about what my future would be with him.

Beatriz commented on my distraction several times before lunch and tried to pry the reason out of me when we finally sat down at our table. Too worried that Morik might be somewhere listening, I shrugged off her friendly concern.

After the final bell rang, I met Beatriz in the hallway and half-listened to the newest rumor she'd heard in gym class.

A random boy I'd never seen before stopped us before we reached my locker. Ignoring Beatriz's smirk, he asked if I'd like to get something to eat after school. I reached forward out of habit to lightly touch his arm and watched our future play out in my mind. He would be good to me and our two children and would love me until the day he died.

Heart heavy, I gently declined his invitation.

"You know," Beatriz said in an unusually serious tone, "for someone who has no boyfriend, you say no a lot."

I wondered where she was going with her observation.

"Maybe you're spending too much time with Morik and not giving other guys a fair chance," she said. "I'd be more than willing to go on a double date with you if you're worried about leaving Morik out."

"You're volunteering to be Morik's date so I could date other guys?"

"Sure." Hope lit her expression.

"Beatriz, if you want to make a play for Morik, go for it. Just don't be upset if it doesn't work the way you hope. He's got some strange rules for himself that he strictly adheres to."

"Oh, like what?"

I snorted.

"Like the girl needs to make the first move." I pulled open my locker and started to sort through my books.

"Seriously? I could do that."

"Without even knowing if he's interested in you or not?" I glanced at her and caught her contemplating the main doors. She was probably picturing Morik waiting out there.

"You bet. How else will you find out?" She didn't wait for my answer. "So you won't be mad if I try?"

"Not a bit. Just be careful, okay?"

She nodded and pushed away from my locker. "I'll see you outside."

I watched her grab her coat and head toward the doors. I envied her confidence.

Not wanting to be a witness to whatever happened, I took my time to get the rest of my books together. The halls started to empty around me.

Glancing at the clock, I joined the stragglers who migrated toward the exit. Outside the doors, the sun shone brightly. Through the glare, I spotted Beatriz talking to Morik. He leaned casually against his motorcycle, his attention on her until the moment I walked out the door.

As if he sensed me, his gaze swept to the entrance and found mine. Beatriz saw his attention wander and turned in my direction. She waved goodbye to him and met me halfway.

"You're right. Weird rules, but what a kiss." She grinned and added, "Too bad it's the only one I'll get."

Before I could question her, Morik started his motorcycle, and she hurried off to catch her ride. Without a word, he handed me the helmet. I climbed on, and he pulled out of the parking lot the second I wrapped my arms around him. His arms were stiff and, under my embrace, his stomach tense. Did Beatriz's kiss upset him? It made me smile, but only for a moment. What if he didn't like kissing in general?

Instead of turning to go home, he turned toward downtown. There wasn't much downtown: a few shops, restaurants, a church, a couple of bars, and a few odd businesses. We drove for another few minutes, and my curiosity grew.

He slowed and pulled into the parking lot for the local bowling alley. I waited until he turned off the bike before I flipped up my visor.

"What are we doing here?" I asked.

"We're going to bowl." Humor laced his voice, and he reached out a hand to steady me as I climbed off the back.

Bowling? I had a hazy picture of birthday hats and pizza mixed in with memories of using two hands to push the ball down the alley. Definitely a happy memory from long ago. Curiosity piqued, I dismounted and pulled off my helmet. He tucked it under his arm, and we walked side by side to the entrance.

The sound of crashing pins and the ping of pinball machines greeted us as we walked through the second set of glass doors. I followed Morik to the counter, and we both exchanged our street shoes for special bowling ones.

While Morik stood at the counter for an extra moment to talk to the cashier, I moved to our assigned lane and quickly put on the shoes. The assortment of bowling balls that lined the back wall of the alley, creating a dotted rainbow of color, called to me. I managed to find the perfect ball. From afar, it appeared to be a solid, vivid orange. However, looking closer, I noticed that silver flecks spiraled in a random pattern around the ball. It reminded me of the color of Morik's eyes when he was upset.

I didn't think it'd taken me long, but when I turned, I saw Morik waiting in one of the anchored plastic chairs surrounding the score monitor. He already had his shoes on and didn't say anything when I placed my ball on the return next to the dark blue one already there.

Above our lane, the score projector showed my name first.

The bowling alley, though not packed, had a steady flow of customers. With the screen above the lane, everyone would see how well, or poorly, I did. That worried me since I wasn't even sure I could roll the ball with one hand like the people around me.

A few lanes down, I spotted a youth squatting to push the ball down the lane with two hands as I remembered doing. As I watched, the ball bounced off a side rail that I hadn't noticed. I looked up at his score projector and saw a note for bumpers. Was it too late to ask for those?

"Are you sure you don't want to go first?"

Morik snagged one of my fingers and used it to tug me toward him.

"I'm beginning to see that Beatriz is right. You don't remember how to have fun, do you?"

I rolled my eyes, not bothering to comment, and he let me go so I could retrieve my ball. The holes in the ball were so snug I worried that my fingers might get stuck. So I picked up the ball, using both hands, and eased my middle and ring fingers into the holes. I only put them in a little bit, just between the first and second knuckles. The image of me sliding down the alley still attached to the ball had me doubting the wisdom of using the holes at all.

My palms started to sweat, and I mentally scolded myself. I had more issues than I could count. There was no way I would add a bowling phobia to the list.

Head held high, I stepped up onto the smooth wood floor and moved into position like those around me. I tentatively swung my arm back while taking a step forward. A buzzer went off. The sound scared me enough that I accidentally dropped the ball on the forward swing rather than smoothly releasing it.

"You stepped over the foul line," an older man from the next lane said with a kind smile. He'd just released his ball as well, but it accurately flew down the lane to crash into the pins. The group of men who waited behind him, all wearing the same shirt, watched me.

"Uh, thanks," I said. My cheeks heated as I turned and walked toward the ball return.

Glancing at Morik, I noticed he was watching the group of men who still watched me.

I nudged his foot to get his attention and whispered, "Told you that you should have gone first." Then, I stuck out my tongue at him playfully. It had the desired result. The orange building in his eyes behind his glasses faded instantly.

I executed the second try with more finesse than the first. The ball sailed straight down the alley and knocked over several of the pins. Relieved that my turn was over for the moment, I sat next to Morik. He grinned at me and stood to retrieve his ball.

He moved with grace and released his ball with a fluid motion that the group next to us noticed. The ball flew down the lane and hit the pins with a crash, knocking them all over. Even over the noise of the games and the music piping over the sound system, the crashing sound seemed a little harsher than the ones around us. I stared at the end of the alley and spotted a tiny piece of something in the pin area.

In the lane next to us, I overheard one of the older men speaking to his neighbor.

"Did you see that?"

When Morik came back to the ball return, I quickly popped up to whisper a warning about our audience. I wasn't sure, but I had the feeling it wasn't exactly normal to crack pins during bowling.

My next turn, I knocked down a total of eight pins between my two tries. Morik again threw a strike. He didn't crack any pins this time, apparently taking my warning into consideration. The men next to us took turns watching us.

Worried that Morik's skill on top of his already unusual appearance would draw unwanted attention, I set out to distract him from his game. Okay, fine. I just didn't want him to score so much higher than me.

I waited until he was already performing his graceful approach before opening my mouth.

"I'm really thirsty."

The quietly whispered words had the desired effect. He turned toward the sound of my voice the moment he released the ball. It veered a smidge off course, costing him a strike, not that he'd noticed.

I struggled not to grin at his distracted gaze.

"A white soda, please."

He came back with two sodas, set them on the table behind our lane, then went to finish his turn. Since three pins remained, one to the right and two to the left, I didn't think he'd get them all. He proved me wrong.

Disgruntled, but hiding it well, I took my turn. I felt more comfortable releasing the ball and no longer worried about my fingers sticking, although I still didn't attempt to put them in any farther. Trying to mimic Morik's fluid form, I managed to get seven of the pins down, leaving three on the far right. By sheer luck, I gained a spare.

Moving out of our bowling area, I picked up my soda and waited until he was about to release the ball before taking a sip. The loud slurp caused a gutter ball, and I almost choked on the soda, trying not to laugh. He turned to look at me, his face carefully blank. When he caught my smirk, he shook his head. The slight twitch of his lips indicated that he knew my game.

After that, he returned the favor. However, with my already poor game, nothing he did made much difference in my performance. As he walked to the ball return, I caught the brown swirling in his eyes and his barely suppressed smile. He enjoyed the game we played.

By the eighth frame, the man behind the counter brought a pizza over to our table. I plucked a piece of pepperoni off the top of a piece and waited for Morik to start his approach to the lane. Then, I plopped the pepperoni in my mouth and hummed with delight. Morik swung the ball back, but I sensed his distraction.

"Do you want a taste?" I whispered as I picked off another piece.

His head whipped around as the ball flew from his fingers. He watched me as I watched the ball sail in a beautiful arc and land in the gutter. The next lane's gutter. Thankfully, no one currently used that lane.

Still holding up the piece of pepperoni, I laughed. Even the group of men next to us laughed, having caught on to our antics.

Morik glanced back at the ball then stalked toward me. He didn't laugh. Black consumed his eyes.

My laughter died, but my smile remained. He didn't worry me.

I playfully held up the pepperoni. He surprised me by eating it from my fingers. His tongue brushed the tips. Eyes wide, I felt my smile fade as we stood there staring at each other for a long moment.

When I didn't say anything, he flashed a small smile then turned away to retrieve his ball. I slowly released the breath I'd held. He confused and unsettled me. And made me nervous sometimes but content, maybe even happy, the rest of the time.

For the rest of the game, I continued to distract him but didn't use the pizza again.

When we finished the last frame with Morik the clear winner, we sat at the table to finish our cooled pizza.

"You've bowled before?" I asked when he sat next to me.

"Yes. Several well-known bowlers have made deals to gain certain abilities. When people start asking for things, I get curious. I studied the game and found that I like it."

I didn't dwell on which bowlers he might have helped.

"How can you bowl, though? There are usually a lot of people in bowling alleys."

"It's been a while," he said quietly before eating another bite of his pizza.

No doubt. With the exception of a new deal, I was the key to his contact with people. I wondered again if choosing him would be unfair to him. Would he be happier with someone else? I understood being lonely and wanting someone to talk to.

We finished the pizza while we discussed bowling and the techniques he'd learned.

"Thank you for this," I said as we waited in line to trade in our shoes.

"Any time," he said, looking at me through his yellow lenses.

I saw the brown floating in his irises and smiled.

Mom stood at the front door, waiting for us when we arrived home. As soon as I saw her angry expression, I realized I'd forgotten to tell someone where we'd be. Though, to be fair, I hadn't known myself until we got there.

Morik killed the bike and waited for me to hop off the back.

"Don't bother turning it off. You can go," Mom said, her curt voice ringing in the yard. "Tessa. Inside. Now."

I pulled the helmet off my head and turned toward Morik.

"Go on, get!" she yelled from behind me.

I froze. Shame flooded me over my mother's behavior. Yet, Morik's face remained impassive despite having just been talked to as if he were a dog.

"Would you mind waiting a minute?" I asked quietly while I handed over the helmet.

He nodded slightly and glanced at my mom.

Steeling myself, I faced her. While I walked to close the distance between us so what I said wouldn't carry to the neighbors, I fought to cool my temper.

Mouth drawn into a tight line, Mom moved back to let me inside. I stopped at the front stoop, which only increased her anger.

"You owe Morik an apology," I said calmly.

"No, I don't. Get inside. Dinner's almost ready."

"Mom, I'm sorry I didn't leave a note. I get that you're mad. But it doesn't give you the right to treat him like that."

"No right? I have every right. You seem to forget that Morik's the reason our family has suffered for over two hundred years."

Did she really still blame him for all our troubles? I closed my eyes briefly instead of rolling them. I'd thought, when I'd explained the story, that they would all see our history and his involvement in the same light I did.

"No. Belinda is the reason. He was lonely and only asked for a chance. She was selfish and wouldn't give him one. Because of her, we've lived in ignorance and fear. That's done now, Mom."

"You've chosen," she whispered in horror.

"I'm giving him a chance," I said. "And you should, too."

"You can't trust him. If he were nice or honest, he'd remove the curse from us instead of continuing to try to get close to you."

She didn't understand the rules surrounding his deals. And, it was my fault for not clearly explaining what I'd learned. But I doubted trying to explain now would help.

"I'll be home before nine," I said.

The door slammed shut behind me before I made it off the stoop. I cringed at the violence of it. Furious didn't seem to cover Mom's current emotion.

Morik watched me approach, his face impassive.

"Would you mind if we went to your house for a while?" I asked.

He handed me the helmet, and I slid it over my head, not looking back at the house. Why couldn't Mom see she was making everything harder on me? I only wanted to do what was right for all of us.

The ride to Morik's passed quickly. We turned into a back alley near my house, he stopped, then suddenly we appeared in his garage, still sitting on his motorcycle. I was grateful I didn't have to endure the icy winds any longer and appreciated his ability to pop in and out of places.

I tugged off my gloves and stuffed them into the helmet that I left on the bike seat. Morik led me in through the side door and immediately went to the thermostat. I watched him set it to seventy-five from fifty-three.

"It will warm up in a bit. Keep your jacket on until it does," he said, moving toward me.

I nodded and looked around his mostly barren yet tastefully decorated house.

"Why don't you have any of your things here?"

"Things?"

"You've bowled, you've created shell combs. Over the years, you had to have collected stuff. Memories."

He reached out, took one of my hands in his, and led me to the couch.

"I keep those hidden away. Neighbors tend to look through your windows. Some of my 'things' would raise questions."

It made sense. Sitting down, I looked up at him and apologized for my mom.

"Your mom has every reason to be angry. She's right. If I were honest and nice, I would release you."

"You said there's always a price."

He shrugged and sat next to me, close, but not touching. Suddenly, I knew that he would be the one to pay if he released me from the original deal. An eternity of isolation. Humans used him to acquire what they wanted, and because of his loneliness, he went along with it. What choice did he really have if he wanted contact, any contact, with another being?

"Morik? You mentioned others like you. Why don't you talk to them?"

He leaned back, resting his head against the back of the

couch, and thoughtfully looked up at the ceiling through his yellow glasses.

"We are all different. Some are so different it is difficult to spend more than a minute together without becoming extremely agitated. Many of my kind before me are violent and confrontational. Not many were created after me. Most of those who were, have already faded into nonexistence." He turned his head to look at me. "Without purpose, they had no reason to exist."

"The older ones have purpose?"

He nodded and looked away. "Many disasters that befall this world are their doing. They are chaos. Nature is control. Together, there is balance. Long ago, humans began to create their own chaos. The younger of my kind, no longer needed, ceased to exist."

"Then, your purpose is to cause chaos?"

"It was, long ago. But I quickly saw what would happen to me and started to make deals with humans, creating a new purpose for myself. It was a loophole that few of us could interact with humans at all. Again, just to create chaos. Some of my earlier deals led to revelations that led to revolutions. Humans interested me. Their diversity and persistence were like nothing I'd witnessed before. I wanted to be a part of that. I wanted a reason to exist."

We sat together quietly, each lost in thought. His own persistence made sense. A two-hundred-year-old deal was the only thing keeping him alive.

I tentatively laced my fingers through his and leaned my

head on his shoulder as I listened to the air blow through the vents. Morik had made the deal because he'd felt lonely. Mom had flipped out because my being with him scared her. Which had more pull on me? His loneliness or her love and concern? Because of my ability to see my future and the consequences of it, I'd felt isolated my whole life. Until Morik came along. Despite my talks with Mom, she didn't see that I couldn't accept choosing anyone other than Morik. I understood her fear, though. What would choosing him bring me?

Soon, the room felt toasty, and I sat up to discard the jacket. My movement broke the melancholy mood in the room. Morik got us both sodas and then dug out a checkers board.

For the next three hours, we talked and played games. After the first game, I insisted he take off his hat and glasses when we were alone so I could watch the different colors that swirled in his eyes. For the most part, brown dominated them with an occasional wisp of black or green.

Just before nine, I put on my jacket. He gathered me in his arms and instantly transported us to a spot just outside my front door.

"What do you do when you leave me for the night?" I asked idly, not yet wanting to go inside.

He looked uncomfortable for a minute then admitted that he never actually left.

"Most nights, I talk to your Aunt Danielle. She doesn't sleep, either."

"You never sleep?"

"Not since finding you. Before that I did, but never for very long. I don't need sleep like you do."

I stuck my hands into my pockets and tried to suppress a shiver from the cold. Leaning against him when we rode kept me warmer than I'd realized.

"I guess I'll see you inside, then."

He nodded with a small smile, and I let myself in even as I wondered if my mom knew he hung around after I fell asleep. Aunt Danielle opened her eyes and winked at me before she closed them again. I suspected that if Mom hadn't caught Morik yet it was because Aunt Danielle seemed to be on his side.

I hung up my things and saw Mom curled on the couch. I debated waking her up. I really didn't want to fight again, but knew she was on the couch because she was worried. So I leaned over her and gently shook her arm.

"I'm home," I whispered.

She opened her eyes, nodded tiredly, then got up and went to bed.

Relieved that we didn't need to fight, I called good night to Aunt Danielle and went to grab my pajamas so I could quickly change in the bathroom. When I finished, I tiptoed back to my room.

Morik stood by the bed, the covers already pulled back.

When he saw me, he started the chant. I stopped in front of him and put my hand over his mouth. As soon as the words stopped, the building lethargy faded.

I removed my hand and flicked the hat off his head with a

grin. He watched me, curious. I plucked the glasses from his face and set them on the desk. He arched a brow at me as I crawled under the covers and then patted the top of the blankets.

"Try and get some rest," I whispered. If he stayed in the house the whole night anyway, there was no reason he couldn't catch a little sleep. It just seemed unnatural that he wouldn't need a little after going so long without any.

He moved to the door. I thought he might leave and felt disappointment. Instead, he turned off the light.

In the dark, I listened to him remove his shoes and jacket. Then, he lay next to me. After spending so much time with him, it felt comforting. I rolled onto my side toward him and laid my head on his shoulder, not asking permission or worrying if he'd mind. His warmth lulled me to sleep as fast as his chant would have.

RELAXED AND WARM, I didn't want to wake up when the sun hit my eyes. My head still lay on Morik, only it'd migrated to his chest. His steady heartbeat drummed under my ear. I'd tossed one arm over his waist while the other remained pinned by my side. He had an arm wrapped around me, and I could feel his fingers lightly running through the ends of my hair.

Something gave away that I was awake because he said, "Good morning."

"I don't want to get up yet," I said, too comfortable to move.

He chuckled.

"You'll be late again."

We'd left his motorcycle behind, which meant I'd be walking. I sighed and lifted my head to look at the time. My internal clock must have still been set to seven. I'd have to hurry. I looked at Morik and lost my train of thought. Black flooded his eyes again, but this time, it had expanded beyond the irises and had completely consumed the ochre.

"It's kind of scary when they do that," I said, moving to free my pinned arm so I could prop myself up.

"Sorry," he rumbled, closing his eyes.

"It's okay. I don't mind." I reached out with my free hand and brushed his cheek. His eyes opened, unchanged. "It catches me by surprise. I haven't figured out what causes it."

He quietly watched me for a moment.

"You do."

I didn't say anything. We were getting into that confusing territory again. Was he attracted to me? Did he want more than a friend? Starting the day very similar to the day before, I chickened out, crawled over him, and grabbed what I needed to get ready.

When I tossed my pajamas back into my bedroom, I saw a neatly made bed but no Morik. I found him at the kitchen table, waiting for me. Gran sat next to him, sipping a cup of coffee.

"Sorry I didn't tell you where I was going yesterday," I said to her.

"Don't worry about it. Danielle told me you were with Morik." She smiled at him.

Apparently, Mom was the only one with a chip on her shoulder regarding him. I wasn't sure about Aunt Grace's opinion since I didn't see her enough to know.

"Where is everyone?"

"Left early for work." Gran picked up her coffee and moved to the living room to turn on a morning talk show. "Better get going or you'll be late."

Tomorrow, the first day of winter break, I promised myself I'd sleep in. Staying up later than I was used to was taking its toll.

When I put on my jacket, I was surprised to feel gloves in the pockets. I distinctly recalled leaving them at his house. Morik opened the door, and I spotted the motorcycle parked out front.

"How did that get here?"

"I got it while you were changing," he said as he held the door for me.

The ability to pop in and out of places at will would have been far handier than seeing my future.

When I got to school, Beatriz waited for us.

"Are you ready for tomorrow night?" she asked with a grin.

I looked toward Morik.

"What time do you want us there?" he asked, surprising me.

"Does noon work for you guys?"

It was his turn to look at me. After how mad Mom had

been, I knew I should talk to her first.

"I'll call you tonight after I check with my mom."

School flew. Before I knew it, I was again settled on the back of his bike as we headed for my house.

We worked on the earrings in my room until Mom and Aunt Grace got home. Despite Mom's rude behavior and refusal to apologize, he accepted my invitation to stay for dinner. Mom was quiet when he joined us.

After dinner, when everyone thought Morik left, I went back to my room to finish the jewelry for my family with his help. Before I went to change for the night, we wrapped the pieces so they'd be ready for Saturday night when we exchanged gifts. I couldn't wait to see their reactions.

When I returned, Morik waited for me beside the bed. His thoughtfulness made me feel guilty that I still didn't have anything to give him. Oh, I knew what he really wanted. If only I knew how to make that happen.

"Did you sleep at all last night?" I asked.

"It was very comfortable," he said, pulling back the covers.

I slid into bed and didn't comment on his evasive answer. The blankets were already warm.

"You're welcome to sleep next to me any time." I grinned up at him. "I don't mind the extra heat."

He returned my smile, pulled the covers up, and repeated last night's routine. Snuggling against his side, I fell asleep.

At some point during the night, I got too warm and tried to kick off the blankets. I felt him shift so I could free my legs. Then, I floated back to sleep.

Chapter Fourteen

WHEN THE MORNING LIGHT HIT MY EYES, I GROANED AND turned my head to burrow into Morik's shirt. His fingers threaded through my hair in slow, gentle strokes, much like they had the morning before. It soothed me from my slightly surly mood because I'd wanted to sleep in.

Sighing, I enjoyed the heat of his skin against my palm and pressed closer. Wait. Skin? More awake, I concentrated on my position, too afraid to look.

I lay against his side with only a thin blanket over us. My hand had found a way under his shirt to his skin. And, at some point during the night, I had casually tossed one of my legs over his thighs.

"I'm so sorry," I said, quickly untangling myself and sitting up.

I caught sight of his eyes as the hand he had in my hair fell to the bed. Onyx pools stared back at me. At least, I thought they did. I couldn't tell the direction of his gaze when they solidified to one color like that.

"I didn't mean to practically lay on you. I must have gotten cold after kicking off the covers."

"I didn't mind."

Something about the way he held himself so still made me nervous. I averted my gaze and saw my hand hadn't just been under his shirt. I'd pushed up his shirt, and his stomach was now exposed. I couldn't look away. I liked the warm color of it and the texture.

Realizing I stared, I forced my eyes to focus on the door.

He'd told me he wouldn't draw any lines for me, but I didn't want to do things that would make him feel uncomfortable, either. He wasn't a toy to be played with.

"I'm going to get ready," I said softly and scrambled over his legs.

I stopped at the door, my arms full of clothes, and looked back at him, unsure of what I was getting ready for. "What are we doing today?"

He rose gracefully from the bed.

"Your grandmother came in a few minutes ago. She covered us up and asked if we'd go shopping with her once you woke."

I glanced at the bed and mentally cringed at what she'd likely witnessed. Better her than Mom, though.

Feeling Morik watching me, I focused on him again. His eyes were still obsidian pools as he folded the blanket in his arms and waited for me to open the door. Even with black nails, the sight of him barefoot in my bedroom started butterflies fluttering in my stomach.

"Do you mind going shopping?" I asked, trying to ignore my reaction to him.

He shook his head.

"Okay."

Leaving him in my room, I used my time in the bathroom to calm down. It wasn't often I could shower in the morning. It gave me time to think. I liked sleeping next to Morik. Maybe a little too much. Would I like doing that for the rest of my life? Would he?

My fascination with him continued to grow each day, and I knew I wouldn't be looking for someone to choose anymore. I wanted Morik as my choice but didn't know how to make it official. Yet, some part of me wasn't in agreement with the rest. Was it my heart or my head? Maybe a little of both.

Though I knew his loneliness inspired the original deal, I wanted Morik to have a choice, too. I wanted him to want to be with me, not out of desperation but because he didn't want anyone else. That part really worried me. What if I was the wrong choice for him? What if we didn't work out? Would he and I be trapped together? Once I chose him, would I still be able to talk to my family or other humans, or would the rules that prevented his interaction then apply to me as well?

I had so many questions, but they all circled back to what I meant to him. And that would be the hardest question to ask. Would his answer change my decision? Selfishly, I didn't think so. I'd take Morik over anyone else just because I didn't want a death on my shoulders, but I still worried about sacrificing his happiness.

After taking some time to apply a little makeup, I stepped out of the bathroom in search of Morik and Gran. The aroma of fried bacon greeted me.

It wasn't often Gran made a big breakfast, but when she did, it was hard to miss. She went old school in the kitchen and used the bacon grease to fry the diced potatoes and onions. When those finished, she put that in the oven and used a little of the grease she'd set aside to cook scrambled eggs. Plated, the potatoes went on the bottom of the pile, topped with the eggs, shredded cheese, then crumbled bacon. My mouth watered.

Inner turmoil forgotten, I followed my nose. Instead of Gran at the stove, Morik stood there, using a fork to scoot the bacon around the pan while he carefully avoided the popping grease. He'd changed clothes while I'd gotten ready, but he left off the hat and glasses. Gran sat at the table, a cup of coffee cradled in her hands as she gave him pointers.

I crossed the tile and peeked over Morik's shoulder. The sight of the browning bacon made my stomach rumble, and he looked back at me. His eyes were normal again. Well, what I thought might be normal for him. Silver with strands of brown swirled in their depths. Without a word, he handed me a piece of cooled bacon from the plate beside the stove.

"Thanks." I broke a piece off and popped it into my mouth.

"You're welcome." He smiled at me then turned his attention back to the bacon.

I sat next to Gran so I could face the stove and watch Morik.

"Did you know he's never had bacon?" she asked as if I were the one responsible for his food options. "Or meatloaf?" She turned her focus back to Morik. "What about a casserole? Ever had any type of casserole?"

I caught the quick quirk of Morik's lips before he answered that he hadn't. He found Gran and her questions amusing.

Gran pushed a pad of paper and pen toward me.

"Write that down, Tessa. We need to get him some variety." She tapped the paper in front of me with an authoritative finger. I dutifully made note of the ingredients we'd need and kept my worry about the cost to myself.

"Morik, set aside a little bit of the grease before you add those potatoes."

I looked up in time to see Morik put down the bowl of dice potatoes he'd been about to dump into the hot, grease-filled pan. Without switching off the burner, he used a spoon to scoop out some of the grease.

"Be careful adding the potatoes," I said just as he again lifted the bowl.

He dumped the cool, wet potatoes into the grease. It popped and sizzled. A large glob of grease flew from the pan and landed on the side of his face and ear.

I didn't think; I reacted. I flew out of the chair, grabbed the towel from the drying rack, and rushed over to him. He calmly put the lid on the pan as I gently turned his face toward me with the tips of my fingers.

Grimacing at the shiny spot on his cheek and ear, I carefully blotted the grease away. However, neither place turned red nor began to welt. I reached out and touched his cheek. It remained his normal warm temperature.

Puzzled, I shifted my attention to his ear and carefully ran my finger along the outer shell. He made a pained grunting noise, and I quickly pulled my hand away.

"I'm so sorry. I'll get you some ice."

He caught me before I could move away. I looked up, worried about him. His eyes had become a void again.

"I'm going to brush my hair," Gran said from behind me.

"I'll help you," Aunt Danielle said, moving to join Gran.

Confused, I watched them both leave the room then looked up at Morik.

"Did I do something wrong?"

"No." He took the towel from my hands and set it on the counter. "You did everything right. Thank you for worrying about me, but I'm fine. The heat doesn't bother me."

"Oh." I felt more than a little silly but still wondered what part of what I'd done had caused the change in his eyes. My concern? I wished I had the courage to ask.

He studied me for a long moment and then asked, "Can you crumble the bacon?"

We worked together to finish breakfast, and Gran came back into the kitchen in time to help serve. We ate together in silence, everyone enjoying the food.

Since Mom and Aunt Grace had arranged for a ride to work, we could use the car to get the supplies we needed for our big holiday meal. Gran insisted that Morik drive, and she sat in the backseat so I could sit next to him. The differences in attitude between my mom and Gran contrasted like night and day.

At the store, Gran tore the list in two and handed us the top half so we could shop faster. Morik studied me as I price-shopped. When he continually glanced at the pathetic small pile of food in the cart, I wondered if I bored him.

After I found the last items at reasonable prices, we met Gran at the register and checked out. There weren't many bags, but Morik loaded everything into the car.

We made it home and helped Gran unload groceries before I packed a bag for Beatriz's house. I didn't plan to spend the night or anything. I just needed normal clothes to wear because Morik had thoughtfully brought the insulated pants for the ride. And, I knew from the last party, it would be too hot to wear them the whole night.

The pants made a huge difference, though. The ride was much more enjoyable when I wasn't freezing.

Beatriz, alerted of our arrival by the noise of the motorcycle, threw open the door and welcomed us with a smile. She told us that Jay and Tommy were already starting to set up in the basement. Brad came upstairs while I changed and enlisted Morik's help outside to clear the snow from the deck.

Beatriz and I worked in the kitchen to prep the food that would be put out in stages throughout the party. My gaze often drifted to the windows to watch Morik as he worked. He and Brad talked a lot, and I saw Morik smile a few times. Did he enjoy spending time with Brad? Was I a means to an end or something more? That question, more than any other, was eating me alive.

The group took a break for a late lunch—takeout pizza again—before continuing with the party preparations. Finished outside, Morik and Brad went downstairs to help the other two. After the last snack was prepped and ready in the kitchen, Beatriz and I joined them so we could check on their progress.

The bar was already stocked with the liquor Brad had somehow managed to purchase, and they were carrying in ice from outside. Since there wasn't anything left for us to do, Beatriz and I took a break on the bar stools closest to the stairs. Brad asked Morik to help Tommy carry down a keg. Morik waved away Tommy's help and said that he'd manage on his own.

Beatriz stared after Morik before turning to me. "Tell me how he kisses."

I couldn't keep the confusion from my voice. "I thought you already kissed him."

She grinned at me. "I kissed him, but he didn't kiss back." She sighed dramatically. "His bottom lip...it's got this little pout to it. I just want to bite it."

I couldn't decide if I was shocked or amused by her openness.

She laughed at my expression. "So tell me, how is it when he kisses you?"

"It's not like that," I said, referring to our relationship.

"Are you kidding me? It is like that. I see how he looks at

you." She studied my face seriously for several moments, and I squirmed under her scrutiny. Dawning lit her expression. "Don't tell me you haven't kissed him yet."

"It's complicated," I said, feeling a little harassed.

"How can it be complicated?"

I looked around the room. Jay was straightening the cue sticks and Tommy was checking the air hockey table. Brad was busy wiping down the soda dispenser behind the bar. The music was loud enough to completely mute our conversation.

"It's new for me," I admitted quietly, looking at her again.

Her mouth popped open for a moment before she snapped it shut. "Seriously?"

I nodded, and a grin spread over her lips.

"That is so damn cute!" She said it loud enough that Brad glanced up from his bottles. I gave her a look, but she didn't pay attention to it. "If you want practice, Brad would be happy to help."

"What's up?" he asked, walking over.

A blush crept into my cheeks, and I gave Beatriz a warning nudge with my foot. She seemed to take it as prompting, though.

"Tessa wants a kiss."

Just then, Morik walked around the corner. The music had masked the sound of his descent on the steps. With his jaw clenched tightly and a keg set over his shoulder as if it weighed nothing, he stopped just inside the room. The timing couldn't have been worse. Had he heard only the last part of the conversation?

His blazing red and orange eyes didn't meet mine. They focused on Brad. I glanced at Brad, who gave his sister an exasperated look. Beatriz winked at her brother. Neither saw Morik's eyes.

I glanced back toward Morik, but he had vanished. Only the keg remained on the floor, standing on its end.

Brad noticed the direction of my gaze. "Awesome. I didn't even hear him bring it down." He waved Tommy over to help him get it into place behind the bar.

I leapt from the stool and raced up the stairs. Beatriz called after me. She hadn't noticed Morik at all. When I made it to the front door, I yanked it open. The motorcycle was still parked where we'd left it, but he was nowhere in sight. He'd obviously just popped out of the basement.

Beatriz caught up to me as I closed the door.

"What are you doing?"

"Morik heard you." I wasn't mad at her. She'd only been playing around, but I was worried about him.

"Oh my God...I'm so sorry, Tessa."

I nodded, accepting her unnecessary apology. I couldn't put off talking to him any longer. I needed to know where we stood. Was he upset because he still thought I was entertaining other choices, or was there more?

She looked out the window and saw the bike as I had. "He couldn't have gone far. Just let him cool off. Maybe this is a good thing. It might help move things along."

She had no idea. I just hoped Morik wouldn't direct his anger at Brad. As we stood there in the entry, the first car of partygoers pulled into the drive. Distracted, Beatriz yelled down the steps to warn her brother then rushed to prop open the door.

I moved back from the cold blast of air, listened to the heat kick in, and hoped the motorcycle meant that Morik would be back. Soon.

Two hours later, I weaved my way through the crowded rooms, still hoping to see Morik. There'd been no sign of him since he'd vanished, and I was worried.

I decided to head upstairs for a drink and some space. The partiers were annoying me. Too often, I accidentally bumped into someone and caused a vision of a future I couldn't care less about. It slowed me down and gave me a headache.

Before I made it to the sink, Brad caught my arm and pulled me through the French doors. When he closed the door behind us and shut in the noise of the party, he sighed heavily. His hair was messed, and his cheeks were flushed.

"You looked like you could use an escape as much as I do." He sat on a chair and ran his hand through his hair. The move explained why it looked so messy.

"Not having fun this time?" I asked, looking away to scan the woods behind the house. Was Morik out there watching, waiting for his temper to cool? His bike still stood parked in the driveway.

"Not really. Bea told me what happened, and I wanted to catch you to apologize for her."

"It's okay, Brad. I know Beatriz didn't mean anything by it."

"Good."

He stood, pulled me into his arms, and before I had a chance to react, he pressed his lips to mine. I stiffened in shock. However, the brief, light touch ended before the kiss really began. I fought to keep all emotion from my face as he pulled back to look at me with a wry grin.

"I just wanted you to know that I'd be happy to help."

He let me go and held the door for me. I moved robotically and struggled to maintain an air of indifference as the vision triggered by the kiss lingered in my mind.

Inside, he winked at me then jogged down the stairs again, probably to take up post behind the bar before things got rowdy.

Once he was out of sight, I went upstairs. There was a sign on Beatriz's bedroom door. In bold, hot pink marker, she said her room was completely off-limits to everyone. The word everyone was underlined several times. After Tommy barfed in her bathroom, I didn't blame her, but I needed a quiet place and didn't think she would mind.

I slipped inside and shut the door behind me. Light from the hall spilled under the door but only enough to see vague shadows. So, I stayed put.

The vision of my future with Brad shook me. He'd be wonderful, of course, but it was my future relationship with Beatriz that truly captured my attention. We would become very close. I'd confide in her before Brad's death, and we'd do impossible things to try to keep him alive. I'd even confide in Brad. He would comfort me and tell me he didn't regret any choices we made as he looked at our two children.

Beatriz would stay by my side through it all. She'd be the best friend I would ever have.

It tempted me so much...and scared me. I'd not only ruin Brad's life but hers as well, trapping her with my choice as securely as my family.

So, I stood there in the dark and gathered my courage. I couldn't play with lives through my inaction anymore. I needed to actively try to make the right choice.

"Morik," I called softly. My palms began to sweat.

"What did you see?" he asked from somewhere in the darkness.

I jumped slightly, and the ninja-kicking butterflies returned. His gravelly voice seemed strained. I couldn't answer his question without hurting him more, and I didn't want to lie. Not to him.

"I need to know something," I said. "Do you want to be with me just because you're lonely or because you truly like being with me?" Silence answered me. "I know you see me as your last choice, but I know what limited choices feel like and don't want that for you. If there's someone else, I'll do everything in my power to help you get the companion you want."

There. Two small pools of rage glowed from the nearby

darkness. Slowly, I moved toward them and hoped that nothing stood between us.

"But, if you do want me as a companion, I need you to tell me what exactly that means." I stood right in front of him. He remained focused on me, his eyes glowing with their unnatural light. "Will I still be able to see my family? What happens if you grow tired of me? What will you do when I grow old and die?"

I reached out my hand and gently touched his cheek. His eyes closed briefly, and he covered my hand with his own. I lifted my other hand and set it on his chest, just over his heart.

"I don't know what you want from me," I whispered.

"A kiss." His breath whispered across my skin, telling me how close we stood.

Heart pounding, I leaned forward and closed the gap. Our lips met, and my stomach flipped. Then, a tingle started at the base of my spine, beneath the beltline of my jeans.

He tilted his head and increased the pressure on my lips. His hands slid into my hair and cradled me gently. I didn't breathe as new sensations swamped me. The smooth, warm texture of his lips. The hot and cold bursts in my chest. The tingle on my spine. I frowned as the tingle grew to an unnatural flare of heat. It scorched my skin until I gasped and pulled away in shock.

"What is it?" he asked, not letting me move too far away.

"Something was burning—"

The door suddenly opened, and before the light from the hallway reached where we stood, Morik disappeared without me. I quickly let my hand drop and looked over my shoulder toward the blinding light.

"There you are. I was looking everywhere for you." Beatriz stood in the lit hall, her expression suddenly curious. "Since when do you have a tramp stamp?"

In the vanity mirror near the door where she stood, I saw the reflection of myself and caught a glimpse of a mark under my shirt. I tugged the material out of the way for a better look. Sure enough. Right where the tingling had been, two thick lines, one strand black, the other a silvery grey, twined twice on their climb up my spine. It looked slightly tribal. Holy crap.

"Uh, it's not something I think about," I said as I turned toward her and tugged my shirt over the new mark.

"I love it! Can we show it to Brad? I want to get one just like it. He's promised to take me."

Morik would just love that.

Beatriz kept talking without waiting for my reply, for which I was grateful.

"What are you doing up here anyway?"

"Just needed some quiet time to think," I said, leaving the room with her. She carefully closed the door behind us. "Hope you don't mind. Nice sign by the way."

"Like it? I had Tommy make it." She grinned cheekily, and I laughed.

After our kiss, I thought Morik might join us again, but he didn't. Back in the basement where the rowdiness of the drunks intensified by the minute, Beatriz started challenging pairs of Brad's friends to a pool game. Jay and Tommy accepted, and she pulled me into the game as her partner. We took turns when it was our team's go.

Jay had too much to drink and kept messing up his shots. After last weekend, Tommy played it cool with the alcohol and presented more of a challenge. That meant Beatriz started to play dirty. She'd stand close to him and talk to him during his shot, pointing out each girl in the room with a short skirt or a low-cut top. For the most part, he ignored her. Then, she talked some of those girls into leaning over the table opposite his shots. He started to lose focus fast.

After we beat Tommy and Jay, she challenged another pair who were too drunk to even hold a cue stick. That game never really got started, so she gave up on them. While she worked the room, looking for another group to challenge, I escaped upstairs again.

Passing the kitchen window, I thought I caught a glimpse of Brian just inside the circle of light on the back lawn. I did a double-take, but he wasn't there. The moment reminded me of my trip to the mall. But this time, I went outside to look.

After the hot basement, the cold air felt good on my face as I stood on the porch and scanned the darkness. At first, I was alone with the wind. Then, I heard faint, racking sobs from the direction of the woods. Girls who went alone into the woods on a dark creepy night usually died. But those girls didn't have Morik.

I quickly stepped back inside to grab my shoes and jacket. No one paid attention to me as I left again. The snow crunched beneath my feet as I stepped off the porch and walked toward the trees, following the distant sound of crying.

I found Brian in the snow at the base of a large oak. There sat the cocky senior who tried to bully me into a date. His knees were drawn to his chest, and his head rested on his crossed arms. Instead of feeling disdain, I felt pity. Without him, I would have never met Morik in time.

Brian lifted his head when he heard me. Enough moonlight filtered through the barren branches to glitter on his tear-streaked cheeks. When he saw me, his tears started falling in earnest.

"Clavin was right. Oh," he moaned slightly as if in pain. "They put him in a hospital because he was talking about demons."

Brian sobbed harder, and I took a step toward him, ready to comfort him. I wasn't sure what to say, but he looked so hopeless.

He saw me move and started to squeal.

"Don't come near me! They're here for you. If he has you, he'll leave me alone."

I stopped my advance and squatted down to Brian's level. He watched me closely.

"Who's here for me?" I asked in a soothing tone, hoping he wouldn't start to freak out again. Was he talking about Morik? I couldn't believe Morik had shown himself to Brian. It didn't make sense.

Brian didn't answer. Instead, his gaze shifted to a place just behind me. Then he ducked his head and began to talk to himself. "This isn't real. This is just a dream. It'll be over soon, and I'll wake up."

"Brian," I said, trying to get his attention. "Who's here for me?"

"I am," a voice rasped. A shiver of fear coursed through me at the sound.

I turned as I stood, one fluid motion. There stood the black apparition that had chased me to my front door so many nights ago. A part of me knew it wasn't Morik, but I still had to be sure.

"Morik?"

It threw its head back and laughed, revealing a mouth illuminated by its burning tongue. Its laughter stopped as quickly as it started. With those glowing, green eyes fixed on me, it glided forward on hazy double columns of shifting smoke.

"No," it said. "I am Ahgred."

The name sounded familiar. Then I recalled why. The second deal Belinda had made.

"What do you want?" I asked.

"You, of course. Morik was clever to find a way into this world. I deserve the same chance."

"Hardly," Morik said as he appeared beside me.

I jumped, and Brian's muttering increased in volume and intensity.

Ahgred turned toward Morik. His flaming tongue snaked out of his mouth in agitation. I kept my gaze locked on Ahgred and again remembered the close race down the driveway of our old house. What would have happened if he'd caught me?

"You can't save both of them," Ahgred said.

When had this turned into a question of saving either of us? Brian whimpered behind me when he heard he wasn't as safe as he'd thought.

Morik spoke calmly as if Ahgred's threat was of no importance.

"I don't need to. I'll save her. If you want any chance, ever, you'll leave the boy alone. She doesn't like us damaging them."

Ahgred whipped his head back and forth angrily.

Morik used his ability to disappear and reappear right behind me. He wrapped his arms around my torso. Ahgred had no time to react before we were gone.

One minute, we stood in the snow under the skeletal oak; the next, we stood in my living room. Gran and Aunt Grace sat on the couch, staring at us with round eyes as their movie played forgotten in the background.

"Chant her to sleep. Now." Morik disappeared as abruptly as we'd appeared.

Before I could protest, Aunt Danielle flew from her chair, her words howling through the house. There was no time for me to say anything, to beg them to stop. My eyes immediately grew heavy as Gran and Aunt Grace quickly joined in.

I had enough time to think two things: What the hell had just happened, and would Morik be able to save Brian? Then, all thought stopped.

Chapter
Fifteen

Like turning on a switch, I woke immediately and sat up in bed, panicked. Eyes wide, my gaze searched the room as I tried to find the source of my emotion. Warm hands gently tugged me back to the chest on which I'd been resting. Morik. My hammering heart started to slow as I willingly lay down. I'd never before woken so disoriented from a chanted sleep.

"Shh. It's okay. You're safe," Morik assured me as he gently ran his hand over my back.

The panic felt so real, and it took me a moment to remember why. The trees. The dark. Ahgred.

"Brian. Is he okay?"

Morik hesitated for a moment, and I lifted my head to look at him. He'd set aside the hat and sunglasses so I could see his eyes clearly.

"Yes and no," he said. "Ahgred didn't do anything to him after we left, but he'd already done plenty before that. Ahgred's been using Brian to watch you. And Brian remembered everything. He needed help. I took him to the same hospital that Clavin's staying at."

Poor Brian. No wonder he'd freaked out when he saw me. The times that I thought I saw him in a crowd, like at the mall, weren't just my imagination then. Ahgred must have been using him for a while.

"And Ahgred?"

"Gone for now."

I rested my head on Morik's shoulder. He continued to stroke my back, and his touch gradually relaxed me as I thought everything over. So Ahgred, like Morik, was tied to me through the deals made by Belinda and her father. Ahgred had found me first, but I'd narrowly escaped him. Then Morik had come into the picture, and for whatever reason, Ahgred had played it cool and had just watched. Why had he made his move last night, though? If Morik hadn't whisked me away, I might have more answers. I didn't doubt that Morik could protect me. So why pop me home like that? And why bark out orders and leave again? He'd left Ahgred behind, after all.

"Why did you have them chant me to sleep?"

"Ahgred is only free at night. He can't touch you when you are protected by your family's chant. Mine isn't as strong."

The mad race to the house the first time I saw Ahgred made more sense. I wasn't out after dark. Ever. Well, except now because of the deal with Morik. Maybe that explained why Ahgred made his move. He was running out of time because my deal with Morik was almost up. Then, I wondered how my family was even able to chant me to sleep. The deal I'd made should have prevented it. Not that it really mattered since tonight was the last night of freedom, anyway.

"Doesn't that break our deal?" I wondered idly.

His hand stilled on my back, and I lifted my head to look at him again. The warm brown that swirled in his eyes abruptly receded, and I idly wondered what colors had dominated his eyes last night when I'd kissed him. Glancing down at his lips, I wondered what he'd do if I kissed him again.

"I'm asking you to release me from our deal."

The way he said it, so formally, forced my attention back to what he said.

"What does that mean exactly?"

"It means you are no longer bound to spend time with me. It also means you will have no choice but to sleep if your family chooses to continue to use the chant on you."

The chanting didn't bother me. I'd gone into the deal with the knowledge my freedom would be short lived. The whole purpose of the deal had been to test whether I could trust Morik. And I did. But to stop spending time with him? He was the reason I'd been able to walk away from the vision with Brad. I needed my time with Morik.

"What if I don't want that?" I asked.

"I will owe you a blood debt. My life for breaking our deal."

"Then, of course I release you," I said, pulling away from him. "I'd rather have you alive and miss you than not have you at all." Maybe I'd be able to make a different deal to spend time with him.

He frowned for a moment before smiling crookedly at me. "You don't *have* to spend time with me, but you can still choose to."

The sadness that had weighed down on me lifted as he spoke. I wouldn't have to give him up, just the stars again...for a while. I slid my hand under his shirt to curl my arm around his waist as I contentedly laid my head back on his chest.

"Perfect," I said, happy with his answer. "What does Ahgred want with me, anyway?"

"He wants a way to interact with humans. If you choose me, we will be connected. You will be my anchor, tying me to your life and giving me purpose. When you choose me, he won't try to touch you."

I definitely didn't want to be Ahgred's connection to this world.

"Will Ahgred try to use someone else to watch me?" I asked, suddenly worried for my family and Beatriz.

"No. He wants to persuade you to choose him. He won't do something that will upset you."

Relieved that everyone would be safe, I idly drew circles on Morik's skin as my mind wandered. We enjoyed a few moments of relaxed silence before Gran knocked on my door.

She didn't open it, but spoke from the hallway. "Since you two are up, you can shovel your mom's car out while I make breakfast."

My eyes rounded in shock. Oh my God...Mom. How would she react when she learned Morik had slept in my room? I almost suggested that we pop to his house but discarded the idea. We'd need to face her eventually. Besides, she seemed to be the only person who had a problem with him.

"Okay," I called back as I scrambled out of bed. "Be right there."

Morik grunted when I accidentally elbowed his diaphragm.

"Sorry," I whispered as I bent to grab the insulated pants from my bag on the floor. Morik must have brought back my things from Beatriz's place.

I tugged them on over my pajamas then paused. Pajamas? I looked at Morik, who watched me, and struggled to remember anything after Aunt Danielle had started the chant. Coming up blank, I decided not to ask who'd changed my clothes. Some things were best left unknown.

"You going to lie around all day?" I pulled a hoodie over my top and arched a brow at Morik.

He grinned at me and disappeared. Shaking my head, I left the room and took a quick detour to the bathroom before I headed to the kitchen. I'd expected to see Morik there but found Gran at the stove, cooking another big breakfast.

"I thought we were out of bacon." The heavenly smell filled the room.

"Me, too. You weren't the only thing that appeared unexpectedly last night," she said.

She moved to the refrigerator and opened the door. Even after shopping, the shelves never looked as crowded as they did now. I even spotted soda. We never spent money on soda. It was milk or water from the tap.

The faint scrape of metal against the sidewalk pulled my attention from the abundance of groceries.

"I better get out there before Morik finishes the whole thing."

Gran closed the refrigerator and winked at me. "I'm letting your mom sleep in. She had a rough night after talking to Morik about what happened. We're all very glad he was with you."

So Mom knew Morik "saved" me. The day seemed a little brighter even though snow continued to fall outside.

After I bundled up, I quietly let myself outside. Morik, as I suspected, already had the path to the stoop clear as well as most of the driveway.

I scooped up a handful of heavy snow and lobbed a ball at him. It hit him square on his back. I'd been aiming for the ground in front of him so it would startle him.

He turned, eyeing me with surprise through his yellowed lenses. Without taking his eyes from me, he leaned to the side and grabbed a handful of snow. He took his time shaping it.

Laughing, I held up my hands to ward off the impending missile. He launched it at me with frightening accuracy. As I tried to move to the side, he disappeared only to reappear right in front of me. I heard the ball hit his back.

The meaning behind the gesture wasn't lost on me.

His eyes met mine, and my smile faded as he lowered his head. My heart leapt in anticipation. Just before his lips met mine, I remembered why I should avoid a second kiss. Too late to pull back, I closed my eyes and braced myself. And nothing happened. Well, not *nothing*.

His lips brushed lightly against mine, smooth and warm.

He gently touched my face, his fingertips tracing my jawline. There was no tingle of pain, only a current of excitement. He tilted his head and pressed closer, distracting me from my concern. Blood rushed to my head. I set my hands on his chest to steady myself, and he moved his lips to my cheek, kissing me there before pulling back.

It took a moment for me to open my eyes. When I did, I saw his satisfied grin. I fought to regain my breath.

"I'll get the other shovel," I said but didn't move. Instead, I stared at his lips.

His grin widened, and he dipped his head again. How was I supposed to think or breathe if he kept doing that? Not that I minded.

A knock on the window near us startled us both apart. I looked over and saw Gran holding up a piece of bacon that she then proceeded to eat with a smile.

"I think that's our warning. If we want food, we better get shoveling."

We worked side by side to clear the snow. When we thought we were done, we turned and saw what he'd shoveled first already had an inch of snow on it. I put my shovel away as he quickly scraped that part again.

Shaking off the snow, we walked inside. Mom and Aunt Grace still weren't up.

"You two have a seat," Gran said, pointing at the two cups of hot chocolate that waited for us on the table.

Morik sat next to me and watched me curiously as I took the first sip.

"Don't tell me," I said. "You've never had hot chocolate?"

Gran clicked her tongue in dismay as Morik shook his head. "Then, I should have done it up," she said. "I wonder if we have any whipped cream." She opened the refrigerator, mumbled to herself for a moment, then remorsefully reported that we didn't have any.

Just like that, Morik disappeared.

Gran looked at his empty chair and steaming cup. "Does he do that often?"

"With increasing frequency. Makes me wonder why he has a motorcycle." I blew gently on the chocolate and only managed three sips before Morik reappeared by the door. He handed a can of whipped cream over to Gran.

She smiled at him and patted his cheek. I caught a fleeting look of surprise on his face at the contact, but he quickly suppressed it. He followed Gran to the table and watched her add a mound of fluff on top of his hot chocolate. Gran and I both watched him take his first sip, which was more of a gulp. I wondered if it burned his throat, but he didn't seem fazed by it. Based on the look on his face, he enjoyed the drink.

By the time we finished breakfast, Aunt Grace had joined us. Morik and I listened to Gran and Grace make plans for a day filled with cooking and baking. It left us with nothing to do but stay out of the way.

"Do you think Mom would mind if we went to Morik's house?" I asked Gran.

"No, she won't mind. Be back by three, though. She's

invited Stephen over for dinner as long as you won't be sleeping early."

I felt Morik glance at me. "Gran, because of what happened last night, it'd be best if we went back to the way things were."

"That's smart of you both," Mom said, walking into the kitchen. "I'll call and cancel. It's snowing too much for him to drive out here anyway."

She couldn't quite keep the disappointment from her face as she fixed herself a plate.

"Mom, if he's willing to drive, we can make this work." I looked to Morik for support. "Before dark we can say we're walking to your house. I can spend the night there."

"Is it safe?"

Her question caught me off guard. I had anticipated an immediate no. Did this mean she was warming up to Morik, or did she want to spend more time with Stephen enough that she could put aside her distrust of Morik?

"Yes," Morik answered before I could. He stood when Mom sat. Old world manners by today's standards, which I found endearing. "Although your chant is stronger, my home is safer."

"Then, if you're willing to take on that responsibility, I'll agree to it. Just for tonight, though." She gave me a "mom" look with that last part. After that, conversation switched to dinner and preparations.

I excused myself from the table and took my plate to the sink. Morik followed suit, helping me clear the dishes. I washed while he dried. Behind us, the conversation didn't flag, and they started to talk decorations. When we finished, Mom shooed us out of the house, telling us they would handle everything else.

Morik followed me to my room, and I packed myself a bag. When I had everything I needed, I called good-bye to my mom and stepped close to Morik.

In a blink, we stood in Morik's living room. This time, toasty warmth enveloped us. He'd turned up the heat for me.

He led me to the guest room, which had changed since my last visit. A large bed with a thick, white down comforter occupied the room and contrasted with the deep brown walls. Heavy white panels covered the room's only window.

He'd changed the room for me, and it looked beautiful. I would have been just as happy to sleep with him in his bed, though, like we'd been doing in my bed the last several nights.

I set my bag down and turned to him.

"Thank you."

"You're welcome."

He watched me for a moment as if waiting for something more from me. Not knowing what he wanted, I quickly thought of a question that had been bothering me.

"Morik, if you're supposed to be an option for me, why doesn't my touch work with you?"

"A future with me isn't natural. What will happen can't be predicted."

That didn't sound very comforting.

"What did you see when Brad kissed you?" he asked quietly.

I hesitated, not really wanting to talk about it but knowing I owed him an answer.

"Beatriz, really. I would confide in her. Instead of turning away from me, she'd embrace my secret and help me raise the kids and prepare them for what would come. We wouldn't hide them from you."

I looked at him with concern. "But it wasn't just about hiding from you, was it? Belinda must have known Ahgred wanted the same thing. If he's only out at night, that would explain why she added that bit about shuttering the windows. That's the only rule that hasn't made sense so far."

"It's possible," he agreed quietly, studying me. "So friendship calls to you?"

"I've had a pretty solitary life," I said, shrugging. Only after I said the words, did I connect them with his existence and his quest for companionship.

He glanced around the room, lost in thought for a moment. When his gaze settled on me, he said, "I want to show you something."

Without waiting, he wrapped his hand around mine, and all light winked out. Cool air surrounded me as if we had stepped outside on a fall morning. Only, it didn't smell crisp and fresh. Dusty, stale air filled my lungs when I breathed deeply. Under my feet, the ground felt hard and uneven. I shifted slightly and heard the slight sound of grit against stone.

"Hold on. Let me find the light." He moved a little, but his hold on my hand remained steady and sure.

A flashlight clicked on. Pointed at the stone wall to my left, the bright beam still blinded me. Blinking, I saw a rough stone floor in the circle of light. The floor and wall of a cave. No water dripped eerily nearby or anything equally creepy, just a cool, quiet cave.

Morik moved the beam of light slowly around the cavern. Items filled the area while walkways trailed through the stacked collections. There were tables, old and new, paintings, pottery, metalwork, hutches, things that looked like old woven sacks, fishnets—was that a bowling pin?

Absently, I held out my hand for the flashlight. He surrendered it with a smile and followed me as I walked among his treasures. Finally, I had a glimpse of his history, the pieces of his life that helped shape him into the Morik I now knew.

"Morik, this is amazing," I said softly, looking everything over. I had a hard time imagining all the things he'd done and seen. A painting caught my eye, the texture of it and the swirl of colors drawing me closer. It reminded me of his eyes.

"I thought we might find something here to add to your room," he said beside me.

I turned with a small smile, knowing he'd seen my interest. "I'd like that."

He let me browse through his things for a while, moving what I liked to the side. I found a vase, an old shell comb that I couldn't quite surrender to him, and a beautiful old chair.

I was still searching for more when I heard something in the back of the cave. Inching closer to Morik, I watched the silver swirl in his eyes as he focused on the area from which the sound originated.

"She is of the line?" a feminine voice asked from the dark.

My heart stuttered. I didn't know if I wanted more attention from any others of Morik's kind. Ahgred's appearance had pushed me enough for the weekend. Make that a lifetime.

"She is. Lurel, come meet Tessa. She is dear to me."

He said the last part quietly, and I thought he meant Lurel. My eyes searched the darkness for her. When she spoke from nearby, I jumped a little.

"Dear to you? Of course she is," she said with a slight giggle.

I didn't like the way she said the last part. Apparently, Morik didn't either.

"Be nice, or leave," he said abruptly, taking me by surprise.

Worried about the reason for his anger, I moved closer to him. Just who waited out there in the dark? He reached out and twined his fingers through mine.

"Ah. I see. Not just a link to your future existence," a tall curvy woman said, stepping out of the shadows.

Dark hair, like Morik's, fell in waves down her waist. I wondered if hers hid horns, too. Wearing a long diaphanous dress, layered over a simply spun, fitted tunic, she glided further into the light. Her stride was so smooth, I looked to the ground to see if she actually used her feet to move. Her skin didn't carry Morik's reddish tone. Instead, her ashen-hued skin made her look sick.

Her eyes swept over me, and she gave Morik a small smile. "I'm truly happy for you, brother."

Brother? My eyes bounced between the two of them. Other than the hair, there wasn't much resemblance. Her eyes lacked the amazing colors that Morik's possessed. Pale white orbs, they lacked any color at all.

Morik seemed to relax. "Tessa, this is Lurel, one of the few of my kind that I can tolerate for more than a minute." Though his tone was affectionate, he didn't claim her as his sister. Interesting. I nodded a mute greeting, not sure I wanted to risk the standard "nice to meet you" greeting. It'd be a lie.

"So what are the two of you doing in Morik's cave of wonders," she asked me, maintaining her impish smile.

Shrugging, I looked toward Morik, unsure how to answer.

"Doesn't she speak?" she asked.

Glancing back at her, I struggled to maintain a pleasant face.

"Yes, I speak. We're picking out things to take to Morik's home."

Her gaze flicked to Morik, her smile growing. "She is adorable."

I didn't particularly care for the way she spoke as if I were his pet.

"Yes," Morik said softly. "I believe Ahgred finds her adorable as well."

Sparks of red drifted into the liquid mercury of his eyes.

Fascinated, I watched the change. Starting from the outer edge, the color began a slow spiral to the center as he spoke.

"He lured her into the dark, using another human." He glanced at me, and the red's saturation in his eyes paused. "I prevented his touch in time." The way he said it sent shivers down my back. He noticed. "We should return," he said to Lurel.

Her brow furrowed with concern. "Call on me if you have need."

Morik nodded and flicked off the flashlight. I blinked at the dark, and when I opened my eyes, we stood in my bedroom, the things I'd pointed out piled at our feet. I glanced at the alarm clock. We'd spent more time than I thought wandering his treasure room. My stomach rumbled as soon as my brain knew it was lunchtime. Funny how that worked.

"So, what's for lunch?" I grinned up at him and noted red still held his irises. "Hey. None of that."

I gently reached up to smooth his hair back. It was a simple touch meant to comfort and distract him. I didn't want him to dwell on what could have happened.

My fingertips brushed a horn. The ridged surface begged for further exploration. I traced it, and he held still for me. The sharp tip scratched against the pad of my finger, and he whispered for me to take care. Yellow replaced any trace of red, and I smiled at him, lowering my hand and accidentally brushing the tip of his ear.

He closed his eyes with a shudder and hoarsely said, "Let's

look in the refrigerator." Then, he vanished, leaving me with a hand still raised in the air.

"Morik?"

"I have many ingredients but am not sure what they could make," he called from the kitchen.

Shaking my head, I wandered out to him. Bent at the waist, he inspected the contents of his refrigerator. The position didn't give me an opportunity to study his eyes, and I wondered what color would dominate them.

I inched closer and looked over his shoulder to see what he had for food. When I rested a hand on his back, the muscles under my palm quivered then settled. His reactions confused me, but I refrained from asking, fearing another rule.

Focusing on the food, I pointed out what we could use to piece together a sandwich. He even had an avocado.

Morik began gathering ingredients and passed them back to me. I stacked them on the counter, and we worked together to make lunch. I noted his eyes once again swirled silver with veins of brown. Struggling to recall all of the color patterns during our time together, I turned to openly study him while he spread mayonnaise on the bread.

Whenever I looked at his eyes for long moments, they pulled me in. The particles of color blended and swirled in soothing patterns. Captivated by the single fleck of violet that appeared, I moved forward. It drifted in from the outer edge and began its slow spiral to the middle. The middle acted as a drain or something because all the outer colors moved toward it. Never away. When they reached it, they disappeared. I inched closer to observe. His breath brushed my face. More violet flooded the iris, and I made a puzzled sound as I watched the center. No, it didn't disappear because there was never a void of color.

His low chuckle broke the spell, and I pulled back with a wry smile along with a mumbled apology. "Your eyes pull me in. I love the way the colors swirl."

He looked at me oddly for a moment. The violet drained, and black and brown crept in.

"I think I know most of them," I said. A wisp of violet came back, confirming his curiosity. Distractedly, I closed the sandwich he'd just finished and handed him the plate. In my mind, I sorted through the colors I'd witnessed.

I expertly assembled a second sandwich, only slightly aware of his intense scrutiny as he ate. Yes, I did think I knew what they meant, but I'd need to test them before I shared my thoughts. Just in case I'd made a mistake.

Putting away thoughts of colored particles, I asked what we should do for the rest of the afternoon. We still had three hours before my mom wanted us home. Once there, we'd decorate the tree together while the meal finished cooking. After that, presents. The thought of presents brought me up short, and I stifled a groan. I'd completely forgotten about Morik. What could I get a four-thousand-year-old man that he couldn't get for himself or didn't already have?

He suggested a movie, and I agreed. It would give me some time to think. Before he led me downstairs, I peeked out the window at the gently falling snow.

"We should go back early and make snowmen in the front yard," I said. "Mom would like that. It could be our gift to the family."

He nodded his agreement, clearly amused by me. Moving away from the window, I followed him down the steps and stared around in amazement. He obviously spent a lot of time down there. There was a huge television centered on the wall; and on the shelves beside it, there were various gaming devices. A pair of recliners sat right in front of the TV.

In awe, I approached the chairs while he used a remote to dim the lights and pull up a movie menu. One chair was well worn, and the other appeared new. He'd gotten it just for me. No bow or ribbon adorned it. It wasn't a gift. He'd bought it, hoping that I'd spend enough time with him to use it.

Settling into the chair, I suggested a Christmas classic. He started the movie then sat beside me. We watched in silence for a moment. The question of his gift bounced around in my skull until I gave in and revisited a topic that had made him run once already.

"I asked you before what you wanted besides a companion, and you disappeared on me. I'm still curious."

He quirked a smile, still looking at the screen. "A kiss."

"You already asked for that and can kiss me whenever you want. Isn't there something else you want?"

His eyes flared in surprise, and his gaze flew to mine.

I quickly backpedaled. "No. No, not that! I mean—" I lost my voice for a second as a neon blush decorated my face. I tried again, slightly subdued. "Is there something else, material, or food, or something that you've wanted to own or try?"

"Nothing, Tessa. You are what I want."

Yeah, I'd figured as much. It would make for a crappy Christmas for him. Then a spark of brilliance ignited a plan. We had one tradition in our family for the men we chose. I just hoped my mom wouldn't throw a fit when I asked her.

WE HAD THE SNOWMEN BUILT IN THE FRONT YARD BEFORE THREE.
I even added one for Morik.

His years of crafting made it easy for him to sculpt the
snow into lifelike human forms whose legs flared into a frozen
mound. The time he spent shaping the face on my snowman
brought a smile to my lips. Flecks of green swamped the silver
orbs behind his yellowed lenses as he finished. It looked
amazingly real.

I turned back to my own very inartistic rendition of Morik.
Three snowballs in decreasing size stacked vertically. I'd
scraped a smile in the top ball to complete my labors. As I
studied snow-Morik, trying to figure out how to add more life,
a snowplow swept by. Snow sprayed far into the yard. After it
passed, a rather large pile of snow blocked the end of the
driveway.

The wind gusted and mixed some of the freshly turned
snow in with the continually falling snow. The blast swept
over me, and I shivered. Wearing my old wool coat hadn't been

the best idea, but I wanted to save the leather jacket for the bike.

Morik noticed my shiver and waved me toward the door, saying he'd shovel before he followed me in. I offered to help, but he insisted I warm up for five minutes first.

I willingly went inside, and inhaled the myriad of aromas that greeted me. Gran stood at the stove, lid in one hand and spoon in the other, giving something a quick stir. When she saw me, she smiled.

"Merry Christmas!" she greeted me. "Take off your things. I have cocoa ready for you two. I saw your pretty work out there."

I peeled off my gloves but held onto them.

"I'm just going to warm up then go back out and help Morik with the driveway. The plow came through and buried it. Stephen won't get in if we don't clear it."

"What?" My mom looked up with dismay. She and Aunt Grace were working to stack the boxes of Christmas decorations.

Gran shifted the curtain to the side and looked out. "Don't worry, Clare. Morik has it clear already. Tessa, he sent you in because he knew he'd be done before you warmed. Take your coat off."

I peeked out the high window by the door and saw she was right. He only had another few moments of work left.

After I hung my jacket, I took the opportunity to whisper in a few ears about the gift I wanted to give Morik. Gran and Aunt Danielle agreed without hesitation. Aunt Grace looked at

Mom with worry before she nodded. I saved Mom for last, knowing she'd be the only one likely to oppose it. But I needed her to agree because she still had the gift in her possession.

She watched me with sad eyes when I approached her. I whispered the words bound to start an argument.

"Can I have the family ring to give to Morik?"

My father had last worn the ring, a plain band worn by most of the husbands who married into Belinda's line. Gran's own husband had never worn it. She'd kept it from him, saying he would have taken it off and lost it anyway. He'd been a cheater. When sisters needed to marry like Mom and Aunt Grace, the first one to marry could offer it to her husband. We'd never lost it in the line. According to Gran, it'd seen at least six generations.

Mom pulled back and studied my face for a moment then reluctantly nodded. I hugged her tightly as Morik knocked on the door. I hurried to answer it and pulled him in with a smile, excited now that I knew what to give him.

Gran shooed us to the living room with our hot chocolate so we could begin decorating. Mom and Aunt Grace had obtained a beautifully pathetic tree. We worked together to transform it into our own Christmas miracle.

An hour later, the lights strung on the thin branches sparkled off the tinsel and ornaments. The tree, lit by those reflections, looked magnificent.

After hearing the plow pass through once more, Morik excused himself to shovel the driveway again. I quickly went to my room, wrapped his gift in a scrap of paper, and tucked it into my pocket. I brought out the rest of the presents, excited to exchange them.

As soon as Morik came back in, we started. There weren't many gifts, so it didn't take long. Aunt Grace scolded me for the shirt but swore she loved it. They all gushed over the earrings, and I quickly said that Morik helped me make them.

Mom gave me a knit hat to match the first scarf Morik had given me. Aunt Grace gave me a bucket of homemade caramel corn and praline mix, my favorite gift from her, which she only made at Christmas. It never lasted long.

Gran and Aunt Danielle gave Morik and me a set of cookbooks. Gran admitted to purchasing it but swore she'd thrifted it. She couldn't stand thinking of things he'd never tried. He smiled, thanked her, and started thumbing through the pages.

When a knock sounded at the door, we all looked at Mom, her face lit with anxious anticipation. Morik slid on his glasses. He tried to honor my request to keep them off when we were together, including around my family, thanks to Aunt Danielle. But I didn't think Stephen would be as open. Not at first, anyway. I hoped it would change if he stuck around and got to know us. I really wanted Mom to be happy.

After taking Stephen's things, she reintroduced him to me —I'd met him once before when I'd gone to work with Mom. Then she introduced Gran, who'd yet to meet him. When I turned, I saw Aunt Danielle had disappeared. Of course.

He shook Gran's hand and turned to Morik. I wondered

how Mom would introduce him and what Stephen's reaction would be.

"This is Tessa's friend, Morik," she said, her excitement over Stephen not dimming.

"A pleasure to meet you, Stephen," Morik said formally, shaking Stephen's hand.

Stephen nodded with a smile, but I noticed his gaze flick over the hat and glasses. I struggled not to frown at him.

We moved to the table to start dinner. For Christmas, we went all-out, content to live off leftovers for a while. There were more dishes of food on the table than people.

I enjoyed watching Morik try a little of everything. His eyes widened in surprise when he sampled Gran's chutneyed chicken. After a bite of Aunt Grace's cheesy-spiced potatoes, he nudged me and asked who made them. I nodded in the correct direction, and he asked for the recipe. I shook my head, smiling.

Christmas dinner was a celebration of flavors. Mom once explained they came up with the idea to signify life's choices still left open to us. Many of the dishes clashed with the main course; but on their own, each held a unique, fulfilling flavor that had you coming back for more.

I noted the fading light as I leaned back in my chair, contentedly full. Unsure how to excuse us, I glanced at Mom, who had skillfully guided the conversation throughout the meal. She caught my look, glanced out the window, and then at Stephen. I could see the worry in her eyes.

"Mrs. Sole, would it be all right if Tessa and I walked to my house?" Morik asked, saving us from having to come up with some lame excuse. For being such great planners, we hadn't planned the details of my leaving tonight.

Mom agreed, and Morik thanked everyone for the wonderful dinner while he took our plates to the sink.

I quickly grabbed my coat, mittens, and new hat. Morik met me by the door, and Gran followed behind him. She kissed my cheek and whispered that she'd see us in the morning. I nervously eyed the dying light through the window. Dusk crept too close. Would I even be safe if I walked out the door?

Morik tugged on his jacket in slow, measured moves, completely relaxed. His calm helped put me at ease.

He smiled at Gran when she moved to block us from Stephen's view. She patted Morik's cheek. He pulled me to his side, opened the door, and blinked us away.

We stood in his living room.

"We didn't close the door," I pointed out.

"That's why your Grandmother came to send you off. She didn't want you stepping outside any more than you wanted to go out." He helped me from my jacket.

I hummed an acknowledgement as I looked around. I didn't want to go to bed yet.

"You said your house was better protection than the chant. Does that mean I can stay up?"

"Yes, if you'd like that."

"Very much. We can watch movies until we pass out, and then I can sleep in until I feel like waking up."

He took my coat and hung it in the closet. With his back to me, I took a moment to dig his gift out of my pocket. When he turned to face me, I had it ready in my palm and held it out to him.

"What's this?" He tilted his head, and violet flashed in his eyes.

"A gift. It's the reason I asked what you wanted. Come on. Take it. Open it." I bounced it in my hand a little.

He reached out slowly as he studied the crumpled, tiny wad of wrapping paper. I agreed it didn't look like much. He closed his fingers around it and plucked it from my hand. I didn't watch him carefully untangle the paper; I watched his eyes. Violet, brown, yellow, and green danced together in their depths.

It took a moment for me to realize his focus had shifted from the gift to me. His eyes questioned, yet I read hope in them, too.

"I know you want me to choose you—and I'm working on that—but until I figure it out, I wanted you to have this." The ring lay in the palm of his hand. I carefully lifted it up for his inspection. "It's something our husbands have worn for, according to Gran, at least the last six generations. It's my promise to you to keep trying." I set it back into his waiting palm. "I hope you'll be the last one to wear it."

Brown dominated his eyes as he slid the ring onto his third finger. It was a tight fit over the knuckle, and I doubted it'd ever come off even if he wanted it to.

"Merry Christmas," I whispered.

283

He pulled me into his arms and kissed me gently.

I truly cared for him. I liked kissing him and being with him. Why couldn't I just choose him already? He pulled back with a wide smile that showed his lower teeth in full detail. Wow. I held my surprise in check and smiled in return. Those were sharp teeth.

Despite all the time I spent with him, I still didn't feel completely comfortable with all of his differences. I needed to work on that.

MORIK GOT us each a soda and led the way downstairs. He taught me how to play a few of his favorite games until our stomachs rumbled again. We drifted upstairs for new drinks, and I thought of my aunt's popcorn and praline mix.

"Do you think you could sneak into my house and grab it?" I asked Morik with a mischievous smile after telling him what I wanted.

His eyes flicked to the windows.

"Yes." The way he drew out the word didn't bode well.

"I sense a 'but' coming."

"It's dangerous to leave you at night."

The disappointment I felt rushed to my face before I could stop it. Ochre flitted into his gaze.

"It's okay," I said, feeling bad that I'd upset him. "We can raid your supplies."

"We can make a deal." The quick, determined way he said it confused me as much as the suggestion.

"But I thought you said we didn't need to use deals."

"You are correct. But this one is important. For your safety. I want you to stay in the house while I'm gone. You may not open a window, a door, nothing."

"Morik, we don't need to make a deal for that. I promise." He was shaking his head before I finished speaking.

"You must name a price."

"How about my popcorn?"

"Your obedience in this is worth far more."

"Like how much? I'm not a deal pro like you." I smiled at him, trying to lighten the mood.

"Priceless, really."

I snorted at that. "Don't these deals need to feel fair to both of us?"

He agreed with a slight incline of his head.

"A new coat for everyone in my family." It was something we could all use. He shook his head, and I narrowed my eyes thoughtfully.

"Priceless?"

He nodded and watched me think.

"I can't go that high for something I would have been determined to do on my own." But obviously, I needed something that could measure up to my "obedience" in his eyes. The thought of anything extravagant made me feel annoyed and wasteful. Fine. Something big yet practical.

"A car," I blurted. "For Aunt Grace. Not new, though. Something nice with good gas mileage."

He didn't respond either way as he considered the deal.

"Seriously, I wouldn't have gone outside," I said, again. Still, he hesitated. "And you can cover the first year's oil changes."

"And any maintenance for the life of the vehicle," he countered.

"Not new, though, right? A beater?"

"Not new," he agreed.

"Deal."

He pulled me into a tight hug and whispered, "I'll be right back." Then he disappeared and left me with my arms wrapped around nothing.

A second later, I heard a knock on the front door.

"Tessa?" my grandma called from outside.

I took half a step toward the door and froze. My promise stopped me. It'd meant so much to Morik that he was willing to buy Aunt Grace a car.

Ahgred wasn't interested in Gran; he was interested in me. So she should be fine out there, I reasoned with myself. But Ahgred could use her to get to me. The thought of him using her now sickened me. The need to protect Gran just made me better understand Morik's need to protect me.

"I'm sorry, Gran," I called, wanting to cry. "I can't let you in until Morik comes back."

"What?" she cried. "He's supposed to be watching you. Wait until your mother hears this."

Morik said he would be right back. The seconds ticked by. I took another step toward the door. He said not to open it, nothing about looking outside.

Creeping to the door, I parted the curtain and almost screamed. Ahgred stood outside, his green eyes glowing. He saw the movement and focused on me.

"Tessa," he hummed in his own voice. "Open the door. I will give you the world."

I dropped the curtain and backed away from the door.

"No thanks." The raw, rasped words were barely audible.

Behind me, something tapped the kitchen window. I spun and saw Morik's worried face. He put a finger to his lips and motioned to the French doors, indicating I should let him in. I calmly walked toward the window, not the door. Through the glass, we stood eye to eye.

"Can you look like anyone?" I asked.

Morik's eyes narrowed and then a grin split his features. "Do you prefer another to Morik?" Ahgred asked. It didn't sound like Morik just looked like him.

"No. Can you sound like Morik at the same time you look like him?" I studied his face, looking for some discernible difference.

Ahgred snarled then changed back into his own shape.

"I won't let you in, Ahgred," I said calmly, waiting for his next move. "Nor will I go outside."

He stared at me for several long moments then faded into the darkness.

I looked at the clock. Just before ten. I wandered back to

the island, took a sip of my soda, and waited. What could have delayed Morik?

Five minutes passed between when he left and when he returned. He reappeared in the same spot, his eyes already focused on me, eyeing me from head to toe. Under his arm, he cradled the plastic container of Aunt Grace's mix.

"You got it!" I moved to him and snagged the container. "What happened?"

His attention shifted to the window then over his shoulder to the door.

"I thought I would be safe to enter your room, but your mom and Stephen were in there."

"What?"

His eyes darted back to me, and he spared me a quick smile.

"My timing couldn't have been worse. I scared your mother. With them in there, I knew I could safely appear in the living room and quickly did so. However, I heard your mother excuse herself and knew I needed to wait to explain my presence."

"Tell me they weren't on my bed," I said, imagining the worst.

"I interrupted a kiss during a tour, I believe."

"A tour? Give me a break. He owns the house. It was an excuse to take a minute to make out." I popped the lid on the container and tossed a tasty morsel into my mouth. It helped ease the painful possibility of what could have occurred if not for Morik's timing.

"Did anything happen here while I was gone?" He stopped studying the doors and windows and focused on me.

I offered him a piece from the tub. When he had it in his mouth, I answered.

"Sure. First, I told Gran she had to wait on the stoop in the cold until you returned, and then when you knocked on the window, I asked you if you could look like anyone else."

He made a choking noise on the popcorn.

Before he swallowed, I quickly said, "She likes red." I grinned at him. His eyes stayed liquid silver, and he gave me a small smile in return.

"Come on," I said. "Let's watch a movie and see how long it takes me to fall asleep."

Chapter Seventeen

THE SOUND OF MORIK'S STEADY BREATHING ERASED THE remnants of sleep and roused my curiosity. Unlike the last few mornings, I lay in my own space because of the bigger bed. But I wasn't alone in the guest room like I'd feared I would be. Morik lay next to me with his eyes closed, actually sleeping. He hadn't needed any more of an invitation to join me in his home than he had in mine.

Carefully, I rolled to my side and studied him. He looked so human, until I spotted his horns peeking through his hair. The sharp tip of one of them rested against the pillow, and I wondered how many pillows died because of them.

My gaze searched for what really interested me, but his ears were completely hidden under his dark hair. I checked the time to make sure it wasn't too early to wake him then reached out to run my fingers through the silken strands. I liked the feel of it. But that wasn't my true purpose. I wanted to find his ear. My fingers found the tip of the one closest to me.

"Good morning." His voice was deep and rough, and he didn't open his eyes.

I paused but didn't remove my hand.

"Morning," I whispered, trying to keep my smile from my voice.

Continuing my exploration, I traced my fingertip along the outer shell to the tip then followed that ridge to the place where the top of his ear joined his head. I repeated the move in reverse. He seemed completely fine with my touch until I reached the tip and began to run my fingers along the outer shell.

His eyes popped open, black voids. I couldn't actually tell if he looked at me but assumed I had his attention. A fine tremor shook him for a moment as I continued.

"Let's get you home before we upset your mother." The words sounded a bit choked.

A moment later, I lay alone on my bed, a smile still lingering on my lips. I looked up at Morik as he stood over me. He shook his head at me and disappeared.

The phone rang.

Muffled through the closed door, I heard someone say, "That girl is driving me crazy."

Curious, I got out of bed and drifted to the living room. A pile of yarn at her feet, Gran sat on the couch. She was far from relaxed, though. Her knitting needles clicked and clacked with her agitated movements.

She looked up from her work when I entered.

"Oh, Tess! I didn't know Morik brought you back. Beatriz has been calling. She called yesterday, and we forgot to tell you to return her call before you left." The phone continued to ring. "Oh, just answer it."

I picked up the kitchen phone.

"Hello?"

"Tessa, what happened to you? You just disappeared. We were so worried." Beatriz sounded more annoyed than worried, though, and I bit back a groan. I'd completely forgotten how we'd left the party.

"I'm sorry for scaring you. Morik found me, and we decided to leave. I should have said good-bye."

A moment of silence carried over the line, and I opened my mouth to apologize again, but she spoke first.

"Brad told me what he did. He thinks that's why you left. Don't get me wrong, I like Morik. But it'd be cool if you liked my brother."

I closed my eyes and felt the lingering pull of our friendship from the vision with Brad. Oh, I knew she wouldn't mind me liking him at all.

"Brad is great, and what he did wasn't the reason I left. I hope he finds someone wonderful, but it won't be me. I like Morik."

"Yeah, I figured." She gave a sad sigh. "What are you doing today? Do you two want to come over?"

Morik still hadn't reappeared, and I began to wonder where he'd gone. Actually, there were a few other people missing, too. I glanced at Gran but didn't want to ask her about Mom or going to Beatriz's while Beatriz was listening.

Aunt Danielle opened an eye to look at me with a large, knowing smile on her face.

"I don't know what we're doing today," I said, answering Beatriz. "I just woke up. Let me talk to my mom, and I'll give you a call back."

She groaned. "It takes forever for you to call back." With that, I knew she'd forgiven me for disappearing.

I laughed, said good-bye, and she unwillingly let me go. Gran's knitting quieted once I hung up.

"Gran, where are Mom and Aunt Grace?"

"Grace is sleeping in, and your mom is still at Stephen's."

Admittedly, the news that Mom went to stay the night at Stephen's took me by surprise, and I stared at Gran for a moment. She returned my look, watching for my reaction. There was none to give.

"Beatriz wanted to know if I could come over today. Do we have any plans here?"

Gran said we didn't and told me to make whatever plans I wanted, assuring me she'd pass them along to Mom. Now, I just needed to figure out what Morik had planned. I debated calling him but decided to leave him alone for a bit. He would show up when he was ready.

After I showered and dressed, I did a load of laundry. Aunt Grace roused herself before the spin cycle finished.

I'd just switched the clothes to the dryer when I heard a car in the driveway. I peered out the kitchen window but couldn't see much because of a sudden gust of blowing snow. A car door closed. Immediately following that, a knock on the door sounded. I smiled and rushed to get it. Only one person could move that fast.

Morik stood in the swirling snow, a small smile on his face. I reached to tug him through the opening and closed the door behind him.

"Where were you?" I asked, taking his things.

"I had to get something for your aunt," he replied, his gaze finding Aunt Grace in the living room.

Having woken up late, she had wet hair from her recent shower and still sipped her coffee on the couch while she watched a talk show. However, when Morik said "Aunt," she looked up and saw his eyes on her.

"Me?" she asked with a startled expression.

"Yes, you." He strode toward her and dropped keys into her hand. "That belongs to the car outside, Tessa's price for a very important promise."

All eyes turned toward me.

"I promised to stay inside last night when he came back for the snack mix." I shrugged as if it weren't a very interesting topic. "What kind of car did you find?"

"Let your aunt look. It's her surprise."

Aunt Grace popped off the couch and hurriedly tugged on her things. Her bare feet slid into her runners. The door loudly clicked shut in her rush.

I went to the window. Between gusts, I spotted a shiny, cherry red car in the driveway with my aunt draped over the hood, obviously in love. I watched her rush to let herself into the driver's side door and listened to the muffled sound of an engine start. She eased the car forward, veering toward the left of our two-car garage.

"It looks kind of new," I said, stepping back.

A moment later, Aunt Grace flew into the house like a lunatic and launched herself straight at Morik.

"I love you!" she cried, wrapping her arms around his neck.

He stood stiffly in her embrace while I stared at them both in amazement. Though Aunt Grace had never shown the open hostility Mom had, she hadn't made an effort to interact with him like Aunt Danielle or Gran, either.

"What was it?" I asked her.

She rattled off something that I didn't understand, but the year caught my attention. The current year.

"That's new, Morik." I frowned at him.

"Technically not. The car has a prior owner, making it used."

"But I said a beater."

"Hey," Aunt Grace scolded, removing her arms to give me a quick frown.

Morik looked relieved she'd released him until she focused on him once more.

"You did good," she said to him as if her enthusiastic hug hadn't already confirmed that.

I continued to scowl at him.

"If she chooses to beat it, she may," Morik said helpfully.

"Best Christmas ever," my aunt said to herself with a silly grin on her face as she shuffled back to her bedroom.

MOM CAME HOME before Morik and I decided what to do for the day. She looked slightly dazed when she walked in the door.

"Saw the car, huh?" I lounged on the overstuffed chair with my feet dangling over the edge as I waited for Morik to come up with a better idea than Beatriz's house.

"Hmmm?" she said absently.

I frowned and watched her hang up her jacket and kick off her shoes. The motions were right but the attitude all wrong. I called her name. Twice. She answered with another noncommittal noise as if her hearing had suddenly ceased to function overnight.

"Gran," I called, getting up and going to Mom. Gran came up from the basement, a basket of laundry in her arms.

"Tessa, you don't need to yell," Gran scolded.

Worried about Mom, I ignored Gran.

"Clare," I said, loudly right in her face.

Mom pulled back as if I'd slapped her. "Tessa! What's wrong with you?"

"What's wrong with *you*? Did you get in an accident?" Despite her now angry frown, I was still worried.

"Don't be ridiculous. Stephen dropped me off."

When she said his name, she smiled a little. That's when I noticed the glint on her ring finger. I grunted at the sudden pain in my stomach. It felt as if I'd been hit.

"Engaged?" I whispered.

She nodded, her smile growing. Gran gasped, and Aunt Grace squealed for Mom to show the ring.

Backing out of the way, I stared at Mom as an alien feeling gripped me. Morik congratulated her quietly then strode toward me. Our gazes locked. How could she do this? Less than five months to go, and I struggled to find the answer to make the choice to set them all free. I was trying. Very hard. She couldn't wait? Didn't she want to know if I'd live with Morik or die as Aunt Danielle had before she threw herself at Stephen?

I pushed away those thoughts along with the angry, bitter feelings that burned my throat. Then, I moved toward her, took my turn to hug her and congratulate her, and listened to her story of how romantically Stephen had proposed after dating a year. A year? I pushed down more bile.

Since it would be Stephen's first marriage, he wanted to go big. So Mom wanted Aunt Grace to be her maid of honor along with Stephen's sisters and me as bridesmaids. Given their age, they wanted a spring wedding. The upcoming spring. My cheeks stung with a sudden, horrible flush. I swallowed hard.

"What do you think of May?" she asked the room with a happy glow.

I quietly went to my room. Morik followed. I waited until he cleared the door and closed it with a click.

"I'm not in the mood for a quiet day. Can I call Beatriz from your house and see if they want to meet for bowling or something?"

He pulled me into his arms as an answer. I felt the temperature change immediately but stayed in his arms for a moment. He tightened his hold minutely, the gesture assuring me that he knew I struggled with something. That he didn't pester me to explain it endeared him to me further.

We passed the remainder of the day at the bowling alley, enjoying the company of Beatriz, her brother, and a few of Brad's friends. When Morik brought me home, I snuck to the bathroom to get ready for bed.

Morik waited for me when I returned. Remembering his warning about my family's chant being stronger, I went to ask Aunt Danielle if she'd help chant me to sleep. She didn't ask why. We both heard the conversation coming from the back of the house. Excited female voices discussed wedding details.

The soft murmur of Aunt Danielle's voice blended with Morik's as they worked together. He lifted me gently into his arms, their touches knocking me out.

The day definitely did not rank in my top-ten-best-days-ever list.

I SHIVERED AWAKE, the space next to me empty and cool.

"Morning," Mom said as she sat, claiming the vacant mattress real estate. "Tessa, I'm sorry about yesterday. I didn't think how it would sound to you."

It sucked that she wanted to discuss this topic before I could even brush my teeth.

"Mom, it's fine. You're doing exactly what I'd want you to

do." I sat up and brushed my hair back from my face. "If Stephen makes you happy, then it sounds perfect."

She pulled me into a hug, sniffling ominously.

I quickly pulled back, telling her I had plans with Morik and needed to get ready. She felt guilty enough for yesterday that she didn't quiz me on the details and left.

Once I had clothes on, I whispered his name. He popped into the room just inside the door.

I didn't bother asking where he'd come from. Instead, I asked if the snow had stopped enough for a bike ride to the Coffee Shop. He took us to his house with a touch and handed me my leather jacket as an answer.

Minutes later, the bell above the Coffee Shop's door rang as we walked in. Its familiar smells greeted me. Mona called hello and hurried behind the counter to take our order. A few older men sat at tables, reading various sections of the shop's single paper.

We ordered one of the shop's specialty drinks and grabbed our own table. The drink warmed me after the ride, but it didn't quite take care of the hungry grumble my stomach kept emitting.

When Mona moved around the tables to fill cups for those who had plain, old-fashioned coffee, I asked if she served anything quick for breakfast.

"I tried making muffins and a few baked things, but the oven and I aren't on friendly terms. Things don't come out looking like the pictures. And ordering from a baker means a minimum for delivery or picking it up myself. Too much hassle for just a handful of people who'd be interested." She changed topics abruptly. "Nice ring, Morik. Someone special give it to you?" She didn't wait for his answer, just winked at me and moved along on her rounds.

I stared after her with a growing respect for her astuteness. Then, I began to contemplate her reason for not offering breakfast items.

"We could do it," I said to Morik. "Gran and I. Well, more Gran than me since I sleep so late. But she could bake, and I could bring it here for her. I think Mona's right about the weekday needs being small, but I bet once people tasted Gran's baking, there'd be a demand for it on the weekends." I slugged back the rest of my cooled coffee and insisted we go back home.

Gran loved the idea when I explained it to her and started to pull out cookbooks. I sat at the table with her and helped calculate ingredient prices, prep time, and baking into estimated costs for her favorite recipes.

The next morning, Morik and I borrowed Aunt Grace's car with promises to return it in an equally pristine condition. We needed it to deliver eight beautifully plastic-wrapped blueberry muffins to Mona. Before we left, Gran insisted we test one of the remaining four that hadn't made the cut. They were delicious and still just barely warm.

When I walked into the shop, carrying the muffins, Mona laughed at me.

"Gran wants you to taste one of these and let her know if

you'd consider a partnership with a bored, home-baker," I said, setting the platter of muffins on the counter.

Mona groaned in anticipation while unwrapping a muffin. Since I knew how it tasted, I grinned when she took a bite and her eyes rolled back dramatically.

"We'll see how well they sell. If not, I'll just gain weight having this stuff here. How much per muffin?" she asked.

We discussed the price for a moment, and I left feeling giddy on Gran's behalf.

"You're giggling," Morik commented on the way home.

"I'm so happy for Gran. This is a perfect way for her to contribute. Maybe they can start to put some money away so it won't be so hard when I—" I stopped myself, stunned by my thoughts. So it wouldn't be so hard when I had babies. But I wouldn't need to worry about that.

Deep down, I found that hidden part of me that denied the possibility of accepting Morik and squashed it with my thumb.

The sudden burning sensation along my spine took me by surprise, and I hissed in pain. As soon as it started, it disappeared.

Morik pulled the car into the garage, watching me while he did it, which made me cringe. He did his blink thing to move us into the bedroom as soon as he cut the engine.

"What happened?" Concern laced his voice.

"I don't know. When I kissed you that first time at Bea's house, a mark kind of burned my back," I said. His brows drew down in a troubled frown. "I forgot about it, but it just happened again in the car."

I unbuttoned my pants, turned away from him, and tugged down the waist of the jeans low enough so he could see the start of the mark. I bent forward slightly and lifted my shirt a little. He moved close and ran a finger over the black and silver twisted lines that decorated my skin.

And that was the sight that greeted my mother when she opened the door. Me, bent over in front of Morik with my pants loose and Morik inches behind me, running his hand down my back.

If I had to guess, I would also add black eyes to the picture.

"Out!" she screeched at Morik.

Wisely, he disappeared and left me to deal with my extremely livid mother.

"Well, there goes my source of a possible explanation for this." I turned and gave her the same view while she still sputtered, trying to piece together a coherent thought.

She gasped when she finally saw the mark. "What is that?"

"Dunno. Morik might know, though. That's why I was showing him...in the privacy of my own room. Didn't want to freak anyone out unnecessarily."

"How long has it been there?"

"A few days," I hedged.

"Why didn't you tell me about it right away?" She tentatively touched it with cool fingertips. I straightened and pulled my shirt back over it.

The distraction of Ahgred and Brian in the woods and then Christmas had wiped it from my mind. But that's not what I told her.

"Why didn't you tell me a year ago that you were dating?"

She remained silent as I buttoned my pants. Tears gathered in her eyes.

"So it's really not okay," she said in a subdued tone.

I sighed. "Mom, Stephen's fine. You getting married is great. You keeping secrets from me for a year while preaching to me the virtues of honesty is not okay. Ever."

"I'm sorry. I thought it would be too much pressure on you if you knew..."

"That you are all looking forward to having a life again? Maybe. Or maybe I would have realized much sooner how important this choice is for the rest of you." Swiping a hand over my face, I said, "If we don't have plans, I'll stay at Morik's for the rest of the day."

She nodded and left the room, closing the door softly behind her.

"Morik?" I whispered. He reappeared in the same spot. "If you can hear me call you, how did you not hear my mom coming?"

His cheeks reddened. A first. "I was a bit distracted."

Understandably. I hadn't heard her either. "What does it mean? The mark."

"It signifies a link we're forming." He said it absently, looking at me but not seeing me. "Once complete, it binds you to my plane of existence and your own. Time will not affect you. Through you, I will have unlimited access to this plane and the people."

"Is this part of choosing you?"

He shook his head, a slight frown marring his brow. "I sought you for companionship. As my companion, once you leave this life, my purpose will vanish, as will I."

"So what's on my back is something different?"

"Yes. According to several of the oldest of my kind, there is a way to form a link, such as what you wear now, that will allow us freedom to interact with humans and a way to maintain our existence after our chaos is no longer necessary. Most do not pursue it."

"Why not?"

"Many heard of the deal I made with Belinda's father and now seek similar deals. But they are having more difficulty. Because I am so close in appearance to humans, humans still willingly deal with me for simple things. However, those who seek a permanent link are not trying to negotiate simple deals for simple things. In order to form the link, the human must willingly give a piece of themselves in exchange for whatever it is they want."

Like giving up a piece of their soul, I guessed. I could understand why a person wouldn't do that with a creature like Ahgred. Why then had Belinda traded with him? Had she been marked like me?

"Wait. That doesn't make sense. Neither time the mark grew on me was related to a deal."

"Correct." He finally focused on me, and the frown cleared. "While I don't understand its existence, I don't see the mark as a bad thing. Once complete, it will protect you from Ahgred and time."

"I thought choosing you would protect me from Ahgred. Once we choose, we no longer carry out the chant to protect us at night."

"I'm no longer sure," he said quietly, his voice laced with apology.

To be bound to the same limitations I now faced for the rest of my life...the idea devastated me. I had thought choosing Morik would gain me more freedom.

"So if we complete this link, then what? How do we know when it's complete?"

"It runs from base to crown. When it's complete, by pact, none of my kind shall harm you."

I sat on the edge of my bed, thinking. Not only did I need to choose with my heart and head, but I needed the link to remove my limitations. That the link would also give Morik free access to my world didn't cause me a moment's concern. Despite his violent possession of Clavin before he first introduced himself, violence didn't live at the core of his nature. Curious and thoughtful, he observed us and learned.

No, Morik wasn't the reason for my thoughtful mood. My pensiveness stemmed from the cause of the link.

"If it's not growing because of deals, then how am I supposed to finish it?" Part of me feared that my inability to choose directly related to the link's growth. Without the link's completion, I was still under my existing time limit.

"I'm not sure." He reached out and ran a hand gently over my hair. "We'll figure it out. We have time."

But how much?

Chapter Eighteen

THE REST OF CHRISTMAS BREAK PASSED IN A BREATHLESS RUSH. Despite Beatriz's begging, I spent New Year's Eve in my enchanted sleep, more aware of the significance of a new year than most other people my age.

I woke New Year's Day and quickly dressed for work. When we'd delivered the muffins a few days ago, I'd questioned Mona to find out if business slowed because of the holiday. She had assured me that she kept the shop open on New Year's Day because the high demand for coffee made it extremely profitable. I looked forward to the work.

Morik waited for me at the table. Optimistically, Gran had made two dozen muffins, and always clever, she'd added two dozen mini-quiches to the delivery. The smell of them made my mouth water on the drive over.

We arrived a few minutes early. Morik carried the larger of the two flat boxes and held the door for me. Inside, the only two customers looked up from their cups at the sound of the bell. Mona stood behind the counter, thumbing through a magazine, but glanced up and caught my disappointed expression.

She laughed aloud. "Remember what this looks like. You'll want a hot bath and a foot rub by one o'clock."

Morik and I set the boxes on the counter. Mona had already invested in a cute, clear plastic display to show the baked goods. She even had paper doilies to place on the transparent shelves, to make the food look fancier.

"What's in the extra box?" she asked, lifting the lid.

"Hangover food, according to Gran."

While I stepped behind the employee door to remove my coat, Morik went to one of the tables. I brought him a cup of coffee, knowing he'd stay until it started to get busy.

Once Mona had set out the majority of the baked goods, she moved the rest to the back room.

The bell rang before she returned. It didn't stop ringing after that.

The crowds of inarticulate, hung-over people hit us like waves on a shore. Starting small, they grew in intensity. At one point, I brought an extra coffee pot from the back. We didn't have a warmer for it, but it didn't matter. We moved a full pot to the counter to sit while the next one brewed. The waiting pot emptied before the next cycle finished.

Gran's baked goods disappeared in the crush of bodies, as did Morik. Before nine, we'd sold every breakfast item. By ten, Morik returned with three stacked boxes, saying Gran had gone back to bed, and we shouldn't expect more.

Mona beamed and refilled, laughed and restocked

breakfast items, took orders and hit the cash button on the register until one forty.

At one forty-five, after the last customer left, she and I collapsed onto chairs. Crumbs littered the tables and floors. The garbage overflowed with coffee grounds. The sandwich board needed serious attention because after we ran out of Gran's goods, people had started to order from the lunch menu. Neither of us moved to clean a thing.

"My feet hurt," I said with a little groan.

Mona laughed. "I'd say you could leave, but I really need your help or I'll be crawling out of here at midnight."

Smiling tiredly, I got to my feet as someone tapped on the door. Morik stood outside.

Mona let him in while I got the wash bucket for the tables. When I came back out, he had a broom in his hand. I wanted to hug him.

Mona turned up the radio, and we set to work again. I never realized how much time all the cleanup and prep I did throughout my shift saved us by the end of the day. It took forty minutes to finish.

Putting the last container of sliced tomatoes into the refrigerator, I grabbed my jacket and hobbled to the front. Mona had just finished counting the tips and handed me a wad of bills.

"Eighty bucks," she said proudly. "I love making hung-over people happy." She also handed me a fat envelope with Gran's name.

I liked the money, but not the achy feet. Morik helped me to the car.

When we got home, Gran sat on the couch while Mom and Aunt Grace worked together in the kitchen to put away the last of the dishes. They had *Miss Congeniality* playing. One of my favorites. After tossing my things in the direction of the coat hook, I collapsed on the couch next to Gran and limply handed her the envelope.

"I couldn't believe Morik when he came back at eight saying you'd need more baked goods." Gran picked up the envelope with a grin. "Did you sell everything in the second batch, too?"

I nodded, eyes focused on the screen. Morik sat on the floor in front of me and nudged one of my legs to the side. Grudgingly, I moved. When he picked up the foot and started to rub it, I sighed and closed my eyes.

"Cars and foot rubs?" Aunt Danielle grumbled. "Idiot Belinda."

My thoughts exactly. But fear tended to make people do strange things.

RETURNING TO SCHOOL FELT GOOD. Though I liked spending the extra time with Morik during break, I craved the normalcy of monotony. Yet, January's piercing cold, the short days, Mom's spring wedding plans, and my dwindling time wore on me.

Morik didn't voice any concern about my lack of choice or the link. He didn't need to. We all knew what consequence loomed if I didn't complete one or both. Everyone dealt with the stress of the wait in his or her own way. Mom and Aunt Grace planned a wedding, Gran threw herself into her baking, and Morik remained extremely attentive when with me.

We only parted company while I was at school, then he went back to my house to spend the day with Gran, planning and shopping for dinner. I loved helping them cook whatever unusual meal they came up with.

Morik's interest in cooking delighted Gran. After exhausting Gran's cookbooks of appealing options, he bought her a laptop so she could research recipes online. It also provided her a way to track the return of investment for her baked goods that he delivered daily to the Coffee Shop.

Despite all the time Morik and I spent together and the closeness we enjoyed, nothing changed. The stunted twist of black and silver, the representation of our link, ended abruptly in the sway of my back. So, by the end of the month, Mom relented on her rule about not spending the night at Morik's. I could see the worry in her eyes. Less than four months until I turned seventeen.

The link's continued lack of growth frustrated me. And, though I tried to recreate the moments I associated with the first appearance of it and its subsequent growth, nothing happened. Well, I shouldn't say that. Morik really liked when I spontaneously kissed him, but despite the consuming black in his eyes, more often I saw a stronger presence of yellow. I didn't let him know his eyes gave away his worry.

Needing a distraction for both of us, we hung out with Beatriz on the weekends after work. Her easy acceptance of Morik gave me a sliver of hope that, if things went wrong, maybe he could endure with her friendship.

We always left just before dark. He would drive to the road, pull over, and pop us into his garage. I loved staying at Morik's. It meant no chant and waking up early enough to make my own breakfast. I was heartily sick of toast.

Thus, when I opened my eyes on the last Monday in January, my first thought was pancakes. My second was how nice and toasty warm sleeping next to Morik made me feel. I didn't get up. Instead, I turned and found him resting with his eyes closed.

His black lashes twitched against his skin. Did he dream? I hoped he dreamt something happy, carefree.

I smirked as I recalled Beatriz's demand to know if I'd "nibbled on his incredibly yummy bottom lip" yet. At school, she constantly hounded me about the details of our relationship. If my seventeenth birthday saw me to the grave, I wished Beatriz's stubborn persistence good luck in winning over Morik.

As I studied him, I decided his bottom lip did need a nibble. Was I bold enough? What did I have to lose? My time was limited. Yet, I didn't move. Why did I hesitate to do the things I wanted to do? Because I still worried about Mom's and Morik's reactions. I didn't want to disappoint my mom or push

Morik into an aspect of our relationship that he hadn't considered.

"You're very serious this morning," he said without opening his eyes.

"Thought you were sleeping." I burrowed in closer to his warmth. Most mornings, I woke on my side with my head pillowed on his shoulder—the perfect spot.

"I was until you woke." He opened his swirling silver eyes and kissed the top of my head. The kiss that usually signaled our time in bed was over.

It suited me fine. I had a lot to think about and didn't want him studying my face while I did.

"ARE YOU SERIOUS?" Beatriz squealed when I admitted I'd spent the night at Morik's.

She leaned against my neighbor's locker, grinning at me stupidly. I rolled my eyes at her and started to pull out the books I needed.

"Yes, but it's not what you're thinking. Mom just gave me a break from wedding plans. By the way, she wants to go dress shopping this weekend," I said to distract her. "Mom wanted to know if you could come with. More opinions."

"Of course I'll go!"

With my arms full, I bumped my locker closed with a hip and walked with Beatriz to our first class.

Thanks to Beatriz's friendship and the reduced use of my

gift, many of our fellow classmates nodded or said hello as we passed. The sea of faces blended as I smiled and nodded in return. A very focused set of eyes caused me to do a double-take. The girl winked at me, and as I watched, she slumped slightly.

Morik? I sure hoped so even though I'd need to scold him for using people again.

A surprise quiz in first hour distracted me so thoroughly that I had no idea what Beatriz was talking about when she whispered to me.

"Are you going to look for a winter formal, too?" She passed her paper forward, and I did the same before giving her a blank stare.

"Don't tell me you're not going. It's the weekend before Valentine's—"

She abruptly stopped talking as Mr. Wammner, our first hour teacher, swung his disapproving gaze in her direction. She smiled innocently in return, and I hid my amusement. The bell rang, and we both scooted from the room before he decided to talk to Beatriz.

"The Valentine's dance," she said, picking up the conversation. "They really do it up here. The student council has the gym cleaned before they start decorating so it doesn't smell like feet. They even bring in a punch fountain and snack table. Come on. We're running out of dances before school's out."

She brought up a good point. As a junior, I hadn't gone to a single dance in my life. Maybe that's why Mom gushed over her wedding plans. She often recalled her only senior dance, after she chose dad, as a magical night. If I was actually considering a human boy, I could count on next year's dances. But, I wasn't.

"I don't know..."

She took a deep breath, and I knew she was winding up for a long-winded list of persuasive reasons I should go. However, the girl who'd winked at me before class approached, interrupting.

"Beatriz, one of the office women asked that I fetch you for her."

I'd forgotten how creepy the double-voices sounded.

Beatriz groaned and rushed away. Once she moved out of range, I turned to Morik with a disapproving frown.

"You know how I feel about using other people."

"I apologize. I missed you."

Yes, I melted a little.

"Would you like to go to the dance?" he asked me, the girl's smooth voice melding with his own deep one.

Damn if the kid from the cafeteria didn't walk by just then. The lesbian rumor would flare again for sure.

"It's after dark," I said to Morik. "I don't think it'll be safe."

"Consider a deal for your safety."

I remembered my thoughts about going for what I wanted. We hadn't heard from Ahgred much in the last few weeks though Morik had said Ahgred waited nearby at night, listening and watching, when he could, through the un-shuttered windows of Morik's home.

"What did you have in mind?" I asked.

"A touch for a night with me."

"That doesn't seem like a fair trade. You can already touch me."

He didn't smile or look away. The grave expression on the girl's face didn't make sense to me, but if he really wanted another deal for a touch, I didn't mind.

"Fine. A single touch in return for a single night, the night of the dance, with you, Morik," I said his name just so I wouldn't be stuck dancing with the girl he currently inhabited.

He laughed eerily and moved quickly to cup my cheek. A burn ignited at the base of my spine and scorched upward. A scream tore from my mouth, raspy, desperate, and full of pain. It stopped all movement around me.

The girl smiled triumphantly as her eyes flashed glowing green. She dropped her hand, and the sensation of being branded stopped. I panted to catch my breath. The pain lingered unlike each time before.

What had I done? How could I have mistaken Ahgred for Morik?

The girl's stance deflated, and she burst into tears. Ignoring my own pain, I focused on her, aware of everyone's attention. I couldn't have another Clavin or Brian on my hands.

"Oh my God, what was that?" she sobbed.

"It'll be okay."

I grabbed her by the arm and steered her through a gawking crowd to the nearest girl's bathroom. The bell rang as I pushed through the door. I eyed the empty stalls while she

315

cried. Someone was bound to tell a teacher. I didn't have much time.

"Morik!" I called softly. He appeared in front of me, and the girl began crying harder. "I don't have much time," I said in a rush. "I accidentally made a deal with Ahgred—I'll tell you about it later. Right now, I need to make a deal to wipe her memory of it." I nodded to the sobbing girl, who, when hearing my plan, made a beeline for the door.

Morik disappeared, and the girl abruptly stopped moving.

"What deal?" they asked in a single discordant voice.

"Ahgred cannot use any more humans during the day to interact with me or watch me. And I want any memory of him wiped from her."

"The price will be steep."

"How steep?"

"It must have value to you," they said.

I already knew that, but having him say it again made me nervous. "What is it, Morik? What's the price?"

"Your family's chant. You must abide by it regardless of where you sleep until you turn seventeen."

My freedom. The key to spending more time with him. Would I have enough time to choose him without it?

"Not until seventeen. A week before my birthday, I want freedom from this deal in case I need to spend more time with you." Whether out of desperation to make the connection or to say good-bye, I wanted those days.

"A deal. Their protection for yours until a week before you

turn seventeen. Your grandmother will come and pick you up shortly."

Then he left.

The girl blinked at me in confusion, and the color drained from her face. She clapped a hand over her mouth and rushed for a toilet. I stayed with her as she emptied her stomach of her breakfast. As expected, a teacher came in to question our lingering presence in the bathroom. My new friend took that moment to heave into the toilet again. Enough said.

"Let's get you to the office," the teacher said. She helped the girl up and led her out. I followed and grabbed my things from my locker on the way.

A stubborn Beatriz stood in the office, waiting for a hall pass. I'd forgotten Ahgred sent her away. When she saw me with the girl who'd misled her, her eyes narrowed.

"Ashley! What the heck? Why did you send me down here?"

Poor Ashley, her skin still horribly tinted green, moaned and shut her eyes as if that would remove Beatriz's irritation. Bea did a head-to-toe sweep of Ashley then looked at me. I had no doubt I looked pale.

"She got sick and didn't want witnesses," I said, hoping Ashley would go with it. I wondered what she did and didn't remember. Her reaction to Morik's tampering made me believe the experience had been less than tolerable.

Gran strode into the office a few minutes later, looking pale and shaken. No one questioned her when she told me to hurry up and held the door for me. Bea waved good-bye while the rest of the office faculty rushed to get Ashley a wastebasket.

Outside, Morik waited for us next to Mom's car. She and Aunt Grace took the new car now, leaving Gran a means of transportation.

He politely opened the door for Gran and quietly apologized to her. She patted his cheek, a little firmly in my opinion, and said she forgave him.

"For what?" I asked when he opened my door.

"My driving."

Gran waited until he pulled away from the school before asking for an explanation.

"Can we talk about it when we get home? I don't want to distract Morik," I said. His white-knuckled grip on the steering wheel conflicted with his sedate driving.

"I MADE A DEAL WITH AHGRED, thinking it was Morik," I said once Morik closed the front door behind us.

I carefully peeled off my jacket. The motion pulled at the sore spot at the base of my spine. Morik's gaze narrowed at my hesitant, jerky movements.

"And I think he marked me." I didn't know what we'd see when we looked; however, based on the area of pain, I feared Ahgred had removed the link Morik and I had forged.

Turning away, I presented my back to Morik and lowered

my pants just enough to expose the scorched area. Gran sucked air through her teeth.

"How bad is it? Did I undo it all?" I felt like crying.

Morik's warm hand traced two twisting lines up the sway of my back. "Our link is still here, Tessa. Don't worry. But he did add his own." Bracing my hands on my legs, I flinched when he touched the tender spot, tracing it only half as far as the other lines.

"It looks raw," Gran said. "Let me get some first aid cream."

"I'll change first." I kept my pants pulled away from my back. Now that I'd moved the material, anything touching that spot hurt.

In my room, I dug out my pajama pants and folded them down low on my hips. On top, I put on a sports bra, not wanting anything to stick to my lower back. I pulled my hair up into a messy bun and shuffled back out to the living room, feeling miserable.

For a while, it had felt like we all had a chance to find our happy endings. Now, I felt like I held the loose threads of an unraveling blanket. How could I have let Ahgred mark me? More importantly, would Ahgred's mark make it harder to finish my link with Morik?

"Tessa, what did you gain from the deal?" he asked as soon as I returned.

Thinking of what I'd gotten in exchange just made the deal worse. My eyes watered.

"I'm not sure what I really got, but what I asked for was to go to the dance with you."

"Can you recall how you worded it? Exactly?"

His suspicion made my stomach churn.

"A single touch in return for a single night, the night of the dance, with you. I said your name, Morik."

He nodded and watched me lay on my stomach on the couch. Gran bustled over with the cream and dabbed it on. Immediate cooling relief followed her touch.

"Gran, with your permission, I'd like to take Tessa to my home."

I didn't turn my head to look at them. Instead, I faced the back of the couch. The material under me shifted from couch cushions to a white comforter, and I sniffled.

"I'm sorry I screwed up, Morik."

"I don't see how you screwed up. You made a deal to spend more time with me. I would never consider that a screwup."

"But the mark..." I turned my head to look at him. He lay on the bed next to me.

"It doesn't mean anything other than he hasn't given up." He smoothed a hand over my hair. "So you really want to go to this dance?"

"Not bad enough for Ahgred's mark."

"There had to be something that you wanted that enabled the deal. If not the dance, then something associated with it."

How could I tell him I wanted to experience things just in case I died? He would think I'd already given up. We still had a little more than three months. Instead of saying anything, I ignored the pain, lifted myself up on my elbows, and scooted closer to him.

I still didn't know where or how far he saw our relationship going or what he expected from me. But I knew I couldn't keep hesitating.

Half-lying on his chest, I leaned in to take a chance. My lips met his softly. Warm. Everything about him warmed me. I brushed my lips over his, feeling the slight rise of his lower lip. No holding back. Heart hammering, palms sweating, I used my lips to catch his lower lip.

As soon as my lips parted, he growled, a low rumble that emanated from his chest and grew in volume.

Clueless beyond our typical kiss, a gentle press of lips, I didn't know if Beatriz's suggestion had been literal, but I went for it anyway and caught his lip between my teeth. The growl turned to a groan. I released him and pulled back.

For the first time in weeks, the void of his eyes assured me. I bent my head and gave his lip the barest lick, a tiny touch of my tongue.

Like touching him first, and kissing him first, I seemed to unlock another aspect of our contact. He wrapped an arm around my shoulders, cupped the back of my head, and lifted his mouth to mine.

At the first touch of his tongue, I forgot to breathe, and my heart skipped a beat. He consumed me with his passion, and his tongue left no space unexplored. I shivered with anticipation and lifted my hands to his hair.

This moment, this kiss, defined the purpose behind my deal with Ahgred. I didn't want to die before I could experience what could have been.

I accidentally brushed Morik's ears. This time, he didn't disappear or pull away. His fingers twitched at the base of my skull then slowly slid down my back. Little shocks crackled along my skin in their wake. Nothing else existed but his urgent mouth and nimble fingers.

He stopped just short of the new mark. I gave up my hold on his hair, tugged his shirt up, and found smooth skin. I glided my palm over the flat planes of his stomach to his ribs.

Seconds, minutes, years...I wanted time to hold still for our kiss. Instead, I tore away from him, desperate for air.

He gave me an inch of space, just enough to turn my head while he trailed kisses down my throat. My skin tingled. More electric charges. His lips met my collarbone, and he growled again. I touched his ear lightly, not wanting him to stop.

Suddenly, I lay on my back, and the weight of him pressed me into the mattress as he continued to kiss my neck.

"Wait," I gasped, and a whiny edge crept into my voice. I hated that it sounded so pathetic, but flames licked the base of my spine. All of the tingling charges he'd planted within me dissolved with my pain. I struggled to push him off me, desperate.

My pain and panic lasted less than a second before the bedroom disappeared and we stood in the kitchen in front of the refrigerator. I blinked at that change of perspective. He pushed the button for ice, caught a handful, and pressed the ice to my raw skin. I immediately felt relief.

"Forgive me," he rumbled. "I forgot for a moment."

"Me too." My hands, still in the same places, convulsed

with the lingering application of ice. I lifted my head from his chest and met his gaze while the soothing water trailed down my back.

Yellow streaked his eyes, no black, and I smiled at him sadly.

AHGRED'S MARK healed enough Monday night that I sported a delicate scab on Tuesday. The vivid red of his mark showed through the scab, and I knew I'd wear Ahgred's color even after the scab fell off.

Ditching jeans, I wore leggings folded down low on my hips and a long sweater. The knitting on the sweater caught on the scab occasionally, but it was better than having anything pressed against the area. The worst pain occurred when I sat or stood because the skin stretched or expanded and affected the scab unpredictably. Thus, Tuesday passed with measured moments of soreness.

Moving from class to class, I struggled to keep the discomfort from showing in my expression. I knew I failed when Beatriz repeatedly glanced my way.

Wednesday should have been better, but instead, the branded patch of skin hurt more.

Before third hour, Beatriz yanked me into a bathroom. Just as the next class bell rang, she demanded to know the cause of my facial gymnastics.

"Remember that tattoo?" She nodded her eyes wide. "Don't ever get one," I moaned and lifted my shirt so she could see.

"Ew! That doesn't look good." She immediately started to rummage in the bag that hung from her shoulder and pulled out tweezers, peroxide, bandages, antiseptic spray, tubes of cream, and more. Everything she found, she set on the stainless steel shelf mounted just below the length of the bathroom's mirror.

Her supplies amazed me.

"Why do you have all of that?"

"Because my friend gimped around most of the day yesterday then left school looking a little flushed. Something had to be infected, and I knew you'd tell me eventually. Turn around."

She picked up the spray and the tweezers.

I *so* did not want to turn around. The white, aerosol cylinder with tiny black lettering screamed hospital-grade, germ-killing fire in a can.

"I'll ask my mom to take me to the doctor," I said quickly, not taking my eyes from the spray.

Bea put her hands on her hips. "Turn around."

Giving her my best puppy eyes, I tried again.

"I'll trade you one more day of let's-wait-and-see-if-it-gets-better for a movie date with Morik."

It'd be dark. He'd be fine.

"Now, I know it's bad. It's me or the school nurse. You're not yet seventeen. Heads are going to roll for an underage tattoo.

And it's not ratting if I'm doing it to save your life," she clarified. Resolve lit her eyes.

Defeated, I turned and angled myself so I could watch her in the mirror while I braced my hands on the white porcelain rim of the sink.

She flipped the edge of my shirt back and hissed in a breath. "Some of the scabs are almost off because of the clothes and cracking. I'm going to use the tweezers to—"

"Bea, just do it quick. I don't want a play-by-play."

She shook her head then ducked closer to her work.

I relaxed my shoulders in preparation for her first assault but it didn't help. I yelped my way through the scab removal. My knees buckled when she sprayed the now open and raw wound. She didn't stop.

Dousing my back in peroxide, she caught the run off with a paper towel and killed every germ. Of course, the peroxide didn't stop at germs. It continued eating its way to my spine, and I clung to the sink to stay upright.

With watering eyes, I looked up as she moved to grab one of the tubes. In a stall off to the side, I caught the blazing red and yellow swirl of Morik's gaze. How had he known? Of course. My pain called him to me.

Beatriz dabbed on some cream then taped thin gauze over the area.

"The gauze will prevent snagging and other stuff from growing into the scab as it heals but will still allow the area to breathe. We should change it again before the end of the day."

I nodded and feebly wiped away the sweat that beaded on

my upper lip. How was I supposed to get through the rest of the day? I wanted to go home, curl into a little ball, and curse whoever taught Beatriz first aid.

"Come on," she said, tossing her supplies back into her bag. "We need to go get a pass."

Motivating my shaky limbs, I followed her out of the bathroom, not looking back at Morik. He'd looked barely contained. Less acknowledgment probably suited the situation.

After the sting of the peroxide and other chemicals she'd liberally applied wore off, the mark began to feel...okay. Still hot and uncomfortable, but not as bad. When she suggested we change the bandage again after the last bell rang, I didn't protest. The process went quickly with little discomfort and no reappearance of Morik.

We stepped out into the afternoon light together. Most of the buses began their slow crawl toward the main exit.

Amidst the slush-filled parking lot, I spotted Morik leaning against his motorcycle. The day, just a hair above freezing, didn't inspire excitement for a motorcycle ride. Or maybe my sore back didn't inspire it.

Beatriz, ever helpful, asked, "Can Morik give me a ride home since I missed the bus?"

Across the distance, I caught his slight nod.

"I'm sure he can. I'd rather walk, anyway."

"I figured." She grinned and took off her jacket so we could trade. When she had the leather one on, she skipped down the steps toward him.

He lifted my helmet and offered it to her when she approached. Beatriz played her chance for what it was worth and lifted her chin in a bid for him to put the helmet on for her.

I shook my head, amused by her, and started home. The winter air ran its frosty fingers over my exposed skin. At first, I welcomed the touch. However, by the time I spotted my house, my cheeks were flushed with cold, and I no longer enjoyed being outdoors.

Morik's motorcycle sat in the driveway, and I knew he'd cheated to beat me home. He opened the door as I stepped onto the front walk. Yellow swirled in his eyes as he followed my progress. I managed a smile, but it probably lacked luster.

"Did Beatriz get home okay?"

He nodded and stood aside to let me pass. While he helped me from my jacket, he leaned close and spoke softly in my ear.

"I never want to feel your pain again." His voice shook with emotion.

I never wanted to feel my pain again, either. As soon as I freed my arms from the sleeves, I turned and wrapped them around his waist. He gingerly embraced me in return.

"I'm okay," I said, enjoying the feel of his hard chest under my cheek.

Gran cleared her throat nearby, and I reluctantly lifted my head.

"Not much time to do homework," she said with an amused expression.

On the off chance I actually lived beyond seventeen, I really did need to keep my grades up. Sighing, I loosened my hold on Morik and drifted over to the table. Morik helped Gran finish dinner preparations while I worked through calculus.

Each time I looked up, I found his focus on me instead of the food he prepared. I enjoyed his attention. With him, I didn't feel desperate or trapped like I did with many of the boys my age. Probably because I knew any serious time with me could kill them. Morik represented hope for a future that didn't involve my husband's imminent death. Thinking of him in terms of a husband gave me a moment's pause.

My focus drifted away from my textbook, and the words on the page danced chaotically. Each generation of Belinda's line produced at least one child. If I successfully chose Morik, it completed the deal. It should then mean additional descendants to my line were no longer needed. But were they wanted? I recalled his reaction when I'd asked what more he wanted before Christmas, and my mind drifted once again into confusing relationship territory.

Morik met my curious gaze when I looked up. Ask or don't ask? I considered the very real possibility of a short life and decided to go for it.

"Will we...do you..." I had his complete attention.

He tilted his head at me as I tried to figure out how to word my question.

"I mean, are we going to have kids?"

Gran turned slowly, her mouth slightly opened in surprise. Her gaze played ping-pong between the two of us.

Morik's eyes darkened. He didn't move or speak, and I felt decidedly uncomfortable. Maybe I'd found a line after all, and not just crossed it but danced on it. Unsure how to take the question back, I sat there and turned a lovely shade of crimson.

Finally, he reached up and ran his fingertips along one of his horns. "Given our differences, I think it unwise to attempt such a thing."

Gran's color matched my own, and I decided to keep any further questions to myself.

He blinked himself beside me and leaned close to my ear. "Having you is enough for me." He kissed the tender skin just below my ear.

My heart beat erratically from his touch and his words, and the tingle that spread up my spine surprised me. Not an extension to the mark, just a good feeling.

"Thank you." I smiled at him and darted forward to catch his lips for a quick kiss.

We both heard the car in the driveway and broke apart.

Chapter Nineteen

I COULDN'T WAIT FOR THE WEEKEND. YET, IT FELT LIKE IT approached with painstaking deliberation.

Ahgred's mark mended slowly. Mom's wedding plans grated on my nerves, and Beatriz's daily questions about dress styles and color preferences tested my patience. It didn't help that I spent very little time with Morik as the week progressed. At least, not any time where I maintained consciousness. The few minutes we had together while he drove me to school and less than two hours after school just didn't feel like enough.

Saturday morning, Morik and I rushed to the Coffee Shop with boxes from Gran. Word had gotten around, and Gran's baked goods had really taken off since she and Mona had started partnering. Our current delivery was double the number of boxes we'd initially provided.

Mona celebrated the increase in business with talk of extending her weekday hours. I declined helping her out after school, but that didn't seem to bother her. She said she might bring in another part-time student but assured me I'd keep my weekend hours.

The workday flew. After I finished the cleanup and prep for the next morning, Morik drove me home where Beatriz already waited, an excited member of the dress hunting party. While I loved the opportunity to spend time with Beatriz, I wasn't overly enthused about the shopping. I would have rather spent the day with Morik, who had quietly disappeared after dropping me off.

The dress-shopping crew rode in Aunt Grace's new car for an hour to reach the first of the three shops Mom wanted to visit before dark. Gran took responsibility for clock-watching. Discreetly, of course.

While Aunt Grace and Mom dug through white dresses, Beatriz and I searched through the winter formals. After seeing a few price tags, I happily let Beatriz pick and try on gowns.

Soon, I found myself in a chair outside two dressing rooms. Mom came out with a first option, and we all agreed it wasn't "the one."

As soon as Mom went back in, Beatriz stepped out in a strappy dress that fell in a silky cascade to the floor. The silver threads woven into the material caught the light as she moved, giving the dress a subtle elegant sparkle. I nodded my approval. She enthusiastically decreed she would not try on the others in the room with her. She'd found her dress.

Aunt Grace and I wandered over to the bridesmaid dresses while we waited for the next round of admiring. It only took a few minutes before we agreed that nothing on the racks tempted either of us. We both favored floor length, but neither of us favored the prices.

"Don't forget we need to eat dinner," Gran said when Mom seemed to be taking a while. It was code for "we need to get Tessa home, so keep it moving."

Mom hurried out with her third option. She glowed in the dress, and we all agreed it at least made the list. The sales associate wrote down the dress information in the register so Mom could return at another time if she wanted to look at it again.

Fifteen minutes later, we stood in a new store. Since Beatriz's dress for the dance rested in the trunk of Aunt Grace's car, she decided to pester me into trying a few on. Aunt Grace found several bridesmaid options for me to try on as well.

When I found myself in a small dressing room crowded with more dresses than I had patience for, I did the unthinkable.

"Morik," I whispered.

"What's that?" Gran called from outside the dressing room.

"Nothing." I wrinkled my nose and reached for the first dress. He probably couldn't have helped me out anyway. If I blinked out of the dressing room, Beatriz would notice, and Mom would flip. No, I needed to endure and just pick some stupid dresses.

The zipper resisted its track, and I struggled to pull it more than halfway up. When I twisted to try to identify the problem, a hidden pin jabbed me in the side.

I swore.

"Do you need help, Tess?" Gran called.

"No. There's a stupid pin in this stupid dress, and it's trying to kill me."

The zipper wouldn't ease back down, and any attempt to tug the dress up over my chest only made the poking worse. I glared at myself in the mirror and tried one more time. Thankfully, I'd bitten my lip to keep from swearing, so when Morik appeared, it prevented a scream.

He stood just behind me, eyes swirling with yellow and red. When he saw the dress, and the fitting room, the red faded. I quickly held a finger to my lips and gestured to the zipper. He expertly eased it down. I motioned for him to turn around then pulled the pin from the dress's lining. After a nudge, he helped zip the dress again. I leaned close, whispered my thanks, and asked him to wait there.

No one liked the dress when I stepped out of the dressing room. Mom poked her head from her own room and agreed. All that pain for nothing. Schooling my disgruntlement, I stepped back into the dressing room and presented my back to Morik.

Understanding his role, he unzipped me then turned to give me privacy. The next dress didn't pose as much of a problem, but I hesitated to dismiss him.

We moved through five of the seven dresses like that. Gran complimented me on my quick efficiency in switching gowns while Mom still struggled with her third.

The sixth dress, a bridesmaid option, elated me. The long gown fell straight from the bust and looked slightly plain from the front. The back was held together with a single strip of fabric that ran from shoulder blade to shoulder blade. Material draped from each shoulder, creating a scooped back that dipped to the base of my mark.

I needed no assistance with the dress. Tapping Morik, I watched for his reaction in the mirror. His eyes lingered on my back, and I felt his gentle touch on my mark.

"Beautiful," he whispered with darkening eyes.

"What's that?" Gran called.

I almost laughed aloud. "I think I found one I like if Aunt Grace agrees." Making a shooing motion to Morik, I mouthed, "I'll see you at home."

He disappeared abruptly, and I smoothed my hands over the material of the skirt. I liked Morik's reaction to the dress and hoped the others would like it. I stepped out, and Aunt Grace squealed right along with Beatriz.

Both Aunt Grace and I agreed the dress was worth the price. We talked colors with Mom and decided on a bold, deep red. I ordered my dress right away, paid for it with my tip money, and asked if I could rush the order so I could wear it to the dance, also.

Mom's gaze didn't quite shine when we finalized the order. When I tried asking her if she didn't like the dress, Gran put her arm around Mom and assured me they all loved it.

Mom said nothing.

WE STOPPED FOR AN EARLY DINNER, took Beatriz home, and returned me to the fortress of solitude with a few minutes to spare. Morik opened the door for us when we pulled into the driveway. No one seemed to mind that he made himself at home.

Mom and Aunt Grace talked about the final wedding dress options while I disappeared into the bedroom to get ready for the chant. Morik followed me.

"How was dress shopping?"

"Boring until you showed up," I said, gathering my pajamas. "What were you doing?"

"Video game. I liked helping you more."

"I bet." I grinned at him then darted to the bathroom.

When I emerged, the soothing cadence of the chant drifted down the short hallway. I hurried to the circle. Morik joined the chant, adding his power to help protect me. He led me to my room after they finished as I strove to keep my eyes open.

"Sleep well, Tessa," he whispered as he eased me under the covers and kissed my forehead.

The kiss sparked an idea, but the spell gripped me too tightly to speak, and I drifted into the void.

I ALERTLY OPENED MY EYES, but I lay in bed alone. That didn't matter, though. The idea still occupied my mind, undisturbed by my visit to the magical abyss that substituted sleep.

A kiss sparked the mark. A thought helped it grow. Both

forged new aspects in my relationship with Morik. Since the last extension, our relationship hadn't evolved. We needed to go to the next step. But what defined the next step?

Both physically and mentally, we'd evolved. I squirmed a little on the inside knowing what we still needed to discover. Emotion. Neither of us ever really talked about what we felt for the other. It made sense as the next step.

Tossing back the covers, I glanced at the clock and groaned. Late again, I rushed to dress.

Morik waited for me in the dining room. Sitting across from him, Stephen sipped his coffee with his back to me. When I saw Stephen, I froze in the hallway, and my eyes darted to Mom, who sat at the head of the table. She looked strained. Tense.

Gran stood to the side with her back to all of us, fixing breakfast.

"Good morning, Tessa," Morik said. He stood, took my coat from the back of his chair, and held it out for me. Averting my gaze from Stephen, who twisted to look at me, I stepped from the hallway and allowed Morik's help.

"Morning, Tessa," Stephen echoed Morik's sentiment pleasantly. "Your mom was telling us about dress shopping yesterday."

I smiled and nodded, turning briefly to slip my other arm into the sleeve. The smile that curved my lips faltered a bit when I glanced at my mom. The very same topic of conversation had her walking around with a perma-grin for the last week. Why the frown today?

Both Mom and Stephen watched me as I zipped the jacket, their gazes making me slightly nervous. Stephen had never been over in the morning before. I felt like I was missing something but didn't ask what.

"Mom has great taste. I think she and Aunt Grace are going to make the final selection this Saturday. That right, Mom?" I asked, trying to pull her out of her funk.

"You're right. She does have wonderful taste," Stephen agreed. He gave Mom a small encouraging smile before he looked back at me. He cleared his throat. "I'm concerned about the bridesmaid dresses she described, though. Do you think, given your age, we should consider something a little more..." His cheeks pinkened slightly. He looked at Mom, again. She dropped her eyes to the tabletop.

"We can talk about this later," Gran said as she turned to look at all of us. Her eyes met mine, and she motioned me toward the door.

I glanced toward the clock and quickly grabbed my scarf, nodding my agreement.

"Nice seeing you, Stephen," I said.

Morik silently followed me out the door.

Ensconced in the car, I turned to Morik. "What was all that about?"

"Your mother was trying to prepare him for the likelihood of a shocking tattoo on one of her bridesmaids. He thought it was Aunt Grace at first, then your mother clarified it was you."

Oh. I looked out the window. The mark had significance to me, to my family, and to Morik, but what would everyone else see? An underage teen with an excessive tattoo. A troublemaker. I sighed and rubbed my forehead. Poor Mom.

Stephen's suggestion of a different dress made sense. But I'd spent the majority of my tip money on that dress. When I'd asked to express ship it, the sales associate made it clear the order couldn't be canceled. Now what?

I would need to talk to Mom after work.

UNFORTUNATELY, when I returned to the house, Mom and Stephen had just left to go out for a late lunch. Aunt Danielle supplied us with the information since Aunt Grace and Gran were also missing. Gran visited with her widower down the road, and Aunt Danielle surmised that Grace left for a joyride.

Finally allotted free time with Morik, I asked Aunt Danielle if she minded if we went to Morik's house. She encouraged me to write a note just in case Stephen returned with my mom first, but she approved of the idea.

As he blinked us from our garage to his, I continued to ponder my mark, the discussion I needed to have with Mom, and the talk I should have with Morik. The Morik talk didn't concern me as much as the talk with my mother. Or how to deal with the outside world's knowledge of my mark.

Morik helped me from the bike.

"You're very pensive," he said as he unstrapped the helmet. "Will you share your thoughts?"

He blinked us into the living room. Very rarely did I

actually see him use a door. I slid the jacket from my shoulders, and he took it with the helmet.

"I was just thinking about the dress I bought." I watched swirls of black invade his gaze.

"I do like that one," he said softly.

"Me too. I thought I could wear it to the dance and to Mom's wedding, but now I'm not so sure."

"Tessa," he said, sounding concerned. "I thought you understood the rules of the deal."

Confused, I shook my head and frowned at him. "What deal?"

"I removed Ashley's memories. The price is the chant until a week before you turn seventeen. There can be no dance."

My expression fell, and my eyes watered.

"Please don't cry," he whispered, setting the jacket and helmet to the side. "I didn't realize you still thought you would attend the dance. I never meant to trick you into agreeing to something that you didn't understand."

I didn't really care about the stupid dance. Well, maybe a little. What really bothered me was the fact I wore Ahgred's mark and now had nothing to show for it. All that pain for nothing. No extra time with Morik.

Yellow flooded his eyes. He watched me with a helpless expression as a single tear slipped over the edge.

Seeing his concern, I swiped the moisture away and reached for his face. He bent, giving me access. My mouth found his, and I teased his lower lip. His hesitant hands roosted on my sides. I smiled at his uncertainty. My mercurial mood probably had his head spinning.

If I couldn't have the extra time during the dance next Saturday, then I wanted to make every minute count today. We needed to have a talk about our feelings, and a kiss was a good way to start.

Deepening the kiss, I inched closer and dropped my hands to his chest. I pushed his already unzipped jacket off his shoulders. He broke the kiss to pull back and study me, his head canted in question. Lingering threads of yellow danced in the darkness of his gaze. I loved his expressive eyes.

Not ready to answer his questions, I tugged him back to me. Again, he gave in willingly.

Our lips met on a warm exhale. He took possession of my mouth, his tongue teasing my own. A tingle spread to my limbs. I found the hem of his shirt and slid my hands under, gliding my fingers along his smooth, warm skin. He shivered. Encouraged, I explored all the way up to his collarbones.

Panting for breath, I pulled away. He released my lips but didn't loosen his hold. Trailing kisses along my jaw, he found the sensitive skin just below my ear. Withdrawing my hands from his chest, I grabbed one of his and pried it from my shirt. He growled faintly, and I smiled.

Heart pounding, I daringly guided his hand under my shirt so his palm rested on my bare side in the exact place it had rested a moment before. He stilled and pulled back. His eyes ran with a kaleidoscope of colors. Every color I'd ever witnessed swirled together toward a black core.

"I love watching your eyes," I whispered.

He made a sound, part groan, part growl. "Ask me for a reprieve the night of the dance. I will give it in return for just a few minutes more of this touch."

The mixed-up colors and the sound he'd just uttered all made sense. He didn't want anything to harm me, but he truly did not want to deny me anything.

Slowly, I stood on my toes, and with my lips almost touching his, I whispered, "Morik, allow me to dance with you at my school with my classmates Saturday night, please?"

"Yes," he breathed. The hand on my skin twitched.

"Morik?" I kissed him lightly. "Don't forget to use your other hand, too."

He claimed my lips again, and my heart ached with what I felt for him.

A tingle started at the sway of my back, just where the old mark left off. When the burning sensation started, I kissed Morik deeply to distract myself. I didn't want the mark to stop growing.

Morik moved his other hand under my shirt and placed it on my skin. The burning began its slow crawl upward, millimeter by millimeter. I pushed the pain aside and focused on what I felt for him and how his touch made me feel. Taking charge, I nudged his hands with my arms and set my own hands back on his stomach, exploring its smooth planes.

The burning intensified. But when Morik moved his hand slightly toward my stomach, the exhilaration distracted me from the conflagration. My stomach quivered. I struggled to breathe.

He pulled back slightly, again kissing my neck. Without the extra distraction, a panting gasp escaped me when the burning sensation hit my bra line.

As soon as I fully acknowledged the pain, it left. The tingle of the new mark remained.

Morik's hands stilled, and he pulled back to look at me. The colors drained from his eyes as I watched, leaving only three. Black, brown, and ochre. I smiled at him.

"The mark grew."

"May I see?"

I nodded and turned my back to him. He lightly tugged my shirt up and ran his finger along the mark's twists.

"It's beautiful."

"It is, but it will also cause problems with people who don't understand," I said. He dropped my shirt so I could turn around again. "People will think it's a tattoo, and someone my age shouldn't have one. At least, not legally in this state. I need to talk to Mom about it. She'll be the one to get into trouble if I wear that dress and people at school see it. We've moved a lot, so the likelihood of us living in a state that approves of a tattoo on a minor with parental consent is high, but I don't know if that will be good enough.

"People might think of her poorly once they see my mark. Like she's a bad mom or I'm a problem child." My stomach chose that moment to growl.

Morik smirked, laced his fingers through mine, and led me

to the kitchen. He directed me to sit on a stool and began to make us a snack.

"Would it hurt you if I tried covering it up for the dance? I'm not ashamed of it," I quickly assured him. "I just don't want to cause any more trouble for my mom. I think she's going to have enough trouble when she tries to explain it to Stephen."

He set a plate with a stacked turkey sandwich in front of me.

"I won't mind at all."

MORIK and I blinked back into my bedroom just before dinner. He listened for several moments then assured me we could join the others in the living room.

Whatever conversation they'd been having stopped abruptly when we walked into the room.

"Okay..." I said eyeing them all. Mom looked especially sad on the couch. "Since when do we clam up when there's an issue? Come on. Spit it out," I said playfully, sitting on the carpeted floor, facing them all.

Morik sat behind me and nudged me so I leaned back against him.

Aunt Danielle, bless her, didn't leave me waiting for long. "Your mark is stressing your mom. Even if you choose Morik, she's not sure how it will affect your school or our lives."

I laughed at Aunt Danielle's choice of words, "our lives," as if she had one. She grinned back at me.

"Well, your lives affect me, too," she said with a wink.

"Morik and I were talking about it. I'm going to try to cover my mark up when I wear the dress."

No one looked overly happy about that announcement.

"Stephen caught a glimpse of it this morning when Morik helped you with your jacket," Aunt Danielle said.

"And?" This time I looked directly at Mom. Why was she suddenly acting like this? She'd never backed down from anything before.

"He was upset. I didn't know what to tell him," she admitted in a teary voice. "I'm thinking of calling off the wedding. There's just too much—"

"Don't be ridiculous," I said loudly, taking them all by surprise. "He doesn't understand. If you want him to, you need to explain. If you want to keep him in the dark, then don't hold him accountable for his ignorance without sharing the blame. He loves you. He probably thinks I'm just trying to find a way to rebel against your plans."

Mom's sniffling stopped.

"Make this work." I looked at all of them. "You all need to make this work. I can't spend time playing guessing games if there's a problem. I'm very aware of the time I have left, and I know you are too. Let me stay focused." Staring at my mom, I added, "I'm trying really hard to do what's right for us." I didn't clarify who I meant by "us."

Morik rested his hand on my leg and gave it a gentle squeeze of support.

Chapter Twenty

MONDAY MORNING, I WOKE CURLED AROUND MORIK, WHO HAD opted to sleep next to me without a shirt. Peeling my cheek from the skin of his arm, I grinned at him.

"Nice look," I said, sitting up.

"Your mother didn't appreciate it when she checked on you," he said.

Both my brows shot up. "I imagine not. Though I'm not opposed to it, maybe we shouldn't push her."

"You kiss me in your sleep," he said with a slight smile, placing his hands behind his head. The move brushed back his hair, exposing his ears and horns. Black and brown swirled in his silver irises.

"Seriously? I thought I just lay there all night. I never remember dreaming."

He shrugged guiltily. "Sometimes, when Ahgred's not around, I lift the spell slightly to check on you."

I shook my head at him and tossed back the covers. "And when you lift the spell, I animate enough to start kissing?"

"Sometimes," he said with a boyish grin that tripped up my heart.

Trying to ignore him, I gathered my clothes and went to the bathroom to get ready. He met me in the kitchen when I finished.

Gran had a quick breakfast waiting for me, which I wolfed down while I put on my coat.

"Morik, can you take the car today?" Gran asked him while I quickly finished my milk. "The temperature dropped further, and I don't want Tessa to get sick."

Morik's eyes slid to mine. I returned his earlier shrug and left the decision completely up to him.

We drove the car.

Beatriz waited for me when Morik dropped me off on the school steps.

"I showed Brad my dress last night." She spoke with a barely contained laugh.

"I thought he went back to school." We made our way to my locker. The first bell rang, and I hurried to switch out my books.

"Video chat," she clarified.

"What did he think of it?"

"He might come home from school that weekend. Want to take him to the dance so I can go with Morik?"

I laughed, shook my head, and closed my locker. "Sorry, not this time. Who are you taking?"

She grew a little serious. "I was hoping I could tag along with you guys and be a third wheel."

"Of course," I agreed as we walked into our first hour class.

Each time we met throughout the day, we talked about the dance.

And again on Tuesday...

And Wednesday...

By Thursday, I begged Morik to help me ditch school. Since he knew Beatriz and her endless chatter about the dance was behind my attitude, he laughingly shook his head no.

At lunch, the boy who firmly believed Bea and I were an item walked over to our table. He didn't say anything, just handed her a note and walked away. Beatriz read it then handed it to me. It simply asked her to the dance. She wore a huge smile when I looked up.

"It's probably to see whether or not we're really lesbians, but I don't care. He asked me, and I'm going." She looked at the boy who sat a few tables away and called back her answer. He flushed pink, but smiled and nodded.

After that, Beatriz spent most of her day catching him in the hallway. I enjoyed the reprieve. We met at my locker after the last bell.

"So, what's his name?" I asked. I quickly pulled out the things I needed for homework and shut my locker.

"Ted Brinnet. Do you know what I like best about him?"

I shook my head as we merged with the other students flooding toward the main doors.

"He doesn't know who my brother is." At my puzzled look, she continued. "Brad graduated last year. That's why most of the boys here won't give me the time of day. He just about threatened bodily harm on them all. Ted's new. He doesn't know."

"Poor Ted," I laughed.

"Poor me," she cried with a smile as we walked outside.

I spotted Morik leaning against Mom's car and said good-bye to Beatriz.

Moving to my side of the car, he held the door for me. "She liked Ted asking her to the dance, then?"

"That was you?"

He didn't answer until he sat behind the wheel. Heat blew from the vents, and I was grateful. The temperature really had dropped.

"Technically, no." We pulled out of the chaotic school traffic, and he smoothly navigated the neighborhood roads to my house. "I caught him watching the two of you walk into school this morning and spoke to him. He just needed a friendly nudge to ask her out."

"I thought you couldn't interact with others."

"I wasn't sure who he watched, so I intervened."

Ah. Protecting me. This time from human interference rather than Ahgred. Morik was a master at finding loopholes.

FRIDAY MORNING, Mom stood by my bed with toast like she used to before Morik appeared in our lives. I smiled at her and accepted the plate. She sat next to me.

"Morik's in the kitchen. I just wanted to let you know

that Beatriz's mom called and asked if she could come here and get ready with you tomorrow evening. I checked with Morik, and he thought it should be fine, but we'll let you decide."

Beatriz at my house after dark? "Has there been any trouble after you knock me out?"

"A few times, we've heard voices outside, but nothing too bad."

"Recently?"

"This week," she said.

I thought back to my vision. Beatriz had accepted me. Could she still, even without me choosing Brad?

"I'll think about it."

Mom nodded but didn't move to leave. "I also wanted to let you know I had a talk with Stephen."

Crunching on a bite of toast, I studied her. She looked happy. "And?"

"He met Aunt Danielle."

My mouth dropped open. "No way!"

She grinned shakily. "He was a bit shocked but kissed me before he left last night. I didn't tell him everything. I figured I'd start small before working up to Morik."

She gave me a quick hug and left me to scrounge up some clothes for the day.

I looked at the clock, wishing I had time to ask Aunt Danielle what she thought of the introduction last night. Her blunt practicality typically amused and enlightened me.

Sighing, I dressed and headed to school with Morik.

Beatriz waited for me on the steps as usual. She called a cheeky good-bye to Morik then dragged me to my locker.

"So, what did your mom say?" she said. Excitement lit her eyes.

"She said it was up to me."

She clapped and bounced on her feet until she saw my serious expression. "What? Seriously, why wouldn't you want me to come over?" she said with a hurt look as she hid her hands behind her back.

Taking her by the shoulders, I hugged her tightly. Of course, Ted walked by. Quickly letting her go, I turned her toward Ted and busied myself in my locker.

"See you at the dance?" he asked Beatriz, his voice laced with uncertainty.

"Absolutely."

Hearing him move away, I stood and smiled at her. "Why is it always him who notices us?"

She watched his retreating form and shook her head, wearing a small smile. "So, about Saturday?"

"You can come over on one condition." She arched a brow at me. "You have to promise not to go outside after dark without me or Morik."

She gave me an are-you-serious look.

"It's important," I said.

Throwing her arms up in surrender, she agreed to my terms.

Despite Beatriz's continual begging throughout the day to spend all of Saturday together, I went to work the next morning. Morik didn't order a coffee or linger. He carried in Gran's boxes then left.

"You two fight?" Mona asked, setting out the baked goods.

"No," I said while I watched the car pull away from the curb. "We're going to a school dance tonight. Maybe he needs to get ready or something."

"He probably forgot to order the corsage," Mona said cryptically.

I hung my jacket to hide my panic. We hadn't talked about the dance in those terms. He hadn't tasted meatloaf until Gran made it for him; why would I think he knew anything about a school dance? I barely knew anything. Would he know how to dress? I didn't want him to feel out of place.

Before I went back out to the storefront, I calmed myself. We had plenty of time to find him something to wear after Mona closed. No worries.

My self-assurance evaporated hours later when Beatriz tapped on the glass of the locked door. She smiled hugely and waved to me, motioning for me to hurry. Brad's car idled at the curb.

I quickly unlocked the door to let Beatriz in. "I wasn't expecting you. I just have to finish up a few tables."

"Morik asked if we could give you a ride home. We can wait," she said, looking around the shop.

My stomach dipped in understanding. I wouldn't get a chance to see Morik before the dance.

"No, you go ahead," Mona called, stepping from the back. "I know how long it takes to get ready for a dance. Have a good time." She tossed me my jacket and shooed us out the door with a laugh.

Beatriz stopped me from getting into the car.

"Tell him he can't stay," she whispered quickly. Then, she opened the back door and slid all the way in so I had room to sit in the back with her.

Confused by her request, I got in and said hello to Brad. "Didn't think you were due to come home until spring break."

Bea reached over and pinched me. It hurt. If she kept that up, she'd witness Morik popping into the car.

"I had to come home for my sister's first date," he said, glancing at Beatriz via the rearview mirror. "I want to meet her mystery man."

"Oh. That's going to be kind of hard since she's meeting him at the dance."

"I was thinking of hanging out with you guys," he said as he turned onto my street.

Ah. Now it made sense. Brad wanted to put some fear into Ted.

"I know what you're up to, Brad." He pulled into the driveway and arched a brow at me. I put an arm around a pouting Beatriz, leaned over, and kissed her cheek. "You see that? Ted keeps witnessing stuff like that and thinks Bea and I are a couple. He's curious about Beatriz. Seriously, he's no threat."

"You're both ridiculous," Beatriz cried theatrically and stormed from the car.

Smiling, I winked at Brad. "I promise to keep an eye on her."

He watched her let herself in the front door then gave me a small smile. "She means the world to me. She escaped the house after just learning to walk. Barely a year old. I didn't close the door tight. My parents found her a few minutes later in the snow, crying. No harm. No permanent damage. But Dad sat me down, and we had a talk about protecting Beatriz."

He turned to look at me. "I took it very seriously."

The intensity of the moment caught me off guard. Would she be safe tonight?

"You have nothing to fear from Ted. I promise." *You just needed to fear everything else*, I thought.

Brad nodded, and I escaped into the house. Beatriz stood at the kitchen window, peeking through the curtain to ensure he left.

"Is he coming back?" she asked, letting the curtain fall back into place.

"Nope. I promised to keep you safe from Ted. So behave tonight."

She snorted and picked up a bag from the kitchen table. Just one of the many that created a small mountain on the wooden surface.

I eyed the bags. "Are you moving in?"

"I wasn't sure what I'd need, so I brought my whole room here."

My mom called from her bedroom that we should bring everything back there. I helped Beatriz carry a few bags and tossed them onto Mom's bed. Everyone sat back there. Even Aunt Danielle. She looked corporeal as long as no one touched her, so I guessed it made sense.

After I introduced everyone, we hung our dresses in Mom and Aunt Grace's bathroom and started talking shoes and hairstyles.

Three hours later, my stomach growled. Gran heard it and ran to get us both something to eat. Mom and Aunt Grace had taken over our preparations for the dance and used us as pre-wedding guinea pigs.

Tweezed and powdered, I rolled my eyes at Beatriz in the mirror. She winked at me. She, at least, didn't mind the attention.

"I saw that, Tessa," my mom said, twisting the curling iron to roll up a length of my hair.

"Are we almost done?" I asked, not trying to mask the whine.

"We have two more hours before Morik said he'd pick you two up."

I glanced at the clock and groaned. Mom playfully tugged my hair. Two hours meant after dark.

"Maybe we can take a break?" I said.

"Sure," she said, giving me hope. "In two hours."

Gran returned with a few crackers and cheese. I scowled and munched my meager portion.

Forever later, my stomach still grumbled as I sat in the kitchen and tried to strap on my shoes all while feeling overdressed and makeuped for the dance. The scary high heels I wore were compliments of Aunt Grace. She wanted us to wear the same ones to the wedding, so she got me a pair for tonight to try them out. Guinea pig.

The doorbell rang, and I stood with relief. Thirty minutes early. Inside, I cheered.

Mom raced to the door and gave Stephen a quick kiss when he walked through it. Inside, I cried. The torture needed to end.

Teetering on the thin heels, I smiled at Stephen and introduced Beatriz, who stood beside me in svelte perfection. She smiled a greeting, her china doll face lighting up.

We did look amazing. After so many hours of prep, how could we not? They'd tweezed our brows, added some light penciling, outlined our eyes, and dusted us with blush and shadow before finishing with several coats of mascara. Then, the sister stylists had agreed both our dresses called for up-dos. For Bea, Aunt Grace had twisted her hair up smoothly to give further elegance to the dress, which currently shimmered softly in the kitchen lights. For me, Mom had created a mass of curls at my crown and allowed several to strategically escape and cascade toward my back, drawing attention to the view.

My back had proved to be a challenge. Aunt Grace had run to the drug store and purchased several varieties of concealer. We'd used them all. With dim lighting and no touching, it should stay intact. I wondered about the car ride to the dance, though.

"Give a spin," Mom encouraged.

She whispered to Stephen as I turned, so I took my

time with the spin. He needed proof we could hide the mark. With my back to the door, someone else knocked. I looked over my shoulder to see Gran open the door for Brad.

Beatriz groaned. She didn't need to though because her brother didn't even look at her. With a camera loosely held in his hand, he stared at me. His gaze swept down my back. I blushed and faced him.

"Here for pictures?" I asked.

He didn't respond immediately, and Bea giggled. It jarred him from his daze.

"Yes. Pictures. My mom sent me," he said to the room.

I put an arm around Beatriz's shoulders, and she carefully wrapped one around my waist, trying not to smudge the makeup.

"Bet you half of me is cut off of each of these photos," she murmured from the side of her mouth as Brad snapped several shots.

I suppressed a laugh as I too noted the canted angle of the camera. Mom ran to get her camera and joined in the clickfest. While we posed for her, Brad moved to the side. I heard a click and glanced over at him. He pretended to look down at the camera.

"I think he just took a picture of my back," I whispered to Beatriz.

"Probably. I'll check the digital for makeup smudges," she promised.

Another knock sounded at the door.

"If that's not Morik, I'm going to scream," I mumbled close to her ear.

Gran opened the door for Morik. He stepped in, wearing a dark suit. His red tie perfectly matched my dress. The yellow tinted glasses again perched on his nose, and the backwards baseball cap adorned his head. He held my gaze as he walked toward me.

Beatriz moved away to speak with her brother.

"Well?" Morik asked quietly when he reached me

"Perfect," I whispered, leaning toward him. Mom cleared her throat, and I pulled back, trying not to frown. She was right. Too many people for that.

He quirked a smile at me and reached for my hand. He slid a beautiful finger corsage on my third finger. A red jewel lay embedded in the center of the miniature white carnation. It sparkled in the light.

"That is so pretty," Beatriz said, once again beside me.

I nodded in agreement, smiling softly at Morik. Pretty and unique. From a man who created beautiful shell combs thousands of years ago and helped me with the jewelry I made for Christmas, I should have anticipated he would know what to bring.

"Ready?" he asked.

"No," my mom cried. "Pictures first, please."

I turned to her, not believing she said that.

She caught my look. "Just real quick. You can keep your hat and glasses on," she said to Morik but meant it as an assurance to me.

"I'm sure he won't mind taking off his hat for you, Clare," Stephen said.

I opened my mouth to protest, but Brad came to our rescue. "When is the dance supposed to start?"

"It already did, technically," Beatriz said helpfully. "We're fashionably late."

"Okay, stand together and then just one of Morik and Tessa," Gran said, issuing orders.

Stephen didn't have a chance to protest further. I flicked a glance at him. He didn't seem to mind. He adoringly watched my mom.

Morik moved to stand between us and put an arm around each of our shoulders. Beatriz giggled. Brad scowled. Mom snapped several photos then Beatriz moved away.

Morik looked down at me, and Mom snapped a picture. He leaned in and kissed my temple. She caught that, too. He winked at me and turned to the camera for the last picture.

I wrapped my arm around him and smiled even though I worried about what was to come.

After the pictures, I'd need to go outside. In the dark.

Chapter Twenty-One

FINALLY, WE PILED INTO AUNT GRACE'S CAR AND MADE OUR WAY to the dance. Butterflies pirouetted in my stomach.

I couldn't believe we'd managed everything without an incident, so far. Where was Ahgred? Was he somewhere nearby, waiting? Had he heard our plans? Did he wait at the school?

Morik reached over and twined his fingers through mine.

"Tonight will be perfect," he promised.

We turned onto the school grounds where droves of attractively dressed girls promenaded from the parking lot to the main doors. Many sported long dresses like ours, but few compared to the elegance of the ones we wore. I nervously fingered the fabric of my dress as Morik guided the car into an open space.

"We are going to *own* in these dresses," Beatriz giggled in the backseat, easing some of my tension. "Oh, look, there's Ted!"

True to her word, she remained in the car and waited for Morik to come around and open the door for her. He helped me out last and wrapped my hand around his forearm. I needed the balance.

"Do you have the tickets?" Beatriz asked. "And the note?"

"Note?" Morik asked as we walked together toward the entrance.

"You're out of school and over eighteen. In order to bring you, I needed to ask permission from the school and bring a signed note from my mom on the day of the dance."

He nodded, but didn't comment.

Only a few lights illuminated the decorated hallway that led to the gym. Faculty stood outside the gym doors to collect our tickets. We waited while the woman read my note. Morik discreetly removed his hat after a look from the principal. I reached up to fix his hair, ensuring his horns and ears remained covered.

Ted and Beatriz went in before us. A photographer for the school paper took their photo, and I rolled my eyes. Hadn't we had enough of this?

When Morik and I entered the gym, I stared at the decorations in appreciation. Someone had spent a lot of time and a chunk of money to turn it into a magical place. More than I thought a high school dance warranted.

Long lines of silver cord dangled from the rafters. Clipped to their lengths, lights flickered softly. With the typical glare of the overhead lights off, the dim twinkling looked like a starry night. Floor lamps against the wall, lent a soft glow to the lower part of the room. Sheeted lengths of pastel-colored material discreetly hid the basketball hoops, scoreboard, and cushioned wall-mats and finished the transformation of the gym into something else entirely.

"What do you think?" Morik asked, giving me a moment to look at everything.

"It's beautiful."

Off to the left, a table laden with elegant tiny sandwiches waited for the malnourished. A punch bowl stood beside it. My stomach growled at the sight of it all.

Morik smiled and, taking pity on me, led me to the table. I gulped down a tiny sandwich and made room for a newly arrived flock of starved girls.

Farther into the gym, a DJ sorted through CDs at a small table surrounded by speakers. With the touch of a button, the music went from background noise to a slow song.

Morik turned to me, and wrapped his arms around me . We danced in the shadows near the back of the room. His fingers brushed the skin of my back.

"I love this dress," he said softly. "I'm glad I get to see you in it again."

I smiled at him and thought of the upcoming wedding. Hopefully, he would see me in it once more.

"You look very fine, yourself," I returned the compliment.

We swayed to the music. Wrapped in his arms, I watched the light play on the liquid silver of his eyes and lost track of time.

He remained equally focused on me. I wished we could spend all of our nights like this. Together and happy. Worry-free. I wanted to spend every moment with him. And not just because I felt our time ran short. No, I needed it. He made me feel alive and loved.

The thought gave me pause, and my eyes widened in surprise. I looked at him with renewed intensity. How hadn't I seen it before? His caring had begun the first moment he touched me with Mr. Jameson's hand and had grown into something more each second we spent together.

I'd wanted to know what I meant to him and what he wanted from me. But I already had the answer. My heart seized heavily for a beat then picked up a faster rhythm.

He loved me.

The mark ignited like flash powder and burned a new segment into my skin. I embraced the brief pain while I swam in an emotional storm.

Something in my eyes gave me away because he pulled me closer and tenderly kissed my forehead. The music changed abruptly from a steady ballad beat to a slow soft symphony.

The heavenly aroma of food tickled my nose. After a rushed breakfast, skipped lunch, and skimpy snack, my stomach rumbled at the smell, but I ignored it and focused on Morik. He watched me closely as we continued to sway to the music.

"Did we just ditch Beatriz?"

"No. I spoke with Brad earlier today. He wanted to pick her up from the dance."

That meant Morik had planned to whisk me away all along. I rested my head on his chest and moved with him, grateful that he was a part of my life.

"Thank you for tonight," I whispered.

His heart beat steadily under my ear, and he placed a kiss on the top of my head.

Knowing that he loved me, and receiving the subsequent burn of my new mark, filled me with guilt. His love should have led to an epiphany of my own for him, but instead, I hesitated to delve too deeply into my feelings.

I still wondered what loving him, truly committing myself to him, would mean. He'd said that as my companion, he would die once I died. But that was without the mark. The mark not only allowed him freedom to interact with humans; it also gave him a way to maintain his existence after his purpose was no longer necessary. Did that mean he wouldn't die when I died or that I would never die, too. The idea of watching my family die terrified me. Yet, as the last in our line, that would be my fate no matter what...if I managed to choose.

Could I choose Morik, knowing I would eventually have to give up my family? I wanted to say yes. I wanted to be so selfless as to give them a chance for freedom through my choice, but something in me stuck on the fear of losing them, and I didn't know how to get rid of that fear.

Rather than focus on my shortcomings, I lifted my head and met his gaze. Brown threads swirled within the black void, proving his complete contentment.

Cupping his face in my hands, I gave him what I could. "I'm so glad you found me. I didn't know it then, but I know it now. That was one of the best moments of my life. It always will be."

A pained noise escaped him a moment before he set his lips to mine. He kissed me tenderly, his lips soft and teasing. This time, I felt the love pouring from him, and my heart flipped over. His fingers skimmed my shoulders then trailed down my spine. My skin tingled, and my stomach twisted. Waves of heat alternated with chills that swept through me.

My stomach growled again, but I willingly ignored it and threaded my arms around Morik's neck. He, however, heard it and pulled away.

When he stepped to the side, I saw a small table elegantly set for two in the dining area. I walked forward and studied the shallow bowl that rested in the center of the white tablecloth. Tiny flowers floated on the surface of the red water. Already, the flowers' petals streaked with color from the dye. Changing. Like me.

The soft glow of the candlelight from the windows caught my attention. Outside the window, I caught a flicker of green and knew Ahgred watched. I didn't like that Ahgred watched us but hid my nervousness.

"It's very pretty," I commented and turned back to Morik.

"So is the new length of your mark." The brown fought for dominance in his gaze and won.

He led me to the table, helped me sit, then went to the oven. He reached in and pulled out two plates covered with old-time silver domed lids. Probably relics from his cave of wonders.

He set both plates on top of the charger plates already on the table and removed the domed lids with a flourish.

"Careful," he said, "the plate is hot."

A tiny little bird, with its crispy brown legs stuck straight in the air, did the dead man's float in a shallow pool of white sauce dusted with green flakes. A fluffy hill of rice rescued the crossed spears of asparagus from drowning. Shreds of yellow sprinkled the rim of the plate. It looked artistic, delicious, and smelled divine.

Morik set the domes on the kitchen island and joined me. I waited for him to sit before I dredged a forkful of rice through the sauce. It touched my tongue, and I groaned.

"This is so good. When did you learn to make this?" I quickly took another bite.

"I didn't. Lurel prepared this."

That didn't stop me from forking in another mouthful.

"Please tell her this is heavenly."

I peeled tender juicy pieces of meat from the bird and savored each bite. The asparagus was cooked to perfection, and the flavor of the sauce complemented the whole dish.

I caught him watching me as I worked my way through the rice.

"I didn't eat much today," I mumbled around my cloth napkin while checking my dress. The sauce didn't like my fork, but thankfully, it had stayed away from my dress.

His brows drew down. "I apologize for that."

"It's not your fault," I said, eyeing the picked over carcass on my plate. It really was a tiny bird.

"I let your grandmother know my plans for dinner. She promised she wouldn't let you eat too much."

That explained the skimpy crackers. "It was worth it. This really was delicious and special. Thank you."

He stood and took both of our plates to the sink. "Do you have room for dessert?"

"Always."

He laughed and carried over two smaller plates. Each held an individual pie. Thin slices of apples had been artfully arranged before baking to form a perfect blooming flower. Brushed with a glaze, the tart glistened. A dollop of whipped cream, topped with a sprig of green, waited on the plate beside the tart.

"Lurel?" I asked.

He nodded, and I picked up my fork.

"Is she really your sister?" I asked before I took the first bite. The buttery, flaky crust melted in my mouth, and the tangy apples played with my taste buds.

"No. She was the one created just before me."

Her reference to him as her brother made sense, then. I took another bite, and too soon, the tart disappeared. I sat back with a sigh.

"Gran would love to take lessons from Lurel," I said.

"Lurel is too...captious."

Yeah, I could agree with that. "Too bad. Gran would have been impressed." I inspected the dress again for any wayward buttery crumbs.

"There is a bag for you on your bed if you'd like to change."

I looked up and caught his amused gaze. "That might be a good idea."

He stood when I stood, and I could feel his gaze on me as I walked away.

In the bedroom, I discovered not clothes but pajamas. Hopes high, I quickly changed. I'd thought that after dinner he would return me home for a postponed chant. I detoured to the bathroom to wash the makeup from my back as best I could and to peek at the mark.

The two lines spun together in an artful twist that ended just short of my neck. So close. I needed to ask Mona about her policy on body art. Soon, with any luck, it would show when I pulled my hair into the usual ponytail for work.

The angry stub of red at the base of my spine pulled my attention, and I scowled at it for a moment before tugging my shirt down. I left the bathroom with renewed determination. Time was too precious to waste.

Hearing sounds coming from the kitchen, I found Morik cleaning up the remains of our dinner. Seeing him barefoot and dressed in flannel sleep pants and a tee did funny things to my insides. I padded toward him, grabbed a towel, and began drying.

Time flowed around us in quiet harmony. With the last dish dried and put away, he took my hand and, with a grin, led me to the game console. We competed against each other in a racing game until my jaw popped with a wide yawn. No wonder Gran hadn't appreciated his driving the day he rushed to school for me.

"Time for you to sleep," he said softly, turning off the game.

The clock flashed one in the morning. Six hours of sleep

before work. I probably should have cringed at the thought, but instead, I focused on the fact that I would be sleeping next to Morik. Not the unnatural sleep I despised but the kind where I could snuggle against him throughout the night.

I nodded and willingly took his hand.

THE TOUCH of his fingers gently running through my hair woke me, and I yawned loudly. I didn't feel like I'd slept at all, but the soft light that poured through the bedroom window told the truth.

"What kind of price would there be to roll back time to give me two more hours of sleep?" I mumbled grumpily.

He laughed softly, but answered seriously. "Time isn't something we can change. Even chaos has its limits."

Sighing, I opened my eyes. "What time is it?"

"After six-thirty," he said.

I flew out of bed, grabbed my bag, and raced to the bathroom. His laugh followed me. When I emerged five minutes later, the house was quiet.

I left my bag in my room with the dress then went to the entry. As I grabbed my jacket from the closet, I heard the scrape of a booted foot outside. My heart did a flip at the thought of Morik waiting for me. Smiling, I opened the front door.

Brian stood in the opening. His crazy hair and sallow

complexion enhanced his surprised expression. His glassy eyes twitched and shifted. He didn't look well.

"Brian, are you all right?"

He lifted his arm and pointed the black handgun he held at my chest. His hand shook violently.

I scrambled backward from the door.

"Where is he?" he demanded in a high-pitched, panicked voice.

His finger twitched on the trigger, and time slowed. The gun jerked backward. A bang filled the air. Brian's eyes rounded in horror, and I opened my mouth to scream.

Morik abruptly appeared before me. He faced me, his expression sad and set. He jerked, and a fine mist showered me. My scream ripped free as Morik fell to his knees, a bloom of red spreading on his chest. I watched as he slowly collapsed to the floor.

For a heartbeat, I didn't move. I couldn't quite register what had just happened. I glanced back at the door. It stood empty. I closed my mouth to stop the pained sounds escaping me; then, I bolted for the door. I slammed it shut. I needed to keep Morik safe from Brian while I called...Who? How could I save him?

A sob escaped as I fumbled with the lock. My hands kept slipping. I wiped them on my pants, twice, and then successfully fastened the lock.

I spun around and spared a glance at Morik, who'd rolled to his back. So much blood. I needed a towel to stop the bleeding.

"Tessss," Morik gasped my name.

It jolted me into action. I dashed for the towels, grabbed several, and raced back to his side. I fell to my knees and pressed all of them to his chest. Another sob escaped.

He raised a hand to touch my cheek. His fingers were cool. I knew that was wrong.

"I love you," he mouthed. Nothing but silver swirled in his eyes.

I nodded and cried harder.

The pool of blood under him continued to grow. Shit! His back.

I blubbered that I needed more towels and dashed back into the kitchen. How could I compress both areas?

Behind me, he let out an agonized breath. Slow and weak.

I spun back toward the entry and blinked.

The place where he'd fallen, marked by his pool of blood, now lay empty. I walked toward the living room. He wasn't on the couch. Confused, I turned back to stare at the congealing blood pool on the floor. No tracks led away from his spot. The towels that I'd left on his chest lay in the blood.

I'd heard him. He'd just breathed.

I recalled the tortured sound, and my heart twisted painfully. Denial tore at me as I realized what I'd heard: his last breath. I fell to my knees and stared at the blood. It made sense that his body had vanished; he didn't belong in my world.

Now, everything was gone. Hope. Love. A chance.

Inside, I broke further. I knew there was nothing here for

me, that I needed to leave. But I couldn't bring myself to move. I hurt too much. So, I stayed on my knees as the tears continued to fall. Eventually, my feet lost feeling.

Then the numbness spread. Everywhere.

I stood stiffly, walked to his phone, and dialed home. Aunt Grace picked up on the second ring.

"I need a ride home." My dull, dead voice echoed oddly over the line. I didn't sound like myself.

"Tessa, is that you?"

"Yes. I need a ride home. Morik," my voice hitched, "is gone."

I gave her the address, and she hung up immediately.

I glanced at the door and noted a smear of pink marring its white surface far above the knob. About level with my head. I swiped at my face and looked at my hand. Gore coated it. Morik. My breath hitched then steadied again even though tears continued to gently stream down my cheeks.

I shambled forward and unlocked the door to look outside for any trace of Brian. The idea of him out there when my ride arrived bothered me; for their safety, not my own. But he wasn't there.

He'd vanished. Like Morik.

I gently closed the door and sat on the couch. The rhythmic tick of the clock mesmerized me. I stared at the tiny black hands.

Time no longer had meaning; for me, time had just run out.

My mind went blank.

I breathed.

I existed.

Inside, I was nothing.

Someone tapped my face roughly, and I tried to blink the clock hands back into focus. My mom's face partially blocked the view, but I saw they'd moved several minutes.

"Tessa. Are you hurt?" she asked. She tugged at my arms as she tried to determine for herself my state of well-being.

The numbness that had protected me fled with her presence.

"Oh, Mom..." It came out a strangled moan. "He died. Brian shot him. It's all my fault." And it was. I shouldn't have opened the door.

"Honey, Morik's not like us. I'm sure he's fine."

"No, Mom. He told me. He can be hurt just like us. Bleed just like us." I felt the tightness on my face from his dried blood. "He's dead," I whispered brokenly, swiping at the mess on my skin and clothes.

The visual reminder of his abandonment tore at me. The pained sounds emitting from my throat sounded like a dying animal.

"Clare, we can't take her out of here like this," Aunt Grace said softly.

I didn't pay them any further attention. My insides were breaking all over again. Everything hurt. Especially my throat. Another sob bubbled out of me.

Someone helped me stand and steered me to the bathroom. Water ran. Someone peeled the clothes from me.

Steam filled the air. A hot spray soaked my skin. I started to shake and blinked at the shower curtain. Mom stood partially outside, using the removable nozzle to hose me down. The water ran clear in the drain. I had expected red.

"Come on, sweetie," she said, coaxing me out of the shower.

She dried me and helped me dress in the pajamas I'd just changed from. They smelled like Morik. Tears streamed down my face in earnest.

Aunt Grace knocked on the door and whispered something to Mom. I didn't pay attention. I didn't care.

Bleakly, I allowed my mom to lead me from the bathroom. She helped me put on socks and shoes. Someone had cleaned them. I couldn't remember Mom taking them off.

The entry smelled like cleaner, and no blood remained.

Movement caught my attention as I shuffled toward the entry. I looked at my reflection in the mirror just behind the door and wondered if the girl staring back at me had figured it out already. We were dead without Morik. How many weeks did we have left? I couldn't think straight but guessed less than five. Then, I would be like Aunt Danielle. No, not like her. I had no twin to tie me here. I'd just die.

Chapter Twenty-Two

I STRUGGLED WITH ANY CONCEPT OF TIME. WHEN PAIN DIDN'T consume me to the point of sobbing dry heaves, a strange numbness invaded and blocked reality. My relief came in the form of the chant I used to hate. I now welcomed the oblivion with open arms. It came too infrequently, though, leaving me to struggle through my regrets.

Too late, I realized my own love for Morik. In the weeks since meeting him, he'd built himself a room in my heart. There, all the memories of him remained to haunt me. Every touch and kiss replayed itself. The playful moments in the bowling alley...the anguished moment our eyes met in the bathroom mirror at school...it all ate at me. Regrets. Missed opportunities for me to tell him of my love.

I stayed in my room and avoided everyone, and any reminder of life, while I dwelled in the darkness of my thoughts.

My solitude didn't remain as long as I wanted. A hurricane broke my reverie.

Beatriz stormed into my room with thunder in her eyes. I

blinked at the unexpected sight. Not just at her presence but also her mood. Everyone had spoken softly since Morik died, tiptoeing around my tears and despondent silence. Not Beatriz. She came in yelling.

"No!" she said as she strode the four steps to my bed. "I won't allow this."

She yanked the covers back and pulled me by the hair from the prone, curled position I'd lain in for I didn't know how long. Then, she got right in my face.

"You reek. Get up now, and shower."

Tears welled in my eyes. I'd cried so much already, but it seemed I wasn't done yet. She didn't understand. My best friend. What I'd always wanted. She didn't understand that I'd lost my heart, that I would be leaving her soon. How could I say good-bye to her, too? It all hurt so much.

"I'm not going to cave because you cry. Up!" She tugged my hair again, and I went with her.

I didn't mind the hair pulling. Its pain dulled the agony I felt inside.

Like my mom, Beatriz helped me undress. But, there was no room in my pain to acknowledge embarrassment, not even when she mumbled something about more lesbian rumors. Unlike mom, Beatriz didn't warm the water. The cold spray jolted me from my stupor.

"W-what are you d-d-doing?" I sputtered at her.

"It's called not giving up. You should try it sometime," she said.

I tried to escape the water, but she pushed me back under it. Something inside snapped, and I narrowed my eyes at her.

"Back off, Beatriz," I growled.

Cold water dripped down my back. I shivered and crossed my arms, my nakedness finally dawning on me. We glared at each other through the gap in the curtain.

"Shower. Then, I'll let you out."

Without looking away, I spun the handle toward hot. The water warmed, and I angrily turned my back to her. As the water heated, my temper cooled. A little.

"What, besides my smell, prompted you to come barging into my room?" I asked. I slowly rinsed my hair, not actually shampooing it. Gross or not, I just didn't care enough to expend the energy needed for a full wash.

"It's been a week. Your mom said to give you time. But I know you don't have that. Enough's enough. You need to find a replacement and stop horsing around."

Her words jabbed deep into my middle, knocking my breath out. I braced a hand on the tile and gagged. A replacement? How could she say that?

Then her words sunk in.

"You know." The statement escaped in a horrified whisper.

"Your mom had your Aunt Danielle tell me," Beatriz said quietly from the other side of the curtain. "She's really awesome. Your whole family is. I want to help you, Tessa. Please."

Tears blended with the water, and I had a difficult time swallowing past the lump in my throat. A true friendship.

Just like I'd seen in my vision. I should have known it wouldn't depend on marrying her brother. It was just the kind of person Beatriz was. Kind and caring...in a scary, cold way.

"I don't know how you can help," I said, turning off the water.

She passed a towel around the curtain, allowing me privacy.

"First, we need to verify he's actually dead," she said practically.

"Watching a bullet pierce him isn't enough?" My voice broke.

"No," she said brusquely. "It's not. And it shouldn't be for you, either. He's not human. Sure, he can be hurt, but what if the same rules don't apply to him? Maybe he can't die."

"I wish that were true." Wrapped in the towel, I stepped from the shower.

"You didn't wash," she said.

I ignored her. "He told me he could cease to exist. That's pretty much how I would define death."

She followed me to my bedroom and waited just outside the door while I dressed. The bed tempted me, but I didn't doubt Beatriz would pull me from it by the hair again. I called her in as I flipped the blankets over the mattress and sat down on its edge.

"What about your mark?" she asked. "It's still there." She sat next to me and gave me a cheeky grin. "I peeked."

I rolled my eyes. "I don't know what it means that it's still there. Morik didn't seem to know much about the link other than it tied us together more than my choice would."

"I think we should take it as a good sign," she said firmly.

I didn't have the energy to argue with her.

"If he is still alive, you wouldn't want him popping in and seeing you like this. You've lost weight and look...well, sick. Let's get you something to eat." She stood decisively and waved me to the door.

With a mulish scowl, I stood and led the way to the kitchen. A smoky, sweet aroma tickled my nose and my memory. Bacon. Nostalgia swamped me, and tears rimmed my eyes. With a sniffle, I stopped in the hallway.

Beatriz stepped around me, grabbed my hand, and held it in her own.

"Trust me," she whispered. "I will pull you through this." Her steely tone indicated her level of determination. She tugged me forward.

Everyone sat at the kitchen table. All, except Aunt Danielle, held a cup of coffee. Their worried expressions changed at the sight of me. Mom started to cry. Gran stood with a watery smile and said she'd fix me a plate. Aunt Danielle winked at Beatriz.

I sat in Gran's vacated chair. Aunt Danielle glided to her usual chair so Beatriz could sit with me at the table. No one said anything, but I could see they all wanted to.

After nibbling halfway through a slice of toast, I set my barely touched plate to the side. Mom's crying had quieted to sniffles, and she cleared her throat for the second time, obviously working up the courage to break the silence.

"Tessa," she said with soft hesitancy. I looked up at her. "Stephen has a nephew we'd like you to meet."

I didn't try to hide my horror. "Isn't Morik's death enough?" A tear slipped down my cheek.

"I don't think now is the time for this talk," Beatriz said. The steel was back. "We need to run. I promised Mona we'd stop in."

Beatriz tugged me to my feet. I followed her like an obedient puppy and put on my things at the door. Gran cleaned up my plate, and I felt a pang of guilt. What had I done to them for the past...How long had it been?

"What day is it?" I asked Beatriz.

"Saturday." She didn't look at me, just pushed me out the door into the snow.

A whole week. I couldn't really remember eating or anything. I frowned.

She led me to a car and held the door for me. I didn't want to get in, but I doubted she was willing to give me a choice. So I sat.

"Buckle up," she said before she slammed the door closed. She joined me a moment later, sliding in behind the wheel. "It's my mom's car, so we need to be good."

I didn't think I had the energy to misbehave but nodded anyway.

A few minutes later, she parked in front of the Coffee Shop.

It hurt to look at it. I thought of all the times Morik helped me with deliveries and waited for me at a table.

Beatriz didn't give me a chance to balk. She pulled me from the car and dragged me inside.

Mona didn't look up at the sound of the bell. A long line waited at the counter. She hustled to make orders and ring up sales. Guilt hit me. I'd never called her to explain my absence. I turned to Beatriz to tell her I wanted to leave.

She'd anticipated it. With determination in her eyes, she held out her hand. On her palm was a hair tie. I stared at it a moment then slowly reached for it.

Mona murmured a quiet cry of joy when I stepped behind the counter with her. Customers watched me expectantly. I turned away, not ready to take orders; but, I could fill them while I bled inside.

The handle of the coffee pot welcomed my palm. Feeling brittle and thin, I strove to slip into our routine. Customers smiled and thanked me as I handed them drinks. I couldn't manage a return smile. The simple monotony kept my hands busy, but I struggled to focus. The noise and the bustle wore on me.

I wasn't sure how long I bumbled behind the counter before Beatriz tugged me to the backroom. She sat me down with a sandwich she pulled from a plastic baggy. It looked like something Gran made. My hand trembled as I ate it. I was numb inside and out.

Beatriz left me alone for twenty minutes, just enough time for me to finish a soda and the shakes to fade. Then she put me back to work. This time, I slid into the routine with more ease.

Beatriz flipped the sign on the door at exactly one. We cleaned in silence. Mona tried giving me tip money, but I saw the pathetic amount in the jar and shook my head. She didn't push me.

Back in the car, I shivered as the chill of the leather seats seeped into the backs of my legs. More guilt weighed me down, and I looked out the windshield.

"I know what you're doing," I said quietly as Beatriz started the engine.

"Good for you," she said sarcastically. Yet, it lacked any malice.

"Pulling me back into my old life won't change anything." She had to know. The sooner she accepted it, the faster she could move on.

"You're right," she said. "It won't. If he's still alive, he'll be back soon. If he's not, you'll die in a few weeks. I just don't see how staying in your room is a better option for anyone. Your life isn't just about you. It's about the people who love you, too."

Ouch.

"I know you're dying. Not just in a few weeks but inside, right now. I can't make that go away. But maybe I can help it fade. Just a little bit every day. If I only have you for a few more weeks, please let me try." Tears thickened her voice.

A few of my own spilled over my lower lashes. Morik wasn't the only one who loved me. I needed to remember that.

I nodded stiffly, vowing that I would pull myself up and live again for as long as I had.

The next week, Beatriz stuck to my side. She used her mother's car to take me to and from school. She sat with me at lunch and met me in the hall after each class. She didn't try to keep a cheery disposition or lighten my mood. In fact, she adopted a snarky attitude that kept most people at bay.

I made an effort to catch up on homework. Also under Beatriz's watchful eye.

While I sat at the kitchen table Wednesday and ignored the snacks Gran placed between us, I listened to Beatriz's repeated sighs.

"What?" I finally asked, setting down my pencil.

"Nothing." She scratched another answer onto her paper. Since she found math easy, I knew the work wasn't the source of her sighing. I continued to wait, and she gave in.

"Ted didn't last more than the dance. I'd really hoped he'd be..." She sighed and shook her head. "Something special."

I hadn't thought much of Ted to begin with. Sure, he would have been nice but a little too boring for Beatriz.

"So find someone better," I said, not wanting to talk about Ted or any other boy. I picked up my pencil, but she wasn't done with the conversation yet.

"That's just it. How do I know if the next one will really be any better? I need a way to see into them. Who they really are. Who they will be." She eyed me expectantly.

I wilted into my chair.

"Mom told you." How much more had my mother told

Beatriz? Since Beatriz stayed until just before the chant, I never got a chance to ask.

"Please, Tessa," she begged.

"Who they are for me might not be who they are for you."

"A wife beater is a wife beater. You can give me the basics," she insisted.

I wrinkled my nose, and she clapped, knowing she'd won.

The next day, I used all the skill I'd acquired over the years to casually touch over fifty boys while Beatriz hovered close by. At first, we started randomly. Then we moved to specific targets. After a touch, I would either nod or shake my head. When I shook my head, I wouldn't give any explanation. Too often, the image of my possible future invoked a bittersweet heartache.

Touching one boy brought me to tears. He reached out to pat my arm in sympathy without even knowing why I was crying. With him, I saw six beautiful girls. Unwilling to suffer his loss, I arranged to die with him. Our six girls, all under the age of eight, went to my mother and Aunt. The largest number of children yet.

By Friday, I begged Beatriz to leave me alone. She conceded but only for the weekend.

With relief, I went to work Saturday morning. Mona welcomed me and Gran's baked goods back, officially, with a smile.

Beatriz and Brad came in just after one. Their parents were once again out of town, and Brad planned another party. Neither would accept no for an answer. Beatriz promised to return me home before dark and coaxed me into Brad's car.

Dressed in work clothes, I went along, thinking I'd help them prepare like I'd done before, then I'd call my mom for a ride home before anyone showed up. Only, when we arrived, the party was already in full swing.

Tommy was running the bar when we went downstairs. He looked at Brad with relief and pulled Beatriz and me to the air hockey table. Beatriz, in her element, started challenging others. Rudely.

When she returned me home just before dark, she waved good-bye with a promise to see me after work the following day.

My family waited for me inside, ready to chant me to sleep. I ignored the hope in my mom's eyes as I stood in the circle, waiting for their touch.

As their fingers brushed my arms, I realized what I was doing. I'd promised myself that I would live for the people who loved me. Instead, I'd been going through the motions, holding myself back because I didn't have the heart to push forward the way they wanted me to do.

I was existing while I waited for the end.

That thought followed me into oblivion and was still in my mind when I woke again at seven. I thanked Mom for the toast and hurried to dress for work.

I'd feared watching my family die. Now, I was condemning them to the hell of watching me die, knowing full well the pain they would feel. Guilt consumed me.

Gran drove me to work, and I took her baked goods from the back seat.

"I love you, Tessa," she said before I closed the door. "I hope you have a good day."

I'd thought it wouldn't be possible for my heart to break any further, but the way it felt when I heard the concern in her voice proved it could. It took effort to continue to go through the motions and not watch the clock as the day progressed.

True to her word, Beatriz walked into the Coffee Shop five minutes before close. Brad was with her.

"Save me," I whispered to Mona.

She gave a small laugh. "No way. She was lost without you for that week. She came in three times, asking questions and planning." Mona abruptly stopped talking and looked at me with worry.

I smiled weakly. "Don't worry. I know what she's doing. I love her too much to tell her to give up."

Mona grew serious and followed me to the back when I went to restock the sandwich containers.

"I don't know what went on with you and your man," she held up her hands, "and I don't want to know. But seeing how it affected you, how you looked when you walked in here last week compared to how you are now...she did what needed doing."

Beatriz came back, interrupting our conversation.

"Hurry it up, slacker." She grinned. "Brad's taking us shopping."

I groaned and started to slice the tomatoes. Slowly. It didn't matter. When it came to shopping, Beatriz had plenty of patience.

Thirty minutes later, we sat in the car headed to the mall.

Brad and Beatriz kept up a teasing conversation about the party the day before. Tommy had defiled Beatriz's room again, and she was refusing to speak to him.

"Did he clean it up?" I asked from the backseat.

"There wasn't anything to clean up," Brad said with a laugh. "Tommy just fell asleep in Beatriz's bed, the only place in the house where he knew no one would bother him. He wasn't feeling well."

"What's wrong with *your* room?" she said.

Brad shrugged.

"Where did you end up sleeping?" I asked Beatriz as Brad pulled into the parking lot.

"In my bed. I managed to shove Tommy to the floor, but he was too medicated to move any farther. I'm just glad he didn't snore."

I caught something in her tone that gave me pause. Perhaps I needed to take a peek at Tommy.

When we arrived at the mall, she led the charge to her favorite store. Brad sat outside the dressing room with me so Beatriz could get his opinions, too.

"So, is Tommy a good friend?" I asked while we waited for her to emerge.

"He is now. We went to high school together but didn't really hang out in the same circles. I really got to know him this year, though. We both picked the same university without knowing it, and we ended up in the same dorm, across the hall from each other."

Beatriz opened her dressing room door, stepped out, and spun for us to admire her outfit. When she ducked back into the room, I turned back to Brad.

"Is Tommy seeing anyone?"

Brad's eyebrows rose an inch. He cleared his throat uncomfortably then shook his head. I took pity on us both and stopped talking. But my mind continued to dwell on those I was leaving behind.

Mom had Stephen. Aunt Grace didn't want anyone; her car made her happy. Gran had Aunt Danielle and the widower down the road. I just needed to solve Beatriz.

The more I thought of Tommy and Beatriz together, the more merit the idea had. A boyfriend would do more than keep her company. He would distract her. I could foresee her crazy determination intensifying as my birthday approached. It would only be a matter of time before she outright suggested that I start to look for a replacement for Morik. I knew that was her intent behind me "looking" for her.

I sat beside Brad for twenty minutes and struggled to contain my agitation. Shopping hadn't been my idea of fun before Morik died. I swallowed audibly.

"Ready for a break?" Brad asked.

"Yes," I whispered desperately.

"Bea, we're heading to the food court to get a drink. Coming?"

Her reply came back muffled. "No, I'll catch up. Just a few more to try on."

The twenty-minute wait while sitting on a hard plastic chair hadn't been kind. Stiffly, I followed Brad out of the store. I rolled my shoulders in an attempt to ease some of the tension.

"I didn't think a girl existed who didn't love shopping," Brad laughed, watching my expression.

"Shopping's okay if you can go in, get what you need, and get back out. The waiting gets a little boring."

Brad grinned and nodded. He bought me lemonade, and we sat at one of the tables and people watched, which suited me fine.

All the waiting had dredged up memories of dress shopping, and I remembered the last time I'd stood in a dressing room with a pin poking my side. A pain tightened my chest. I missed Morik so much.

Brad reached over and laced his fingers through mine. The unexpected gesture took me by surprise, and I pulled back.

"Sorry," he said. "You looked like you needed a friend."

Quickly scrubbing my hands over my face, I wiped away the visual traces of my misery.

"Thanks. I'm okay."

We both knew that was a lie, but he didn't push it.

Beatriz didn't have her brother's tact, though. She cornered me the next morning by my locker.

"Let's skip first hour and go to the library."

"I just got caught up with homework," I protested weakly.

She shrugged. I sighed and tossed my books back into the locker.

The librarian didn't look up when we walked in. It was the one place they didn't take attendance.

Beatriz led me to the overstuffed chairs near the back.

"So," she whispered. "I've been patient, but now I need to know." She looked at me expectantly.

"Know what?"

"What happened. Your mom said you didn't say much before you went catatonic."

I glowered at her, feeling a true pinch of anger toward my friend. "Maybe that's because it hurts too much to talk about it."

She leaned forward. "There may be something you overlooked that can help us figure out—"

"If he's coming back," I finished for her. "The answer is no. When he first started driving me around on the motorcycle, he told me he could be hurt just like us."

She kept looking at me expectantly, and I exhaled heavily.

"That morning, I'd just come out of the bathroom, ready for work. I thought I heard him outside on the front walk. But it wasn't him; it was Brian, a kid from my old school." I swallowed hard against the pain eating my middle. "He had a gun in his hand and asked me if 'he' was there. He pointed the gun at me. His hand shook so much. He looked like hell. Like he hadn't slept since—"

I looked at Beatriz in astonishment.

"Ahgred."

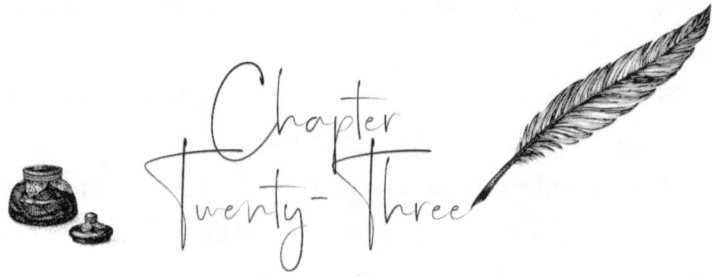

Chapter Twenty-Three

"You lost me," Beatriz said, confused.

"Ahgred is like Morik but not. He's bad. He'd been using people to watch me. Possessing them. Remember Ashley?"

Beatriz's eyes rounded. "Possessed?"

"Yes, and because of that, I made a deal with Morik, trading my freedom to keep Ahgred from using people to watch me or speak to me. The people Ahgred used remembered everything. He'd been using Brian. When I saw Brian last, before the shooting, he'd been crying, curled in a ball in the woods. Morik told me that he'd gotten Brian help. But, I think Ahgred tried using Brian again after that. That's why Brian showed up at the door. How else would he know where Morik lived?"

"Does that help us?" Beatriz asked, still clearly confused.

"Yes and no. It doesn't give us an answer, but it gives me a place to start asking questions."

"Whoa, wait. You want to talk to Ahgred? Didn't you just say he was bad?"

The librarian shushed us. Beatriz picked up a book and pretended to read.

I chewed on my lip and considered her very valid point. I'd spoken to Ahgred when safely inside Morik's house and had been fine. However, I hadn't fared as well when he'd used Ashley, and I wore his mark because of it.

The deal I'd made with Morik cut off the possibility of daytime contact. That meant nighttime contact only. Without Morik around, if Ahgred found me, he would try to finish burning his mark into my skin.

I shivered, and we sat there in silence, each lost in thought until the bell rang.

After school, Beatriz gave me a ride home.

"Maybe you could make a deal with Ahgred to get information," she said, pulling into my driveway.

"No. That's how he marked me the first time. Whatever he could tell me isn't worth the price. Like you said, either Morik's alive, or he isn't. Knowing won't change anything."

She sighed and said what I knew she'd been working up to for a week now.

"You would know if you should start looking for someone else."

"No, Beatriz. I won't kill someone so I can live. And I won't pass on Belinda's stupidity to another generation. It ends with me."

She nodded but didn't look like she took me seriously.

I got out of the car and waved as she left. Down the road, a figure abruptly turned and walked away. I recognized the back of Brian's head and felt a shiver of fear. He moved stiffly, a slight twitch to his walk.

Belinda's deal wasn't the only threat to my existence.

THE NEXT DAY, Beatriz made school slightly uncomfortable for me. Boys continued to stop over during lunch and ask me on dates. The whole time, she sat across from me, and with a beaming smile, she countered every excuse I gave.

During a pause between boys, I growled at Beatriz. "What are you offering them? Money?"

She waved away my scowl with a laugh. "No way. I said you're easy."

"Beatriz!" I hissed.

"Oh, calm down. I needed to give them a fast motivation." She dragged a fry through a mound of ketchup and plopped it in her mouth. "You're the only one who's accepted your fate. I haven't. I'll risk our friendship until the end just for a chance to have you around long enough to apologize."

Unwilling to yell at her, I rubbed my head at her brusque attitude.

"Let's make a deal," I said, not wanting this to continue. "You talk Tommy into coming home this weekend to be *your* date, and I'll agree to go on a double-date with you two."

Her mouth dropped open. "Tommy?"

"Yep, and you can pick my date."

"Deal," she said the word with the tone of a dare.

After that, Beatriz stopped prodding me to say yes to any date requests. She also stayed close-mouthed about the identity of my date and our destination. On the off-chance she might forget about it, I didn't bring it up either.

I should have known better.

Friday, after school, Brad and Tommy waited for us outside. The image of Morik leaning against his motorcycle as he waited haunted me for a moment. I wrapped my arms around myself as I followed Beatriz to Brad's car.

Brad held open the front door for me, his presence not unexpected. I didn't imagine he liked the idea of his sister going anywhere with Tommy without him. Tommy, looking very uncomfortable, held the back door for Beatriz.

"So, what are we doing, Bea?" Brad asked once we all sat in the car.

She grinned at him. "Roller skating."

Both guys groaned. I couldn't ever remember roller skating and didn't think the date would end well for me.

Ten minutes later, Brad parked outside a nearly deserted roller rink. I wanted to ask Beatriz who we were meeting, but Brad hung back to hold the door open for us. Rather than bring it up in front of him, I followed Beatriz into the building.

Inside, multi colored lights flashed in time with the music. Beatriz led the way to a long counter that guarded several racks of skates. The man leaning against the counter asked what kind of skates we wanted, and Beatriz asked for her size in a speed skate.

I looked at the rink. A worker sped around the loop. I

definitely didn't plan on any speed, so I asked for regular skates when it was my turn.

Beatriz laughed, but Brad elbowed her. With a smirk, she picked up her skates and moved away. Tommy grabbed his skates and sat beside her to lace up.

Brad and I took our skates and went to a separate area, away from Beatriz and Tommy.

"Have you done this before?" Brad asked.

I shook my head and stuffed my foot into a skate. Another new experience. The prospect didn't thrill me as much as it probably should have.

"Don't worry," he said. "Beatriz used to beg me to bring her here all the time. With enough time and practice, you'll catch on."

I nodded and tried standing. Brad, already laced, stood with me to offer his support. I pin-wheeled my arms numerous times as we made our way to the glossy wood floor. Beatriz hovered in front of Tommy, encouraging his movements while she effortlessly glided backward.

Brad wrapped his hand around mine. His firm grip steadied me, and Beatriz's diabolical plan flashed clearly.

"So, what did Beatriz say to get you here?" I asked as Brad and I inched our way along.

"That you wanted a double-date with me and Tommy. I wasn't too thrilled about the idea of Beatriz and Tommy; but if they're within sight, it's not so bad." He gave my hand a gentle squeeze.

I couldn't speak. Beatriz would sacrifice her brother like

that? My gaze darted to her. She caught my glance and gave me a sad smile.

"I'm dying," I said flatly, looking at Brad.

He laughed, probably thinking I referred to my pathetic attempts at skating.

"Beatriz isn't accepting it. I wanted this date because I'm hoping that Tommy will distract her from it. In a good way."

Brad spun in front of me, stopping us both, his expression serious.

"She's the first real friend I've ever had," I said. "And I don't want her to dwell on this. I didn't think she'd pull you into it."

"She pulls me into everything," he said with quiet affection. "What do you have?"

Bad luck, I thought.

"It doesn't matter. What does matter is the time I have left. She's going to need you and," I looked toward Tommy who now held her hand, "Tommy, too, I think."

"When?"

"About two weeks."

Brad's eyes widened briefly. Then he turned and helped me around the rink. When we finished the loop, we sat together to watch Beatriz and Tommy skate by several times. Brad kept his hand wrapped around mine, and I didn't mind. I felt less lonely that way.

They took me home before dark. Beatriz grinned as she walked me to the door. Tommy and Brad stayed in the car.

"I saw," she said knowingly.

I shook my head, said goodbye, and walked inside. Her

laughter echoed through the door as I leaned my head against it.

She'd witnessed me holding Brad's hand and took it as hope. My throat closed, and a tear spilled over. I would never do that to her or Brad.

"Everything okay?" my mom asked behind me. I heard hope in her voice, too.

"Yes," I said, keeping the devastation from my voice. "Can we start the chant early?"

I needed the peace of oblivion.

I RUSHED out the door with Aunt Grace's keys in my pocket and two boxes in my arms.

Across the street, the sight of Brian brought me up short. This time, he didn't walk away. He stood there shaking and watching me. Anger pierced me.

"Didn't you do enough?" I screamed at him.

He visibly jumped and turned away, quickly putting distance between us.

While I could understand his trauma after being used by Ahgred, I couldn't understand why he'd gone after Morik. Morik had never touched him. Why not go after Ahgred? Perhaps facing Ahgred in the dark proved too risky. Hadn't I shied away from the same thing? Whatever Brian's reason, his continued strange behavior worried me. I didn't like that he watched our house. Could he be waiting for my family?

Dropping the boxes into the backseat of the car, I dashed back into the house to tell everyone about the encounter.

"Ahgred mentioned that," Aunt Danielle said, surprising us all.

"What do you mean?" I said.

"Brian's been trying to watch you. Each time he gets too close, Ahgred turns him around."

"No, I mean why are you talking to Ahgred?" I asked. I wasn't the only one staring at her as if she'd gone crazy.

"It keeps him quiet so the rest of you can sleep. He can't hurt me anymore," she said softly.

"Just be careful," I said to everyone before leaving.

I didn't see Brian again throughout the day, and given everything that I'd been going through lately, Mona didn't mention my distraction.

A few minutes before closing, Brad came in.

Since Mona was already in back, cleaning up, I moved behind the counter to take his order. Instead of ordering, he asked if I wanted to walk the few blocks to the theatre and catch a movie.

"Beatriz?" I asked suspiciously.

"No. She's at home with Tommy, chaperoned by our parents. I thought you might want to get out and enjoy something a little less intense than roller skating."

I really didn't want to, but something in his expression told me he had just as much determination as Beatriz. So, I nodded and told him it would take me a few minutes to clean up.

As soon as Mona saw him waiting, she gave me Gran's

money, my share of the tips, and sent us on our way. We walked together, not really talking, which was a good thing. A light rain had obliterated all traces of winter's snow. The visual reminder of the passing time tightened my throat and stung my eyes.

By the time we reached the theater, I was more composed. We chose a comedy and spent the next two hours sitting side by side.

Smiling with the closing credits, I turned to Brad to see his reaction to the movie. His eyes already watched me. No smile lit his face. Before I could ask why, he leaned in and kissed me. The kiss differed from the one he'd given me on the porch. One, it lasted longer. Two, it lacked any playful flavor. It tasted of good-bye and regret.

He pulled back slowly, sorrow lining his face.

"She wouldn't talk about it last night other than to say she wasn't giving up on you," he said.

"I know she won't. That's why it will hurt her the most."

He nodded and took my hand. Wordlessly, we left the theatre.

BEATRIZ DROPPED me off after school on Thursday, and I watched her pull away with relief. Four weeks had passed since the shooting, and tonight marked the first night of my last week. No more chant. No more hiding.

I walked into the house and dropped my books on the floor.

"A lot of homework?" Gran asked. I shrugged and went to sit by Aunt Danielle, who watched me closely.

"Giving up the pretense?" she asked quietly when I sat.

"Maybe," I whispered back, closing my eyes. "I don't know."

They left me alone through dinner. I stayed next to Aunt Danielle, not wanting to eat. Restlessness grew. My mom noticed and suggested I go for a quick walk around the block before dark. I tugged on my jacket and slipped out the door, pretending not to notice her tears or Gran's consoling embrace.

My feet decided on a long walk and carried me to Morik's house. I stood outside and stared at the dark windows, remembering the fun we'd had inside.

"I didn't look up that night," Brian said behind me, startling me.

I whirled to face him. He stood a few steps away, his hands empty and at his sides. He didn't look at me but watched the house. He looked clean and amazingly composed. The sallow complexion and weight loss remained unchanged, though.

"What night?" I asked, eyeing his bulky jacket. Did he have the gun hidden? I blinked against the sting in my eyes.

"The night of that party. When they take over, you can't see them."

I remained quiet as I understood what he said. He'd meant to shoot Ahgred.

"He still controls me, or tries to. I figured out how to keep him out." His tone was pleased, but his flat, lifeless gaze didn't look it.

Shivering, I struggled to maintain eye contact.

"It's you," he whispered. "He can't control me when I think of you or watch you."

My deal with Morik had protected Brian, but not the way I'd intended.

"I'm so sorry, Brian."

He nodded absently and went back to watching the house. "Will that one come back?"

I turned away so he wouldn't see the grief in my eyes. "I don't think so."

"I watched you with him," he admitted. "The night before I shot him. You danced with him. Why?"

A slight rustle of material indicated he moved. I glanced back at him, worried, but he had only placed his hands in his pockets.

"He's different than the other one," I said cautiously. The vibrant colors of the sun cut through the evening clouds, reminding me of the time. "I have to start walking back, Brian."

He nodded but didn't move out of my way. "Not safe for you after dark, is it?"

The way he said it froze my insides with fear.

"Brian?"

"Tell me why, Tessa," he said. "Why did you dance with him?"

Something within me let go. It didn't matter anymore. This fear and uncertainty. I'd already determined my family would be fine without me. Sad, yes, but they would survive losing me.

So I gave Brian the answer he wanted. The truth.

"I love him."

Fire ignited on the surface of my skin, connecting the base of my skull to the end of my mark in an instant. Instead of fading, the burn intensified, sinking deeper into the tissue. I gasped in pain.

Brian watched me dispassionately as he pulled something from his pocket.

"That's what I thought." He nodded to himself and pushed me toward Morik's house.

I stumbled along and struggled to focus. Morik's link. Completed. If he were dead, that shouldn't be possible, should it? Excitement and hope bloomed.

Brian reached around me and indicated the door with his gun, killing my hope.

"Open it," he directed. "Sun's almost down. We're safe in there."

Numbly, I twisted the knob. The door swung open. The foul smell of rancid garbage permeated the air. Dirty dishes mounded in the sink. I frowned at the sight.

"Ahgred can't reach us in here. It's the only place I've been able to sleep in weeks."

Brian's cleaned-up state made more sense. I stepped inside and heard him enter behind me.

"Now what?" I asked, without turning.

"We wait just a minute. It won't take long." Moving around me, he positioned himself so I stood between him and the door.

We watched each other as the bold pink highlighting the sky faded to a dusky blue. A sound like a distant train caught my attention. Before me, Brian quivered, and his skin took on a grey hue. His gaze didn't waver from what he watched just behind me.

I faced the door, fearing the dark more than Brian's gun. No lights flickered to life outside the house as the sun completely fell behind the horizon. Darkness consumed everything through the open doorway.

Two green lights blinked into existence in the street. Behind me, Brian made a small, frightened noise.

Ahgred.

"We need to close the door," I gasped, rushing forward. Brian caught me from behind.

"No," he shrieked. "He's been waiting for you. It's time to end this."

I struggled, but Brian held me tight. Outside, Ahgred approached the house, his dark smoky form invisible until he reached the pool of light that illuminated the area just before the front step.

Brian pushed me hard out the door. The threshold tripped me, and I fell to my knees on the stoop. Ahgred hesitated just a few feet away. He didn't look at me but, instead, focused on Brian.

I risked a backward glance and saw that Brian had the gun

leveled at me. My heart thumped heavily.

"If you're gone," Brian whispered, "they have no reason to come back."

A light flared at the end of the gun.

An invisible hand knocked me off balance, and heat flared where it had hit me. The boom of the gun echoed around us.

Ahgred gave an inhuman cry and sprang toward Brian. I watched the terror on Brian's face grow as Ahgred stepped through the door. Locked in fear, Brian didn't try to run. Ahgred sank into Brian.

I fell back onto my butt, struggling to breathe. Whatever had hit me had knocked the wind out of me.

Ahgred, in possession of Brian's body, lifted the gun to fire it once more. Brian crumpled to the floor, sightlessly staring at the ceiling.

Ahgred had killed Brian, and I understood why as I collapsed onto the cement. Brian had shot me.

A fine tremor started in my hands and worked its way through my limbs.

"Morik is fortunate to have you," Ahgred said nearby.

I blinked at the stars that shone above me.

"He feels your pain and struggles to return. I can ease your discomfort, for a touch," Ahgred offered.

I laughed, a dry sound that brought a wave of pain.

"No deals. Never again. What will be will be."

Dizzy and suddenly too tired to keep my eyes open, I floated in a pain-filled void until the pain, too, began to fade.

Somewhere in the darkness, Ahgred roared.

Chapter Twenty-Four

"TESSA."

The voice echoed softly in the darkness, barely a whisper of sound against my consciousness. It comforted me at first. But each gentle wave grew in volume, amplifying the sound of my name to a roar. With it, my pain swelled back into awareness, robbing me of breath.

I fought to crawl back into the void, away from it all.

"Tessa," the familiar voice called again.

Something gently brushed my cheek.

"Forgive me."

The physical pain radiating from my shoulder was nothing compared to the emotional torture that consumed me at the echoing of that familiar, soft rumble.

Morik. He was calling to me. No, not calling to me. He was touching me.

I forced my eyes open, not believing what I heard. Yet, I didn't doubt what I saw.

Morik leaned over me, looking wan and worried. Yellow dominated his eyes.

"You died," I said weakly.

"Not quite. Lurel took me before I bled out. I'm sorry I was gone for so long."

In the background, I heard sirens. "You need to leave."

He shook his head.

"Never again."

I wanted to argue more, but the cut-off wail of the siren distracted me. Instead, I whispered the words I should have said weeks ago.

"I love you."

A pained smile crossed his face as he clasped my hand.

Closing my eyes, I listened to the voices that approached. Morik released my hand. Someone started to tug at my shirt and talk to me. I answered until they pushed on the source of my agony. Then, I cried.

MOM CAME RUSHING into my hospital room with a huge smile and tears in her eyes. She didn't wail about my condition or ask how I felt. She knew the bullet wound wouldn't kill me. And that was all that mattered.

"Morik is in the waiting room," she said, kissing my forehead.

"Can you talk to the doctor and see if he can stay here with me tonight?" I asked weakly.

She nodded and touched my hand.

"Everything's good now, right?" she asked quietly.

A nurse came into the room before I could answer. She and Mom started to discuss when I would be discharged.

Brian, in his fear, hadn't taken time to aim. Or maybe he'd aimed, but his shaking hand messed it up. Either way, he missed anything vital. I'd have a nasty scar just below my clavicle and would need to be careful for a while because the stitches pulled every time I moved it.

The police had pieced together the story they'd needed. Brian, a bully from my past and the reason behind my switch to a new school and my family's relocation, had tracked me down to finish what he'd started. I'd asked about Clavin during the interview and had expressed my concern over his well-being. They hadn't told me much but had promised to check in on him. I hoped that he would recover from Morik's uninvited influence in his life.

During the interview, I cried for Brian. What would have happened if I'd chosen him last fall instead of shunning his attention? I would have most likely saved his life. Well, extended it, anyway. In the process, I would have condemned our daughter to the same life I'd led up until Morik.

Even though I regretted what happened to Brian, I couldn't regret my decisions. My stomach did a crazy flip just thinking of Morik.

"Morik, Mom?" I said, reminding her.

She and the nurse disagreed on what was best for me and left the room, still debating Morik's presence overnight. A few minutes later, he walked through the door, wearing his ball cap and yellow glasses.

My bottom lip quivered at the sight of him.

He bent and kissed me softly, bumping a few of the cords connected to me.

"Don't cry," he begged.

"It's a good cry. I can't believe you're here," I said.

The nurse strode into the room and started to lay out the rules to Morik. No messing with my cords. She'd apparently witnessed the kiss. No giving me anything to eat or drink. If I asked for anything, he should get a nurse. No trying to sleep in the bed with me. I almost rolled my eyes at that one.

He listened to everything with a serious focus and promised the nurse he would cause me no duress. I already knew that.

WITH MORIK and Mom by her side, the nurse wheeled me through the hospital doors a few days later. The colors of another setting sun decorated the sky.

Morik helped me into the car while Mom put all my stuff in the front seat. Despite his gentle care, his eyes swirled yellow and ochre behind his glasses by the time I was settled. He'd witnessed a few of my flinches even though I'd tried to hide them.

"I'm fine," I whispered.

He made a non-committal noise, closed the door, and waved to the nurse before going to the other side to get in back with me. Mom met my gaze in the rearview mirror and smiled.

"We'll be home soon."

Morik wrapped one arm around my shoulders as she pulled forward. I rested my head against his chest and listened to the steady beat of his heart. How I'd missed that sound.

Once we cleared the parking lot, Mom said, "All right. Get her home."

In a blink, I lay in my twin bed with Morik stretched out next to me.

"Finally," I sighed, relaxing.

Morik chuckled softly and kissed my temple.

Alone for the first time in days, I slipped a hand under his shirt and ran my fingers lightly over his scar.

"Tell me what happened."

He stayed quiet for a moment as he tangled his fingers in my hair.

"I felt you put pressure on my chest and knew it wouldn't be enough. As you moved away, I called for Lurel. She took me back to the cavern and fought to keep me alive for days. Even after I started to heal, I was too weak to return to you. She stayed with me. When I felt you—" He sighed. "Nothing could have kept me away." He kissed the side of my head again. "Sleep. Your mom will be home in an hour with dinner and Stephen."

I wrinkled my nose. Stephen had removed himself, unwillingly, from our lives after Brian shot Morik. Now that Morik had returned, everyone was putting their lives back in order, which meant wedding talk had resumed. And, everyone agreed I'd have no problem walking down the aisle in a few weeks.

After sleeping so much for the past several days, I couldn't do more than doze next to Morik. When I grew uncomfortable, I shifted slightly. Morik immediately lifted me and moved me so I didn't strain the stitches. I sighed when he settled me more firmly on his chest.

Someone tapped on the door, and he rumbled permission to enter. His easy presence here made me smile.

"She awake?" Mom asked.

"Mostly."

"Can you bring her out?"

I felt him nod. In an instant, he stood with me in his arms. The abrupt shift from horizontal to vertical left me dizzy.

Opening my eyes, I looked up at him. He watched me, his silver eyes swirling with yellow. That color had been present to some degree since he'd returned.

"Can you hand Tessa my glasses, please?" he asked my mom while watching me.

She moved around us and grabbed the glasses from my desk. She handed them to me with a smile and left the room. I carefully fitted them on his face, using my good arm. As soon as they sat on his nose, he strode out toward the living room.

I could smell the sulfur of a freshly struck match.

"Surprise!" Beatriz and a few other familiar voices yelled when we emerged from the hallway.

A cake lit with seventeen candles glowed in the center of the table. My family, Beatriz, Tommy, Brad, Stephen, and

Mona stood around the table. They all started singing to me, and I smiled as I tried to count back the days in the hospital. Had that much time really passed?

Morik set me on the couch and claimed the space next to me. Beatriz handed me several gifts while Mona and Gran cut the cake. I took my time opening the presents.

Beatriz gave me a gift card to her favorite store in the mall. A trap if I ever saw one. Gran, Mom, and Aunt Grace gave me a quilt for a larger bed, handmade following our tradition. Knowing they meant it for our bed, I blushed when Morik held it up for my inspection.

Brad and Tommy each gave me a card. Tommy's thanked me for including him on the double-date. I could feel Morik's eyes scan the card and blushed. He and I had a few things to talk about. Brad's card simply stated, "I'm glad it's no longer a count down. Get well soon and happy seventeen."

I smiled and thanked everyone. No one stayed long. While the rest of my family quietly cleaned up, Morik carried me back to my room.

After he set me on the bed, he produced a small, brightly wrapped gift.

"Happy birthday, Tessa."

Nestled in a soft bed of silk, a thin chain held a sparkling stone teardrop, clear and beautiful.

"Just having you back is enough," I said, closing the lid on the box.

His lips twitched, and he set the box with the necklace still inside on the desk before lying on the bed with me.

"I know," he said softly, touching his lips to my hair. "I felt the moment you chose me. Then, I felt your pain. Again."

His eyes blazed bright red at the memory. I reached up and ran my fingers through his hair, accidentally—on purpose—touching his sensitive ears. Black obliterated any color.

"That's what I wanted to see again," I whispered, stretching to kiss him.

Our lips touched lightly, and I sighed. The kiss warmed me. Playfully, I nipped his lower lip. He pulled back and shook his head at me.

"Everything's the way it should be. Stop dwelling on the past," I said.

He smiled at me and nodded. "It's finally time to start thinking of a future."

MORIK'S EYE COLORS

Throughout the book, Tessa keeps noticing the shifting colors in Morik's eyes and begins to associate them with what he's feeling for her. To take the guesswork out of it, I've created a quick little cheat list.

Green-Satisfied/Content
Violet-Curiosity
Brown-Happy
Black-Desire
Red-Anger
Orange-Jealousy
Ochre-Frustration
Yellow-Concern

AUTHOR'S NOTE

I just want to hug Morik and Tessa! They went through so much together. If you're like the majority of my readers, you're desperate to know if there will be more from these two. I sincerely hope so. I love how cute they are as a couple and see so much opportunity for a sequel. I'm just not sure when I'll be able to get to it, though, because there are so many more stories crowding my head.

The original version of this book was first published in 2013 as Touch. Finishing it sparked a change in career, though I didn't know it at the time because I was still working in the IT department for a company I'd been at almost 15 years.

I'd gotten into writing when my third child was born. Before my second child, I'd read a lot. We're talking a two books a day kind of obsession. Once the family grew and I pulled back on my work hours (because daycare is freaking expensive!), there wasn't any fun money left for books. Oh, I know...there's the library, right? Yeah, I'd gone through our small town library selection already. Remember, two books a day! ;)

Anyway, because I wasn't able to obtain as many books, I started making up my own stories. While I loved writing, I never really thought my stories were good enough to share with others. After a lot of encouragement from family and friends, I put on my big girl pants and published Touch.

I would have never thought back then, that it would be the first of many or how much I would learn along the way. In 2020, I re-edited Touch and rebranded it as Dealing with a Demon to better reflect what the book was about.

Revisiting a world I'd created all those years ago was humbling. I'm so glad I took a chance and published, and I'm eternally grateful for every reader who not only read the book, but bravely put their thoughts about the book into writing and left reviews.

Without those reviews and ratings, I would have never known I had a story worth sharing. I would have never kept writing. I would have never published 30+ books and counting.

Thank you. Writing has changed my life in a very positive way. I hope reading this story touches yours in a positive way too.

If this is your first time reading this story, please consider leaving your thoughts for others on any of the retailer sites where my titles are found, or on Goodreads. Each review not only supports me, but is greatly appreciated by me and prospective readers.

For more information regarding other titles, to sign up for my newsletter, or to read exclusive content, please visit my website http://melissahaag.com/subscribe.

Happy reading!

Melissa